THE
SHADOW

ALSO BY AJAY CHOWDHURY

THE
SHADOW

AJAY CHOWDHURY

Harvill
Secker

1 3 5 7 9 10 8 6 4 2

Harvill Secker, an imprint of Vintage, is part of the
Penguin Random House group of companies

Vintage, Penguin Random House UK, One Embassy Gardens,
8 Viaduct Gardens, London SW11 7BW

penguin.co.uk/vintage
global.penguinrandomhouse.com

First published by Harvill Secker in 2025

Typeset in 10.75/15.75pt Scala Pro by Jouve (UK), Milton Keynes
Printed and bound in Great Britain by Clays Ltd, Elcograf S.p.A.

The authorised representative in the EEA is Penguin Random House
Ireland, Morrison Chambers, 32 Nassau Street, Dublin D02 YH68

A CIP catalogue record for this book is available from the British Library

HB ISBN 9781787304031
TPB ISBN 9781787304048

Penguin Random House is committed to a sustainable future
for our business, our readers and our planet. This book is made
from Forest Stewardship Council® certified paper.

For Kaikobad

Salt of the earth

Old sins cast long shadows

Agatha Christie, *Nemesis*

Map of Mumbai

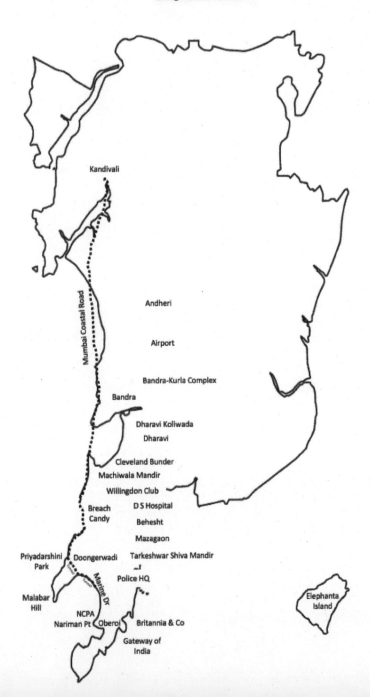

The Mehta Family Tree

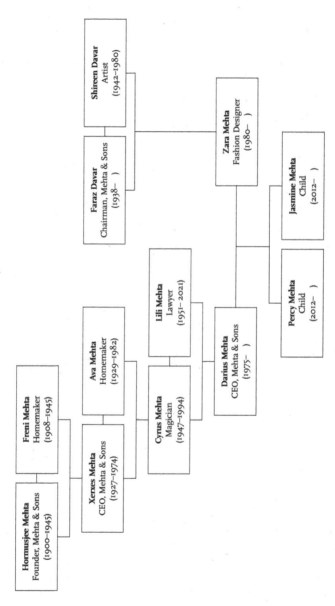

Hormusjee Mehta
Founder, Mehta & Sons
(1900–1945)

Freni Mehta
Homemaker
(1908–1945)

Shireen Davar
Artist
(1942–1980)

Faraz Davar
Chairman, Mehta & Sons
(1938–)

Xerxes Mehta
CEO, Mehta & Sons
(1927–1974)

Ava Mehta
Homemaker
(1929–1982)

Cyrus Mehta
Magician
(1947–1994)

Lili Mehta
Lawyer
(1951–2021)

Zara Mehta
Fashion Designer
(1980–)

Darius Mehta
CEO, Mehta & Sons
(1975–)

Percy Mehta
Child
(2012–)

Jasmine Mehta
Child
(2012–)

Employees and Associates of Mehta & Sons

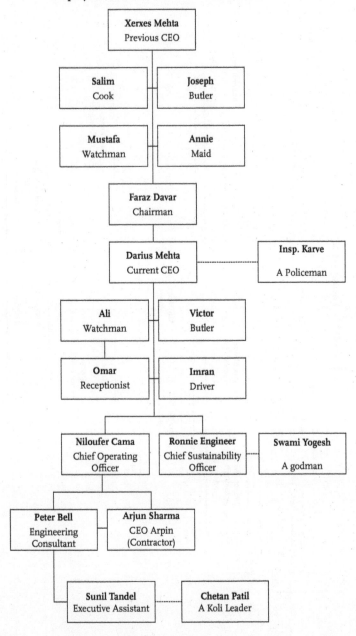

Then

*For he who looks upon evil with tolerance is
no other than evil himself*

Zoroaster

Xerxes

Bombay. Friday, 15 August 1947. Just before midnight.

'*L*ong *years ago, we made a tryst with destiny; and now the time comes when we shall redeem our pledge, not wholly or in full measure, but very substantially. At the stroke of the midnight hour, when the world sleeps, India will awake to life and freedom.*'

Pandit Nehru's voice crackled through the wireless, his patrician accent battling against a sea of static. Xerxes leaned closer, straining to decipher the words amidst the interference. The faint applause and roars of the crowd made it even harder to hear.

'*A moment comes, which comes but rarely in history, when we step out from the old to the new. When an age ends, and when the soul of a nation, long suppressed, finds utterance.*'

'Soul of a nation,' Xerxes muttered under his breath. 'The bloody fool doesn't grasp how good we have it under the British. Just wait till he sees the carnage that's coming.'

He glanced at the portrait of Sir Hormusjee Mehta, Baronet, GBE, KCIE (1900–45), on the wall. The extravagantly moustachioed face stared back, cold and haughty. 'You would have been horrified, Father. Perhaps it's fortunate you didn't live to see this day.'

'. . . *cause of humanity. At the dawn of history, India started on her unending quest . . .*'

Xerxes's attention was snatched away by faint shouts from within the house. His heart quickened. Leaping from his chair,

3

he rushed down the dimly lit corridor, the polished floors echoing his hurried steps. He paused momentarily, steeling himself before knocking on his wife's door.

It creaked open. Annie's wide eyes shimmered with excitement as she clutched the door frame.

'Well?' he prompted, breathless.

A smile spread across her fourteen-year-old face. 'A boy. It is a boy, Mr Xerxes. You have a son.'

Relief flooded through him, melting the tension from his shoulders. 'And Ava?'

'Madam is well. Resting. Do you wish to see the baby?'

He nodded, his voice thick with emotion. 'Yes.'

A banging on the front door.

'Now what!' he barked, bounding down the grand staircase to the main hall, where his butler was engaged in an urgent conversation with a shadowy figure on the porch.

'What is it, Joseph? Don't they know what time it is?'

His butler turned, face pale. 'Mustafa says there's trouble outside the compound. People are begging to be let in.'

Xerxes stepped forward, peering past the burly watchman to the high wall enclosing their property. The sky had an eerie orange glow, the night air heavy with the scent of burning wood.

'Jab mulle kaate jayenge, woh Ram Ram chillayenge. Jab mulle kaate jayenge, woh Ram Ram chillayenge.'

'Who's out there? What are they saying?'

'A gang of Hindus, sir. They are shouting . . .' Joseph swallowed. 'When the Muslims are killed, they will scream Lord Rama's name.'

For a heartbeat, Xerxes was paralysed, staring at Joseph in horror. Then he raced up the stairs. From the window, he saw a mob approaching, brandishing tridents and swords, their flaming torches casting dancing shadows on the walls of the shantytown outside his mansion.

He tried to suppress his panic. 'What should we do?'

'Maybe . . . maybe they will just chant and move on?' said Joseph, who had followed him up.

The rabble was closing in. The chanting subsided. A few seconds of silence. Then screams. Breaking glass.

'Call the police!' Xerxes shouted over the din.

'The Muslim families outside are terrified,' Joseph yelled back. 'They believe the Hindus will burn down the mohalla. They've asked to come inside for safety. Can we let them in?'

Frozen by the destruction unfolding before him, Xerxes forced himself to look away. He staggered back down the stairs, followed by Joseph, to see Mustafa pacing agitatedly.

He turned to his butler, his voice a strained whisper. 'Tell him . . . tell him to make sure the gates stay barred. It's too dangerous. There could be looters. Keep them out. My wife has just given birth. My family must be safe.'

Joseph hesitated, then relayed the message to Mustafa. The watchman's eyes pleaded as he replied, voice quivering.

'He says it is hell outside,' said Joseph. 'He begs you to let in people he trusts. Family. He promises they won't disturb Madam.'

Xerxes couldn't meet the Muslim watchman's beseeching look. He knew what his father would have done. He would have opened the gates and saved lives. But his father wasn't here. Xerxes was. 'I'm sorry. I cannot risk it. Ensure my orders are followed.'

Joseph cast a look of sympathy at the watchman's stricken face and delivered the message. The front door slammed shut with a finality that made Xerxes's stomach lurch.

Unable to face his wife, Xerxes retreated to his bedroom, trembling. He lay under the covers, the distant screams penetrating the walls and seeping into his thoughts. He closed the blinds to block out the world outside, and whispered the Ashem

Vohu prayer, seeking its calming embrace. But his mind remained a storm of fear and guilt.

Morning arrived, shrouded in an unsettling silence. Xerxes sat on the balcony, eyes gritty with exhaustion, waiting for Ava to wake. He should have seen his son. She would wonder why he hadn't come.

The mansion was wrapped in a strange quietude, the usual chatter of birds and monkeys replaced by the incessant buzzing of insects, mirroring the thoughts rattling round his head.

Why were there so many flies?

The peculiar haze brought back a memory of how he had once glimpsed the world, hiding behind the gauze of his mother's sari. He was an innocent child then, unaware that, after the car accident killed his parents, he would stumble haplessly into manhood at eighteen.

He coughed as the acrid stench of smoke invaded his nostrils. He could delay no longer. Steeling himself, he crossed the house to the wing overlooking the street. His hand hovered over the closed blinds, fingers trembling.

What kind of man was he, unable to even open a window?

Clenching and releasing his fist, he turned away and headed to Ava's room. She was sitting up in bed, cradling their son, Annie by her side.

He forced a smile. 'How are you feeling?'

Ava looked up, weary but content. 'Tired. What was all that commotion last night?'

'Nothing. Just troublemakers,' he lied. 'So, this is our son?' He took the boy from Ava's arms, marvelling at the tiny mouth, the eyes squeezed shut, the perfect little nose. Relief surged through him. He had made the right decision. His son was fragile, too vulnerable to face the world. He had kept him safe. 'Hello, Cyrus,' he whispered. 'I'm your father.'

The baby's lids fluttered open, meeting his gaze. Then his face contorted. A reedy wail occupied the room. He handed the boy back to Annie, who gently rocked him while Ava prepared to nurse.

Filled with newfound resolve, Xerxes hurried out to find Joseph. 'Summon Mustafa. I need to see what's happening outside.'

When they returned, the watchman's face was a mask of fatigue and anger. 'All dead,' Joseph translated.

Xerxes's heart clenched. 'Is it safe now?'

Joseph nodded.

'Show me.'

They walked down the driveway towards the massive, gated entrance. Mustafa unlocked it, stepping aside to let Xerxes pass.

He froze.

The scene beyond his lush, tree-lined drive was a war zone. The usually bustling street lay in an unnatural silence, the mohalla reduced to smouldering ruins. Xerxes looked up at the sky, dense with smoke, filled with distant cries.

'We were fortunate the flames did not engulf Behesht,' Joseph said softly.

Numb, Xerxes walked through the devastation. Since childhood, he had been warned of the dangers lurking in these alleys of Mazagaon, his father adamant that he never venture out unaccompanied, lest the outside world taint him. To assert his independence, Xerxes sat by the gate in the evenings, observing the lives led beyond the walls under Mustafa's watchful eye, until Salim would fetch him for his favourite chapatis with cream sprinkled with sugar.

'Why didn't the police intervene? I told you to call them.'

Joseph looked down at the path littered with burnt wood and shattered glass and said simply, 'They are Hindus.'

7

Catching his gaze, Xerxes gestured to the ground. 'What is all this?'

'The rioters filled bottles with kerosene, set them alight, and threw them into the houses.'

'O Khodai!'

They approached a tin shack, miraculously still standing amidst the ruins.

'Isn't this where . . .' Xerxes's voice faltered.

Joseph nodded. 'Yes. Mustafa's brother Salim, his wife and two children lived here. Mustafa pleaded for their safety last night, but I followed your instructions and refused.'

The watchman stood rigid, staring straight ahead, refusing to meet Xerxes's gaze.

'But you never told me it was for Salim!' Xerxes's throat constricted. 'I would not have turned my own cook away.'

He peered into the shack's open door. The roof had been incinerated, exposing to daylight the dented tin plates and mugs scattered across the floor. A grimy wooden cricket bat lay, desolate and abandoned, stirring a memory: a smiling tousle-haired boy in a blue shirt and shorts, hitting a ball in the mansion's gardens, his little sister chasing after it, her faded pink dress fluttering in the breeze.

Xerxes stepped inside. Slipped. Joseph grabbed his arm, steadying him. The ground was slick with gore. The pungent scent of iron and burned fabric hit him. He retched. Through tears, he saw three bodies covered in blood-soaked shrouds. In the corner, Salim sat, knees bent, back against the wall, staring vacantly at the corpses of his family. Xerxes blinked when he noticed the sword jutting out from his cook's flank. Swallowed a sob. Turned to leave this place of horrors.

A sound.

Xerxes turned.

Salim's eyes, filled with fury, locked onto his. The cook raised a trembling finger. 'You . . . you . . .'

'You're alive! Thank god!' Xerxes shouted to Joseph. 'Run to the house. Call a doctor!'

Salim's stare drilled into him, holding Xerxes in a grip of guilt and terror. 'You did this,' the cook rasped, his voice cracked and broken. 'You could have saved us, but you did not. Because of you, they are all dead.' He struggled to his feet and stumbled towards Xerxes, the sword sticking out from above his hip like an obscene handle.

Before he could react, Salim's hot, blood-soaked hands clamped onto Xerxes's face, the same hands that had fed him as a child and a man. The cook's voice was a haunting whisper, laced with agony and rage. 'Xerxes Mehta ke upar lanatullah. Xerxes Mehta ke upar lanatullah. Xerxes Mehta ke upar lanatullah. A curse on you and all your descendants. In this forty-seventh year of hell, you killed my family. You will burn to death on your forty-seventh birthday. Your children will burn to death on their forty-seventh birthdays. Burn like I burned. Burn like my wife Zebu burned. Burn like my children, Ameira and Zafar, burned. A life for a life. Burn in the scorching flame of al-Saqar in Jahannam.'

Salim's iron grip tightened, his eyes ablaze with fury and pain. Xerxes screamed and wrenched himself free. Salim fell, driving the sword deep into his side. He collapsed, lifeless, his final curse hanging in the air like a spectre.

The lane was a blur as Xerxes fled, Joseph and Mustafa racing behind him, all three scrambling to reach the sanctuary of the compound.

As they stumbled through the gates, a dark shadow painted the ground and flowed after them.

Now

Everything is so sudden in India, the sudden twilights, the sudden death. A man can be talking to you at breakfast and be dead in the afternoon – and this is one of the things you have to deal with.

Charles Allen, *Plain Tales from the Raj*

After

Kamil

London. Monday, 12 December.

Eight days have passed since his terrible death, and I've barely slept.

Were the Mumbai murders my fault?

What if I'd responded differently to Darius's text? What if I'd identified Felix quicker? What if I'd stayed in the shadows? What if I hadn't insinuated myself into Bell's murder investigation? What if I'd just kept my big trap shut?

What if? What if? What if?

The questions spin around, getting louder and louder as they crash against each other inside my head, until all I can hear is that last, most terrifying, what-if:

What if the monkey hadn't hit me with that mango?

I know the answer to that one.

Anjoli and I would be lying dead at Shiva's feet in that dark, dusty cave.

Two Weeks Ago
Kamil

London. Monday, 28 November.
Six days to go.

'Are you sure you still want to do this?' Anjoli's knife hovers in mid-air as I pour milk over my cornflakes.

'Absolutely,' I lie, trying to muster more conviction than I feel. 'I'm excited!'

She gives me a look and goes back to slathering butter on her toast. 'You don't have to, you know.'

'Why? Are you having second thoughts?'

'No. It's just . . .' She puts the knife down, takes a bite. Stares at the steam swirling up from her coffee. Am I supposed to guess the rest? I shift in my seat. The creak is loud in the silence that's settled between us.

'It's just what?'

She sighs. 'Don't feel you have to. I'm fully capable of doing it on my own. I don't need you alongside me.'

'I know that. But this is definitely something we should do together.' I shovel a spoonful of cereal into my mouth. The milk is cold, the cornflakes soggy, but it's a distraction from her gaze, heavy with an emotion I can't quite name – scepticism? Disappointment? My good intentions always seem to crumble around

Anjoli, like a house of cards in a gust of wind. Is that what she's afraid of now?

If so, she's right.

Of course I'm bloody having second thoughts. And third and fourth thoughts. What possessed me to blurt out that I was leaving the force . . . so we could start a detective agency together? Was it because I knew she was bored running the restaurant? Or was it the sour taste of being overlooked at the Met?

Four murders solved, an assassination attempt thwarted, yet here I am, stuck, a lowly detective constable, drowning in a sea of under-appreciation and systemic racism. The cigarette burn on my arm still stings from that last undercover op. My leg still aches where the bullet wound reminds me of past mistakes. And the guilt of my complicity in the death of the grandmother and her sons . . . the weight of that bears down on me like a relentless anchor.

Is that why I did it? No. I'd made the offer because I saw us in some rosy future – partners at work, partners in life. Hearts and flowers and happily ever after.

Well, half of my ridiculous plan worked. She agreed to be my partner at work. Partners in life? Not so much. Hearts and flowers morphed into discussions of private investigator licences, legal partnerships and probate disputes.

But before I could take a deep breath and tell her I was reconsidering, that I needed time, she was interviewing for a replacement manager for Tandoori Knights. And I was on the phone with Abba. His disappointment was palpable, even across the crackling line. 'So, Mr Big Police Hero, you have given up already, without taking advice from your father, even? So much for my son joining Scotland Yard.'

'It's complicated, Abba. There's the racism and—'

'Racism! Pah! You think I didn't face discrimination for being

Muslim? Fight it from within. Show them you are as good as anyone.'

Anjoli's voice pulls me back to the present. 'Kamil? You've gone awfully quiet.'

I look up, the cereal forgotten. The room feels like it's closing in on me. Okay. I have to be honest. 'Well, since you ask . . .'

My phone buzzes, slicing through the moment. Darius. Strange. We haven't spoken in months. I answer quickly. 'Daru! Hi. It's been a while. What's up?'

His voice is strained, urgent. 'Kamil, listen, something's happened. I . . . I need your help.'

'Of course. What's going on?'

'There's been a murder. I want you to . . . hang on.' Muffled voices in the background. 'I have to go. Please come. I need you.'

'Come where? Need me for what?' But the line goes dead.

Anjoli looks up. 'Who was that?'

'Darius. He said he needs my help. Something about a murder.'

Her face lights up. 'Hey, maybe it's our first case? That would be cool.'

'Maybe.' I glance at the clock. 'Damn, it's late. I'm meeting Rogers at ten.'

This is it. My last chance to confess my doubts. I open my mouth, but the words stick. Instead, I pat my jacket pocket and gulp down my coffee, its bitterness mirroring my state of mind. 'I've got my resignation right here.'

Anjoli stands with me, her hand reaching for mine. 'You really do not have to do this. I'm worried you think this is a way to win me over and . . .'

Our eyes lock. For a moment, the world narrows to just the two of us. 'What if it is? Would it work?'

She looks away. Murmurs, 'It might.' Hope sparks like a

struck match, but then she adds, 'But working together day and night . . . it could ruin our friendship.'

Screw it. I'm in. If there's even a sliver of a chance, I have to take it. Five years of waiting for something, anything, to click with her. If diving into the murky waters of probate is the price, I'll pay it. Abba's opinion be damned.

I squeeze her hand to convey all the certainty I don't feel. 'Look. If it's a mistake, well, my life has been a series of dead-end rabbit holes. We'll figure it out. What's the worst that can happen? You always have the restaurant, and who knows, maybe Rogers will take me back.'

She returns the squeeze, throws me a tentative smile. 'If you're sure . . .'

'Dead sure.'

Decision made.

Anjoli

Anjoli slipped on her Marigolds and turned to the sink, the warm soapy water a soothing contrast to her churning mind.

The cereal bowl clinked against the metal as she soaked it. Kamil was so having second thoughts about the agency. It was obvious in his enthusiastic *absolutelys* and *definitelys*, but that final *dead sure* had sealed it. Kamil had never been dead sure about anything in his life. Whether it was a new job, the latest gadget, or his romantic relationships, he was always chasing something brighter, just out of reach.

She scrubbed the bowl with a fierce intensity, the brush moving in rapid circles. She had seen that look so many times before – the one that said he was convincing himself as much as anyone else. 'Bloody idiot,' she muttered affectionately as she placed the utensil on the draining board. He could be such a child sometimes, bumbling through life with that puppy-dog exterior. But beneath that, there was a sharp detective brain capable of slicing through to the essentials. They were a good team. After all, they had solved four major crimes together.

Her likeness in the window looked back at her, eyes reflecting the same doubts she'd been harbouring for weeks. Was she making a huge mistake? Should she just set sail on her own?

Kamil would always be there to help when necessary. One less complication on their tortuous journey.

She sighed and rinsed her mug. 'Am I trying to convince myself now?' she asked aloud. The empty kitchen offered no answers, just the hum of the refrigerator and the sound of delivery vans on Brick Lane. Oh god! She was as bad as he was. Why couldn't she whole-heartedly commit? She certainly had feelings for him that were at least . . . love adjacent.

Maliha's memory surfaced, unbidden. She shook it off. Kamil had chosen *her*, Anjoli. That had to mean something. Could she meet him halfway, bridge the gap between their friendship and a deeper bond?

Her hands stilled in the suds. She cared for him more deeply than she had for anyone in years. But letting him keep his job while she embarked on this adventure alone? That was terrifying. What did she know about being a detective? Sure, she'd had moments of brilliance, but Kamil was the seasoned professional. He understood the intricate dance of procedure and interrogation, observation and analysis, skills honed over years. All she had was a smattering of knowledge from countless hours scouring Google. She watched the water swirl away her indecision. That was the heart of it – she needed him. Both professionally and personally.

The laptop on the counter beeped softly, reminding her of the upcoming interview. Okay, Anjoli. Focus.

She wiped her hands and brushed a few stray crumbs from her T-shirt, which declared, *The Universe Is Made Up Of Two Things: Matter & Shit That Doesn't Matter*. The irony wasn't lost on her.

Pulling up the candidate's CV, she scrolled through his impressive qualifications. Her cheek twitched in irritation at the thought of Chanson's inevitable resistance. He had been hinting for weeks about wanting more control, even suggesting she sell the restaurant to him. His dissatisfaction at being 'just' head chef was palpable, and his not-so-subtle advances added another layer of stress. Instead of addressing his inappropriate behaviour head-on, she'd carefully managed his expectations, keeping his hopes alive just enough to avoid him flouncing off to another restaurant. Tandoori Knights was her parents' legacy, and she still needed this life raft in case the detective gig didn't pan out.

Her work and personal lives were hopelessly entangled, and it seemed she was the one weaving the web. Her psychology degree had taught her to recognise these patterns, yet here she was, embroiled in them. She had to clarify things with Chanson and finally commit to Kamil. But something inside her . . .

'Right.' She slammed the laptop shut and stood, her resolve solidifying. 'Enough psycho-bullshittery. Time to sort your life out, Anjoli.'

She glanced at the clock. An hour left until the interview. She could still salvage the day and maybe find clarity along the way.

Kamil

I barrel through the station, heart pounding, just making it to Rogers' office by 9.55. Slowing my pace outside his door, I lean against the wall to catch my breath. The corridor smells faintly of disinfectant and coffee – a strangely comforting blend that momentarily calms my nerves.

Tahir saunters by. 'A'right, mate? Any idea what this is all about? Rogers didn't say when he asked me to come in. Very cloak-and-dagger.'

I swallow hard, guilt tightening my chest. 'Sorry, Tahir. I didn't know how to tell you.'

His eyebrows shoot up. 'What is it? You terminally ill or something? Spit it out.'

Rogers steps out of his office and gestures us inside. The door closes behind us with a soft thud, sealing us into his cluttered room. We sit on the worn sofa opposite him, the leather creaking under our weight. He gives me a warm smile before I can launch into my prepared spiel. 'I'm glad you arranged this, Kamil. I was planning to call you in. First, congratulations on your work with MI5. You got very positive feedback.' Tahir tries to conceal a sardonic smirk. It doesn't work. 'And second, now that you're back with us, I've got a special assignment . . .'

'Sir,' I interrupt. 'Before you go on, there's something I need to say.'

'Oh?' He leans back, eyebrows raised. Tahir's gaze sharpens.

I clear my throat. 'Well, I've been giving it a great deal of thought, and . . .'

Rogers' expectant look deepens. 'Yes?'

I take a deep breath, trying to quell the storm in my gut. 'I hereby present my resignation from the Metropolitan Police.' I pull the folded letter from my pocket, my hand trembling slightly as I place it on the desk in front of him. It sits there, like a tiny bomb ready to explode.

Rogers blinks, stunned, as if I've just sprouted an extra head. 'What? Why? You're a talented officer with a bright future ahead of you. Is this about the suspension? I explained that was beyond my control. It's all behind you now. We need role models from your background. Isn't that right, Tahir?'

I catch a flicker of disappointment on Tahir's face as he nods his assent. I hadn't anticipated such a heartfelt response. Why didn't Rogers say all this before I'd made my decision? My left hand twitches, eager to snatch back the letter, but I clamp it down with my right. 'Thank you, sir. I appreciate everything you and DI Tahir have done for me. But I'm looking to pursue another opportunity.'

'Oh really? And what opportunity might that be?'

I hesitate, feeling foolish. Should I mutter something vague about 'security services'? No. 'Anjoli and I . . . you remember Anjoli. We're planning to open a detective agency.'

For a moment, the room goes silent. Then Rogers guffaws, the sound loud and surprising in the small space. 'A detective agency? Why on earth . . . why? That's what people do when they can't make it in the force or when they retire. Not when they're starting out!'

I can hardly tell him it's because Anjoli's bored and I'm a prat. I settle for a po-faced, 'We'd like to give back to the community, sir.'

He's not buying it. 'You'll do far more good as an outstanding Muslim police sergeant. Yes, lad, you're up for promotion. You'll have to take the exam, but you have my full support. I've even put you in for a commendation.'

My heart leaps. Abba will be ecstatic – super-fast track. Then I remember why I'm here. 'I'm sorry, sir. I appreciate that, truly. But my mind's made up.'

Rogers sighs. 'Kamil, have you thought this through? There are hundreds of detective agencies in London, most barely scraping by. The work isn't glamorous. Divorces, eviction notices, insurance fraud. No homicides or the cases you excel at. Is that really what you want?'

A wave of doubt crashes over me. This is not how I expected this meeting to go. I thought I'd submit my letter. Rogers would nod, maybe shake my hand, and we'd part ways. Tahir would call me an idiot and then we'd grab a pint.

But now what? What if the DCI's right? Do I really want to spend my time chasing ambulances and spying on benefit claimants? Have Anjoli and I been carried away, imagining ourselves as the brown Strike and Ellacott?

'Well, sir . . .' My voice falters.

Rogers seizes the moment. 'Tell you what.' He stands, takes my letter, slips it into his drawer and shuts it with a definitive click. 'Let's hold on to this for now.' Walking around his desk, he looms over me. 'The Foreign Secretary got a call from the High Commission in Mumbai yesterday. A British citizen was murdered three days ago. They need one of our officers to shadow the police in Mumbai. They specifically asked for you.'

I blink. 'For me? Why?'

He shakes his head. 'I'm as puzzled as you are. But someone senior in the Indian Police Service requested you. I'm guessing because of all that business with the Indian PM?'

A lightbulb goes off. Darius. He must have pulled some strings to get me involved. But why?

Tahir breaks his silence. 'Who was killed?'

'A man named Peter Bell. A boring expert.'

Tahir knits his eyebrows. 'Why is he boring? Do you know him?'

Rogers chuckles at his own joke. 'No. He's an expert in boring. Tunnelling for construction. Underground.'

Tahir barely suppresses an eye-roll. I bite my lip to keep from laughing. 'And how was he killed?' Tahir asks.

Rogers' expression turns grave. 'Apparently, he was shot by an arrow.'

'An arrow?' Tahir and I exclaim together.

'Exactly. It sounds unlikely, but that's what the report said. His next of kin have agreed for you to represent them. You're to shadow the local investigators, establish the circumstances of Bell's death and return the body to the UK.'

Their eyes are on me, waiting.

'I appreciate the opportunity, sir. Can I think it over and get back to you?'

'By lunchtime,' Rogers says. 'They need an answer right away.'

So decision not quite made.

Back at Tandoori Knights, I slip quietly through the restaurant, trying not to disturb Anjoli and Chanson as they interview another manager candidate. Chanson, with his perpetual hyper energy, is gesturing wildly, probably spinning tall tales of his culinary exploits in Bangkok. I can't shake the suspicion he might be on something stronger than coffee, although I'm not sure what I'd do if I caught him at it. Even though I know he fancies Anjoli, I wouldn't want to destroy her cash cow (£135 Indicular gastronomy tasting menu, £200 with wine pairings), cokehead or not. I once asked her point-blank if she liked him, and she deflected the question in classic Anjoli style: 'I like a lot of things and a lot of people, Kamil.' Well, starting the agency could get her out of his orbit and into mine.

Stomach rumbling, I go into the restaurant kitchen, where I find some of his leftover prawn and asparagus salad with za'atar new potatoes. Although Chanson is a tosser, I will reluctantly admit he's a dab hand at unusual flavour combinations – the smoky Middle Eastern spice goes brilliantly with the sweet prawns and the earthy asparagus tips. I slope upstairs to the flat, throw myself onto the sofa, and scarf it down while scanning my phone for any news about Peter Bell's murder. Nothing comes up about his death, but a quick search reveals he's a top-tier tunnelling expert at Metcalfe Engineering in Leeds. How does a guy like that end up dead in Mumbai, impaled by an arrow? Should I take this last assignment? It sounds exciting. Maybe Anjoli's reaction will help me sort out my priorities.

Why has Darius pulled me into this? I dial his number, but it goes straight to voicemail. I google him. Still CEO of Mehta & Sons, the construction giant (*Building India for over a hundred years.*). A press release shows him glowering at the camera, arms folded, celebrating some new road project along the Mumbai coastline.

I smile at the memory of our last night together, drunkenly belting out 'never gonna keep us down' as we weaved down Marine Drive, a bottle of Johnnie Walker passing between us. Now he's a serious corporate honcho, and I'm seriously contemplating becoming Philip Marlowe. Well, I'll find out soon enough if I'm destined to be a gumshoe hired by a sultry dame to find her dead husband or a dick hired by a rapacious landlord to serve some poor sod with an eviction notice.

I head back down to the restaurant. The next twenty minutes will determine my future.

Anjoli

Anjoli sat across from Chanson, listening to him ramble on about the latest applicant's shortcomings, his fingernails tapping an erratic rhythm on the table. 'I don't know, Anj. Let me play devil's avocado for a second. She has a good CV, sure, but it's all Mayfair and Knightsbridge. How will she fit in? And why does she even want to be here? She came off as really aggressive.'

Just as she was about to slam her hand down on his fingers to shut him up, Kamil plopped down next to them.

'Come on, Chanson!' she said. 'She's perfect. Assertive, not aggressive. She's worked in Michelin-starred restaurants. She was probably trying to impress you.' She leaned in, her voice taking on a soft, encouraging tone, the kind she knew he responded to. 'And she wants to be here because of you. Who wouldn't? You're one of the top chefs in London. Besides, we need someone who can handle stroppy customers.'

'I can handle stroppy customers!' Chanson shot back. 'She'll just throw a Spaniard in the works!'

Anjoli glanced at Kamil, who was struggling to hide a grin. She turned back to her chef. 'You're not supposed to handle customers. You terrify them! And the staff. If I could, I'd lock you in the kitchen!'

'That's because I'm the squeaky wheel that gets the cheese!'

Kamil disguised a laugh as a cough, as Anjoli rubbed her temples, trying to stay composed. 'Enough with the nonsense!' She raised a hand, cutting off further debate. 'I'm making her an offer before another restaurant snaps her up.'

Chanson leaned back, crossing his arms defiantly. 'Let's see a few more candidates first. If she really wants to work with me, she'll wait.'

She blew out her cheeks in frustration. 'We need a competent manager now, not someone you can steamroll when I'm not around. I wish you'd stop arguing with me for once!'

'If wishes were horses, beggars would not be choosers.' He batted his eyelids at her, which, combined with his shaved head, thick neck and numerous tattoos, made him look like a bizarre GIF come to life.

She couldn't help but laugh. 'All right, take your high horse back to the kitchen. I need to talk to Kamil.'

Chanson winked at her and sauntered out. Kamil watched him leave, then turned to Anjoli. 'What a cowboy, eh?'

'Huh? Oh, right, high horse.' She humoured him with a sympathetic smile. 'He's impossible. Our candidates are either too aggressive or too meek. They either don't understand great cooking or aspire to be chefs themselves. He wants someone who's a cross between Stalin, Mother Teresa and Jay Rayner!'

'He has high standards after working with you. Can't blame him.'

She lifted her eyes heavenwards. Kamil's blatant apple-polishing never worked on her. 'Anyway, how was Rogers? Got your P45?'

His silence made her heart sink. 'You didn't do it, did you? I knew you'd bottle it.'

'No, I did. I did. But . . .'

'Am I wasting my time with all these interviews?' She sighed, stacking her notes into a neat pile. 'Go on.'

Kamil looked down, choosing his words carefully. 'I went in and told Rogers I was resigning to start our agency. Gave him the letter we wrote. Tahir was there. They were both shocked. But then . . .'

'Mmm-hmm?'

'He pointed out that running an agency would be tough, and—'

'We knew that. We said we'd go for it.'

'Let me finish! He said it'd be mostly insurance claims and eviction notices, which we *haven't* discussed. Then he asked if I could stay for one last case . . .' Kamil launched into an account of the meeting, finishing by saying, 'Oh, and he said I was going to be promoted to Sergeant.'

Anjoli mulled over what she'd just heard. This sounded like an amazing opportunity, but was it also his exit strategy? 'Mazel tov. But I thought you didn't want to work there anymore because of racism and all the bad shit that the Met has been doing?'

Kamil hesitated. 'That's true of course.'

'They probably want you to stay out of tokenism. To show they are changing. Which they aren't.' She saw his face tighten and quickly added, 'Not that you don't deserve the promotion.'

'Thanks. So what do you think I should do?'

She paused. 'Why did Darius ask for you? Why can't the local police handle it?'

'Dunno. He runs a massive construction company. Maybe Bell worked for him and got killed? The only way to find out is if I go.'

'How do you know Darius?' she asked to buy time.

'I met him during my posting in Mumbai. He's older than me, but we hit it off. Stayed in touch. He's a Parsi, married to Zara, a well-known fashion designer. They're fun, easy-going people. You'd like them. So, what do you think?'

Silence filled the space between them like a vacuum.

'An arrow?' Anjoli stood, smoothing the tablecloth absently. 'That's . . . freaky. And you want to go?'

She knew she was being less than supportive, but couldn't help it. It felt like Kamil was abandoning their agency, blowing a gaping hole in her plans. What if he ended up returning to India permanently, leaving her to manage everything alone?

'Honestly? It's flattering to be asked. But I'm conscious of my commitment to you, to us . . .' He came over to her, gently placed his hands on her arms, and turned her to face him. 'Why don't you leave the chancer in charge here and come to Mumbai with me? We could get into the rhythm of working together again. Think of it as a trial run for our agency.'

A tiny spark flickered in her chest. Enthusiasm? She had never been to Mumbai, and it did sound tempting. But leave Chanson running Tandoori Knights? That was a hell of a risk.

'Don't call him that. What would I do in Mumbai? I'd be in the way. A shadow of a shadow.'

'You won't. You always end up helping me. I couldn't have done half of the things I've achieved without you.'

She gave him a tiny smile. '*Most* of the things. What's Mumbai like?'

'Beautiful. Awful. You spend hours just stuck in traffic. But very special.'

'Where would I stay? Pretty sure the Met won't spring for my air ticket and hotel.'

'We'll cover the flight. Consider it a business expense. Daru has a massive house. We'll stay with him. Mumbai's lovely this time of year. We can escape Brick Lane's cold and damp. Plus, I'll earn another month's salary, which we can invest in our partnership.'

She could feel her doubts being titrated by his increasing enthusiasm. It would be their first trip together, a chance to figure out their relationship. But she couldn't let him think he'd won too easily.

'Not *un*interesting. I suppose a temporary delay wouldn't hurt. I'd need to manage things remotely.'

'Couldn't one of our waiters step up?'

'No. I'll have to Zoom in every day.'

Kamil's face lit up with a Cheshire Cat grin, making Anjoli hide her own smile. 'Okay, it's settled,' he said. 'Can we leave today? Rogers said it was urgent. He wants to know urgently.'

'Today? Is that even possible?' She glanced at her watch, ran her fingers through her hair, and let it fall loose. Weighed her next words. 'Did Rogers really say it'd be all eviction notices and insurance claims?'

'He did. I was googling.' Kamil handed her his phone. 'Most agencies advertise things like employee theft, absenteeism, watching nannies, unfaithful partners. What do we know about that?'

Anjoli stared at the screen, feeling the weight of her sandcastle dreams being washed away by reality. Was she doomed to run the restaurant forever? 'We can discuss all this later. Right now I've got shitloads to sort out if I'm really coming with you to Mumbai. Call Rogers. Tell him you'll do it and book the tickets. Check with Darius if it's okay for us to stay at his place.'

Kamil's face brightened with a mixture of relief and elation. As he reached for his phone, Anjoli turned away, a cocktail of emotions swirling within her. This was a leap into the unknown, but maybe, just maybe, it was the jump start they both needed.

Kamil

Mumbai. Tuesday, 29 November.
Five days to go.

The stars outside the aircraft window gleam like scattered diamonds against the velvet night, mirroring the flickering lights of the cities far below. The faint hum of the engine and the rhythmic breathing of Anjoli, her head nestled on my shoulder, are oddly soothing. Her hair smells faintly of jasmine shampoo, a scent that cuts through the sterile tang of the airplane cabin and makes my cramped middle seat a little more bearable.

Mumbai.

The name echoes in my mind, pulling me back to Abba's voice eight years ago. 'Kamil, you need to expand your horizons. I've arranged a secondment for you in Mumbai with Inspector Naik. You leave next week.'

Back then, the idea of Mumbai had been exhilarating. A city alive with energy, twice the murder rate of Kolkata, and a desperate need for more hands. I looked forward to solving cases that were more gripping than the routine burglaries and traffic violations I'd been dealing with. But Naik's not-so-silent resentment at an outsider foisted on him turned my days into a cage of paperwork and dead-end desk duties and, after a few months, I retreated home, tail plastered between my legs. Maybe that's when I learned to run when things got tough. Anjoli would have a field day psychoanalysing that habit.

A gentle tap on my arm pulls me out of my reverie and a steward proffers a glass of water. I shake my head and glance down at Anjoli, careful not to wake her. My arm's gone numb under her weight, and my restless mind needs calming. I reach into the seat pocket and pull out the stack of documents from the Foreign Office on body repatriation procedures. The words blur as I skim through them, my thoughts drifting between my past and the uncertain future awaiting us in Mumbai.

The next thing I know, the pilot's message crackles through the intercom, announcing our descent. The sudden jolt of the landing stirs Anjoli. She blinks against the harsh sunlight flooding through the window, her voice thick with sleep. 'Did you rest?'

'Dozed off a bit,' I reply, trying to mask my fatigue. 'Didn't want to disturb you.'

At immigration, we split into different lines – me with the Indian passports, Anjoli with the foreigners. My queue is interminable, a snake of weary travellers inching forward. By the time I rejoin her, she's already collected our bags. We wheel them out of the terminal and I'm immediately assaulted by Mumbai's sensory overload. The heat wallops me first. Then an embrace from the humidity saturates my clothes and skin in its sticky grip. A jab from the air follows, stinging my eyes and nostrils with the acrid effluvium from diesel exhausts. The finishing touch is a punch to the ears from the cacophony of taxi drivers shouting for fares.

Anjoli's face is a study, her wrinkled nose betraying her discomfort. I can't help but smile. 'Welcome to Mumbai,' I say, giving in to the city's familiar, chaotic grasp.

'There,' she points, spotting a tall, athletic young guy in a pristine white uniform, gloves and shiny black shoes. He holds a sign with my name, his hesitant smile widening as we approach.

'I'm Kamil.'

He snaps to attention, offering a salute that's almost comically eager. 'Welcome, saar. Myself Imran. Darius saar send. I take bag?'

Before I can respond, he deftly grabs our luggage and leads us to a sleek blue BMW 6 Series. Sinking into the luxurious seat, Anjoli immediately plucks at her T-shirt and directs the air conditioning vents towards her. 'Nice car. Your friend is certainly pulling out all the stops.'

Imran hands us cold bottles of water. 'Where are we going?' I ask.

'Office. Nariman Point,' he replies, his English heavily accented but clear.

Anjoli takes a long swig of her water. 'You sure you want me to come?'

'Absolutely.'

The drive to Nariman Point is a gruelling crawl through a sea of vehicles. The sky above is a dull, overcast grey, punctuated occasionally by rumbles of thunder. We weave through narrow streets and wide boulevards, the city's relentless honking and the constant jostling of cars, scooters and buses taking its toll on my sleep-deprived body. We pass a billboard depicting a serene lake with mountains in the background. The slogan reads: *Kashmir. You can't have enough of it!*

Anjoli catches my eye. 'What?'

'What, what?'

'You had a funny expression.'

'Just thinking of Kashmir and all the terrible stuff I saw there.' I tap the driver on the shoulder. 'Tell me, Imran. You're Muslim. Have things changed much for you since the PM resigned?'

Imran pauses, choosing his words carefully. 'Do not know, saar. Hoping. Maybe better life for my small daughters. Difficult for us now. Not so much money. But Faraz saar, Darius saar,

33

Niloufer madam, very good people. Look after us.' I catch his eye in the rearview mirror. 'You are man who save PM, no? I see on TV.'

'Yes. But I was just doing my job. I don't like him.'

'I no like, also. He no good.'

A wave of melancholy washes over me, and the bullet wound in my leg pulses with a dull ache. What have all my efforts been for if the situation for minorities remains unchanged? Is this trip going to be another exercise in futility?

We finally reach Nariman Point, its glass and steel towers gleaming against the stormy backdrop of clouds. The reception at Mehta & Sons is on the twentieth floor, and after a brief check-in with a young receptionist named Omar, Anjoli excuses herself to freshen up.

I wander over to the large window, mesmerised by the view of the crashing waves and turbulent skies. Dim lights from cars crawl along the distant roads, and tiny black umbrellas bob on rain-slick pavements.

'That's gorgeous!' Anjoli's voice startles me. She stands beside me in a fresh T-shirt that reads *Luke, I am Your Sister*, her gaze fixed on the horizon. 'I could stand here for hours and just stare.'

A young man in a sharp suit appears. 'Mr Kamil Rahman?'

'Present.'

'I am Mr Darius's executive assistant. Please follow me. Sir is waiting for you.'

My friend is a shadow of the man I knew. The once towering figure with a commanding presence is now standing before me in a crumpled suit with his tie askew, looking gaunt and tired, his hair streaked with grey and weariness drawn on his pale face. Suppressing my concern, I say, 'Hi, Daru. This is Anjoli.'

'Welcome. Nice to meet you finally. Kamil's told me a lot about you.' His smile is faint, almost forced. 'Please, sit. Coffee? Tea? Something stronger?'

'Tea would be good,' Anjoli replies as we settle onto his sofa. The assistant hurries off to fetch the drinks. Darius stares at us, as if unsure of what to say.

'Are you okay, Daru? You seem . . . tired. Working too hard?'

Another rictus of a grin. 'Or hardly working. Haven't been sleeping too well.'

'What's going on?'

'Ah. Chai.'

The assistant lays out tea and biscuits for us. Darius rises and pours himself a glass of Scotch from his drinks cabinet, the amber liquid catching the light as he moves. 'You're sure . . .'

'No thanks.' A knot of worry tightens. 'What's this all about? Why am I here?'

He downs his drink in one gulp, the alcohol bringing a fleeting spark of life back into his visage. Refills his glass. 'All in good time. You tell me. I read how you saved the PM's life. That was impressive. Did you get the Padma Shri for your heroism?'

'Hardly. What's been the reaction to his resignation?'

'*I'm* pleased. Never liked him, although he was good for business. But he still has a hard core of supporters who say he was set up. Elections are in eighteen months and they are desperate to win. We'll see what happens. How's Maliha? She was all over the airwaves, talking about him. Very brave.'

'She's fine.'

He glances at Anjoli. 'So, are the two of you . . .'

An awkward silence. Anjoli shoots me a look. Her lips twitch. 'We're partners.'

Trust her to be creatively ambiguous.

'And the commissioner? Still disappointed in his only son?'

'Abba is Abba. He'll never change. I think he was happy I got some public recognition, even though I could have done without it.'

Darius is lost in thought, focused on his whisky. 'So, what's the urgency, Daru? Why did you bring us to Mumbai? I was told a strange story about a murdered Englishman?'

He gathers his thoughts. 'Yes. Peter Bell. Have you heard about the Mumbai Coastal Road project?'

'I read something about it on your website.'

'You experienced the awful traffic coming from the airport? It's an ambitious plan to build a road over the sea, a massive billion-dollar scheme awarded by the municipal corporation. We are the prime contractor. Everything was going smoothly, on plan, on budget. Then, three weeks ago, we brought in an English expert to advise us on building a tunnel that's part of the project.'

'Bell?'

Darius nods, his expression darkening. 'An exceptional engineer. He was found dead last Friday on the rocks off Marine Drive, across from the Hindu Gymkhana, where we are planning to start the tunnel.'

'Shot with a bow and arrow? Is that right?'

'Actually, he had eighteen arrows jammed into him.'

Anjoli gasps. The air seems to solidify. The room grows silent and tense. I clench my fist. *Eighteen arrows.*

Darius swallows hard. 'It was . . . shocking. The local police are investigating, but I requested your involvement as a liaison. To shadow them.'

'Why?'

He hesitates, his leg bouncing nervously. Takes another sip of his drink. 'I feel responsible for Peter's death. We asked him to consult for us. He died on my watch, and . . . I'm not sure how effective the Mumbai cops will be. A dead Englishman isn't high on their priority list.'

'Do they have any suspects?'

'There was a similar murder in Bandra recently. They think it may be connected. Ritual killings committed by a fundo.'

'Fundo?' Anjoli asks.

'A religious fundamentalist. Hindu fanatic, maybe.'

I lean forward. 'So, they believe it's a serial killer?'

'Do two deaths make a serial killer? Apparently, the number eighteen is also significant. I can't think who'd want to harm Peter, especially in this horrible fashion. You couldn't have met a more inoffensive fellow. Quiet. Kept to himself. This was his first trip to India. He didn't know anyone here.'

'How come the press hasn't picked it up? Seems like quite a juicy story.'

'It's been in a couple of local papers. They haven't connected it to the Bandra killing. I only hope our name is kept out of it.'

'Anything strike you about Bell? Something you noticed? Any arguments with others?'

Darius looks pensive. 'He . . . he did seem concerned about something.'

'What?'

'I . . . don't know exactly.'

'How do you know he was concerned?'

'Just a sense I got.'

Anjoli interrupts. 'What does shadowing the police mean? What would Kamil's role be? I can't imagine your cops being thrilled about him second-guessing their investigation.'

'You're not wrong. I had to lean on them to allow him to come. Luckily, I have some clout in this city. Technically, you're here to sort out the admin to ship Peter's body back to the UK.' A sudden intensity enters his gaze. 'Look, maybe you won't be able to help, but I owe it to Peter to find out what happened.'

Something feels off. Seems odd to summon me from England for this. What is he not telling me?

'Where was he staying?'

'We put him up at the Oberoi. Round the corner from here.'

'Who found the body?'

'Some fellow taking a sunrise walk on Marine Drive. He called the police, and they contacted me.'

'Who's handling the case?'

'An Inspector Karve. I've arranged for you to meet him tomorrow morning at the station. He'll bring you up to speed.' Darius looks away, the weight of the conversation settling heavily on his shoulders.

'Hey,' I say after a pause. 'Daru, there's something else, isn't there? Come on. I know you. Why am I really here?'

He takes a deep breath and meets my gaze. 'The thing is, Zara doesn't think I should have bothered you. Maybe she's right. Perhaps I shouldn't have. But there is something else you could help with. Or maybe you can't. You'll think I'm crazy, but . . .'

His desk phone rings, cutting him off. He slams a button, his voice sharp. 'I said I wasn't to be disturbed!'

'Sorry, sir, but Sunil Tandel is in the office now. You said you wanted to know as soon as he got in?'

He freezes. Shoots me a calculating look. 'I have to take this meeting. Listen, why don't we reconvene for lunch in an hour? I'll ask Zara to join us.'

I want to press him, to get to the heart of what's troubling him, but it'll have to wait. 'All right. We'll go for a stroll and get some fresh air. Where should we meet?'

'Britannia. You'll love it.' His smile is ragged. I squeeze his shoulder, giving him a speculative look. What's my friend hiding that's transformed him into this shell of his former self?

Anjoli

'What did you make of that?' asked Kamil as he and Anjoli walked out of the marble lobby of Mehta & Sons. Anjoli stretched, trying to shake off the fatigue from their lengthy flight. The prospect of lunch with Darius and his wife was a lot less appealing than a hot shower and a long nap. 'Not sure. He doesn't seem much like the fun, happy-go-lucky guy you described.'

'Yeah, something's definitely not right. I've never seen him this way before.'

She turned the conversation over in her mind. 'Although to be fair, it's pretty terrible for someone you've employed to drop dead. With eighteen arrows in him. What's that about? It's like something from a Dan Brown novel!'

'I know, right? But that only just happened. Daru looks like he's been ill for months. I still don't understand why he sent for me.'

'Hey, who wouldn't want Kamil Rahman, super sleuth, to investigate the Case of the Perforated Engineer? But he did intimate that there was something else.'

'True. No idea what it could be, though. And why this elaborate rigmarole? Why not just ask me directly?'

The sun made an appearance as they walked onto the seafront, ocean stretching before them in a vast, restless expanse. Anjoli took a deep breath, trying to wake herself up. 'Were you and Darius close, then?'

'We were pretty good mates. I met him at some party, and we got on. He was a great guy to get drunk with. I didn't know many people in Mumbai, so he and Zara took me under their wing. Introduced me to their friends. I owe him for making my life bearable when the job got too boring.'

Anjoli raised her arms over her head, feeling her muscles loosen. 'Well, maybe he thinks it's payback time.'

'It would help if I knew exactly what it is I'm supposed to be paying back with. Hopefully it'll become clearer over lunch. Anyway, let me show you Marine Drive. It was one of my favourite places to come to when I was miserable in Mumbai.'

'*Miserable in Mumbai*. Is that the sequel to *Cop in Kolkata*?' Unable to help herself, she felt a twinge of jealousy. 'Did you come with Maliha?'

'No, she was back in Kolkata. Always wanted someone to walk hand in hand with here, though – it's so romantic. And by the way,' he added with air quotes, 'partners?'

She chuckled. 'Aren't we?'

'Are we?'

'Sure. In our detective agency.'

A flash of disappointment crossed his face. Anjoli felt a stab of guilt. Why was she toying with him? It would be so easy to just give in and become a couple. He was good-looking, smart, funny, moral. He really cared about doing the right thing, even though he often didn't do the thing right. They had a spark. So what was stopping her?

She breathed in the sea air, still damp with the petrichor remnants of the rainstorm, and impulsively took his hand. He stiffened for a second, then squeezed it. The graceful curve of the road around the bay, the tall buildings gleaming across the restless water, the smell of the briny ocean – all lifted her spirits.

40

Kamil looked out over the sea. 'I remember perching on the parapet one evening after a stressful day. I was staring blankly at nothing. Then I noticed the sky was a blue I'd never seen before. The thrashing of the waves filled my ears. I felt the spray fly up at me and dust my cheek. Smelt the ocean. Tasted it. And at that moment, something extraordinary happened that I've never experienced again.'

Anjoli turned to him. 'What?'

'My mind stopped.'

'Huh?'

'The little voice in my head that had been missing Maliha, obsessing over my career, wondering if I should go back to Kolkata, it went totally silent. I felt the most incredible peace. I sat here, bathed in quiet joy. And then – poof – it was gone. Followed by despair at being unable to maintain it, like all the good things in my life.' He squeezed her hand again, as if to anchor himself in the moment.

Strangely moved by this revelation, Anjoli squeezed back. 'Y'know . . . you can maintain the good things in your life. You still have me, remember?'

His gaze lingered on her. 'I know.' He pointed across the ocean. 'Forget the traffic and imagine what Bombay was like centuries ago. A tiny fishing village that grew into the heart of the British Empire.'

'It's beautiful. I love the palm trees.' She twined her fingers into his, intensely aware of his body moving next to hers. She could smell his aftershave and knew he was as conscious of her as she was of him.

They walked in comfortable silence, their steps matching the gentle rhythm of the sea lapping against the rocks. The city buzzed around them, a hive of activity, but in this moment, it was just the two of them.

Half an hour slipped by as they strolled, hands still interlaced.

The seafront was abruptly cut off by a yellow hoarding with jaunty navy-blue waves at the base. It read: *Mumbai Coastal Road Project. Connecting People & Places.*

Anjoli gently disentangled her fingers. 'This must be what Darius was talking about.'

'You're right.' Kamil scanned the area. 'The Hindu Gym's just there. They would have found Bell's body somewhere around here.'

The spell between them broke. Anjoli scrambled up the embankment, Kamil following. Looking down at the strange, black, sausage-shaped concrete blocks that made a levee between the seawall and the ocean, she said, 'No sign of anything untoward happening here.'

'If it was here, they killed him somewhere else, then threw him over,' Kamil speculated. 'They'd hardly shoot him full of arrows on this busy road in public view.'

Anjoli pointed. 'Maybe they did it inside that bit that's boarded off? There's an access gate there, look.'

They peered through a crack in the padlocked door. All she could see were fragments of a metal shack surrounded by random bits of equipment.

'Bell was working on the project. He may have had a key,' she mused. 'The killer could have taken it from him and forced him inside. Then he could do what he wanted in private.'

'I'll ask Daru. It'd take some strength to drag Bell from in here, haul him over the parapet and throw him onto the rocks when he was riddled with arrows. I saw his picture online. He wasn't a small man.'

'Maybe it was more than one person?'

'Maybe. Question is, was he randomly chosen or was he targeted?'

'Or is it a serial killer?' She stretched once again and let out a pleasurable groan. 'Where's this restaurant? My stomach's rumbling. And it's getting hot.'

Kamil rattled the lock on the door in front of them. 'I'll call the driver.'

As they waited for the car, a shaft of sunlight broke through the clouds and illuminated the tops of the palms. They looked like they were on fire.

Kamil

I mran drops us off outside Britannia and Co. Restaurant, nestled among the grand, ageing British-era buildings of Ballard Estate. The verdant branches overhead sway gently in the wind, droplets of recent rain glistening on the lush leaves. It's been years since I've set foot in this part of town, but it looks exactly as I remember – a hidden enclave, reminiscent of a time when Mumbai was Bombay. The warmth of Anjoli's hand in mine still lingers like a glove.

We cross the road and step inside, passing a sign that boldly proclaims:

EXOTIC PARSI AND IRANIAN CUISINE.

This is no lie, going by the specials on the blackboard.

Iranian Kesar

Fry Bombay Duck

Gaz

Sohan

Drink of the Century - Sosyo

Darius isn't here yet, so we pick a table covered with a red-and-white checked plastic tablecloth. The high ceilings and peeling bottle-green walls tell tales of a place that hasn't changed in decades. On the back wall, three full-size flags – Indian, British and Iranian – twitch in the breeze from a ceiling fan that looks like it's exhausted from years of service. Portraits of

Gandhi, Queen Elizabeth and Zoroaster dot the other walls, casting their doleful gazes over the sparse lunchtime crowd.

A dog sprawls on the cash counter, one eye lazily tracking our movements as we settle into our seats. In the corner, a group of bow-tied waiters lounge like indolent penguins, smartphones in hand. The scene could easily belong to any era if not for those tiny screens.

A prominent sign on the wall catches my eye:

SORRY

NO TALKING TO CASHIER
NO SMOKING
NO FIGHTING
NO CREDIT
NO OUTSIDE FOOD
NO SITTING LONG
NO TALKING LOUD
NO SPITTING
NO BARGAINING
NO WATER TO OUTSIDERS
NO CHANGE
NO TELEPHONE
NO MATCH STICKS / LIGHTER
NO DISCUSSING GANBLING
NO NEWSPAPER
NO COMBING HAIR
NO BEEF
NO LEG ON CHAIR
NO HARD LIQUOR ALLOWED
NO ADDRESS ENQUIRY
NO PHOTOGRAPHY
ANY INDIVIDUAL OR ARTICLE WILL BE
CHECKED ON SUSPICION

I nudge Anjoli, who grins and immediately breaks a rule by taking a sneaky photograph. 'I have this sudden urge to comb my hair, put my leg on the chair and loudly discuss ganbling,' she whispers.

'And I'll start a fight with you over what the address of this place is.'

'Lol. There they are.'

I turn to see Darius and Zara walking in through the door. They look almost ethereal, backlit by the day, but there's a heaviness in their steps.

'Sorry we're late. Anjoli, this is my wife, Zara. Zara, Anjoli. She's Kamil's,' Darius winks, 'partner.'

The old Darius seems to be breaking through the gloom.

I lean in for an air-kiss, noticing the artificial smile and the strain lines on Zara's face. 'How do you never age? You look even more beautiful than you did all those years ago.'

Slimmer and shorter than her husband, wearing jeans and a smart red shirt, Zara's long black hair frames her dimpled cheeks and oval face. She shakes Anjoli's hand while Darius flops into the chair opposite me, ignoring its groan. 'This is our favourite restaurant. Best Parsi food in the world. Other than Zara's, of course.' He pulls four cold beers out of his bag. 'They don't have a liquor licence, but you can bring your own.'

Anjoli unfolds her napkin. 'I was hoping to try the drink of the century.'

'Avoid Sosyo unless you want to rot your teeth,' Zara says, her smile wry, but not quite reaching her eyes.

A burly man in a white shirt gone grey, who's been standing at the entrance staring out at the empty street, ambles over.

'Hi, Neville, meet my friends, Kamil and Anjoli,' Darius says. 'This is Neville Irani, the owner. His grandfather started the restaurant . . . when was it?'

Neville claps Darius on the back with a hearty laugh. 'Over a century ago. And we are still a mixture of Iran, India and Britain.'

Anjoli smiles. 'I'm British.'

Neville's face lights up. 'Oh, very good, very good. We have always been partial to the English. We called the restaurant Britannia for a reason. What can I bring you, Darius?'

'The usual. Sali boti and chicken berry pulao for everyone.'

Darius takes a swig of his beer as we wait for the food to arrive. 'Many Parsis were unhappy when India got independence. We had real status under the British. My great-grandfather Homi was even knighted.'

Zara interjects acidly, 'To be accurate, he bought his baronetcy.'

Darius grimaces. 'Well, yes. The Raj required a twenty-five lakh contribution. But he deserved it. He founded Mehta & Sons, and my grandfather, Xerxes, built it into one of India's biggest construction companies.'

'How much would that be in today's money?' asks Anjoli.

'Around two and a half million pounds,' says Darius.

'Gosh. Your family has an impressive pedigree.' I detect a hint of sarcasm in Anjoli's tone and give her a sideways look, but no one else seems to notice.

'After the British left,' Darius continues, 'Parsis started losing their standing. And on Independence Day in 1947 . . .' his voice trails off. He sneaks a glimpse at Zara, who studiously ignores him.

Anjoli catches the awkwardness. 'What happened?'

Darius looks at his wife again as the food arrives. 'Eat. Before it gets cold.'

The sali boti turns out to be meltingly tender mutton in a rich brown masala, thick with onions, ginger, garlic and chilli, topped with fried shoestring potatoes that provide a satisfying crunch. The chicken berry pulao is the highlight – a decadent tomato sauce envelops the delicate chicken, hidden inside flaky basmati rice, scattered with cashews, slightly sweet caramelised onions and tart barberries. The contrasting textures and layers of flavour are an orchestra in my mouth. All conversation grinds to a halt as Anjoli and I dive into the food. Darius and Zara barely touch theirs, ingesting bird-like quantities, while pushing the rest around their plates.

Sated, I sit back. 'That was absolutely incredible, Daru!'

'Wait till you try the caramel custard.'

'I don't know if I can,' groans Anjoli. 'I'm totally stuffed.'

'Nonsense. You can't miss it. Neville, four caramel custards, please.'

I steer the conversation back to the matter at hand. 'We walked down Marine Drive to the Hindu Gymkhana. Where exactly was Bell's body found? Was it near your boarded-off construction site?'

Darius flinches. 'Next to it.'

'Could he have been killed inside there? We saw a locked door. Did Bell have a key?' Anjoli asks.

'No.'

'Who does?' I press.

'The site's not ours.' He hesitates. 'It's run by one of our sub-contractors, Arpin Industries. But Karve said the lock was quite basic. Anyone could have bypassed it.'

'What does Arpin do?'

'Demolitions. The police looked inside the site but found nothing.'

'Did Bell have any interaction with Arpin?' I push further.

He looks away. 'Don't see why he'd need to.'

There's something in his tone, but the rich food, beer and lack of sleep are making my head swim. Zara's also strangely silent – normally, she's always chattering away. 'Have you partnered with Arpin a lot?'

'First time. They bid against us for the Coastal Road contract. When it was awarded to Mehta & Sons, they kicked up a stink. Said we won by underhand means. Threatened to sue.'

Anjoli's forehead wrinkles. 'So how come you're working with them now?'

'They . . .' he pauses, clearly struggling with what to reveal, 'unexpectedly dropped the suit. And surprisingly, their CEO agreed to become a subcontractor.'

'Why surprising? Presumably he thought they wouldn't win in court?'

'It was out of character for him. He's a really arrogant guy. I think he may have an ulterior motive.'

Anjoli leans in. 'Which is?'

Darius glances at Zara, who is now staring at the table, and just shakes his head. There's something not quite right in this conversation, an edginess I can't place and undercurrents that keep threatening to drag us down. Is Darius nervous because Zara doesn't want me here? What was the other thing he said he wanted me here for? The beer has given me a headache, and I'm tiring of these half-hints. I bite back my irritation. 'Who else was Bell working with in your company? I should speak to them.'

'I can arrange that. But I doubt any of my people were involved with his death.'

Zara finally breaks her silence. 'It's hit Daru really badly. Peter was a nice man.'

I look at her, sensing more beneath her words. 'You met him?'

'Yes, we had him over for dinner one night.'

'How did you come across Bell, Darius? Had you worked with him before?' Anjoli asks.

'No. Faraz partnered with his company, Metcalfe, on a project we did in London. I contacted them and they recommended Peter.'

'Faraz?'

'My father-in-law. Zara's dad. Chairman of Mehta & Sons. He's eighty-four now. Been in the company since my granddad's time. Sadly, now he's . . . very ill.'

Zara's jaw tightens. 'Lung cancer. He doesn't have long.'

Ah. Maybe that explains her closed-off demeanour. Poor thing.

'I'm so sorry, Zara,' says Anjoli, her voice soft with genuine sympathy.

Zara nods and turns away, dabbing at her face with a paper napkin.

I'm terrible at offering consolation. 'I'm sure he's had a good and fulfilling life,' I say.

'It is what it is,' Zara replies. 'He lives with us. We're trying to make his last days as comfortable as we can. He's coming home from hospital tomorrow, so you'll get to meet him.'

'Did you two meet through your dad, then?' asks Anjoli. 'Because he worked with Darius's grandfather?'

Darius gives Zara a warm smile. 'Yes. We grew up together. She was the annoying little kid with braces and plaits. Then she went off to college and came back as this gorgeous, talented designer. Boom! I was smitten. And the rest is chemistry.'

Zara looks down. A tear drops onto the plastic covering.

'Are you okay?' I ask, concerned.

'I'm fine. It's a difficult time with Puppa and Daru and . . .' she bites her lip, 'everything.'

Dessert arrives, and we eat in silence. The slightly bitter caramel and silky, sweet set custard slide down my throat, but the unease around us is deepening. Darius's leg is jiggling under the table and Zara hasn't touched her dessert. Anjoli's glancing from one to the other, clearly also wondering what's going on.

Enough. I have to know what's underneath all of this. I push my plate aside. 'What's the story, Daru? You seem very different from before. You've lost weight, you're incredibly stressed. I mean, come on. Whisky at eleven in the morning? Beer for lunch? Have you really dragged me across the world to solve Bell's murder? You said in your office there was something else. Spit it out. What is it, really?'

My friend flinches at my barrage of questions, shrinking into himself. His eyes look haunted. He sighs heavily. 'Perhaps Zara was right. Maybe I shouldn't have asked you to come.' Another deep breath. 'But you're correct. Peter Bell's death was an excuse.'

'An excuse for what?'

He pauses. Zara looks up, her voice sharp with frustration. 'Oh, tell him, for god's sake.'

'Tell me what?' I ask, my patience fraying.

'Nothing. It's stupid,' Darius mumbles, looking away.

Zara slams her palm down on the table as the dog lets out a startled bark. 'If you don't tell him, I will. I told you not to call him all the way from London. We could have made our own arrangements. But now that he's here . . .'

Darius exhales a long, defeated breath. 'All right. Kamil, I'm going to die on Sunday. And I need you to stop it from happening.'

Anjoli

The air in the room seemed to coalesce after Darius's pronouncement and Anjoli felt goosebumps rise on her arms. Kamil's laughter shattered the spell, jarring in its harshness. 'Well, if you don't stop hoovering up these berry pulaos and sali botis, the cholesterol will kill you. But deciding it's going to happen on Sunday? That's oddly specific.'

Anjoli nudged his foot under the table. His face flickered with confusion, unaware of the anxiety that had enveloped his friends. She forced herself to ask, 'What's happening on Sunday, Darius?'

'Please, call me Daru. Everyone does. It's my forty-seventh birthday.'

Kamil's brows knitted together, his gaze darting between Darius and Zara, searching for an anchor in this sudden tonal shift. 'So?'

Darius hesitated as Zara leaned forward. 'Just tell him!'

'Tell me *what*?' said Kamil, clearly annoyed now.

Anjoli felt a coil of unease tighten in her stomach. Whatever this was, it wasn't trivial. She wished Kamil would listen, see the storm brewing behind Darius's eyes.

'There's a curse of death on my family,' said Darius. 'It's already taken two people.'

The words hung there, floating like a surreal cartoon bubble over them. Anjoli felt as if their table had become enveloped in a force field which dimmed the light and caused the clink of cutlery and murmur of conversations to fade into a distant hum. Reality seemed to pause, waiting for an unseen power to restart it.

What did Darius mean? She knew superstitions were as common in India as chai and street vendors. Curses, ghosts, rituals, charms to ward off the evil eye – they were all part of the cultural fabric. But it was weird to see such fear in this modern couple.

'Curse? Oh, come on! What are you guys playing at?' Kamil's bravado was tinged with uncertainty.

Darius responded with a fierce intensity. 'It's *not* a joke, Kamil. A spirit has been killing my ancestors, and I'm terrified I'll be next.'

Anjoli's breath caught. She turned to Kamil, who was poised to pooh-pooh the idea again, and interjected quickly, 'Tell us, Daru.' Anything to prevent Kamil from dismissing it outright. He glanced at her, irritation flickering, but then nodded slowly.

Darius exhaled deeply, the story spilling out in a rush, as if he could no longer contain it. 'It started on Independence Day. 1947. The riots . . .' His voice grew quieter as he got lost in a past he had never witnessed but was bound to by blood. 'My grandfather, Xerxes, took in as many people as he could into our house. But many Muslims died just outside the walls. His cook's entire family was wiped out. Before he died, the cook cursed my grandfather and his descendants to perish by fire on our forty-seventh birthdays.'

The temperature of the force field surrounding them dropped and Anjoli felt a chill. She leaned closer, her gaze never leaving Darius's. 'What happened?'

'Xerxes didn't believe it. But on his forty-seventh birthday . . .' Darius's voice cracked. 'He burst into flames.'

Kamil's gasp cut through Darius's agitation. 'He . . . what? He spontaneously combusted?'

'Yes. My father and Faraz both witnessed it firsthand. Then, exactly the same thing happened to my father on *his* forty-seventh birthday. Zara and I were there. I swear to you it occurred.'

Anjoli's gaze shifted to Zara, who was methodically shredding a napkin into minuscule pieces, her face as pale as the paper in her hands.

'You and Zara actually saw the spontaneous combustion of your father?' Kamil's scepticism was straining against the growing weight of the story.

'That's terrible, Daru. How old were you?' said Anjoli.

'Nineteen. Zara was fourteen.'

Zara's eyes shimmered. 'It was horrible. I still have nightmares about it.'

Anjoli's chest tightened. She wanted to reach out, to somehow bridge the chasm of pain separating them. 'I'm so sorry. How awful for you both.'

Darius's expression hardened. 'An extraordinary thing, right? Both dying by fire? On their forty-seventh birthdays? As predicted? Over the past year, my fear's been growing. I'm next in line. And this weekend . . .'

Anjoli felt a strange kinship with this man whose life was underpinned by a date and a fire. 'You turn forty-seven. No wonder you're scared.'

Darius nodded, his grip on the beer glass tightening until his knuckles whitened. 'I've been going crazy. Is it a curse? Coincidence? Conspiracy? I don't know anymore. But I read about you saving the PM, Kamil. And for some stupid reason, I thought if there was a detective . . . a friend I trusted . . . by my side, then maybe I'd be safe. And if . . . if your being here doesn't work, if there really *is* a curse and it kills me, you can investigate my death. Stop this ghost before it gets my kids.'

'How old are your children?' Anjoli asked.

'Twins,' Zara's voice cracked. 'Boy and girl. Ten.'

Darius continued. 'I know it makes no sense, but nothing in this nightmare does. Then when Peter died, it gave me an excuse and . . .'

'You got your police contacts to ask Scotland Yard to send me,' said Kamil. 'You could have asked me directly, Daru.'

Darius's shoulders sagged. 'You'd think I was bonkers.'

'No, I wouldn't.'

A wounded look entered his friend's eyes. 'You already do! You called it a joke. And you know what? I don't blame you.'

'Daru,' Kamil said softly, 'it is a coincidence, though. Curses aren't a thing in the modern world. They are just excuses people resorted to in mediaeval times when no one knew about science and medicine.'

Anjoli bristled. 'Don't be so dismissive, Kamil. We don't know everything. Strange things happen all the time. *I* believe you, Daru.'

Darius said wearily, 'No, he's probably right. I'm sure it'll all be fine. I dragged you here for no reason.' He looked at Zara. 'You were right, jaan. As always.'

Zara looked away, her expression unreadable.

'So you don't actually want me to investigate Bell's murder?' asked Kamil.

'It's complicated. His death was tragic, and I really hope it has nothing to do with Mehta & Sons, especially given the other similar killing in Bandra. But if there's the slightest chance it does, then I need to know.'

Kamil nodded slowly, the pieces falling into place. 'And you're worried the police will just assume the two killings are connected and go down that line of inquiry?'

'Exactly. Not that I want them to investigate us. I know you're here primarily to shadow the Indian cops, but I thought you could pursue your own inquiries. Discreetly. Just ensure Peter's death is unconnected to his work for us and then leave it to Karve.'

'Do you think it might be connected?'

He looked away. 'I . . . I don't know.'

Kamil gave him a sharp stare. 'Okay, I'll do some poking around.'

Darius grabbed his arm. 'And if something happens to me on Sunday, you'll try to save my children from the same fate?'

Zara was audibly sniffling now.

Kamil patted his friend's hand. 'I promise. But nothing will.'

Darius exhaled a slow, trembling breath. 'Thank you, my friend. I knew I could rely on you.'

Anjoli watched this exchange, a lump forming in her throat. She had never seen Kamil so earnest, so vulnerable with anyone. She envied their bond.

'What are your plans for your birthday, Daru?' she asked.

Zara pulled at her hair in despair. 'A massive party on Saturday. Can you believe it? Outside catering, live band, fireworks, the lot. I've told him it's a terrible idea, but will he listen?'

'Zara's right,' Anjoli said to Darius. 'It's better you don't have people around.'

'And especially stay away from fireworks!' Kamil added.

'I've already invited everyone,' Darius protested. 'I planned it for Saturday because that's the day before the curse is due to strike. I figured if I'm fated to pop it, I might as well go out with a bang. What do I tell them? That I'm scared I'll die, so the party's off? They'll all have a good laugh at that.'

'Tell him, Kamil. He pays zero attention to me,' Zara pleaded.

'Daru,' Kamil's voice was gentle but firm. 'I've promised to help, so I'm advising you to cancel. Sorry about this, Zara, but Daru, perhaps you can use your father-in-law's illness as an excuse. Say you don't feel right celebrating when he's so ill.'

'That's a great idea,' said Zara. 'And it happens to be true. Listen to Kamil, Daru. You're the one who involved him.'

Darius said, 'Hmm. I guess I can go to that other function then . . .'

Zara let out a frustrated cry. 'He's up for an award at this Businessman of the Year thing. I told him to decline that, too. Daru, you can't say you're cancelling the party because of Puppa's health and then happily swan around town. Just stay home and stay safe. Please!'

Darius raised a hand, cutting off her protest. 'If I'm not having a party, I'm getting my plaque! I'll return home before midnight.'

Zara said nothing.

'All right, that's settled.' Kamil let out an enormous yawn. 'Sorry. It was a long flight.'

Anjoli caught the yawn and threw it back. 'Jet lag's hitting me, too.'

'Of course,' said Darius. 'Sorry. Stupid of me. Let me get the bill.'

'Let me,' Kamil insisted. 'You are putting us up at your place, after all.'

'They only take cash, dude. Anyway, you're here because of me, and it's Anjoli's first trip to Mumbai. Least we can do is treat you.'

The four of them climbed into the car, Darius in front, Anjoli and Zara with Kamil in the back. As they wound through the busy streets, Anjoli's thoughts swirled with the ramifications of Darius's story. Mysterious curses, spontaneous combustion, communal violence – her rational mind fought against the absurdity of it all. But one thing was evident. Real or not, the curse had cast a long shadow over Darius and Zara's lives.

Twenty minutes later, they entered a warren of narrow lanes. Anjoli peered out at the vibrant shops, their displays spilling over with everything from medicines to flowers to pots and pans. The crowds moved with purpose, a living, breathing tide. The car navigated a tiny gully, the BMW barely making it through the tight confines, people pressing themselves against the walls to let it pass. At the end of the lane was a set of large metal gates, *Behesht* wrought on the iron in elegant script. The white-suited watchman glanced at the car, threw a sharp salute, and rushed to open the barrier.

'What's Behesht?' Anjoli asked.

'The name of our house,' Zara replied. 'It means heaven.'

And it was heavenly.

As soon as the gates clanged shut, the noise of Mazagaon's streets faded, replaced by a serene silence. They drove up a long driveway, glimpsing manicured lawns and flowerbeds through the ancient trees. A peacock strutted on a flowerbed, its feathers shimmering in the sunlight.

When the car came to a stop, Anjoli stepped out, her breath catching at the sight before her. 'Wow. This I did not expect.'

'My great-grandfather built it,' Darius said, a note of pride in his voice. 'My family's lived here ever since.'

She took a step back, absorbing the mansion's vibrant yellow facade. The intricate carvings and inlaid glass on the upper floor's wooden-framed windows that created rainbows on the ground. The white shutters that gleamed. The towering wooden pillars encased the front entrance. In the courtyard, a tranquil fountain murmured.

Two servants in white uniforms, eager as politicians, hurried to retrieve their bags. Anjoli followed them into the house, stepping into a foyer of dark wood and vaulted ceilings. Through a door on the right, she saw a spacious drawing room bathed in light. To the left, a dining room with a long table flanked by a dozen chairs on each side.

Kipling was wrong. East and West definitely meet here, she thought. English trinkets filled carved dressers, Persian carpets covered blue and white tiled floors, and South Indian brassware adorned end tables.

'These are my family's possessions, amassed over a century. I'm just a caretaker for those who are to follow,' said Darius.

Zara smiled ruefully. 'Obssessive's not the word for him. A place for everything and everything in its place. It drives me crazy.'

'I like things to be tidy. These are some of my ancestors.'

He led them to a huge grand piano in the corner, its top crowded with sepia photos of people standing stiffly, staring at the camera. There were individuals, folks in pairs, in groups; men in high collars and ceremonial headgear looking pleased that they owned the world; women gazing wistfully into the distance, wishing they were somewhere else; children grinning widely with gappy teeth, delighted to be in front of the lens. Anjoli paused at a photo of Zara and Darius garlanded with flowers. 'Was that your wedding?'

Zara's face softened at the memory. 'Yes. In the agiary. Our fire temple.' She pointed at another photo. 'That was Daru's navjote. The priest is tying his kusti, the sacred thread.'

'That's Xerxes with Faraz.' Darius showed them a picture of a man in a well-cut suit with an arm around the shoulders of a young man in his late twenties in front of a building site.

'Show them to their rooms, Daru,' Zara said. 'I'll check on dinner.'

Anjoli followed Darius past two massive, four-foot, white and blue Chinese porcelain floor vases at the foot of a sweeping staircase with an incongruously ugly stairlift. Darius hesitated at the top of the stairs. 'Um, I wasn't sure if you wanted one room or two. So both are made up.'

'Two please,' Anjoli interjected quickly, before Kamil could speak.

Darius smiled, and they walked to the end of the corridor. 'Okay. This is yours, Kamil, and next to it is Anjoli's. There's a connecting door. That you can lock. Or not.' Another smile, this one playful. 'Our room is at the end of the corridor, past the stairs, on the other side of the building, next to my study. Zara's dad is adjacent to the study. If you need anything, just let me know. There are fresh towels in your bathrooms. There's no Wi-Fi password and there's a library downstairs if you want something to read.' He opened the door to the room. 'You guys freshen up. We'll be in the living room. Unless you want to take a nap?'

'No, we're fine. We'll come down soon,' Kamil replied as Darius left.

Anjoli entered Kamil's room, appreciating the view of the grounds through the open windows, as the breeze rustled the white lace curtains. The furnishings were simple – a spacious double bed, a writing desk, a sofa and an antique wooden wardrobe. Their bags stood upright in a corner.

She threw off her shoes and hopped onto the bed. 'Look at this place. He must be loaded.'

'Yeah, he's not short of a few rupees,' Kamil said, unzipping his suitcase.

'What do you make of this curse?' she asked, wiggling her toes.

'They obviously believe it. Sometimes we will bad things to happen.'

'You're such an idiot, laughing at him like that. You need to have your antennae up and read the room.'

Kamil flushed. 'It *was* pretty insane. Why don't you spend some time with Zara and get her to shed more light on what happened to his dad and grandfather?'

Anjoli considered this. It would make her feel more useful, and she was certainly intrigued, if a bit freaked out. 'All right. Bloody weird though. One guy shot through with arrows and now ghosts chasing people down and burning them alive. This trip's almost a parody of what you expect in India.'

Kamil took his toiletries into the bathroom, saying over his shoulder, 'Nonsense. This is a modern, thriving country, not some ancient superstition-ridden backwater. Let's freshen up.'

Anjoli grabbed her shoes, dragged her case through the connecting door, and shut it behind her. But she didn't turn the key in the lock.

Then

When their specified time arrives, they cannot delay it for a single hour

The Qu'ran

Xerxes

Bombay. Wednesday, 2 October 1974.

Xerxes woke with a deep, satisfied groan, and stretched his limbs languidly. The warm, golden sunlight filtered through the curtains, and cast a soft glow across the carpet. Beside him, Ava mumbled something incoherent, turned over, and tugged the sheet up to her neck.

Forty-seven years old today. The thought lingered, heavy and unsettling. His parents hadn't reached this milestone. Lying in bed, he reflected on his life, a ritual he performed every birthday.

Health. Seven out of ten. He patted the belly straining against his pyjamas. He needed to eat less ravo and dudh-na-puff and exercise more. But overall, he was in decent shape. At least, physically.

Wealth. Nine out of ten. No worries on that front. Mehta & Sons was flourishing under his leadership, the legacy of his father cemented. He had provided his family with a good life – memorable vacations in London, New York and Paris; the finest education for Cyrus; and Ava, although not extravagant, lived in comfort. He had built a solid foundation for them all.

Family and friends. Eight out of ten. He and Ava had weathered twenty-eight years of marriage, and, though not without challenges, she had been a wonderful companion. Cyrus was grown, a clever man of twenty-seven, though his obsession with magic still bewildered Xerxes. He remembered the child's amazed expression when he had shared the story of how three powerful Zoroastrian mages had visited Jesus with gifts. Cyrus's fascination with the Magi had blossomed into a lifelong passion for sorcery, one that had distanced him from the family business. Luckily, Xerxes had Faraz. His younger brother in all but name. How lucky he had been twelve years ago, to take a chance on this young Parsi boy fresh out of Cambridge who was now his right-hand man in growing Mehta & Sons.

Community. Ten out of ten. His contributions had been generous, endowing scholarships and building housing for poor Parsis. In this, he could find no fault.

And finally, the big one. Happiness.

He paused, the number elusive. By all measures, he should be content. Yet, a whisper inside him said: *five out of ten.* How much of his success was truly his own? Ava had been chosen by his parents. The business thrived on foundations laid by his father. Cyrus's upbringing was because of his mother's efforts. Maybe that's what made the boy . . . he didn't want to say the word. But he *had* turned down every girl Ava had found for him. Let it go. His son would live the life he was destined to.

The memory of the tiny baby with screwed-up eyes floated into his mind. And fast behind that, the shadow that was always lurking beneath the surface. The night he had been found wanting. The night of . . .

Nausea surged. He bolted to the bathroom, barely making it to the sink before vomiting violently. The sour taste burned his throat.

'Are you okay, maari jaan?' Ava's sleepy voice floated from the bedroom.

'Yes,' he managed. 'Go back to sleep.'

He washed away the sick, gripped the porcelain, and stared at his reflection. The lines etched on his face were deeper, more

66

pronounced. Stress and guilt had left their indelible mark. He attempted to smooth out the furrows, but they stubbornly resisted.

A movement caught his eye – a fleeting shadow across the sunlight streaming through the bathroom window. His pulse quickened. Was it a bird? In the garden below, he saw Mustafa conversing with Joseph and visions of that terrible, terrifying night twenty-seven years ago returned.

Xerxes Mehta ke upar lanatullah. You will burn to death on your forty-seventh birthday.

Was the curse of Allah real? Had Mustafa forgiven him? He had considered firing the watchman, unable to bear the weight of that blank, hooded gaze each morning. But that would have been piling injustice on injustice. He shivered. Dug his fingernails into his palms. Stupid superstition. Well, today was the day. Que sera sera.

After showering and shaving, Xerxes donned his white sudra vest and carefully tied the wool kusti around his waist, reciting his daily prayers. He whispered an additional prayer for safety. Nothing to fear, he assured himself. Everything would be fine.

Back in the bedroom, Ava was sipping tea in their breakfast nook, the aroma of freshly brewed chai mingling with the morning air.

'Happy birthday, my darling.' She stood and hugged him.

'Thank you, my love.'

'All ready for the big bash tonight?'

'I'm looking forward to it.'

'I still don't understand why you couldn't wait for your fiftieth, but if it makes you happy . . .'

Xerxes felt a wave of relief that he had never shared the curse with her. Why burden her with such dark thoughts? 'I'll have an even bigger celebration then.'

She smiled and handed him two beribboned presents. 'I've got you some gifts, my love.'

Eagerly, Xerxes opened the first, revealing a silver picture frame showcasing a family photo outside Buckingham Palace.

'Asprey! How marvellous! I'll keep it on my desk at work.'

'Faraz bought it for me in London.'

He tore open the second, larger box, uncovering a cream suit from Gieves & Hawkes.

'You needed something special for your birthday, so I ordered it. I had them adjust the measurements. I hope it fits.'

The soft linen felt luxurious under his fingers. 'Beautiful. Let me try it on.'

He changed into the suit and struck a James Bond pose. 'Well?'

Ava laughed. 'Perfect. I have the handsomest husband in the world. Put it away now.'

The evening unfolded in Behesht's opulent drawing room, where chandeliers sparkled like starlight. Guests mingled beneath the soft glow, their laughter blending with the gentle strains of Mozart played by a pianist in the corner. Outside, the full moon peeked through the branches, casting long shadows across the room.

The formal dining area was set for the birthday feast, crystal glasses and silverware gleaming under the ambient lighting. Champagne flowed freely as waiters circulated with trays of canapés, discreetly overseen by Joseph, whose watchful eye missed no detail. Xerxes smiled, noting how his butler swiftly removed an ashtray just as a guest stubbed out a cigarette.

A sudden tapping of a spoon on a champagne flute drew everyone's attention. Silence fell as Cyrus stepped into the centre of the room, beaming with pride. 'Please come up here, Father,' he called out. 'I'd like to say a few words.' Xerxes walked up to his son, beaming. 'Thank you all for joining us on my father's forty-seventh birthday.'

Xerxes and Ava shared a secret smile. Cyrus was enjoying the limelight, as always.

'You may not know this, but he is the best father a son could have. My mother would agree he's the best husband a wife could ask for, and you all know him as a great friend and employer.' He turned to Xerxes. 'I only hope to achieve as much in my entire lifetime as you have in half yours, Puppa.'

Applause erupted, and Cyrus took a little bow. 'So, happy birthday, Father, and may you have many more.' He handed Xerxes a heavy box wrapped in vibrant red and gold paper. Xerxes opened it to find an antique Persian chess set, the board inlaid with colourful gems.

'It's exquisite!' he exclaimed. 'You know how much I love things that connect us to our heritage. Thank you, Cyrus. But all I really need is the love of friends and family.'

Cyrus winked. 'Although the wealth of Mehta & Sons doesn't hurt.'

Xerxes laughed. 'Love of friends and family is easier when you're well off! Faraz and I are going to build the biggest construction company in India.'

'Why stop at India? Why not the world? These are for you too,' said Faraz, waving his cigarette at Joseph and Mustafa, who carried in two large blue and white Chinese floor vases. 'I thought you could place them at the bottom of the staircase.'

'Beautiful,' Xerxes murmured, running his fingers over the porcelain. 'Joseph, please put them there.'

Joseph nodded, and they transported the vases away.

'Hang on, something's missing,' Cyrus said suddenly.

'What?'

'The blessings of the gods.' Cyrus clapped his hands, and golden confetti cascaded down upon his father.

The room filled with applause. Guests sang 'Happy Birthday' as the lights dimmed and a cake, ablaze with forty-seven candles, was wheeled in. Xerxes gazed at it, the dancing flames casting flickering shadows on the walls.

As he lifted the knife to cut the cake, he saw Salim's face, contorted in agony, reflected in the silver blade. He spun around, but only saw his friends, family and servants. His gaze flicked to Mustafa, standing on the side, watching him impassively. He made a silent wish and blew out the candles with a powerful breath.

As the last notes of 'Happy Birthday' faded, he cut a slice of cake, feeding it to Ava and then to Cyrus. He embraced his wife, son and Faraz.

Truly, he had been blessed by Ahura Mazda.

Stepping back, he allowed Joseph to serve cake to the guests. Suddenly, he felt a searing pain across his right ear. A gasp rippled through the dining room as Xerxes raised his hand, staring in disbelief as the elegant cuff of his new suit ignited, a snake of fire curling up the sleeve.

Then his head was alight.

A howl of agony erupted from his throat as the pungent smell of burning flesh and hair filled the air. Screams and shouts echoed around him, but he didn't hear them.

Ava, Cyrus and Faraz stood frozen, horror etched on their faces as they watched Xerxes burn. Recovering, Faraz grabbed a water jug and doused him, but the flames only seemed to grow fiercer.

Panic gripped the room as it overflowed with choking smoke. Joseph and the servants rushed in with buckets of water, but each attempt to put out the fire was met with explosive steam, the liquid soaking the plush Persian carpets.

Faraz tackled Xerxes to the floor, and threw a rug over him to smother the conflagration, but it was too late. Then, abruptly, the fire subsided as quickly as it had started, leaving the carpet smouldering and Xerxes's head glowing with an eerie orange light. This was no ordinary fire. The air around him shimmered with an unnatural intensity.

Ava tried to kneel beside her husband, but the scorching heat drove her back. 'Fetch a doctor! Please!' she cried, her voice breaking.

A servant ran to the phone.

Joseph, pale and trembling, whispered, 'The curse. It has come true.'

Mustafa, unmoved, stared at Xerxes with an inscrutable expression. 'Salim's spirit has returned for vengeance,' he intoned. 'Just as he said he would.'

Faraz shook Mustafa by the shoulders. 'What curse? What are you talking about, man?'

Joseph's voice was barely audible. 'Independence Day. Salim cursed Mr Xerxes. He would die by fire on his forty-seventh birthday because of what he did. It has come to pass.' He broke into sobs.

Mustafa pulled himself away from Faraz's grip, stepped forward, and pointed at Cyrus. 'My brother said you too would burn on your forty-seventh birthday. And your child, and your grandchild. Your lives for their lives.'

Cyrus stood gaping as Faraz glared at Mustafa. 'Get out!' he shouted. 'Don't listen to this nonsense, Cyrus! It's rubbish. It was an accident. Nothing more.'

Xerxes's consciousness faded, his last thoughts a whirl of memories. A wooden cricket bat on a blood-soaked floor. A shadow outside his bathroom window. Salim's eyes in his knife.

Then he was on the back of an enormous black vulture flying into an azure sky.

Now

This is not India. There are people here from every part of India, but Bombay isn't India. Bombay is an own-world, a world in itself. The real India is out there.

Gregory David Roberts, *Shantaram*

Kamil

Wednesday, 30 November.
Four days to go.

Anjoli yawns, stretching like a cat after a long night prowling alleys. Her hair spills in all directions, defying gravity, but it frames her face in a way that makes sleep deprivation look almost glamorous. We're alone in the grand dining room, attended by servants who glide around in white jackets and gloves like apparitions in Manderley. Darius has gone to work. Zara's taken the kids to school. It's just us and the ghosts of breakfasts past.

'Didn't sleep well?' I ask, more to break the silence than out of genuine worry.

'Nope. I was exhausted, but sleep wouldn't come. Bed was too soft. Oh, thank god, coffee.' She clutches the cup like it's her last connection to the waking world.

The butler, Victor, sweeps in with an English breakfast that would make a condemned man weep. Fried eggs glisten with golden yolks, sausages curl invitingly, bacon crisps at the edges, and beans sit smugly in their tomato sauce. The table is set with Wedgwood china and silverware polished to a blinding sheen. Toasts, both brown and white, stand at attention in a silver rack, with pats of butter arranged neatly beside tiny cubes of ice to keep them from melting into oblivion.

'This is a setup, right?' says Anjoli. 'Our personal Ritz? Only without the tourists.' She digs into her bacon. 'Do you think this is the daily grind for Daru and Zara, or is this special treatment for us?'

'I wouldn't put it past them. They enjoy living well.'

'Well, there's well and there's *well*. What are your plans for today?' She stuffs a bite of sausage into her mouth.

'See the police. Meet the people Bell was working with.'

'Ah yes. *Poking around.*'

'My poking's probably a waste of time if it *is* a serial killer. But since Daru asked and all . . .' My hand hovers over the toast.

'Can't decide?' she grins.

I opt for the brown, spreading butter with deliberate precision. 'How about you? What are you going to do?'

'Zara mentioned taking me to her boutique and then to lunch. So I'll do some subtle digging. I also need to check Chanson hasn't burnt down the restaurant. Apart from that, I'm open.'

'It would take him longer than a day to wreck it. He's not that efficient. Make some time for yourself. Explore Mumbai. You deserve a holiday.'

'Listen, this ain't no va-cay.' She waggles her knife. 'I'm here on work. Detective work. Got to sort out this curse business. Any ideas?'

'A murder conspiracy over fifty years is pretty unlikely. Has to be coincidence. We'll stay close to him this weekend. Make sure he's safe.'

She drops her voice. 'Could Daru have anything to do with Bell's murder? I mean, I know he's your friend and all, but . . .'

'Why bring me to Mumbai if he's involved?'

'Good point. Highly risky bringing the brilliant detective Kamil Rahman in to investigate. He'll swoop in, poke around, triumphantly unmask his friend Darius Mehta as the mad archer, then return to London trailing clouds of aftershave.'

'I thought you liked my aftershave.'

'In tiny quantities. Not when you bathe in it. It would stun a cow.' A warm smile salves the sting. I take a surreptitious sniff. It doesn't *seem* overpowering. I switched from Lynx to Tom Ford at her suggestion.

'Thanks for the constructive feedback.' I pause. 'Why *not* make it a vacay?'

An eyebrow goes up.

'Once I've sorted Bell's body and we show this curse is bunkum, let's go on a trip.'

'A trip? We are on a trip.'

'No, a trip trip.'

'Where?'

Easy. Don't scare the horses. Casual shrug. 'Goa? Jaipur? Taj Mahal? I'll temper the cologne.'

'Aren't you supposed to take the body back to London?'

Oh yeah. That.

'I'll see if I can send it unaccompanied?'

She thinks for a moment. 'Might be nice. *After* Daru's birthday. But don't get into trouble on my account.'

A gentle smile. Nod. No need to show her the fanfare that's lit up my heart. Who cares if she doesn't like my aftershave? I can change that. Again.

When I worked in Mumbai before, the Crime Branch was holed up in a grimy, hundred-and-twenty-year-old Gothic building. Now, it's in a shiny new six-storey tower that looms over the British relic like a bully over a schoolyard runt, a testament to the city's relentless march forward into the twenty-first century.

The reception area is sleek, all glass and steel, a stark contrast to the dinginess of the old place. I ask for Inspector Karve and take a seat. Seconds stretch painfully into minutes, which soon become an hour. The receptionist's polite but firm 'He's still busy' grinds my patience to dust. The message is loud and clear: I'm not welcome.

Just as I'm about to call Darius and vent, a skeletal policeman in a crumpled khaki uniform comes down the stairs. A turmeric tilak sits on his forehead conveying his religious superiority. He looks past me, dismissing me before I even open my mouth. 'Constable Rahman?'

Has this ability to make a title sound like an insult served him well in his career? Maybe it's something I should give some thought to practising.

'*Detective Sergeant* Rahman.' Well, my promotion is imminent. 'Inspector Karve?'

'Follow,' he barks. I fall in step behind him, my irritation simmering. The inside of the building smells of sweat and the stale air of crushed dreams. Cops sip chai at battered desks, their blank looks following us as we pass.

Karve strides into his glass-walled cabin, and I seat myself on a steel chair that feels like a mediaeval torture device. He opens a file, shouts, and a peon scurries in. Karve's eyes flick to my ear, avoiding direct contact. 'Cha?'

I shake my head. The peon vanishes, and Karve flips through the file with deliberate slowness, savouring each page as if it's the last he'll ever read. The silence stretches, heavy and uncomfortable. He looks up and stares at the fan as if looking for answers to the existential questions of the universe. Finally, he deigns to speak. 'Why will I let a Muslim from Scotland Yard shadow me?'

It's going to be like this, is it? I bite back my irritation. Beam. 'Honestly, Inspector, I'm as much in the dark as you. I was told by *my* senior to jump on a plane and come here, so I jumped. I will assist in any manner you prefer and not get in your way. I'm just here to liaise.' And if you don't want me to liaise, fuck you very much. I have better things to do.

A sigh to show me how much of his precious time I'm wasting. 'What is your connection with Darius Mehta?'

'He's an acquaintance. The Met would have sent someone anyway, and he felt more comfortable with a familiar face. I've served in Mumbai.'

A flicker of interest. 'When?'

'Eight years ago, with Commissioner Naik.' I drop the name, hoping to spark recognition. 'I helped him solve the case of the woman who was strangled in Bandra. And you also might have read, I saved the PM's life in London.'

'No. Didn't read.'

Liar. I take a deep breath, resisting the urge to wipe the smirk off his face. 'Let's focus on Bell's murder. As I understand, his body was found near Marine Drive by a morning walker. How did you identify him?'

The peon brings in Karve's tea. He stirs it slowly. Takes a noisy sip. Placing the cup carefully back on its saucer, he scratches his right armpit. 'Oberoi keycard in pocket. Mehta & Sons paying. Mr Darius Mehta inform us Bell employed by him. Then I am told you will shadow me.'

'Great detective work.' I apply some strategic maska-polish to butter him up. 'Any findings from the post-mortem?'

'We are waiting for you. You need to formally identify the body and authorise post-mortem. It is arranged at D S Hospital. You can proceed there now.'

'Thank you. Where was Bell killed?'

'No blood in hotel room or on the rocks where he was found,' Karve's tone is as dry as the Thar Desert.

'Well, it's unlikely someone would carry a body through the Oberoi's lobby unnoticed,' I say, my mind sifting through possibilities. 'No attempt to hide the body?'

'No.'

'Could he have been killed inside the Coastal Road construction site?'

'Fingerprint and footprint squad find no evidence. He was not killed there.'

I frown, not convinced. 'Nothing at all on the body? Hair? Fibres? Scraping from under his nails?'

Karve stiffens. 'Listen, Mr Muslim sergeant from London. We have a murder every two days. I work for people of Mumbai, not people of London. I do not stop everything to work for Parsis and Muslims and Christians.'

His words are bait, but I refuse to bite. I smile, the kind that barely reaches my lips. 'I understand, Inspector Karve. And there was no evidence at the site?'

'Hundreds of people in and out of that area. Impossible to find anything.'

'Did you speak to Arpin, the company controlling the site?'

'I talk to CEO. He assures me Arpin has nothing to do with it.'

Incompetence or cover-up? I let it slide. 'What lines of inquiry are you pursuing?'

'It is a ritual killing by a madman. Human sacrifice.'

'What?'

A sip of chai. 'Some year ago, a woman is murdered in ritualistic sacrifice. She has paralysed son. Tantric tell husband an offering to gods will cure him, so he kill his wife. Another fellow offer up a child. Stab body with arrows. Drill hole in head to make goddess happy. Only one month past, we find Christian man beheaded in Bandra. Number zero carved on forehead. In Hinduism, zero is bridge between reason and faith. We are looking at killings to appease gods.'

Not *implausible*. Especially in India. 'Darius mentioned you thought the eighteen arrows were significant?'

Karve folds his arms over his scrawny chest, waggles his head, and delivers a sermon. 'The war of Kurukshetra in the Mahab-harata last eighteen days. That book is eighteen sections. Conflict fought with eighteen army divisions. Eighteen people survive the war. Shrimad Bhagavad Gita has eighteen chapters. Lord Krishna say ideal man has eighteen traits. Hinduism is triumph of good over evil – dharma over adharma.'

He gives me a significant look. I guess I'm the evil one here.

'So eighteen arrows signify . . .'

'That good has conquered evil. But may not be a Hindu. Muslims and Jews also make these sacrifices. Killer can be pretending he is Hindu.'

Karve's knowledge of Hinduism is impressive, his prejudices even more so. 'The national newspapers aren't covering the story?'

'The commissioner does not wish to cause panic.'

Smart move. Though, I'll bet Karve craves the spotlight. 'Can you tell me more about the Bandra murder? Was that body concealed?'

His face closes down. 'It was not. Listen, you can shadow on Peter Bell death. Other killing not your concern. You take Bell back to London. Let me do my job. Do not poke your nose in my business!'

'Can you estimate the time of death?'

'Pathologist says between eight p.m. and midnight.

'Any suspects from Bell's work? Witnesses? Persons of interest?'

Karve seems torn between telling me to fuck off and displaying some iota of professionalism. Luckily, he opts for the latter. 'Not connected to his work. I interview people he work with. No one know anything. Driver drop Bell off at hotel on Thursday around six thirty p.m. Bell request pick up at nine a.m. on Friday. But by then,' a flick of his wrist, 'he dead.'

'Did you find Bell's mobile?'

'No.'

'And there's no way to ascertain when he left the hotel on Thursday night?'

A pause. Extracting information from Karve is like chipping away at a block of granite. Whether a sculpture will emerge or just a hot mess remains to be seen.

'An outside call to his room at 19.03 on Thursday evening. The operator does not know who from.'

'Man or woman?'

'She thinks, man. But not sure. Then doorman see Bell leaving shortly after. He does not want a taxi. Says he will walk. No one see him return.'

Makes sense. The coastal road site's close to the Oberoi. 'Anything interesting in his hotel room?'

He stares at me mutinously. 'Room was mess. Someone searched it.'

This makes me sit up. 'Any idea if anything was missing?'

A piercing glare, as if he suspects me of searching Bell's room myself. Another scratch of his underarm. The left this time, to mix it up a bit.

'Don't know.'

'So, the killing *must* be connected to Bell's work if they were looking for something. How did they get in if you found his keycard on the body?'

Karve shrugs.

'Any fingerprints in the room?'

'Arre, it is a hotel. Thousands. We do not know what is useful or not.'

'No CCTV?'

'Oberoi is a top hotel. Of course there is CCTV.'

'And?'

'My people found nothing.'

That doesn't fill me with confidence. In my experience,

Indian cops watch cricket on their phones while the hours of CCTV they're supposed to be monitoring plays in the background.

'Interesting that someone called him at the hotel. Implies they didn't have his mobile number. Or didn't want a record. That and the room being searched also makes it unlikely to be a random serial killer.'

The inspector makes a show of gazing at his watch. Stands. 'Bell went for walk. Was in wrong place. Wrong time. Same fellow who did Bandra killing saw him. Killed him. We will find the man and jail him. You go to the post-mortem now. Here is paperwork and the address. Then take corpse to London and leave me to do my work, Mr Scotland Yard.' He hands me a chit with the address and a sheaf of documents, and dismisses me with a wave.

As I leave his office, I press my palm to my back, easing the strain from Karve's chair. I feel somewhat up to speed. Karve's analysis makes no sense, given the call and the search, but he seems to want to ignore that. Why? Is it just irritation at my presence, or is he hiding something?

Either way, this case just got a lot more interesting.

Kamil

I sit in the back seat of the BMW, scrolling through the sparse details about the Bandra murder on my phone. The decapitated head of a man, Thomas Eapen, a local Goan lottery seller, was found outside the Mahadev Shiva temple on the twenty-seventh of October, a zero or an 'O' carved on his forehead. The rest of his body is still out there somewhere, playing a grim game of hide and seek. The police haven't made much progress, but I can see why Karve may want to link it to Bell's death. However, I'm not about to swallow that hook without some concrete proof. Hopefully, the post-mortem will shed some light on the shadows swirling around this case.

Imran pulls up outside Dadabhai Sethna Hospital. The name has an antiquated ring to it, an echo from the days when Mumbai was Bombay, and hospitals were charitable institutions run by rich patrons.

As I wait, my mind wanders back to the horror I'd encountered the first time I'd visited a post-mortem hospital. It was a macabre scene, straight out of a fever dream, with bodies stacked like unwanted books in a dusty attic, some doubled up on stretchers, neglected and forgotten. When I joined the homicide division, Abba had drilled into me the importance of a good post-mortem doctor. *The bad ones miss things all the time, and you'll be chasing your tail.*

After what seems like an eternity of restless pacing, a dishevelled, prematurely balding man in a stained doctor's coat, thick-framed glasses perched precariously on his nose, rushes towards me. 'You are finally here,' he grumbles, as if I've kept him waiting. 'Inquest papers?'

'Here you go. I'm Kamil Rahman, with Scotland Yard. I was sent to Mumbai to accompany Peter Bell's body back to London.'

The doctor couldn't look less interested as he gives my documents a cursory glance, stuffs them into his pocket, then leads me down a corridor that seems to grow colder and more decrepit with every step. We arrive at a room that reeks of neglect and disinterest, decidedly at odds with the glossy reception I'd been waiting in.

'They have not bothered to do up this part of the hospital – wealthy patients don't come here. "Prioritise the living over the dead. Corpses will not care," says my administrator. Although if you see some people they get up there – living corpses.' The doctor lets out a hacking laugh, lights a cigarette and offers me one.

'No thanks, I don't smoke.'

'You're sure? It helps with the stink.'

Under the glare of a harsh thousand-watt bulb, a lifeless body lies on a stone slab. A tag on its right big toe reads *Petter Bell*. The stench of decay is an invasion. A cocktail of earth, musk and rot that turns my stomach. I carefully avoid puddles on the wet floor that are leaking from large metal containers in the corner, filled with melting ice.

The doctor follows my gaze. 'Watch your step. We need those to keep the bodies cold. During power cuts, the freezers stop working, and the generators are reserved for critical equipment. Circumstances might be a little different from what you're used to at Scotland Yard.' His tone carries more than a hint of sarcasm.

Bell looks deader than dead – skin grey and papery with a sickly green hue, hair looking like the artificial tresses of a doll, some of it missing. His lower body is dark, where blood has settled. The arrows still lodged in him are a surreal touch, like relics from some mediaeval horror story. I could be in a museum, staring at a macabre exhibit, but there are no explanatory plaques here.

Trying not to breathe too deeply, I force myself to look closer. The eighteen arrows seem to follow a deliberate pattern – head, trunk and limbs each have their fair share. The arrangement speaks of ritual, of something sinister. In some places, the arrows are so close together, their fletching is intertwined. I begin to understand Karve's human-sacrifice theory.

Beside the slab stands a man dressed in shorts, a stained white vest, rubber flip-flops and yellow kitchen gloves. He has the air of a hapless domestic handyman come to fix the toilet using string, hope and jugaad. I catch a powerful whiff of alcohol as he coughs. On a nearby table are arrayed three rusty knives – two small and one large – with broken handles tied with twine; a compact iron wedge and an ordinary household hammer. No long-handled plunger in sight. The doctor dons a gown, surgical gloves and a mask, then hands me similar gear. The mystery man gets nothing. 'He is the mortuary sweeper. He does the cutting,' the doctor says, catching my look at his companion.

'Are you not performing the post-mortem yourself?'

'I am a Brahmin. I don't cut.' He gives a disdainful sweep of his hand, sprinkling ash onto the damp floor. 'I will analyse the results.'

'But he's *drunk*!'

'Would you want to do his job sober? Please formally identify the body.'

I examine Bell's face. It matches the description on the Metcalfe website. I nod, fulfilling my duty to the UK Government.

The doctor circles the corpse, recording notes on his phone with the cigarette dangling from his lips. 'Body: white male, 195 cm tall, weight?'

'103 kilos,' supplies the sweeper.

'Black hair, greying at the temples, eye colour unclear due to arrows in eye sockets. Naked. Significant livor mortis. Rope marks on arms and wrists. Blunt force trauma to the back of the head. No other suspicious marks on face, arms, torso and legs.' He barks a short laugh. 'Other than the arrows. One in each eye and ear, one in mouth, one in throat, one in heart, one in palm of each hand, one in crotch, one in each foot and six in abdomen.' He jerks his head at the sweeper. 'Tyanna kadhun taka.'

The sweeper, seemingly well-practised in post-mortem arrow removal, wiggles them out delicately, one by one. Some come out relatively easily; others, jammed further in, take more effort. It's a time-consuming process, leaving the corpse raw and grotesque. The doctor motions for the sweeper to reposition the body, aligning the incisions under the light. He fetches a magnifying glass from a steel chest of drawers, an oddly sanitary and modern instrument amid the gothic tools. With great care, he examines the punctures, extracting minuscule objects with tweezers.

'Tiny metal fragments in the wounds, most likely from the arrows. He was rendered unconscious by a blow to the head, bound, and then one arrow pierced his heart. The others were inserted post-mortem. Some in a hurry, by the looks of it. Blood loss would have been minimal. More seepage than spurting.'

I peer at an arrow. It's around two feet long, made of sturdy wood, with sleek feathers at one end and a sharp metal point at the other, not the triangular head I'd expected.

'Why?' I ask, more to myself than as a question.

'How should I know why? You're the detective,' the doctor snaps.

'Could they have been shot with a bow?'

He scrutinises the wounds again. 'No. They appear to have been put in manually. Carefully positioned. Shooting arrows would have left them more random. I'll send them to FFPS for fingerprinting.'

'The arrow in the heart would have taken some force if jammed in by hand. The perpetrator must have been a male adult, surely?'

He checks the gash once more. 'It went between the ribs, so no, it doesn't have to be a male. A determined woman could have done it.'

'Could the tips have been poisoned?'

'I will know once I have the toxicology results.'

'Is there any significance to the placement of the arrows? Could this be some sort of ritual killing?'

'Again, I give a medical opinion of *how* the person died, not theories about *why*.' He looks at his assistant. 'Kapanyasathi tayari vha.'

The sweeper lifts the knife and places it against Bell's chest, ready to cut.

'Is he trained?' I put my hand against my nostrils in anticipation of further foul smells.

'What training? Nobody is trained to do this. Twenty million population in Mumbai. You know how many people die every day? We could train for a hundred years and still not have enough. At least we are competent here. In Bihar, I have seen them perform PMs wearing plastic bags on their hands because they have no gloves. I'm an oncologist who has experience in forensics, so am wheeled out for important cases. In other places, anyone can do a post-mortem – paediatricians, dentists, family doctors. Ridiculous state of affairs. Training! Ha! Tu kasachi vat baghat ahes?'

The sweeper gets to work, his knife creating a neat incision

88

down Bell's chest. The act of cutting releases a noxious burst of gas, intensifying the already unbearable stench. The doctor's glasses fog up, and he wipes them on his coat. The sweeper continues, carefully removing and weighing the organs, then placing them on the table.

The floor tiles glisten under the harsh fluorescent light, and I focus on their worn patterns to avoid the macabre sight at the periphery of my vision. The doctor glances at the organs, touching none of them. He nods to his assistant, who methodically replaces them in the body cavity and sews it up with slow, laborious stitches, occasionally using his forearm to wipe the sweat and hair plastered to his forehead despite the cold. When he's finished, he covers the body with a sheet and takes his instruments to the sink to be washed.

The doctor switches off his recorder with a click and crushes his cigarette underfoot, the scent of burnt tobacco mingling with the odour of death. 'We're done,' he says, his voice flat and unfeeling. 'I'll conduct the toxicology report and send it to you later. What should we do with the corpse?'

Oh yeah. That's my responsibility and the whole reason I'm here. It had slipped my mind as I grappled with Bell's strange death and tried to avoid vomiting my guts out. 'The family wants him repatriated to England as soon as possible. I'm looking into his insurance to see if it covers the cost. Can you provide a cause-of-death certificate? I need it for registration. And we'll need the body embalmed.'

The doctor nods, his face inscrutable. 'I'll inform Inspector Karve. You'll need to arrange for an undertaker to do the embalming. We can store the body for now, but make it quick. Space is limited.' His gaze returns to the corpse. 'He was working for Darius Mehta, right?'

I look at him in surprise. 'You know him?'

He nods. 'I'm treating his father-in-law, Faraz Davar. Actually, there's no more treatment needed. He's been in the ICU for two months and is on his last legs now. All we can offer is palliative care. I doubt he has more than a few weeks left. They are taking him home today so he can die there. Sad, when you see a titan of industry in that position, barely mobile, mind going. But it will happen to all of us.' He eyes me with a mix of pity and detachment, patting my shoulder with one hand and pointing to his nose with the other. 'You might want some Vicks.'

As I run to the toilet to throw up my breakfast, I try not to think how Bell's family will react when they get his corpse back, looking like Frankenstein's monster. At least I got a PM doctor who seemed to know his stuff and hopefully the embalmer will hide the worst excesses of the sweeper-cum-post-mortem-surgeon-cum-alcoholic. The acidic taste of bile lingers in my mouth as I stumble to the pharmacy and slather Vicks under my nose, the sharp menthol cutting through the nauseating odour that clings to my skin and clothes.

Back in the car, the city blurs past the windows, a swirl of colours and sounds that barely register as I replay the scene in my mind. Bell's body, the arrows, the cold efficiency of the doctor – it all seems unreal, like a twisted nightmare I can't wake from.

One arrow through the heart makes sense, a quick, efficient kill. But seventeen more? Placed with such precision, post-mortem? They speak of something far more baleful. A ritual? A message? Is Karve right about the significance of the number eighteen? If so, the connection to Darius's company seems tenuous at best.

This isn't the Mumbai I wanted to show Anjoli. The city I remember was vibrant, chaotic, alive with possibility. But this trip, with its shadows and secrets, feels like a descent into a darker, more dangerous world. I stare out of the window as the buildings close around the hazy, cloud-strewn sky.

Anjoli

The silk fabric slipped through Anjoli's fingers like a whisper, cool and smooth. She couldn't tear her gaze away from the vibrant floral print draped over the mannequin in Zara's boutique. Her fingertips traced the delicate patterns as if memorising every petal. 'This dress is stunning,' she murmured, imagining herself wrapped in its lush colours, a bold departure from her usual T-shirts and faded jeans. 'Did you design it yourself?'

'All the pieces in here are my creations,' Zara replied without looking up, her hands deftly arranging a stack of kurtis. The air was filled with the subtle scent of jasmine, mingling with the rich, earthy aroma of fresh fabrics. 'I trained at the National Institute of Fashion Technology and caught the bug. Puppa helped me start the business, and Shireen took off.'

'Why Shireen?'

Zara gave a half-smile. 'The brand Zara was taken. Shireen was my mother. An artist, though I never knew her. She died giving birth to me.'

Anjoli felt a connection forming. She knew the ache of parental loss all too well. 'I'm sorry. It must have been hard growing up without her.'

Zara's look was distant. 'Puppa raised me alone while building his business.'

'It's nice you and your dad are so close. I miss mine terribly.'

'He's everything to me. Only child with no mother, you know. No cousins, even. We just had each other, and he shaped every part of who I am today. I owe it all to him. But who knows how long he has. With that and Daru's birthday . . . it's been hard.'

The heaviness in Zara's words settled into the space between them. Anjoli reached for a change of topic, searching for something lighter. 'Your clothes. Where do you manufacture them?'

Zara's face brightened, as if a switch had been flipped. 'All across India. I work with indigenous artisans who excel in traditional crafts. Look at this lehenga.' She held up an intricately embroidered piece adorned with tiny mirrors that caught the light. 'This level of craftsmanship is rare. You won't find it on the high street.'

Anjoli looked closely at the delicate stitching, absorbing the texture and detail. 'Exquisite. How much does something like this cost?'

Zara hesitated. 'In pounds, around two and a half thousand. But for you, I'd offer a special discount.'

'Oh, I couldn't,' Anjoli protested, secretly thrilled.

'No, really, it would be my pleasure.' A smile twitched her lips. 'Your T-shirt is fab as well.'

Anjoli glanced down at her blue T-shirt with *Religion is the Opium of the Asses* emblazoned across it. 'Believe it or not, I design these myself. I could send you a few.'

'I'd love that. Want to try the floral dress on? It's about fifteen thousand rupees after your discount.'

Anjoli did a quick calculation. Hundred and fifty quid. Manageable. 'Well, if you don't mind, that would be lovely!'

In the changing room, Zara's assistant brought the right size, adjusting the dress so it fit Anjoli perfectly. The mirror reflected a version of herself she barely recognised – elegant, vibrant, alive. She wondered what Kamil would think of it.

After the fitting, Zara said, 'Let's go for lunch. The dress will be altered and ready soon.'

'Oh my gosh. That's so nice. You must let me pay for that, too.'

Zara laughed. 'All part of the service! Can't have you walking around in an ill-fitting Shireen garment. Bad for my brand.'

The drive through Mumbai in Zara's sleek Mercedes was a journey through contrasts. The city unfolded like a vivid tapestry outside Anjoli's window: Victorian Gothic buildings stood shoulder to shoulder with modern shops, and the Art Deco facades along Marine Drive gleamed under the midday sun. The ebb and flow of the honking traffic was a rhythmic pulse that mirrored her growing fondness for Mumbai. It had a vibe she could relate to: laid-back yet on-the-go.

The Willingdon Club was another story. A relic of Raj grandeur, all dark wood panelling and comfy sofas. Anjoli wandered up to a portrait of a man with a white Hercule Poirot moustache sporting a natty cravat, complete with pearl tiepin. A plaque underneath read 'Freeman Freeman-Thomas, 1st Marquess of Willingdon, GCSI, GCMG, GCIE, GBE, PC. Viceroy and Governor-General of India.' Good to know he was a Freeman, she thought, as opposed to the millions he enslaved. Britain is busy tearing down relics of Empire, while the Empire still celebrates their overlords.

A uniformed waiter led them to a covered patio where elderly men and women lounged on rattan chairs, the soft strains of classical music playing in the background. 'This is . . . different,' Anjoli commented, absorbing the serene yet oddly colonial setting.

Zara settled into her chair. 'One of our havens in Mumbai. Would you like a beer?'

'Maybe a fresh lime soda?'

Anjoli's stomach growled in anticipation of Indian delicacies.

Instead, Zara ordered a peculiar mix: fish fingers, cucumber sandwiches, ham sandwiches and something called Eggs Kejriwal. Anjoli suppressed her disappointment, hoping the conversation would be more satisfying than the food. 'Do you believe in the family curse?'

Zara's eyes flickered with unease. She glanced around, her voice dropping to a near whisper. 'Not here. There are always ears present. It's not something we discuss openly.'

'Sorry.' Anjoli modulated her tone. 'It just sounds so unreal.'

Zara's expression went taut, and Anjoli could feel her discomfort. She felt guilty forcing her to relive what were obviously traumatic memories, but she needed to understand what had occurred. She'd have to grow a thick skin if she was serious about being a detective. Pushing through her own reluctance, she persisted. 'What was Daru's father like?'

'Can we not talk about it here, please? Look, the khana's arrived.'

The waiter laid out a selection of dishes, all toast, bread or breadcrumb adjacent, on the table. The Eggs Kejriwal turned out to be eggs and cheese on crunchy toast. Everything else was exactly as its description. The food was unusual, and Anjoli was puzzled why all the Indian uncles and aunties surrounding her were devouring their meals with gusto. She suppressed a grin as she recalled a sketch from *Goodness Gracious Me* where an Indian diner dared a waiter in an English restaurant. 'Give me the blandest thing on your menu!'

They ate in silence, Anjoli rehearsing some benign questions to ease Zara into divulging more than she might be comfortable with. Just as she gathered the courage to speak, Zara jumped up. 'Shehnaz, Rux, darlings! You never told me you were back!'

For the next hour, Anjoli sat smiling and listening to the lilting articulations of Mumbai socialites catching up after a 'such a long time!' Their preening and chirruping filled the air like a chorus of brightly plumed parrots perfectly at home in Zara's peculiar, anachronistic world.

Back in the car, Zara merged without slowing down into the Mumbai traffic as Anjoli clutched the edge of her seat, trying not to squeal. When her heartbeat returned to normal, she said, 'Are you ready to talk about the curse now?'

Zara's grip on the steering wheel tightened. 'It's been such a lovely day. Must we ruin it?'

'I don't want to ruin anything, Zara. But Kamil and I are here to support you. I can't help you if you won't let me.'

No reply. The honking and beeping did nothing to quiet the awkward and resounding silence inside the car. Anjoli gave Zara a minute, then spoke again. 'You mentioned being there when Daru's father died. Can you tell me about it?'

Zara's face was a mask. 'He was performing a magic trick. Suspended in an empty box above the stage. Then he burst into flames. It was horrifying.'

Anjoli's stomach clenched, but she kept her voice steady. 'What did the police say to you?'

'Nothing. I was just a kid.'

'Did they suspect foul play?'

'I don't believe so. No one could explain it.'

'And the curse? How did you learn about that?'

The traffic slowed to a crawl. 'It was always there, a shadow over our family. But when Daru turned forty, it became real. Too real.'

Anjoli tried to piece together the fragments. 'What do you know about the cook who cast the curse?'

Zara shook her head. 'Salim? Not much. Daru attempted to uncover the truth after his father died, but it's all bits and pieces.'

Anjoli wondered what else she could ask. She tried to think logically. There were three options: curse, coincidental accidents, or murders. If it was one of the first two, there wasn't anything she could do. But if it was murder . . . 'Can you think back? Was anyone present at both deaths?'

Zara thought for a second. 'Mustafa, Salim's brother. He was there when Daru's grandfather died and again at the magic show.'

Anjoli's pulse quickened. Brother? Was there a thread here? 'What happened to him?'

'He died ages ago.'

'Was Mustafa fired after Daru's dad passed?'

'No. No one accused him. What could he have done? Cyrus Uncle just . . . exploded. We saw it all.'

'What if the box was rigged with an explosive?'

'It was totally empty. Daru and I both saw inside it when we went to wish Cyrus Uncle good luck before the show.'

'How mysterious. And when you looked inside did you see—'

Zara interrupted, 'The thing is, we've always taken care of our domestics and their families. It's something my father inculcated in all of us. Generations of people have worked for us. In fact, Mustafa's grandson, Ali, now works as our watchman. He took over from his father when he died. Victor, our butler, is the grandson of Joseph, who was Xerxes's butler. So if there's one thing I'm sure of, it would have nothing to do with any of them. They would not risk the job security of their family.'

Anjoli made a mental note to check out Ali and Victor. 'Who else knows about the curse?'

'Just Puppa, Daru and me. It's been hell trying to keep it quiet from the kids. I don't know . . .' She slammed on the brakes and blew her horn as a motorbike swerved in front of her. 'FUCK-ING IDIOT! Sorry, Anjoli, are you okay?'

Anjoli regained her composure. 'I'm fine.'

'This damn traffic!' Zara's voice was tight with frustration as she honked at the bus ahead, which hadn't moved despite the green light. 'Sometimes I want to move out of Mumbai and just live in a quiet hill station. Away from curses and horrific murders and familial responsibilities. Do you mind if we don't talk about all this stuff anymore? It's quite upsetting.'

Anjoli shifted topics, hoping to ease the tension. 'Why is there so much traffic? It's not even rush hour, is it?'

'Roadworks. You can thank Daru for that because they're building the coastal road. Once it's built, it'll be better.'

'How come you don't have a driver? How do you do this every day?'

'Imran normally drives me when Puppa doesn't need him, but we assigned him to Peter and now Kamil, since Puppa's in hospital.' She laughed darkly. 'At least I can release all my frustrations this way. Without scaring the children.'

'Lol.'

Zara navigated a hazardous turn, and Anjoli let her concentrate for a minute before speaking again. 'Ali and Victor might know about the curse. It could be family lore if their grandfathers were at the first death?'

A shrug. 'I guess.'

'Maybe you should give them the day off on Sunday? Make sure they're nowhere near the house? Just to be safe.'

Zara seemed taken aback, but nodded thoughtfully. 'Perhaps. I'll think about it.'

Well, at least I'm being marginally useful, thought Anjoli. 'Daru said you were hesitant about Kamil and me coming here. I hope we're not imposing.'

Zara looked embarrassed. 'He's an idiot. Sorry he told you that. I was sceptical. How can anyone help with a curse? But I'm glad you're here. You've lightened his mood, and it's good to have you both. Listen, since you're in India, make the most of it. See Mumbai together. Go to Elephanta Island. It's one of my favourite places.'

'What is it?'

'Ancient cave temples carved from solid rock, over fifteen hundred years old. The sculptures of Shiva are breathtaking. Very special. It's just an hour away by ferry. Don't get sucked into our drama. You and Kamil deserve your own bit of drama.'

It was Anjoli's turn to be embarrassed. 'What do you mean?'

'What do you mean?' Zara mocked, batting her eyelashes. 'Come on! Anyone can see Kamil's got a major thing for you. Put him out of his misery, for god's sake. We're fond of him and he deserves someone like you.'

Anjoli laughed, feeling a mix of embarrassment and warmth. 'Okay, maybe. But only after we make sure Daru's safe.'

'Good. Because life's too short, I can tell you that for nothing. Okay, let me drop you home. Then I need to get back to work before we bring Puppa home this evening.'

As they pulled up to the house, Anjoli stared at the grand facade, unsure what she had learned from the day's conversations. But something inside told her that all she had to do was find the right thread and the knot of this curse would unravel.

Kamil

'You look terrible,' I say, as I step into Darius's office.

He runs his fingers through dishevelled hair and gestures wearily towards the sofa. 'Not sleeping. Neither is Zara.'

The lines on his forehead seem deeper today, etched by worry and exhaustion. I settle next to him, trying to project confidence. 'Well, just four days to go, then this nightmare'll be over. I won't let anything happen to my best friend in Mumbai.'

He turns towards me and attempts a crooked smile, rubbing his bloodshot eyes with the heels of his palms. 'Your *only* friend in Mumbai. What have you been up to?'

'Gathering info. Saw Karve. Was just at Bell's post-mortem.' My shudder inadvertently adds flesh to my skeletal facts.

'Oh? How was it?'

'Did you see his body?'

'No.'

'A pin-cushion. And being at the post-mortem . . . Jesus. It was a nightmarish, vomit-inducing experience that'll stay with me till the day I die.'

He goes pale. 'Oh god.'

'Karve believes it was some kind of ritual human sacrifice. As you said.'

'I really hope so. I mean . . . well, you know what I mean.' He turns away, his gaze flitting around the room, unable to settle, as if trying to escape our discussion.

'The ransacking of Bell's hotel room bothers me, though. Yesterday you said he was concerned about something. Do you really have no idea what it could be?'

'No. No idea.'

He knows *something*. I'm about to push, but his ravaged face makes me hold fire. 'All right. Why don't I talk to the other people who Bell dealt with in your company?'

He nods, relieved. 'There were three. Niloufer Cama, Ronnie Engineer and Sunil Tandel.'

'Tell me about them.'

He looks distracted. 'Niloufer's one of our top talents. Super smart. Faraz and I are grooming her to take over as CEO when I become chairman after he dies. Or if ... well, if I go prematurely ...'

'Daru ...'

He sits up. Shakes himself like a dog after a bath. 'Let's stay on topic. Ronnie's ambitious. He'd like Niloufer's job. But I worry he cuts too many corners.'

'And Sunil?'

'He's very junior. We made him Peter's assistant for the duration of his trip. Bright boy. Go easy on him. He's taken Peter's death and Faraz's illness badly.' He clears his throat, trying to regain his composure. 'He was off for a few days, but came back to work yesterday. I'll tell them you're here from Scotland Yard, shadowing the investigation. I'm sure they'll co-operate.'

'Any reason they wouldn't?'

'No, of course not. See me when you're done.'

Ronnie Engineer exudes an air of easygoing elegance with his trim goatee, smart jeans, open-necked white shirt and fashionable unstructured jacket with an abundance of flapped pockets. Is this what Anjoli's always suggesting for me? *You should buy a utility jacket, Kamil, update your look a bit. It's either suited and booted or T-shirt and jeans with you. You need to find the casual middle.* Well, my casual middle is currently hanging over my belt. Pretty sure the next few days living under Darius's silver-service roof won't help.

I take a sip of my second coffee and organise my thoughts as I assess Ronnie adjusting the chair opposite me. He sits side on with an almost performative grace, legs crossed, elbow casually resting on the table. *Look at me, I'm the future, not a suit-and-tie dinosaur like everyone else here.* I decide to disrupt his facade with a rapid-fire interrogation. 'What's your position in the company? Is it engineering?'

'Haven't heard that one before,' he says with a congenial smile. 'As it happens, I *am* an engineer. Got a first from IIT Bombay. Nominative determinism, eh?' He leans forward, face now serious. 'I've been at Mehta & Sons for a year as Director of Sustainability. Responsible for all our environmental initiatives. I ensure the work we do doesn't damage local wetlands and has minimal impact on the ecosystem. Darius and Faraz have set an ambitious target for us to become a net-zero company within ten years. I'm tasked with making it happen.' He re-adjusts the angle of his chair, leaning back. His constant shifting betrays a restless energy. What's he worried about?

'What was your association with Peter Bell?'

His expression turns sombre as he strokes his beard. 'Man, I can't believe what happened. Such a solid guy. He'd only been here a few weeks. I was looking forward to getting to know him better. He was highly respected in his field, you know. Shared my concerns about sustainability. We were working on plans to minimise the carbon footprint of the project. We have to be careful with the tunnelling as it goes under sensitive areas.'

'What was your contact with him in the days before he died?'

'We had regular check-ins twice a week. I met him Thursday

afternoon as scheduled. We were reviewing the plans and making some tweaks.'

'How did he seem in the time leading up to his death?'

His gaze shifts, fingers tapping restlessly. 'It felt like something was bothering him. His mood changed.'

'Changed how?'

'Hard to say. He became quieter. More thoughtful. Questioned me on *why* we were doing the project. I thought it seemed a little odd. I mean, it's pretty obvious why we're doing it. You've experienced the traffic.'

'When exactly did you notice this change?'

Ronnie thinks for a moment. 'Three or four days before he died? It was quite obvious.'

I make a note. 'If you were to hazard a guess, what was his concern?'

A shake of the head. 'I really don't know. He asked about Arpin a couple of times. They're a contractor who reports in to Niloufer. They own the construction site where . . .'

'Yes. What did he ask?'

'Um . . . how involved they were with the project. Exactly what their role was. Things like that.'

'And your answer?'

'I gave him the facts. They are our demolitions contractor.'

'Did he meet with them?'

'He planned to discuss demolition strategy for the tunnel with them. I offered to go with him, but he said he'd go on his own. I don't know if he actually had the meeting or not.'

Seems straightforward. So why was Darius so cagey about Bell meeting Arpin?

'Any issues with the construction?'

He purses his lips. 'With any project of this scale, there are going to be issues, you know? The important thing is to allay all concerns through consultation and education. But . . .' He opens his hands and there's that smile again. 'You can't make everyone happy. Understand what I mean? As long as intentions are clean . . .'

'Mr Engineer, who—'

'Please, call me Ronnie.'

'Mr Engineer. Who wasn't happy?'

A slight tic appears on his left cheek. 'There was some minor apprehension about tunnelling under Malabar Hill from the Parsi priests, for instance.'

'Go on.'

'You see, the tunnel skirts Doongerwadi – the Parsi funeral grounds. There are long shafts inside the Towers of Silence that lead down through the hill to the sea. The priests were worried our tunnel would desecrate their holy site.'

'And how did you allay their concerns?'

'We conducted a thorough assessment and found there would be no effect on the towers. Darius made the priests understand before it escalated into a full-scale protest. Those can be quite challenging to handle. The government wants to avoid any unrest, given the upcoming elections. They need all the votes they can get and the last thing they want is thousands of angry Parsis voting for the opposition because they're annoyed with our project. Once the elections are over, people can protest as much as they like. The ministers know this initiative is for the good of the city.'

The good of the city – that's a laugh. Palms in the assembly will have been well greased. Indian politicians have two priorities: win their seat and then make as much money as possible while keeping it. Rinse and repeat. I refocus. 'Did Mr Bell meet these Parsi priests?'

'Yes. Darius asked him to show them the tunnel plans. They were quite satisfied.'

I'm not letting him off the hook yet. 'No other issues?'

He shifts in his chair. 'There are always issues. Anything specific you want to know?'

There's an evasiveness in his tone that catches my attention. 'You tell me.'

He scratches his goatee. Wonder what Anjoli would think if I grew one. 'Well, there's always some noise from the locals, concerned about construction and all that. But nothing major.'

'Locals other than the Parsi priests?' He's definitely hiding something.

He fidgets, his gaze darting to the window. He's trying to act casual, but it's not working. 'Well, yes, there was something. But it's really nothing significant. Just another routine matter.'

'A routine matter? Sounds like you've got a story there. Care to share?' My eyes drill into his, forcing him to look at me.

He sighs and resigns himself to the inevitable. 'Swami Yogesh. He has a small temple in Priyadarshini Park.'

'Mm-hmm.'

He measures his words carefully. 'His temple is in the tunnel's path. I proposed a plan to avoid it, but Peter had other ideas.'

'What ideas?'

'He recommended demolishing the temple. He said curving the tunnel around it added too much risk.'

Now we were getting somewhere! 'And how did the swami take it?'

'Not well. He threatened to take legal action. Said he'd lie down in front of the bulldozers.'

'That's a pretty powerful reaction,' I observe, watching him closely. 'Did Bell meet with him?'

A slight hesitation. 'Yes. We both did, on the Monday before Peter died. Peter offered a compromise. Suggested relocating the temple for free. But the swami refused. It's been there for decades.'

'And Darius? What was his stance?'

'He sided with Peter and Niloufer.' His nervousness eases slightly now that the story's out.

I push one last time. 'And what do you think? Should the temple be demolished?'

He says quietly, 'I believe we should respect the swami's wishes. Go around the temple like I originally planned. There's a pond there with important bird and frog life. But I was overruled.'

The room falls silent as I absorb the implications. A swami with a grudge. Ronnie overruled. Religious tensions and threats. 'Thank you. Did you tell Inspector Karve this?'

The alacritous smile returns, tinged with relief. 'Of course. Why would I be anything but transparent with the police?'

I shift my line of questioning, keeping him off balance. 'Did you ever meet Bell outside work hours?'

'For dinner. Twice.'

'Just you two?' He nods.

'What did you discuss?'

He pauses for a second. 'Work. He mentioned he missed his wife and kids in London.' He makes sure I catch his emphasis.

'Was there an issue with his wife and children?'

He leans back with a bland expression, lacing his hands behind his head. 'No. Why would there be? Ask Niloufer. She spent more time with him than me.' The implication hangs in the air, unmistakable. A possible affair? I make a mental note.

Ronnie frowns at a corner of the room, then speaks slowly. 'There *was* one other thing.'

'What?'

'It happened some days earlier. Peter was late for our usual meeting on Tuesday evening, so I went looking for him. He was in Darius's office.'

'And?'

An uncomfortable look. 'They appeared to be having an argument.'

'About what?'

'Don't know. But it was pretty heated.'

'And you couldn't hear anything at all?'

Another slight pause. 'Not really. I knocked on his door and opened it. Peter was talking about someone called Felix.'

'Felix?'

'Yes.'

'What exactly did he say?'

He hesitates. 'Look, it's entirely possible I misheard.'

'I understand. Just tell me what you think you heard.'

'Well . . . I heard Peter say, "Are you going to kill Felix or not?" Then Darius saw me, gestured, and Peter went quiet.'

Silence stretches between us. '*Kill* Felix?'

'Yes.'

'Do you know anyone by that name?'

'No.'

'And it was definitely Tuesday?'

'Yes.'

'What do you suppose it could mean?'

'No idea.'

I file it away. 'Where were you Thursday night?'

'I went to see a performance at the NCPA around the corner.'

'With someone?'

'Alone.'

'What was it?'

'A play. *Love Letters*.'

'Do you often go alone?'

'Sometimes. Nothing wrong with that, is there? Anyway, it wasn't a good play, so I left in the interval and went home.'

'Can anyone vouch for you?'

'No. I live on my own.'

'Any idea why Bell's room in the hotel may have been searched?'

'Searched? No idea.'

My sharp questioning is undermined when I let out an enormous yawn. 'Sorry. Jet-lag.'

Ronnie stands. Smooths down the multitude of flaps on his jacket. 'Are we done?'

'Thank you. I'll be in touch. Please send Niloufer Cama in.' I stare after him as he leaves. Who is this Felix that Bell wanted dead?

Kamil

The woman strides into the office as if she owns it, a towering figure in a midnight-blue bespoke trouser suit that clings to her frame with an air of authority. She's easily six feet tall, with a presence that could stop conversation in a room. Her slim, silver-framed specs catch the light, glinting against her penetrating gaze. Discreet diamond earrings sparkle beneath the office's washed-out lights, hinting at wealth, much like the gold chain around her neck. A simple wedding band and an engagement ring with a blindingly large solitaire complete the image of calculated elegance. The epitome of cool, competent professionalism – every movement precise, every detail meticulously arranged. She extends her hand, assessing me with eyes that miss nothing. 'Niloufer Cama.'

'Sergeant Kamil Rahman. Nice to meet you, Mrs Cama.' We shake hands. She has a firm, no-nonsense grip.

'Ms,' she corrects with a raised brow, taking a seat opposite me. I take a deep breath and sip my third coffee of the day. The caffeine does little to cut through the fog of fatigue clouding my mind, but I need to stay sharp. Use different tactics with this woman. The hectoring I used for Ronnie won't work here. I decide to play to her authority – friendly, but slightly subservient. 'I appreciate you making time in your busy schedule, Ms Cama.'

'So shocking what happened to poor Peter.' Her voice is even, controlled. 'I don't know how much help I'll be, but I'll answer any questions I can.'

'Thank you.' I pull out my notepad and pen. 'Can you describe your role at Mehta & Sons?'

'I'm Chief Operating Officer – number three in the company. Been here for over seven years.'

'What does the Chief Operating Officer do?' I scribble down notes, though I already have a good idea. It's not just about her answers – it's about how she gives them.

'Faraz, our chairman – well, he's mainly a figurehead now – manages the board. Darius, our CEO, sets strategy, wrangles investors, raises finance. I run the day-to-day operations. I'm currently overseeing the Coastal Road project.'

'And in line to become CEO soon, I hear? Being mentored by Darius and Faraz.' I throw out the bait.

Her composed facade slips for a moment, as she tucks a lock of red-highlighted hair behind her ear. 'They have been extremely supportive of my career progression, but I'm very happy in my current role. Mehta & Sons has a truly excellent CEO in Darius.'

How often has she rehearsed that line in front of her bathroom mirror? 'If – I'm sure we can speak frankly, Ms Cama – *when* Faraz dies, Darius will become chairman and you'll step up and take his place, if asked? Right?'

She doesn't miss a beat. 'Darius may choose to keep both roles – chairman and CEO. As I said, I'm very happy in my current role.'

Oh good. I'm happy you're happy. She's a smooth operator, I'll give her that. 'Can you explain the Coastal Road project to me?'

She looks relieved as she launches into her well-oiled spiel. 'The Mumbai Coastal Road project is one of the most ambitious construction projects the country has ever undertaken. We are building a twenty-nine-kilometre, grade separated, eight-lane expressway along and in the sea off Mumbai's coastline from Marine Drive to Kandivali. We expect around a hundred and thirty thousand vehicles to use it daily and it will cut travel time from two hours to forty minutes. And reduce a significant amount of congestion and pollution from cars not sitting in traffic.'

She's polished, rehearsed. 'Impressive. And what was Peter Bell's role in the project? When did he arrive in Mumbai?'

She consults her mobile. 'Peter arrived on November seventh. So just over three weeks ago. He is – was – an expert in boring and reported to me. We're utilising a unique machine made by his company to bore an underground tunnel from Chowpatty Beach to Priyadarshini Park, passing beneath Malabar Hill. It will be the deepest road tunnel in India.'

I whistle, impressed despite myself. 'That's quite a task. Are the residents aware of the plans? I can't imagine they're all thrilled?'

A grim smile. 'You're right. We call them numbys – not under my back yard. It's a high-class area, and managing their concerns has been delicate. There was some grumbling, but we managed it. Everyone will benefit from the reduction in congestion.'

'How was Bell to work with?'

She takes a moment, her mien softening just a fraction. 'Friendly. Easy to get along with. Extremely knowledgeable. We were collaborating well.'

'Did he express any concerns about the job?'

Is that a slight tightening around her mouth? 'Not really. It's complex, but we have a good handle on it. Peter was confident in our ability to deliver.'

'And how was his demeanour in the days leading to his death?'

'Fine.'

Hmm. Not what Ronnie said. 'Mr Engineer said he was having doubts about the project? He said Peter asked him *why* you were doing it?'

Her brow furrows. 'Why we were doing it? How odd. No, he didn't mention any worries to me.'

'When did you last see Bell?'

'Thursday afternoon.'

'And he seemed normal to you?'

'What is normal, anyway?' Her voice breaks. For a fleeting moment, a child-like vulnerability leaks through the professional armour.

'Are you okay? Would you like some water?'

'I'm fine.' She waves off my concern. Plucks a tissue from a box on the table and dabs at her nose. 'It's just a shock. I can't believe what happened. It hasn't sunk in.'

I'm warming to Niloufer. It can't have been easy rising to her position as a woman in this industry. Especially in India.

'He was one of the good ones.'

Something in her voice? I recall Ronnie's insinuations. 'Were you *close*?'

'What do you mean?'

'Were you and Peter Bell involved? Romantically?'

A flash of anger. 'Oh my god! Can't a woman simply have a positive working relationship with a man without it being romantic?'

Her sudden aggression surprises me. Have I struck a nerve? 'Sorry, I had to ask. Just eliminating theories, you understand.'

'Theories? Now I'm a suspect?' She crosses her arms, her gaze icy. 'Ridiculous.'

'That's not what I said. Give me your overall impression of Bell. Anything you can tell me. I'm trying to get a picture of who he was.'

She considers her answer. 'Peter was unlike most men you meet in construction. They tend to be very macho and uncomfortable with women in senior positions. But Peter treated me as an equal from the get-go. He loved his job, took it seriously, and cared deeply about the environmental impact of his work. Was genuinely concerned about the stakeholders.'

'Meaning the owners of the companies?'

'I mean everyone affected by the construction – residents, workers, the environment.' She gives me a small shake of her head, probably thinking I'm an idiot. 'He really cared. It's rare in this field. Most just want to lay down cement, take the money and run.'

'Ronnie Engineer mentioned a Swami Yogesh causing problems?' I slip the question in casually. A flicker of something – fear?

'He's been a thorn in our side. A dangerous man.'

'Dangerous how?'

'Unpredictable. Potentially violent. Ronnie went out of his way to placate him. Too far, in my view. Darius, Peter and I agreed we needed to demolish his temple, regardless of the outcome. It made much more sense than Ronnie's plan.'

'But Ronnie disagreed.'

'Yes.'

'Why?'

She shrugs, a hint of disdain in her expression. 'He's close to the swami. Didn't want to anger him. Didn't know what he might do. It's a risk we have to take. Ronnie was not willing to.'

Clearly, no love lost between them. Ronnie must know he's on thin ice if she becomes CEO. 'Who's Felix?' I ask abruptly, trying to catch her off guard.

Her head jerks up, startled. But at what? My knowing about this Felix or the unusual name. 'Who?'

'Felix.'

'Felix?'

'Yes.'

'I don't know any Felix.'

'No one by that name's associated with the project?'

She shakes her head.

'Ronnie said he heard Bell telling Darius to kill Felix.'

She stares at me. '*Kill?*'

'Yes.'

'I don't know what that means.'

I give her a direct look for a few seconds. She looks straight back at me. I can't tell if she knows this Felix or not. I move on. 'Fill me in on Arpin.'

Her eyes narrow. 'What about Arpin?'

'Did Bell meet them?'

'No reason for him to do so.'

'So he didn't?'

'Not that I know of.'

'Ronnie mentioned Bell needed to see Arpin to discuss demolitions?'

'I'd already sorted all that out. Peter didn't need to be involved.'

These inconsistencies are bothering me. Darius was evasive about Bell meeting Arpin as well. There's something beneath the surface here. Is it just professional jealousy between her and Ronnie? I've seen enough of that in my career. Or is it something else? I scribble a final note and drain my coffee. 'Where were you Thursday evening?'

Her answer is immediate. 'Home.'

'Anyone there with you?'

'My husband and daughter. So I'm not a suspect, but you think I was having an affair and you want to know if I have an alibi for the night Peter was horribly murdered?' Her voice drips with sarcasm.

'It's only a formality, I assure you.' Her demeanour hardens, arms crossing defensively. 'Did you go home straight after work?'

'I did.'

'What time?'

'Seven.'

'Where do you live?'

'Bandra.'

'How did you get home?'

'My driver took me. Obviously.'

'Do you know where Bell was staying?'

'The Oberoi.'

'Round the corner from the office?'

'It's the most convenient place for visitors to Mehta & Sons.'

'Did you phone him that evening? Call on him?'

'No.'

'Did you ever see him outside work hours? Visit his hotel room?'

I'm expecting another monosyllabic negative, but now she considers her answer. 'We worked late sometimes, had dinner together. He didn't know many people in Mumbai. I never went to his hotel bedroom.'

'And it was purely a business relationship?'

Indignant, she shoots back, 'Again! I'm very married! Now if you're done, I'll—'

'Just a couple more questions. Bell's hotel room was searched after his death. Any idea what the perpetrator might have been looking for?'

'Searched? No. Peter had no confidential documents. But,' she straightens up, 'Sergeant Rahman, I have a question for you.'

'Certainly.'

'What is your business here, exactly?'

'Darius has asked me to investigate Bell's murder.'

'Nothing else?'

'What else is there?'

'So you're saying Peter's death is not connected to the killing in Bandra?'

She's sharp as a needle. 'What do you think?'

'Looks like they might be, no? First a beheading, now,' a little shiver, 'a horrific death with arrows? So why has Darius asked you to investigate?'

I shrug. 'Call it due diligence. Making sure that nothing connects to Mehta & Sons.'

Mollified, she lets her shoulders drop. 'Yes, well, I can see that would be bad for us. But I'm sure it isn't linked.' She glances at her watch. 'I have another meeting.'

'Thank you. Can you please ask Sunil Tandel to come in?'

I massage my neck, trying to shake off the tightness. Impressive woman. Does she have something to do with the murder? She's strong enough to have embedded the arrows in Bell. And she got defensive when I asked if they were intimate. What does she stand to gain?

Niloufer Cama warrants a little more investigation.

Anjoli

Anjoli paced the wooden floors of Darius's library, the phone pressed tightly to her ear. She could feel the snake coiling in her stomach, that familiar mix of frustration and exasperation. 'There are two new one-star reviews on TripAdvisor about the chef being rude. What the hell did you do?'

Chanson's voice came back, laced with a casual indifference that only fuelled her irritation. 'I wasn't rude. I just politely pointed out that if they wanted chicken tikka masala, they should chicken tikka hike from my restaurant.' His smugness was apparent, even over the phone.

She took a deep breath and reminded herself that Chanson, despite his antics, was a culinary genius. 'It's not your restaurant, it's mine. And you can't kick people out. What happened with the other diner?'

A pause. She could almost hear the gears turning in his head. 'Okay. Maybe I went a little over the board there. They sent the first two courses back from my tasting menu because they didn't like the taste. So I informed the woman that looking at her companion she obviously had no taste so it was pointless them continuing with the meal. Can you really blame me?'

Despite herself, Anjoli stifled a chuckle. She forced her tone to remain stern. 'Behave, Chanson. This is why I wanted to hire the manager. I'll be back next week, so please try not to destroy what's left of our reputation before then.' She hung up. Chanson was a nightmare, but he had a knack for amusing her even amidst chaos.

The room around her was thick with the scent of old paper and furniture polish, filled with the quiet dust of age and knowledge. Her eyes drifted to the cluttered table in front of her, littered with copies of the *Parsi Times* and *Parsiana*. She picked up one with a cover story about Darius.

As she read about his achievements in philanthropy and business, a grudging admiration grew within her. The journalist had captured Darius's essence without a hint of the curse that hung over him, although the article mentioned '*tragic deaths by fire of both Xerxes and Cyrus Mehta*'. She lingered over a photo of Darius shaking hands with ex-Prime Minister Jaideep Sanyal. Better not let Kamil see that, she mused. He'll never shake Daru's hand again. Another picture showed Darius, Ava and her father, Faraz, at a reception the previous year, their formal smiles and carefully composed postures telling their own story.

Her gaze shifted to a photograph of Darius's father, Cyrus, inside a transparent box. The caption read, *Cyrus Mehta, one of India's greatest magicians, performing his signature trick minutes before he was tragically killed in an onstage accident.* She squinted at the grainy image, trying to see if anything seemed off. The photographer had captured Cyrus looking down at his feet instead of at the audience. Had he spotted something that shouldn't have been there? Or was he preparing his escape?

She moved on to a black-and-white photograph of two men – one young, the other older – signing a document: *March 1970: Xerxes Mehta and Faraz Davar, marking the contract to construct the Ava Mehta Parsi Orphanage in Fort.* Then a picture of Darius, his arm casually around Niloufer: *CEO Darius Mehta with his protégée, COO Niloufer Cama.* Did their easy familiarity suggest a bond that went beyond the professional?

Setting the newspaper down, Anjoli wandered across to the shelves, her fingers trailing over the spines of the books. One caught her eye – a creased, well-read volume. She pulled it out. It fell open to a page on the *Importance of Fire in Zoroastrianism*.

Settling back on the sofa, she drew her legs up to her chest and began to read. The text described fire as the most primordial, god-created element of existence on earth. It was sacred because it retained the characteristics of the otherworldly, endless light of god's abode, and its purity was a physical representation of truth. It was a focus for worship for Parsis because they believed a conscious spirit lived in the flames that linked the material and spiritual dimensions.

Anjoli closed the book and leaned back, analysing what she'd read. So, did it mean anything that two Parsis had died in flames and the curse was about fire? Was it some way of moving them from one dimension to the next? She shook her head and stood. 'Pah! This is all too fanciful! I need to get real and do some proper investigation.' Feeling like the chatelaine of Downton Abbey, she reached for the electric bell by the sofa. Moments later, the butler appeared.

'Ma'am?'

'Hi, Victor,' she said, feeling awkward. 'I was wondering if I might ask you a few questions?'

'Of course, ma'am.'

Downton Abbey or not, sitting on the couch while Victor stood there like a servant from a bygone era didn't work for Anjoli. 'Why don't you take a seat?'

Victor raised an eyebrow, his posture stiffening slightly. 'I prefer to stand, ma'am.'

Her attempt at casualness falling flat, Anjoli got up, trying to bridge the gap between them. 'I believe your grandfather worked for Darius's grandfather?'

'Yes, ma'am. And my father served Mr Cyrus. The Mehtas have been very good to us.'

'Have you heard anything about,' she lowered her voice, 'a curse on the family?'

Victor's face remained impassive, but there was a flicker of calculation behind his eyes. 'Curse, ma'am?'

'Yes. A fire curse.'

For a long moment, Victor was silent. Finally, he spoke. 'I have heard rumours of deaths on forty-seventh birthdays.'

'And do you believe it?'

Another pause. 'It is not my place to believe or disbelieve, madam. I just pray that Mr Darius remains safe on Sunday.'

'Did you hear about the curse from your grandfather?'

'Not in any detail. I . . . I was at the show when Mr Cyrus passed. The staff were invited, so my father took me. I was in my early twenties.'

Curiosity piqued, Anjoli leaned in slightly. 'Did you notice anything odd that day?'

'It was a long time ago and quite a terrible event. Will there be anything else? I must prepare the household for Mr Faraz's return.' Victor's tone suggested he had said all he was willing to on the matter.

Anjoli nodded, not entirely satisfied but unsure what else to ask. 'Where can I find Ali the watchman?'

'Please follow me.' He led her to the front gate, where he introduced her to a man in his late forties, dressed in the usual Behesht white uniform, gloves, peaked cap and shined black shoes. To her slight surprise, the butler didn't leave but stood, listening.

'Tell me, Ali,' she said, turning her attention to the watchman. 'I understand your grandfather, Mustafa, was Salim's brother and watchman here?'

Ali looked at her curiously. 'Yes, madam. And my father after him.'

'And did Mustafa tell you much about Salim's death?'

Ali nodded solemnly. 'The curse?'

Well, at least he's admitting it. 'Yes.'

'Yes, madam.' Ali's voice was matter-of-fact, as if discussing the weather.

'And what do you think about it?'

'Curses are dangerous, madam. Mr Darius needs to be very careful on his birthday on Sunday.'

From the corner of her eye, Anjoli saw Victor give a minute shake of his head. Ali continued, 'I mean, he will be safe, of course, alhamdulillah. But these are messages from God and we cannot meddle in them. Fire is a powerful force.'

'Do you live in the servant quarters in Behesht?'

'No, madam. In Andheri. Excuse me.' He went to open the gate for a delivery man.

Anjoli walked up the driveway back to the house. After a few steps, she turned to see Victor and Ali, heads close together, whispering. Victor glanced up, and she looked away. She couldn't shake the feeling that both of them were waiting for Sunday. Whether it was with anticipation or dread, she couldn't say.

Kamil

The smell of stale coffee hangs in the air, a reminder of my unrelenting sluggishness. I lean back in the creaky chair, the fabric cold against my skin, and contemplate whether another caffeine fix might clear my jet-lag. Vivid images from the morning's post-mortem refuse to leave my mind. My hand drifts towards my mug when a hesitant knock breaks my reverie.

A young man steps into the room, his movements cautious, like a deer venturing into a predator's den. He's slim, with close-cropped dark hair, a pencil moustache and a soft face that hints at boyish innocence. His outdated bush shirt and trousers don't fit with the slick execs I've been dealing with – an odd puzzle piece in this grim picture.

'Mr Kamil Rahman? My good name is Tandel. You want to see me?' His voice is almost a whisper. He lingers by the door, eyes darting around as if unsure whether to retreat or advance.

Weariness settles deeper into my bones. I motion him to a seat, trying to shake the lethargy clouding my mind. 'I understand you were Peter Bell's assistant while he was here in Mumbai. Can you tell me about your work with him?'

He moves forward with a nervous energy, his hand trembling slightly as he pulls out the chair. He offers a tentative smile, eager to please. 'Yes, sir. I used to be Mr Faraz's executive assistant. But when he fell ill, he didn't need me anymore. So, Mr Darius asked me to look after Mr Peter. He is – was – a very kind man. He treated me very nicely.'

'What were your responsibilities with Bell?'

'I arranged his meetings, took notes and managed his diary. Anything he needed.' Sunil's voice grows softer, almost reverent.

'You were one of the last people to see him alive.'

A distressed look. He shifts uncomfortably in his chair. 'In the office on Thursday, yes. He met Mr Ronnie, and I came to collect him at four p.m. We discussed his appointments for the next day. Then he went back to the hotel. I didn't see him after that.'

'Ronnie Engineer mentioned Bell had some doubts about the project. Did he share any of those with you?'

Surprise crosses his features. Genuine or feigned, it's hard to tell. 'Mr Peter *told* him that?'

Bingo.

'What were those doubts?'

A hesitation. 'I don't know exactly.'

I raise an eyebrow. 'Really?'

He avoids my gaze, staring at his hands instead. I try to let the silence do the talking, but he stays mute. Eventually, I say, 'What *were* Bell's appointments for the next day?'

Relief floods his face as he retrieves his phone, eager to provide a concrete answer. 'That I can exactly tell you. On Friday, at eleven a.m., he had a meeting scheduled with the CEO of Arpin Industries. Then he was seeing Mr Darius for lunch.'

Arpin again. 'Why was he meeting with Arpin?'

'I don't know. He simply requested I organise it.'

'Were Niloufer or Darius aware of this Arpin meeting?'

A shrug.

'Please email me Bell's full diary for when he was in Mumbai. Did you meet him outside work?'

'No.'

'No dinners together?'

'No.'

'Where were you Thursday night?'

'At home with my parents.'

I sit back, studying him. 'You spent a lot of time with Bell. What did you talk about during those long car rides through Mumbai's traffic?'

A deferential nod. 'Traffic will be better when the coastal road is constructed, sir.'

I'm not falling for it. 'What did you discuss?'

He looks down at his fingernails, reflecting. 'Normal things. Work. He was interested in my community.'

'And where is your community from?'

'Dharavi.'

'India's biggest slum?' The words slip out before I can catch them.

He looks up, his face a blank canvas. Have I offended him? Nice job, Kamil.

'Yes, sir. Dharavi Koliwada. I'm the first in my family to go to college. I met Mr Faraz at a job fair. He always tries to help lower castes, minorities. Has given many of us work – our receptionist, his driver, his watchman, other servants. But he told me he was impressed by my potential and *that* is why I got the job, not because I'm underprivileged. He doesn't do it for the sake of doing it, like others.' His voice cracks. 'We will all miss him very much. He takes care of us and we all look up to him. Once he goes, I don't know if Mr Darius . . .'

'Mr Darius what?'

He shuts down, the vulnerability replaced by a blank mask. 'I was the first Koli ever employed at Mehta & Sons.'

'What does that mean, Koli?'

Pride enters his voice. 'Kolis were the original inhabitants of

Mumbai. Fisher people. We have been here for almost a thousand years. But the British removed us from our traditional fishing grounds.'

'I didn't know that. Where were these fishing grounds?'

'All around the island. Now we can only fish in a few places.'

'So Bell was intrigued by your background and Dharavi? Why did he find it so compelling?'

He looks away.

'Sunil?'

He meets my look reluctantly. 'All foreigners are fascinated by Dharavi, especially since *Shantaram* and *Slumdog*.'

'Did you take him there?'

'Yes. He wanted to see it.'

'When?'

'Friday? The week before his death. Eighteenth.'

'What did he think of it?'

He frowns. 'He said it wasn't as bad as he expected.'

I feel like I'm chasing shadows. Time to switch gears. 'Have you heard the name Felix in relation to this project?'

'Felix? No, sir. I know nobody by that name.'

'Bell never mentioned Felix to you?'

'I'm certain I don't know a Mr Felix.'

A slight stress on the name? Is he hiding something? Or am I tired and hungry and inventing signs that aren't there? 'Darius said you took time off after Bell's death. Why was that?'

'I . . . I was sick.'

'Sick how?'

'Bad stomach.' He clutches his midsection for effect.

'Did you sit in on Bell's meeting with Swami Yogesh?'

He looks confused by my questions, which are more of a scribbled zigzag than a straight line. I'm confusing myself. My gut releases a loud gurgle. 'Sorry. Go on. Were you there? Swami Yogesh . . .'

'That fellow. Yes. He was very angry. Made many threats.'

Ronnie hadn't mentioned that. 'Oh yes? What threats?'

'He swore the tunnel would never be built. He would not let them destroy his temple. The wrath of Shiva would come down on those that crossed its threshold.'

Eighteen arrows. The wrath of Shiva. My mind tries to piece together the fragments.

'Can you think of anything else that might be relevant to the inquiry into Peter Bell's death? You must tell me, Mr Tandel. Even if it seems insignificant.' I stifle a yawn, trying to project authority while battling my exhaustion. The words feel hollow. How would he know what insignificant detail could be crucial?

He blinks. Looks away. 'No. Nothing.'

My stomach rumbles again, insistent. I need a break. All I can think about is a table laden with Darius's delicious food. I give up.

'You can go. If anything else comes to mind, please reach out to me via WhatsApp.'

I let out an enormous, eye-watering yawn as soon as he leaves. Leaning back, I stretch, trying to get rid of the fatigue, then glance over my notes briefly, and head over to see Darius. His assistant informs me he's somewhere in the building but will return shortly. She hands me yet another coffee and waves me into his office to wait.

The city sprawls below the window, a chaotic tapestry of life. I sip the hot beverage, feeling the caffeine buzz through my system, a temporary reprieve. Darius's desk is unnaturally tidy, almost sterile. An open laptop sits beside a photo of Zara and the kids. My eyes are drawn to a dusty folder with *New Mumbai Relocation and Redevelopment Plan* scribbled on it. Darius's laptop isn't password protected and, on a whim, I type 'Peter Bell' into the search bar of his email. Dozens of messages pop up. I scroll through the most recent thread in reverse order.

From: Darius Mehta <darius_mehta@mehtaandsons.in>
Date: Wednesday, 23 November 2022 at 04:43
To: Bell, Peter <peter.bell@metcalfeengineering.co.uk>
Subject: Our conversation

Hi Peter,

Just following on from our conversation yesterday which as you can imagine took me by surprise. Can you please give it to me? I need to understand it further.

Best,
Darius

From: Bell, Peter <peter.bell@metcalfeengineering.co.uk>
Date: Wednesday, 23 November 2022 at 09:27
To: Darius Mehta <darius_mehta@mehtaandsons.in>
Subject: Re: Our conversation

Hi Darius,

I no longer have it. You have yours. As I said, if you don't take action immediately I will.

Best,
Peter

From: Darius Mehta <darius_mehta@mehtaandsons.in>
Date: Wednesday, 23 November 2022 at 10:19
To: Bell, Peter <peter.bell@metcalfeengineering.co.uk>
Subject: Re: Our conversation

Peter,

Where is it? It doesn't belong to you and is company property. I need it back. Immediately. Or there will be consequences.

Best,
Darius

From: Bell, Peter <peter.bell@metcalfeengineering.co.uk>
Date: Wednesday, 23 November 2022 at 12:11
To: Darius Mehta <darius_mehta@mehtaandsons.in>
Subject: Re: Our conversation

Darius,
You do what you need to and I'll do what I need to.

Peter

Nothing after that. The timeline fits: Ronnie mentioned they discussed killing Felix on Tuesday. What had rattled Darius so much that he emailed Bell at four the next morning? I quickly photograph the emails and type 'Felix' into the search bar. No hits.

The door handle turns just as I'm about to delve into his documents. I slam the laptop shut as Darius strides in. His gaze flickers from me to the closed computer. Damn. It was open before. Has he noticed?

He growls, 'What are you doing?'

I lift my coffee cup in a casual salute. 'Admiring the view. Drinking endless cups of coffee.'

His scowl deepens, but he doesn't push it. 'Well, admire it from somewhere else.'

I stand as he settles in his chair, his gaze still fixed on me with suspicion. I meet his eyes blandly and perch on the edge of his desk.

'How are the interviews progressing?' he asks, his tone clipped.

'Okay.' I'm careful not to reveal too much, unsure how to broach the emails without admitting I've been snooping. Instead, I pivot. 'Was something going on between Niloufer and Bell? Could she benefit in any way from his death?'

Confusion flickers across his tired face. 'Going on? Like,

romantically? Oh. I hadn't considered . . .' He trails off, lost in thought.

'Well?'

He dismisses the idea. 'She's married. With a kid. So is Peter, I believe. Highly unlikely she'd get it on with him. We have a strong policy against company relationships in Mehta & Sons. We had a bad experience a few years back. She would have to resign.'

I mull this over for a second. 'Who's Felix?'

'Huh?'

'Ronnie said he heard Bell asking you to kill someone called Felix? Who's Felix?'

He stiffens, the reaction almost imperceptible but there. 'Ronnie said that? Felix?'

'Yes.'

'Oh.' He shakes his head, too emphatically. 'I don't know any Felix. When did he claim he heard this?'

'Tuesday evening.'

He looks me straight in the eye. 'He's mistaken.'

One of them is lying. And from the way Darius reacted, my money's on him. The emails don't paint him in a trustworthy light either. 'All right. Leave that for now. Ronnie said Bell asked *why* you were doing this project. Did he ask you that?'

'What a strange question.'

'You don't know what he meant?'

'No.'

'Was there anything you . . . needed him to give you?'

'What do you mean?'

I can't bring up the emails directly. 'Some company property he took or something?'

He stares at me. 'Has someone said he took something?'

'Not as such.'

'So, what do you mean?'

I let it go. 'Never mind. Where were you on Thursday evening?'

'Me? You don't think I . . . I was at work till late, then went home.'

'What time?'

'I got home after nine. Zara was there. She'll tell you.'

'And before nine?'

'I was here. But most people had left, and I was alone.'

'And you didn't go out?'

'No. You can check the CCTV in the lobby if my word's not enough for you.'

'I'm not accusing you of anything.'

'I should hope not.' He's defensive. 'So, do you think Bell's murder is connected to his work here, or was it just a serial killer?'

'I can't tell yet. There are a few anomalies. Ronnie and Sunil believed he was worried about something. You said you thought that, too. But Niloufer thinks he was fine. There's this godman . . .'

'Swami Yogesh. Yes, he's been a pain in the arse.'

'Could he be involved?'

He cracks his knuckles as he considers this. 'It's possible. He's a nutcase. Threatening all kinds of things.'

'Does the Coastal Road project have anything to do with Dharavi? Sunil Tandel mentioned he took Bell there.'

His mouth turns down. 'Dharavi? No. The coastal road goes nowhere near there. It doesn't impact that area at all. He was probably being a tourist.'

Maybe. I continue, 'And Arpin keeps coming up. Bell wanted to meet with them. Ronnie thought it could be about demolition strategy.'

'So?'

'Yesterday you said there'd be no need for them to meet? Niloufer said the same. Arpin is popping up a few too many times for my liking. Can you introduce me to someone there?'

He hesitates, his reluctance evident. 'They're not on the best terms with us . . .'

His caginess is grating on me. I know my friend's going through a lot, but I've altered the course of my career, my relationship, and after this morning's horrendous post-mortem, probably my psyche, all as a favour to him. I wish he'd let me do my job. 'I have to talk to them. And, Daru, I know it's a tough time, but you're acting seriously weird.'

'All right, all right. I'm sorry. I've got a lot on my mind. I'll put in a call to Arjun Sharma and set something up.'

Arjun Sharma! The name hits me like a sucker punch, my exhaustion evaporating in an instant.

'Arpin's CEO is Arjun Sharma?' I whisper. 'Son of Rakesh Sharma?'

'You know him?'

My heart's pounding like crazy. And it's not the coffee. 'Er, yes? I investigated the death of his father in London some years ago. He's a childhood friend of Anjoli's.'

'Really? That's a hell of a coincidence.'

'Their parents knew each other. She fell out with him after Rakesh Sharma's murder. Because of me.'

'You? What happened?'

'He believed I caused his dad's death and never forgave me. I thought his construction business went bust?'

'It did. But he rebuilt it successfully. Friends in high places, if you catch my drift. Listen, if you've met him, then you know he's a nasty character. If you want my advice, steer well clear.'

I'm all too familiar with Arjun's brutality. Our paths crossing again can't be mere chance. 'I appreciate that, but will need to speak to him. Something's not right here. Don't give him a heads-up. He won't meet if you tell him it's me.' I rise. 'Now I need to head back and get some rest.'

Darius gets up as well. 'All right. Imran can drop you home, then he needs to go with Zara to pick up Faraz. We'll discuss this more over dinner.'

I nod absently, my mind churning. Why has Arjun reappeared? What did those emails mean? Did Darius search Bell's room to find whatever it was Bell wouldn't give him? Did Bell reap the consequences he was threatened with if Darius didn't find it? And why the hell am I really here?

Kamil

Arjun Sharma is a ghost materialising from the fog of my past. I grip my armrest as the car inches through the traffic, unresolved questions pressing against my temples. The memory of his actions in London threatens to drag me down a familiar path of resentment. I can't afford to be distracted now.

I force my attention to the present, letting my gaze wander out the window. The sun dips low behind the looming skyscrapers, casting elongated shadows that stretch like fingers across the teeming streets. Light suffuses the air from the top down, highlighting the crowns of the hundreds of dark heads milling about. I trace the buildings upwards and see a tiny reflection of sky and fiery clouds in the upper windows, gleaming through the layers of grime. It's almost cinematic, a fleeting moment of calm amidst the turmoil.

I lean back, the hum of the air conditioning offering a cool reprieve from the outside heat, and close my eyes briefly, willing the jittery buzz of caffeine and adrenaline to subside. My thoughts drift to Dharavi. Why did Bell visit that sprawling slum? I lean forward and catch Imran's eye in the mirror. 'Imran, did you take Peter Bell to Dharavi?'

He waggles his head. 'Yes, saar. Two times. Big place, very confusing. Small gullies everywhere.'

Twice? Sunil didn't mention Bell going there twice. The first trip could be a poverty tour, but why return a second time? 'When exactly?'

'On Friday, then again . . .' he stretches his mouth downwards in the mirror. 'Monday?'

'Who did he meet?'

He shakes his head.

Monday was when Bell's behaviour changed. Did Dharavi change it? 'Where else did he go?'

He ponders for a moment. 'Lot of places, saar. Mehta office. Oberoi. Construction site. Chowpatty. Priyadarshini Park. Arpin office. Doongerwadi. Wherever he want to go.'

Arpin office. 'When did he visit Arpin?'

'Maybe . . .' Imran pauses to recollect. 'One day before he is no more? Wednesday?'

A chill prickles the back of my neck. A day after his heated argument about Felix with Darius and those emails. The timing is too close to be mere coincidence. Why didn't anyone mention this? Did Darius know? Did Sunil? Niloufer? Or did Bell hide it from all of them? 'Was Sunil with him when he went to Arpin?'

'No. Peter saar go alone.'

The driver is a mine of information. I kick myself for not interrogating him sooner. 'Did you overhear any conversations between Mr Bell and Sunil?'

'No, saar. My English is not good. I don't understand.'

'Did he ever talk about a man called Felix?'

'I think no, saar, but not know.'

I nod, my mind racing. 'Can you take me to Dharavi? To where Mr Bell went?'

He frowns at me in the mirror. 'Where you want go, saar, in Dharavi? It is big only. And no clean for you.'

'Wherever you went before.'

'I try remember . . .'

'I'll ask Sunil to join us. Oh, and Darius said you need to take

Zara to pick up Faraz from the hospital after dropping me home.'

'Faraz saar coming home today?' His face lights up.

'Yes.'

'Mashallah! So worried, we are. Great man, Faraz saar. Very good to me and my family.'

'I'm looking forward to meeting him,' I say absently, my mind spinning with the new discoveries.

We arrive at Behesht just after six. I head straight for a long, hot shower, hoping to will my fatigue down the plughole. As the water scalds my skin, I try to piece together the jigsaw of the day's revelations, but the picture remains frustratingly incomplete.

Anjoli's door is ajar. She's propped up in bed, engrossed in her book. Her fingers brush a stray lock of hair from her forehead, a small smile playing on her lips. My heart swells at the sight, sweeping away the detritus of the day. I could stand here for hours just staring at her. Sensing my presence, she looks up with a start. 'Hey, you. How was your day?'

I slide onto the bed beside her, letting her proximity anchor me. 'It was . . . enlightening.' I recount the day's events, skirting around the grim details of the post-mortem. No need to drag her into that darkness. Then I drop my bombshell. 'Guess who's mixed up in all this? Only your childhood playmate, AKA the piece of shit bane of my life when I came to London.'

She looks confused. 'Huh? Not . . . Arjun?'

'Yep. He's the CEO of Arpin, the company that owns the construction site where the body was found. Bell visited him secretly. Had another meeting set up for the day after he died.'

She falls silent, processing the information. 'You don't think . . .'

'I don't know what to think yet.'

'Very restrained of you.'

'We need to meet him. Will you come? He might be more open with you there. I wasn't his favourite person, if you remember.'

'Lol. Understatement of the year. Of course I will.'

'And Bell went to Dharavi twice. We need to go there too.'

She wrinkles her nose. 'Not sure I want to visit a slum. You know how I feel about poverty porn.'

'I can go on my own, don't worry.'

'So, are you moving away from the serial-killer theory? And who is this Felix that Daru was supposed to kill?'

I shake my head. 'No idea. Those emails also showed Daru's hiding something. But I'm not ruling anything out yet. There are still similarities in both killings. The bodies weren't hidden. The ritualistic elements. The proximity in time.'

'What does it mean that the bodies weren't hidden?'

'The killer wanted them to be seen. Was sending a message.'

'To whom?'

'That's the million-dollar question. Bell was clearly hiding something, but whether that led to his death? I don't know. What did you do today?' I ask, trying to shift the focus.

She leans into me, massaging her neck. 'Zara took me out. I spoke to Chanson.'

'And?'

'He's hanging on by a thread. He could unravel everything I've built.'

'Good,' I murmur absently, distracted by her bare legs folded under the denim skirt.

She shoots me a look. '*Good*? What the hell do you mean, good?'

I blink, refocusing. 'I mean, not good. He's a loose cannon-ball. I've always said that. Did you get on with Zara?'

'She's sweet. We had lunch at her posh club, met her friends.'

'Did you learn anything about the curse?'

'A bit. I think there might be something to it.' Her eyes shine with a mix of excitement and trepidation.

I raise an eyebrow. 'Really? You believe in it now?'

'It may not be a curse, but it could be murder. Salim's brother, the old watchman, was at both deaths. His grandson works here now. And Victor the butler was at Cyrus's death.' She pauses, letting the implications sink in. 'What if it's an old family feud?'

I consider it. 'Sounds like a stretch. Probably just coincidences. Nevertheless, interesting.'

Her cheek twitches in irritation. 'Anyway, I suggested Zara send the watchman and Victor away on Daru's birthday.'

'Smart move. Well done.'

Mollified, she continues, 'Zara mentioned we should visit Elephanta Island. Have you been?'

'No. What's there?'

'Ancient caves.' She flips open her book to a picture of a dancing Shiva. 'I thought it could be our mini-break.'

My heart flutters. 'Just you, me, the sea, the sand and Lord Shiva.'

'The god of destruction. Perfect.' She grins mischievously.

'Good point. Maybe we'll find sculptures of Kama instead.'

'As in Sutra?'

'The god of love. And pleasure.'

'That's more interesting.' She leans against me, her weight a comforting presence. Her eyes close. Should I take my chance? As I angle my head towards hers, a gong sounds, and she springs up.

'Dinner time. This place is like Downton Abbey. Better put on your tailcoat.'

Always the tortoise.

Anjoli

The dining room's grandeur was almost oppressive. A massive rosewood table stretched out like a dark river, its surface gleaming under the soft flicker of three silver candelabras. The flames danced beneath the slow-turning fan, casting long, wavering shadows over the polished silverware and ornately painted plates. Each placemat bore intricate etchings of the British Isles, a subtle nod to the family's colonial past.

Anjoli leaned close to Kamil. 'Toto, we're not in Mumbai anymore.'

Darius and Zara sat with their children at one end of the table, flanking a ghostly old man in an electric wheelchair, with an oxygen cylinder beside him, who peered at them through cataract-clouded eyes.

'There you are,' Darius called, waving them over. 'Come. Wet your nose. Puppa, this is Kamil, my friend I told you about, and his partner, Anjoli. Guys, meet my father-in-law, Faraz Davar. He's our chairman. Just back from the hospital.'

Faraz seemed more wraith than man, his skin pale and fragile, like parchment draped over brittle bones. Deep lines on his forehead and the sides of his nose looked as if they had been scraped with a rake into wet snow. Anjoli shook his hand gently, wary of its attenuated frailty, and noted his neatly combed hair and pressed shirt. Someone had taken care to present him well.

'A pleasure to meet you, sir. I hope you're feeling better,' said Kamil.

Faraz's voice rasped out, reedy and thin. 'Piffle and nonsense. Poking and prodding at me like I'm a lab rat. They wanted to keep me another week, but I told them I'd rather die at home, with my family.'

'Stop it, Puppa,' Zara scolded softly, patting his arm. 'You're not going anywhere.'

'Every soul shall taste death,' Faraz countered, a shadow of defiance on his face.

'. . . and only on the Day of Resurrection will you be paid in full,' Kamil finished the quote. Faraz's face flickered with a spark of recognition before a fit of coughing seized him. He hacked into a napkin, speckling it with rusty drops of blood. Anjoli averted her gaze as Zara gently took the cloth away.

Kamil turned to the children. 'Percy. Jasmine. How you've grown!'

'Thanks, Kamil Uncle,' they chorused.

Zara rang a small bell, and Victor appeared. He poured wine with practised grace, while another server presented plates of fried chicken. Percy's face lit up as he reached for a drumstick. 'Yummy, chicken farcha, my favourite.'

Anjoli bit into the crisp breadcrumb coating, savouring the burst of spices, garlic and lemon that followed the initial crunch. This wasn't the bland imitation from a chain restaurant. This was authentic, vibrant. She licked her fingers, unable to hide her delight. 'This is amazing. So crispy and delicious.'

Zara smiled. 'It's a Parsi recipe. I can write it down for you if you like.'

Her mouth too full for words, Anjoli gave her an enthusiastic thumbs-up.

As the meal progressed, the children's chatter turned into a familiar sibling argument, their voices rising above the clinking of silverware. The butler hovered, refilling glasses with silent efficiency.

Kamil said, 'Bell visited Arjun Sharma two days before he died. Did you know that?'

Darius paused mid-bite, surprise flickering across his face. He carefully placed his drumstick down and wiped his hands. 'Really? Puppa, do you know why Peter Bell would visit Arjun Sharma?'

Faraz adjusted his hearing aid. 'What did you ask me, dikra?'

'Why would Peter see Arjun?'

'Who is Peter?'

'Peter Bell,' Zara said patiently. 'The consultant for the Coastal Road project?'

'Oh. I do not know him.'

'I know. He's from Metcalfe. You used to work with them and ... actually, don't worry about it. Just relax and eat your food.'

Kamil pressed on. 'Anjoli and I are planning to visit Arjun. He's an old friend of hers.'

Faraz waved away a servant who was refilling his water glass. 'Rakesh Sharma's boy? Rakesh was murdered, you know.'

'Yes, Puppa,' Darius interjected. 'We're talking about Arjun, his son.'

'Rakesh was a bad egg,' Faraz's voice grew fainter. 'The egg doesn't fall far from the chicken. Arjun is also not a good egg.'

Anjoli caught the brief look Darius shot Faraz, a fleeting flash of discomfort.

'In what sense?' she asked.

'I never liked that family.' Faraz turned to Darius. 'You shouldn't have done a deal with him.'

Darius's face tightened. 'We didn't have a choice, Puppa. We needed to move ahead with the project.'

Faraz waved a thin hand in the air. Repeated, 'You should

never have done a deal with him. It will not turn out well. More delays. Delays, delays, delays. What a country. Things were so much easier in my day.'

'We've started building,' Darius replied, his tone edged with frustration. 'I hope there are no further delays.'

'Hope is just postponed disappointment,' Faraz muttered.

Anjoli smiled inwardly, filing away the phrase. That would make a perfect T-shirt slogan.

'Sorry,' Zara murmured to Anjoli. 'He has good days and bad days.'

At Zara's signal, Victor brought in the next course. She looked at Anjoli, suddenly anxious. 'Do you eat brain? I'm not sure it's common in your country.'

Anjoli laughed. 'My new chef's adventurous, but I've never had brain. Happy to give it a go. Whose brain is it?'

'Goat. Made into cutlets. We also have rice and tarkari ni curry.'

Anjoli poked at the wobbly fritter with her fork, cutting off a piece and tasting it. The texture was delicate, almost silky, encased in a crispy breadcrumb shell. It was surprisingly good, a cross between a spicy custard and bone marrow. 'This is unlike anything I've had before. Do you think your cook would share some recipes? I'd love to feature them in my restaurant.'

Zara laughed. 'We Parsis are magpies with food. We borrow from everyone – Hindu spices, Gujarati seafood, Muslim meats, Portuguese potatoes, tomatoes, chillies and British custards. Even your St John in London has a Parsi head chef.'

'Maybe you need to replace Chanson with a Parsi, Anjoli,' Kamil needled.

She shot him a bright smile, spooning more curry into her mouth. The table fell into a companionable silence, broken only by the sounds of chewing, Faraz's laboured breathing and the quiet clink of cutlery. After a simple fruit salad dessert, the children asked to be excused and scampered away.

'They're so polite,' said Anjoli.

Zara rolled her eyes. 'That's what you see now. They're quite a handful. Puppa spoils them rotten.'

'I spoiled you, and it didn't do you any harm,' Faraz mumbled. 'I must spread the love. You cannot have it all.'

'Very funny.'

'I regret being so busy with work,' Faraz sighed, his voice thick with emotion. 'I should have spent more time with you.'

Zara squeezed his hand. 'It's my turn to take care of you.'

'I don't need taking care of.' His fingers trembled as he lifted an orange segment to his mouth. 'But in the end, family is all that matters. Remember that.'

'I know, Puppa.'

'Give me a cigarette, maari jaan,' he wheedled.

'Absolutely not!'

Silence settled over the table until Darius spoke again. 'Have you thought more about this weekend, Kamil?'

'I still think it must be a coincidence,' he said. 'Regardless, we'll keep you safe. Don't worry.'

Anjoli could sense the strain these dinners must put on them. Each one could be the last time they shared their favourite meals with Faraz and the children. She ventured, 'What's your view on the curse, Uncle?'

Zara's glare was like a slap, but Faraz seemed to take her question in his stride. 'What curse?'

Anjoli felt a sudden panic. Had she overstepped? Was it going to upset this infirm old man? Last thing she wanted was for him to keel over because of some stupid comment she'd made. But Darius had brought it up, not her.

Darius's voice was gentle. 'Salim Sinai's curse, Puppa.'

Faraz's expression darkened. 'Oh, that. I never believed in such things. But as I grow older . . .' Anjoli looked at him questioningly. 'I know Ahriman exists. The evil spirit. We worship

Ahura Mazda. Ahriman is his opposite. Pure evil. I will find out soon after I die.'

'Stop talking like that, Puppa,' Zara admonished gently. 'Let's discuss happier things.'

Faraz's chuckle became a coughing fit. 'Then I'll come back and haunt you.'

Kamil cut through the tension. 'Can you tell us about the deaths, sir? If you don't mind, Daru.'

Darius sighed, draining his glass. 'It helps to talk about it. Makes it seem less real. Puppa, would you?'

Faraz reached for the oxygen mask attached to the cylinder and took a blast. 'So many years ago . . . Xerxes was my oldest friend. You know, he was only eighteen when he inherited the family business? So young. What do people know of life at that age? What did I understand of life when he hired me straight from college years later? I studied in Cambridge, you know. Xerxes mentored me. Like I mentored Darius and now, Niloufer. Taught me all I know. I went through all the divisions of Mehta & Sons, constructing, altering, repairing, extending, demolishing. Of course, it was much simpler in those days. But Darius's father, Cyrus, was not interested in business. So Xerxes asked me to take over. He wanted to make me an equal partner. Give me half the shares in the company. But I said no! No, Xerxes, I said, *your* family owns the company. I will run it for you. But only as a salaried employee. And when your grandson is old enough, he will take over. Family.'

'And you did an amazing job, Puppa,' Darius said.

'I did what I had to do, and handed you the company ship-shape. Xerxes and I were going to build the biggest construction company in the world! We failed, of course. I didn't even manage to build the biggest one in India. Could not leave you the legacy I had hoped. But who knows . . . with this new contract and what might follow . . .'

Darius looked distracted. Had another sip of wine. 'I offered you shares in Mehta & Sons too, Puppa, but you refused again.'

Faraz's visage softened. He smiled. Took on an almost ethereal glow. The creases on his face seemed to vanish. 'Arrey dikra, what do I need with money? I have a few clothes on my back, a small roof over my head and a little food in my belly. You are my son and are looking after Zara and my grandchildren. Wherever I go after my death, I will take nothing with me but a soul to be judged.'

'And the curse?' Anjoli prompted, avoiding Zara's stony face.

The creases in Faraz's face returned. 'Imagine my horror. I was standing right there, with a hundred other guests at the party, raising a glass to Xerxes, when he burst into flames. I swear by Ahura Mazda there was no fire near him. His head just ... ignited. It was like a halo. I doused him with water, but could not save my mentor.' A tear traced a path down his cheek. The room fell silent. Zara reached out and gently wiped his face.

'And Cyrus?' said Anjoli.

'I was not there when Cyrus passed. I was ...' Confusion crossed his countenance. 'Where was I, maari jaan?'

'London,' said Zara reluctantly.

'Oh, yes. London.' Another tear. 'I regret I was not here. Maybe I could have done something. You had to go through all that on your own. That was not a situation a child should experience. If I knew then what I know now, I would never have left you.'

Darius squeezed Zara's hand. 'I tried to help her.' His voice trailed away as they sat, looking at each other awkwardly.

The fear that had taken root in Anjoli's gut ballooned. It had to be a coincidence. Curses didn't exist. But this ghostlike old man with his milky, near-blind eyes talking of good and evil made her believe something truly strange had happened in this house. She broke the silence. 'We'll make sure nothing happens to Darius. We'll wrap him in cotton wool this weekend.'

'That's very flammable,' chuckled Darius. 'Maybe asbestos.' There was an edge to the laughter.

'Tea? Coffee?' said Zara.

'Not for me,' Kamil stifled a yawn. 'Long day tomorrow. Still fighting jet lag.'

'What are your plans?' asked Darius.

'Seeing Arjun. Meeting this swami. I might go into Dharavi with Sunil. Find out why Bell was so interested in it.'

Darius shook his head. 'You can ask Imran to drive you past, but avoid going all the way inside. It's not a pleasant place.'

'You've been there?'

'Years ago. It was awful. Don't go.'

A gentle snore came from the end of the table. Faraz had fallen asleep, chin resting on his chest. Zara moved to his side. 'It's too much for him,' she said softly. 'Come on, Puppa, let's get you to bed.'

Faraz mumbled, 'Fuss, fuss. You all just fuss.'

Everyone rose, watching as Zara accompanied her father out of the room.

Then

Now I know what a ghost is. Unfinished business, that's what.

Salman Rushdie, *The Satanic Verses*

Cyrus

Bombay. Friday, 12 August 1994.

As the sun dipped beneath the horizon, a strong breeze carried the concerto of the unreal city – the blaring racket of horns and hawkers mingling with the roar of the ocean. Night fell abruptly, as it always did in Bombay. The streetlights flickered on, engendering the road's nickname – The Queen's Necklace. Street food vendors, already at their posts, infused the air with tantalising aromas of garlic, roasted spices and fried delights.

Darius walked alongside Zara towards the NCPA auditorium, the anticipation and anxiety in their minds as palpable as the scent of roasting corn.

'Want some bhutta, kiddo?' he asked.

Zara's lips tightened. 'Don't call me that.'

Darius chuckled. 'You shouldn't have worn your school uniform and that pink backpack then. Do you want some or not?'

'I'm not hungry,' she muttered, her voice edged with unease.

Darius gave her a sidelong glance. 'Are you okay? You seem on edge.'

Zara's eyes darted nervously. 'I just can't stop thinking about . . . you know . . .'

He waved a dismissive hand. 'It's all nonsense. Nothing's going to happen. Especially not in front of an audience full of hundreds of people.' He signalled the vendor, who expertly plucked a perfectly roasted ear of corn from the coals. Butter melted into the kernels as the man sprinkled it with chaat masala and chilli powder before adding a squeeze of lemon. Darius handed over two rupees and took a bite, savouring the sweet and spicy flavours that burst in his mouth. 'I just love this part of Bombay,' he said, tossing the bare corncob into the sea with a casual flick of his wrist.

Zara shot him a reproachful look. 'Don't litter!'

He grinned. 'Never mind, the vultures will have it.'

'Or a dolphin will choke on it,' she retorted.

'Sorry, I won't do it again.' He raised his hands in mock surrender. 'You know, this place is a microcosm of Bombay. The young and old, rich and poor, Hindus, Muslims, Christians, Parsis, atheists – all here for the same cool breeze and the sea.'

'You can say that, living in your mansion. Most people here have nothing.'

'You're one to talk. Cathedral School isn't exactly admitting paupers these days. Anyway, here we are.' He wiggled his fingers in front of her face. 'Wooooo. I'm a ghost and I have the Mehta family in my sights.'

'Stop it! It's not funny,' she snapped.

They stepped through the doors of the auditorium, pausing before a vibrant poster of a man in flowing robes, his eyes glowing with supernatural light. Lightning bolts shot from his hands, and above him, in fluorescent yellow letters, were the words: THE GREAT CYRUS: PERFORMING THE MOST START-LING MYSTERY OF ALL INDIA.

Darius shook his head. 'Could he be any more over the top?'

'Let's go backstage and make sure he's all right.'

Navigating a labyrinth of corridors and staircases, they emerged in the wings. Before them stood the man-sized Perspex box that would feature in the show's climax. It glinted ominously under the stage lights, like a predator waiting to pounce.

'Here it is.' Darius rapped his knuckles against the box. 'The most startling mystery of all India.'

Zara stepped closer, pressing her palms against the cool surface. 'How does he escape? There's nothing in here. No trap doors. Nothing.'

'Let's go inside and see if we can figure it out.'

'Are we allowed?'

'Probably not,' Darius admitted. 'But no one's around.'

They squeezed into the cube, their breaths fogging the Perspex. The bottom third was shielded with copper, but the rest was transparent, revealing every detail of the empty interior. Darius gazed up at the air holes in the top and the ropes that would hoist it fifteen feet above the stage.

'It's scary. How does he get out?' Zara's voice was barely above a whisper. 'I wish he wasn't doing this.'

'Maybe it *is* magic.'

'Hey! What are you doing?' a voice shouted from the stage.

They scrambled out, Darius mouthing a hasty apology to the stagehand as they ran down the corridor to Cyrus's dressing room. Inside, his father was adjusting his silk robes, preparing for the performance.

His face lit up. 'You made it! Your mother was just here. She's gone to her seat now.'

'Break a leg, Daddy,' Darius grinned. 'What a cool poster.'

Zara hugged Cyrus tightly. 'You look wonderful, Uncle.'

Cyrus patted her face affectionately. 'Thank you, dikri. Now go take your seats. Lili will be wondering where you've got to, and you shouldn't be backstage. I need to prepare.'

'All right.' Zara slipped away, but Darius lingered. 'I know you don't believe in all this, Daddy, but you were there when Motta Pappa passed away. The curse said . . .'

Cyrus's smile faltered as memories of that horrific day resurfaced – his father's screams, the frantic efforts to extinguish the flames, the chaos that ensued. 'It's just a myth, son. Nothing will happen. I know what Joseph and Mustafa said about the curse. But it was a freak accident with birthday candles.'

'Zara believes in these things,' Darius insisted. 'She's been stressed for weeks. And Mustafa's been winding her up, saying he saw the ghost of Salim Sinai walking in Behesht's gardens. It really upset her. Why have you kept him on?'

'Salim was his brother, dikra. We can't just throw him out. He's a good watchman, and we've always had generations of servants at Behesht. They've all brought their families to see the show tonight.' Cyrus grasped his son's face, planting a kiss on his forehead. 'Don't worry. I'll be careful. We've taken all the necessary precautions. Now go to your seat. I'll see you after the show.'

As Darius left, Cyrus turned to the mirror. Playing at the National Centre for the Performing Arts was the pinnacle of his career. He had proven that magic was more than cheap tricks – it was an art form that could inspire wonder. Tonight had to be perfect. At forty-seven, it was his moment to shine after years of slogging in small theatres and fairs.

He had sacrificed so much for this. Had hidden his true self from his parents, married Lili out of duty, and only fathered Darius to fulfil his mother's wishes. The secret liaisons in back rooms, the guilt, the lies – they had all taken their toll. If tonight was a success, he could start anew. He could finally come out, get a divorce, and live authentically. Lili knew, perhaps had always known, and he suspected she had her own secrets. Her freedom would ease his shame.

He reached into his bag and pulled out a worn letter, its edges frayed from years of handling. The neat handwriting read:

Dear Mr Cyrus. I saw a ghost today and wanted to warn you that—

A shadow flickered at the open door, and Cyrus jumped. He rushed over and peered into the dimly lit corridor. 'Is anyone there?'

Silence. The only reply was the distant hum of the crowd gathering in the auditorium. The stage manager's voice crackled over the intercom. 'Ten minutes.'

Cyrus folded the letter and slipped it back. Should he have heeded Annie's warning? But how could he believe in a ghost when he had spent so many years debunking frauds?

And yet here was the curse.

This ghost tormenting his family.

Mustafa's story.

Maybe dark magic existed.

Darius waved at Mustafa and his son, who were sitting next to their butler and his son Victor at the back of the auditorium, then squeezed past the people in the front row, joining Zara and Lili. Zara sat on the edge of her seat, knuckles white as she gripped the armrest. 'I wish Puppa was here,' she said, her voice small.

'When is he back from London?' Darius asked. 'Maybe we can catch another performance with him?'

'He called this morning,' his mother replied. 'He returns Monday and has tickets for Friday's show. He said he'd bring you that M&S shortbread you like.'

'I feel sick,' said Zara.

'Relax,' Darius said, patting her arm. 'It's a stupid superstition. Dad will be amazing, and we'll celebrate his birthday afterwards. He was fantastic in rehearsal yesterday, remember?'

'I really want today to be over,' Zara's voice quivered. 'I wish he'd broken a leg, so he didn't have to perform.'

'Why do they say "break a leg" for luck, anyway?' Darius asked Lili. 'It's so stupid. What if you were a dancer?'

'Actually, dancers say "merde" for luck.'

Darius laughed. 'Really? That's "shit" in French, right?'

'It is.'

Darius noticed her distant gaze. 'You seem upset, Ma. Did something happen at work?'

Lili shook her head. 'I'm fine. Just busy with this UK deal, but Faraz has it under control. Let's enjoy the show.'

The lights dimmed, and the curtain rose. With a dramatic puff of smoke, Cyrus appeared on stage, the audience erupting in applause. 'Ladies and gentlemen,' he announced, his voice commanding. 'Tonight, you will witness the greatest illusions known to humanity. Prepare to see me catch a bullet in my teeth, survive a pit of vipers, and vanish from a transparent box suspended in mid-air. But now . . .' He extended his arms, and flames shot out from his sleeves, eliciting gasps from the crowd. Zara recoiled, eyes round with fear.

Darius was spellbound for the next hour as Cyrus performed one mind-boggling trick after another. Each illusion seemed more miraculous than the last, the live audience's energy amplifying his father's performance. The atmosphere was electric, every moment charged with wonder.

'He's incredible, isn't he?' Darius said during the intermission, sipping his drink.

Lili stared at her nails. 'Your father's magic may drive me crazy, but he's always been a brilliant performer. Your grandfather would be so amazed to see him now.'

'Well, construction was never his thing,' said Darius. 'Imagine him climbing scaffolding in those robes.'

Lili chuckled. 'What about you? Have you decided if you're going to take over the family business?'

'They should have made you CEO, Ma, not just general counsel.'

'I know where my talents lie. Keep learning from Faraz and join after college. Let's head back; the second half is starting.'

Darius drained his glass, and they returned to their seats as the lights went down once more. The show built towards its climax with seamless precision. Finally, Cyrus stepped forward, his voice elevating the suspense. 'And now, the moment you've all been waiting for. The most astounding illusion in all of India.'

Four assistants wheeled the transparent cube onto the stage. Cyrus announced, 'Behold, a perfectly ordinary box. I will enter it, and it will rise in the air. There, it shall hang. And from there . . . I. Will. Vanish.'

Applause thundered through the auditorium as he entered the box. An assistant padlocked it from the outside. Darius noticed a flicker cross his father's face as he glanced at his feet before he refocused on the audience. With a groaning creak, the box ascended, swaying gently as it rose above the stage.

The music swelled to a dramatic crescendo. Zara leaned forward, holding her breath. Darius reached for her hand, but she pulled away, eyes glued to the spectacle.

Cyrus raised his hands. 'Alakazam!'

Flames erupted within the box, engulfing him. Cyrus's eyes widened in terror as he screamed, his voice piercing the air. The audience clapped, thinking it part of the act. Darius felt the blood drain from his face. He turned to his mother. 'That didn't happen yesterday, did it?'

Lili and Zara were frozen, staring at the box, now a blazing inferno. Cyrus pounded desperately on the Perspex, his robes aflame, fire licking out from the holes on top of the cube. Stage-hands rushed in with fire extinguishers, spraying foam upwards, but it barely dented the blaze.

Horror seized Darius as he saw the ropes holding the box

aloft fray. The stage manager shouted, 'It's going to fall! Get out of the way!'

Everyone scattered as the ropes gave way. The box plummeted to the stage, shattering on impact. Shards of Perspex and debris flew everywhere as the stagehands rushed back, dousing the conflagration with extinguishers until it subsided.

Pandemonium erupted as the audience stampeded for the exits. Darius fought through the chaos, and scrambled on the stage, Lili and Zara close behind. Cyrus's body lay in the wreckage, his skin blistered and charred, the stench of burning flesh filling the air. Zara collapsed, retching, while Lili tried to shield her from the gruesome sight.

'Call an ambulance!' Darius yelled, his voice breaking over Zara's keening wails. 'He's still alive! Daddy, stay with us!'

But Cyrus's eyes were vacant, his body lifeless. Reality settled over Darius like a suffocating shroud.

The curse was real.

And he was next.

Now

If you want to live in the city you have to think ahead
three turns, and look behind a lie to see the truth
and then behind that truth to see the lie.

Vikram Chandra, *Sacred Games*

Kamil

Thursday, 1 December.
Three days to go.

The car jerks to a halt in the traffic, and the city presses in. Four young kids rush towards us, small hands outstretched, faces full of feigned desperation. Anjoli isn't carrying any cash, but she pats her pockets anyway, eyes apologising, conveying the disturbing discovery of her own inadequacy in the face of abject need. Imran catches her troubled look in the rearview mirror, reaches into the central console, and cracks his window just enough to slip out packets of biscuits. The kids snatch them up eagerly, and we move on.

Anjoli smiles at this kindness and adjusts her necklace, which has somehow got caught in her hair. I watch it all blankly, pre-occupied with the sense of foreboding that's been growing since I heard Darius utter Arjun's name.

'Shouldn't we have called first?' Her voice breaks the spell. 'What if he won't see us? What if he's not in?'

I damp down my anxiety. Flash my best Ronnie Engineer grin. 'I didn't want to give him a chance to say no. If he's out, we wait. I'm counting on his curiosity. And his delight at the opportunity of catching up with you, his beautiful childhood sweetheart from London.'

'Shut up! We were never sweethearts. We just grew up together because of our parents.'

The car falls silent, the hum of the traffic filling the void. Anjoli turns her gaze out the window. 'The strain's really getting to Daru and Zara. I felt bad asking all those questions at dinner.'

'It's a lot – this curse, Bell's death, Faraz's declining health. Daru's holding up well, all things considered. I'd probably be screaming under my bed.'

'What did you think of Faraz?'

'Impressive guy. He's accomplished so much. I hope I can face the end with that kind of dignity when my time comes.'

'Zara's struggling, though. It was obvious yesterday.'

'Who wouldn't be? It's a lot to handle.'

She sighs. 'I wish there was more we could do. These immolations don't seem like murder, do they?'

I shake my head. 'The only links are the watchman and the butler. If Ali's seeking vengeance for his great-uncle, Darius should be safe. We won't let anyone near him on Sunday.' Shifting gears, I pull out my phone. 'By the way, about our mini-break. There are no hotels on Elephanta. How about Goa instead? Beach, sun, relaxation. What do you think?'

'Is this the right time, Kamil?'

I show her the screen. 'It's the perfect season for Goa. Rogers won't keep me here indefinitely. We have two tasks: ensure Daru's safety and confirm Bell's death isn't linked to Mehta & Sons. Then it's up to Karve. Why not take a couple of days for ourselves before heading back to London?'

She considers this. 'Hopefully Chanson won't burn down the restaurant while I'm AWOL.'

'So, that's a yes? Should I book one room? To save on costs, since we're investing in our new business?'

In for a penny . . .

She rolls her eyes. 'Show me some options.'

All right! That was *not* a no.

As we enter Bandra Kurla Complex, the scene shifts. This

isn't the Mumbai I know. Sleek skyscrapers of steel and glass rise from lush gardens, their reflections shimmering in the sun. The broad, tree-lined boulevards teem with the usual traffic, but the pavements are crowded with well-dressed professionals walking to work past massive sculptures between the buildings and colourful murals that tell the story of the city's past and stretch out towards its bold future. On a continuum from developing to developed, here at least, it feels as if India is well beyond the halfway point. Imran pulls into a basement car park. 'Arpin in this building, saar. Message when you need pickup.'

The contrast between Arpin's reception and Mehta & Sons is stark – tired furniture, faded decor and a bored receptionist. 'Mr Arjun Sharma,' I say.

'You have appointment? What is your good name?'

'No appointment.'

She sucks her teeth. 'You cannot see sir without an appointment. He is very busy.'

Anjoli steps forward. 'Please tell him Anjoli Chatterjee is here from London. I'm an old family friend.'

Looking dubious, the receptionist picks up her phone and murmurs into it. Her eyebrows rise slightly as she hangs up. 'Sir will see you.'

We're led through a maze of cubicles, mostly empty, their occupants looking like bored automatons. At the end of the corridor, the receptionist knocks on a nondescript door. I brace myself.

Arjun Sharma appears a decade older, even though it's been half that time since I last saw him. I'm disappointed to see he's still got his rugged good looks that probably come from his childhood access to a full gym and swimming pool in his house and membership in some rich-people tennis club in adulthood. No paunch in sight, unless he's wearing a waist trimmer under his shirt. But his face is lined with deep crevices, offset by a determined greying at the temples. Maybe the intervening period has had a similar effect on me and I just haven't noticed? Lucky bastard. How is he not morphing into the corpulent, hairy goblin that was his father?

'Anjoli!' He walks up with a pasted-on smile and embraces her. 'What a wonderful, wonderful surprise.' Turns to me. Pumps my hand vigorously. '*And* the great Mr Kamil Rahman. Saviour of the Prime Minister of India. What a great honour. Please have a seat. When did you arrive in Mumbai? To what do I owe this visit?' That private school cut-glass British accent. He has to be putting it on after all this time.

Given the receptionist didn't mention I was with Anjoli, I'm astonished that Arjun hasn't shown the surprise – or anger – I'd expected at his seeing me. Did he know we were coming?

'You look great, Anjoli, as always. Still doing your T-shirts, I see!' He nods at her chest, which is emblazoned with *Anagrams don't know their ears from their bowels*.

'Yeah, passes the time when I'm not running an award-winning restaurant.'

'I know. Tried to get a table when I was last in town, but you were fully booked.'

Lying dipshit.

'Oh! You should have called. How've you been?'

'Great. Really great. Busy.'

I realise he's more anxious about us dropping in unannounced than we are of facing him. I lower my guard as he pours tea, his hands steady but his eyes watchful. 'I know your parents passed. I'm so sorry. You know how fond I was of them.'

'Thank you, Arjun. How's Pinky Aunty?'

'She's great. Getting older, but still a force of nature. You must come for dinner while you're here. She'd love to see you. And you too, Kamil! She was so impressed when we saw you on TV. What a hero! Come over and give us the full story. Have a biscuit.'

Have a biscuit? When we last met, this guy attempted to have

160

me deported from Britain, so it's more than discombobulating for him to be treating me like his oldest buddy. I'd better get down to business before he invites me to play golf. 'Arjun, this isn't a social call. We're here for work.'

An eyebrow goes up. 'Oh?'

'I'm in Mumbai as liaison for the UK Government investigating the death of Peter Bell.'

His expression shifts to one of sympathy. 'Awful, what happened. A serial killer, right? I heard about another similar death in Bandra. Why are you involved?'

'I'm a friend of Darius Mehta. He asked for me to look into it.'

'Ah, yes. Dear Darius.'

'I understand Arpin is a subcontractor to Mehta & Sons on the Coastal Road project?'

'*Arpin*! *Ar*jun and *Pin*ky. I get it now! That's clever.' Anjoli breaks my flow, irritating me. I want him off balance. 'When did you set it up, Arjun?'

He stretches his legs out. 'Yes, Ma was happy with the name. Dad's business didn't survive all that ... unpleasantness in London.' Gives me a quick look. 'So I had to start from scratch. Rather than becoming a full-fledged construction company, I focused on demolition. We've been quite successful in that arena.'

'But you bid for the entire project against Darius. Not just the demolition,' I say.

He laughs, a rich, practised sound. 'You're well informed. You have to be in it to win it.'

'You sued when *they* won it.'

His jaw clenches briefly. 'True.'

'How did you end up working for Mehta & Sons?'

A hint of irritation. '*With*, not for. Darius is a smart businessman. He realised we were the best demolition partner for him. We reached an amicable agreement.'

'But Faraz wasn't happy with you working *for* him?' I needle.

This takes him aback. I see confusion for the first time. 'What do you mean?'

'Something he said last night.'

'He's out of hospital, then?'

'Yes.'

'How is he?'

'Not well.'

'I saw him a few weeks ago. He looked terrible. I'm glad he's home, though. I didn't realise he was unhappy with us. But Darius makes the decisions now.'

'Why did Peter Bell come to meet you the day before he died?'

He pours himself another cup of tea, stirring slowly, buying time. 'He wanted advice.'

'On?'

'How to demolish a temple in the tunnel's path with minimal environmental impact.'

Is he lying? I can't tell. 'Why did you meet him? Couldn't someone else in your team handle it?'

He straightens his jacket, his demeanour suddenly more guarded. 'It's an important project. I like to be hands on.'

'Who's your day-to-day contact at Mehta & Sons?'

'That would be Niloufer Cama.'

'But she didn't know about this meeting?'

Arjun shrugs.

'What else did you two discuss?'

'He asked why the temple wasn't scheduled for demolition. I explained the tunnel went around it.' He lowers his voice conspiratorially. 'The original plan surprised me, to be honest. Bell's plan was more sensible. Although the swami who runs the temple is troublesome.'

'How so?'

'He incites protests and violence. Not someone you want to cross. Maybe that was the reason for Ronnie Engineer's plan.'

'Why did Bell schedule another meeting with you for the day after he died?'

Arjun's eyes flicker with something – surprise? Guilt? 'Did he? I didn't know.'

He's lying.

'Did you have unfinished business with him?'

'Not that I know of.'

'What were you doing the night Bell died?'

He looks at me in mock horror. 'Are you suggesting I'm a suspect? You do like to persecute me, don't you? I was at a party from eight to eleven.'

'Where?'

'Ziya. At the Oberoi.'

'That's where Bell was staying.'

'Was it?'

This guy's definitely playing games.

'He was found dead next to your construction site on Marine Drive.'

He shudders dramatically. 'Shot with arrows. Horrifying.'

Terrible actor.

'Who has keys to that site?'

'I don't. My site foreman manages it. He has the key. But we haven't worked there for a month. We've moved down to Chowpatty now. Karve investigated and came up empty. Now, if we're done . . .'

'You know Karve?'

A beat. 'Yes. He's helped me before.'

'From before this murder?'

'Yes. If we're finished, I have another—'

'Who's Felix?'

'What?'

'The name means nothing to you?'

He shakes his head, standing. 'No. Felix doesn't ring a bell.'

He extends his hand. 'Look, Kamil, I'm sorry for everything after my father died. I was wrong. Grief made me act out. Can we move past it?'

I take his hand reluctantly. It's clammy. 'Of course. Water under the bridge.'

'Good. So, dinner on Tuesday? I'll text you the address.'

As we drive away, Anjoli turns to me, eyebrows raised. 'Well?'

'Great. Really great. He's such a great guy.'

She laughs. 'Weird, all that warmth. What did you make of his story?'

'Did you ever have a thing for him growing up?'

'Seriously? He was like my brother.'

'Cain?'

'Focus, Kamil!'

'He was expecting us.'

'Yes. I got that feeling too. But who could have told him? Darius?'

'Maybe.' I ponder. 'He lied about Bell's second meeting. Why *did* Bell want to see him again? Arjun could have killed him, then gone to his party. The Oberoi isn't far from where Bell's body was found.'

'He'd have to be a psychopath to kill someone with arrows, then party like nothing happened. What about the swami?'

'Everyone's pointing us that way. We should visit him next.' I glance at my watch. 'I'll call Ronnie Engineer.'

Our car glides along the Sea Link. Mumbai's skyscrapers loom like shadows on the horizon, a ghostly outline against the gauzy haze. The sea sparkles beneath, a deceptive beauty concealing the undercurrents of sewage, debris and secrets below. Just like Arjun's smile.

Kamil

Bulldozers rumble and excavators groan as they carve through Priyadarshini Park, turning its leafy serenity into a chaotic construction site. Dust hangs thick in the air, shrouding the scene in a gritty haze. The once public space is now off-limits, closed off by blue tarpaulins that flutter like forlorn flags in the sultry breeze.

'They've started prepping for the tunnel,' Ronnie yells over the din, his voice swallowed by the cacophony of drilling and machinery. He glances back at us, his face strained. 'I've messaged the swami to say we're on our way.'

The idea of a godman on WhatsApp makes me chuckle. Anjoli pulls her T-shirt over her nose, trying to filter out the dust, revealing a glimpse of her pierced belly button. 'Talk about a health and safety nightmare!' she mutters, her voice muffled behind the fabric.

We push through the turmoil, the noise gradually fading as we approach the end of the site. Workers disperse, leaving behind a strange, unsettling silence. Before us lies a small pond, its murky green water stagnant and uninviting. No sign of the birds and amphibians Ronnie's so keen on.

Beside the water stands a modest temple, its orange stone paint peeling, the structure perched on a raised platform overlooking the sea. The shikhara, the temple's spire, is roughly carved, tapering to a point, with patches of faded paint flaking off. It looks ordinary. One of countless such structures scattered across the city. Nothing worth fighting for.

A tall, muscular man draped in saffron robes stands at the shrine's entrance, his gaze fixed on the horizon like a sentinel. The air vibrates with an almost tangible anticipation. Ronnie's demeanour shifts as we climb the steps, his usual bonhomie replaced by a visible unease.

'This is Swami Yogesh,' he says, his voice low. 'Do you need me to translate, or are you okay with Marathi?'

'Translate, please.'

My eyes lock on the swami. He has a formidable presence. His face and hair are coated in ash, his forehead marked with a white stripe and a red slash. The medallions and necklaces draped around his neck catch the light as he moves. In his hand, he grips a curved sword, the blade gleaming ominously. He seems to be powered by a coiled energy waiting to be unleashed. This is not the smiling Maharishi you see on Discovery Channel documentaries. This is some kind of deadly avenger. I've seen plenty of godmen before, but this guy's different. Hypnotic.

He beckons us wordlessly. Flows into his shrine. We follow him through the narrow entrance, ducking to avoid hitting our heads. The air inside is redolent of incense and fresh jasmine, mingling into a heady perfume. The inner sanctum reveals a jet-black shivalingam adorned with vibrant marigold garlands. On the wall, a fierce mask of Shiva glares down at us, teeth bared and eyeballs bulging, surrounded by coiled snakes and skulls. Sunlight streams through gaps in the walls, casting intricate patterns on the uneven floor, lending the room an otherworldly atmosphere. The swami's eyes bore into mine, black as night. 'Mussalman?' he rumbles, his voice like distant thunder.

I nod, an inchoate anxiety forming in the pit of my stomach. He says something to Ronnie, who looks embarrassed.

'You can't enter the holy room because . . .' Ronnie trails off, clearly uncomfortable.

'That's fine. We can talk here.'

Anjoli's gaze darts to a pile of weapons in the corner – arrows, swords, maces, tridents, axes. 'Why do you have those?' she asks.

The swami's expression is inscrutable as Ronnie translates. 'Protection.'

Right. Protection. Or for mowing down unbelievers who cross him.

The swami motions for us to sit, and we lower ourselves onto the dusty floor, the stone cold beneath us.

'Swami Yogesh, I believe you met with Peter Bell?' I start, watching Ronnie translate.

The swami's gaze remains unflinching. 'I saw the Englishman. With the Koli.'

'Sunil Tandel,' Ronnie explains. 'Bell's assistant.'

'You had concerns about his plans for the tunnel?'

'He would not understand,' the swami replies through Ronnie.

'Understand what?'

'A Shiv Mandir has stood on this site for centuries. It is sacred land. Ronnie Engineer understands this. We had an agreement. Your tunnel would go around god's house. But this man Bell broke the agreement.'

I turn to Ronnie, who shifts uncomfortably. 'What agreement?'

'Just an understanding to respect the temple. Environmental impact. Because of the pond,' he mumbles.

'Did you know Bell was found dead, with eighteen arrows in his body?'

The swami nods, his expression unchanged.

'What do you think about that?'

He raises his palm and intones a Sanskrit verse. '*Jātasya hi dhruvo mṛityur dhruvaṁ janma mṛitasya cha tasmād aparihārye 'rthe na tvaṁ śhochitum arhasi.'*

Ronnie looks puzzled, but translates after a brief exchange in Marathi. 'Death is certain for one who has been born, and rebirth is inevitable for one who has died. Therefore, you should not lament over the inevitable.'

'Do you believe Bell's death was inevitable?'

'He wanted to destroy my temple.'

'Did he deserve to die for that?'

A cryptic gesture with his hands. 'It is all written. When your time is up, it is up.'

'That's what my dad used to say.' Anjoli changes position to swap her tucked legs to the other side. The floor is hard. She looks as uncomfortable as I feel. The swami looks at Ronnie. 'You don't need to translate that,' she adds quickly.

I wipe the sweat from my brow, trying to steady myself. The oppressive heat and the thick incense are making me dizzy. Or maybe it's this man's intense presence. 'Are you familiar with ritual sacrifices?' I ask, flipping through my notebook for Karve's notes.

A brief nod.

'Have you heard about the beheading in Bandra?'

Another nod.

'Did you know that victim?'

A shake of the head.

'What were you doing Thursday night?'

'Meditating.'

'Where?'

A head jerk towards the inner room.

'Alone?'

'I am never alone. Lord Shiva is with me always.'

Anjoli mutters under her breath, 'He's not available for an alibi interview anytime soon.'

Before I can respond, the swami cuts me off with a sharp

wave of his hand. He barks something at Ronnie, who gets flustered and mumbles in Marathi. The word 'paise' catches my ear, repeated several times. Money.

'What's going on?' Anjoli whispers to Ronnie.

'Nothing.' His forehead gleams with sweat.

'What's he saying about paise?' I ask.

'Just . . . just that it will cost a lot to build a new temple.'

'I thought you offered to rebuild it for free and he refused?'

'Ya, we did. He's not making sense. We should leave. He's upset.' Ronnie rises, but the swami grabs his arm, turns to me and, to my surprise, breaks into English. 'He lie. Take money. Make god promise. Bell break promise. Now this man also break promise.'

Ronnie goes pale. 'I don't know what he's talking about.'

'Did you tell Bell this?' I ask the swami.

'Yes. I say everything arrange with Engineer. He not listen. And now . . .' The swami releases Ronnie, grabs his scimitar with a fluid motion, and jams the blade under his neck. 'Now, he die also.'

Anjoli jumps to her feet. 'Oh my god!' she yells as Ronnie stumbles back, terror etched on his face.

The swami's eyes, illuminated by a sliver of light, seem to shoot sparks. He hisses. 'Listen! I warn. You hurt temple, you die also. Shiva anger fall on you like thunder and lightning. With storm and fire. This is war. Good against evil. Good will win always. Against Christian. Against Muslim. Against Parsi. This is your last warning.'

Is this for real? Ronnie's face is ashen, and even I feel a flame of fear. I step in front of Anjoli, my heart pounding. 'Is that why you killed Bell?' I try to keep my voice steady, but it's an effort.

The swami swivels. Presses the tip of the sword against my chest. I feel the pressure of the weapon on my breastbone. Hear Anjoli's breath catch behind me. His skin smells of some pungent oil, and the heat of his body radiates through the blade. I stare into his black eyes, trying not to blink. We stand frozen, locked in a silent battle of wills.

Suddenly, his mouth twitches into a smile. He tosses the sword onto his pile of armaments and claps me hard on the back, almost knocking me off balance. 'You are Aurangzeb fighting Shivaji,' he declares, his expression shifting to one of calm. I take a moment to recover from this transformation. The vengeful Shiva has been supplanted by a peaceful, smiling deity in a matter of seconds. Did he realise he went too far? Gave too much away?

'How much did you pay Ronnie?' I ask, my voice hoarse.

'Enough. He make promise and . . .' The swami shakes his head. 'But I will fight. And win. You will lose. Or die. Now go.'

I raise my hands defensively. 'We're going.' We leave him standing outside the temple, his figure silhouetted against the sky like a general on the battlements of a besieged fort.

We walk back to the park entrance in silence as my mind races. This man is dangerous, capable of great violence. He's fit, quick, and seems utterly devoid of fear. He'd feel no more at killing us than swatting a mosquito. Is he Karve's serial killer? I fix Ronnie with a hard stare. 'So. He paid you off. You altered the plans to accommodate the temple. Darius didn't understand why. Now it makes sense.'

'No, no,' Ronnie mutters, his voice desperate. 'Nothing like that.'

'Bell found out, didn't he? Was he threatening to expose you?'

'Nothing happened, I swear.' Ronnie's eyes are wild. 'If you want to know what's really going on, ask Niloufer. She and Bell were having an affair. That's the truth.'

I've suspected as much, given Ronnie's earlier insinuations, but it doesn't constitute proof. It's also beside the point. 'Bell was going to tell Darius about the bribe, wasn't he?'

Ronnie can't meet my gaze. 'I need to talk to the site supervisor.' And with that, he bolts.

In the car, Anjoli bursts out, 'Jesus! What a nutter. Those arrows! The sword!'

'It was almost like he was mocking us. Niloufer was right. He's dangerous.'

'Dangerous? He was fucking terrifying. It was as if he could see into my soul. I actually thought he was going to impale you. Are we in danger?'

'I don't think so. We've done nothing to him. Ronnie's the one in trouble if the swami feels betrayed.'

'You held your own, though,' she says, a hint of admiration in her voice.

I puff out my chest. 'A man's gotta do what a man's gotta do. I think he's just pissed his bribe didn't work.'

'Do you think he killed Bell?'

'It's possible. Sometimes the obvious suspect is the right one. He's got the means, the motive, and no alibi.'

'But why? How would killing Bell help save his temple?'

'To scare people into leaving him alone? He said this was our last warning. These religious fanatics aren't rational. Or maybe Karve's right, and Bell's death is just some twisted ritual unrelated to the project.'

'Do you really believe that?'

I shake my head. 'Too many people could have had a reason to want Bell dead. The swami, Ronnie, Niloufer, even Arjun and Daru. Any of them could be hiding something.'

She grins. 'Maybe it was like that Agatha Christie film we saw. Eighteen killers. Each shoving an arrow into him.'

'Yeah. *Murder on the Mumbai Local.*'

The moment of levity lifts our mood somewhat.

She scrunches her forehead. 'Why was Bell's room searched? Can't see the swami doing that?'

'True. Daru's emails implied Bell had something *he* wanted. I'd like to check the CCTV from the hotel.'

'Didn't the police do that already?'

'Karve says they did. But I don't trust him.'

'So, what's our next move?'

She's fired up on adrenaline. As am I. This experience has unleashed something in both of us.

'See Karve.' I dial. 'Inspector? Kamil Rahman here. I'm organising Bell's repatriation, but I wondered if you'd made any progress on the case? No? I've just seen the swami at Priyadarshini Park. Did you interview him? Not yet? I think you should. Also, could I learn more about the other tantric death you mentioned? It would help if I could report back with some solid leads. Oh, you're busy. No problem. I'll call Commissioner Naik. Maybe he can help. You have time now? Excellent. We'll be there soon.' Have I made a mistake mentioning Naik? Last thing I want is for him to know I'm back in Mumbai.

Anjoli looks at me questioningly. I force a laugh. 'Always good to invoke the bigger dog. He'll see us.'

'Who's Naik?'

'My old boss when I was here. He doesn't like me much, though, and—' My phone buzzes with a text. 'Rogers. He's asking for an update and sent Bell's insurance details. Give me a sec.'

The charged atmosphere from the temple dissipates as I'm pulled back into mundane bureaucracy. I dial the funeral director to arrange the collection of Bell's body. He's professional and efficient, sending a list of documents he needs. I text Rogers that everything will be ready in a few days.

Good. I'll expect you back next week. I show the message to Anjoli. 'Maybe the week after. We're taking our holiday, no matter what. You'll need time to recuperate from seeing Shiva's junk.'

'Huh?'

'The black stone sculpture in the temple. The shivalingam. It represents Shiva's, uh, undercarriage. It's symbolic of creation.'

'Blimey. And that ash-covered dude worships it?'

'Yep.'

'I guess a swami's gotta do what a swami's gotta do.'

Anjoli

Anjoli sat cross-legged, her ankle bouncing with nervous energy. The lobby of the police station felt strangely oppressive despite its clean appearance and the presence of uniformed cops working diligently. She couldn't shake the feeling of being watched. One policeman, seated behind a windowed office, caught her eye and licked his lips. Her stomach churned in response. The muffled sound of shouting echoed through the corridors, angry and drunken, adding to her unease.

She glanced at Kamil. He seemed lost in thought, probably rehearsing his upcoming conversation with Inspector Karve. He had ignored her most of the drive over, his anxiety simmering since their encounter with the swami. She tried to push the memory aside, focusing instead on the here and now.

When they were finally ushered into Karve's office, Anjoli's expectations of a sullen, surly officer were upended. The inspector was a mild-mannered man who looked like a stick figure made of coat hangers. The religious mark on his forehead seemed oddly out of place with his crisp uniform, but he greeted them with a reserved nod, not fazed by Anjoli's presence. Settling behind his desk, he addressed Kamil, 'You have organised the return of the body?'

'It's in process.'

'You will go back to London now.'

'Soon. Did you follow up on Swami Yogesh?'

Karve's eyes narrowed. 'I have looked into him.'

'He had an obvious motive for killing Bell. His temple was about to be destroyed by the tunnel. He had arrows and a sword that could have been used in the Bandra murder.'

'No connection between him and Eapen. This is clearly a killer targeting Christians for tantric reasons. Non-Hindu,' he added, glancing at Anjoli as if she might need clarification.

Her irritation flared. 'That's exactly why it could be the swami. He just threatened us with a sword!'

Karve's look turned withering. 'Madam, I know Swami Yogesh. He is not a murderer. His weapons are legally held in the mandir. You two return to London and tell the family we will find the killer. Not to worry.'

'Not to worry?' Anjoli's frustration bubbled over. 'Is that what you say to families when their loved ones are murdered? The swami also threatened to kill—'

'Listen, Inspector,' Kamil interrupted, irritating her even more. 'We won't interfere with your investigation, but I would like to review the CCTV footage from the Oberoi.'

Karve looked affronted. 'Why? I said already. We look at it. Find nothing.'

'An extra pair of eyes is never a bad thing. Always good to double check. Is it a problem?'

'That is not your job.' The atmosphere in the room had gone from neutral to adversarial within minutes. 'You go back to your Scotland Yard. You cannot access the CCTV.'

'I can get Commissioner Naik to give me permission.'

Karve's face contorted in fury. Then he waved a hand. 'Waste your time. What do I care?' He barked an order in Marathi to his peon, who led Anjoli and Kamil through a labyrinth of corridors.

'Maybe we shouldn't have pissed him off,' Anjoli whispered as they walked.

Giving her a dismissive wave, Kamil said, 'We got what we wanted, didn't we?'

Her annoyance simmered. They arrived at the IT department, where a young man in jeans and a Rolling Stones T-shirt was fiddling with a computer. The techie barely acknowledged Anjoli as he spoke to Kamil. 'Bell. Oberoi,' he said, gesturing them to a desk with two monitors. Connecting a hard drive, he set the video playing. 'There are two views. This monitor shows the lobby cameras. Date and time stamps are in the corner. The other is the lift on the murdered man's floor. Rewind, pause and fast-forward with these keys. What time do you want to start?'

'Six p.m. Last Thursday,' Kamil said. 'Did you examine the footage?'

'Not my job. The video was delivered by the hotel, but you're the first people to see it.'

The stifling atmosphere was weighing down on Anjoli. Her throat felt parched, but she hesitated to ask for water. Kamil oozed self-satisfaction. 'I knew Karve hadn't checked it!' He fixed his eyes on the screens. 'Right. Let's see what we have here.' Anjoli didn't think that merited a reply. Just stared at the monitor.

Kamil looked at her. 'You okay?'

She shot him a glare. 'You sure you need my help? You seem to have it all under control.'

'Huh?'

'Why didn't you tell Karve what the swami said? About threatening Ronnie? The bribe? And whatshername, the affair woman?'

'Shit, that reminds me. Wait a minute. Sorry.' He dialled his phone, causing Anjoli's fury to boil over. What was *wrong* with him? Was the casual sexism of Indian cops rubbing off on him?

'Hi, Sunil? This is Kamil Rahman. You mentioned taking Peter Bell to Dharavi. Could you accompany me there? I'm curious about why he went. Darius said you'd help ... Okay, tomorrow morning then. Good. WhatsApp me a meeting place.' He hung up and turned back to Anjoli. 'Want to come?'

Her face set, she said, 'Is this how it's going to be?'

'What do you mean?'

'Me tagging along as if I'm some sort of accessory.'

'You *are* my accessory and I'm yours. We're partners, remember?'

'Accessory. Like a hat or bag.'

'You're not an old bag.' He attempted a smile, but it fell flat.

Her anger gave way to resignation. 'Kamil, why am I here?'

'Huh?'

'It's not like I'm not needed back home. You barely spoke to me in the car, interrupted me with Karve, and just now, you dismissed me and took a call. If we're partners, shouldn't we discuss our moves together?'

'I'm sorry.'

Her anger flared. 'Sorry's not good enough. You keep saying we're partners and I'm a good detective. Fine, you've got more experience, but I'm logical and understand people better than you do. You know the nuts and bolts of investigating, but I can get into people's heads. So, be honest. Can we work together or should we forget the whole thing?'

Kamil glanced at the techie, who gave him a slight grin and left. He raised a placatory hand and whispered, 'I really am sorry. I'm stressed and trying to get on with it. I do think you're a good detective, or I wouldn't have quit my job to work with you. I love you, but I'm not stupid enough to throw away my career on a whim.'

Anjoli froze. Although she was well aware of Kamil's feelings for her, he'd never said the words before. Her irritation dissipated like smoke and was replaced by a warm glow. She felt like laughing. *Here?* In a grubby room in a grubby police station. Was this

177

what she'd been waiting for? For Kamil to actually come out and say it? She knew he'd been about to kiss her when the gong had sounded for dinner the previous night. In fact, she'd wanted him to. Maybe this was the push she needed.

Kamil continued, oblivious to the impact of his words. 'Look, I don't trust Karve. There's no point in telling him our theories if he's just going to follow his own ideas.'

Anjoli hid a smile and collected herself. 'You think he'll fudge the investigation?'

'Probably. It'll end up as another unsolved case. I've seen many cops like him. They do the minimum to cover their asses until retirement. He might have an agenda.'

'Like what?'

'You saw the tilak he was wearing. He's a devout Hindu and seems close to the swami and Arjun. Maybe he's okay with these tantric killings.'

She raised an eyebrow.

'I know how corrupt the police can be. If the swami's paying Ronnie, it's not a stretch to think he might bribe Karve, too.'

She chewed on this for a moment. 'Bell didn't deserve to die like that.'

'No, he did not. I want to find out why he went to Dharavi. Please come with me. I honestly need you.'

I love you *and* I need you. The words echoed in her mind, and she nodded, feeling the connection rekindle between them.

'Thanks. And sorry,' said Kamil. They turned their attention back to the screens. 'There! That's Bell!' Kamil exclaimed. The time stamp read 18.26. Bell entered the lift in the pristine white hotel lobby and exited on his floor. Forty minutes later, he did the same in reverse, rushing into the lift and leaving the lobby.

'That matches the timeline Karve gave us,' Kamil noted. 'Must be in response to the mysterious call he got.'

Anjoli stretched, feeling the weight of the day. 'How much longer?.'

'Fast forward a bit.'

She pressed the key, watching the time tick by: 19.10, 19.15, 19.20, 19.25.

'Wait! Go back.'

Anjoli squinted at the tall woman carrying a large handbag entering the lobby at 19.23. 'Who's that?'

Excitement coloured Kamil's voice. 'Niloufer Cama.'

Her heart pounded. They watched as Niloufer exited the lift on Bell's floor. For twenty agonising minutes, nothing happened.

'Go forward.'

At 19.46, she re-entered the lift. By 19.50, she had left the hotel.

They looked at each other and breathed again. 'She searched his room,' Anjoli whispered. 'Can you tell if anything's in her bag?' They replayed the footage, scrutinising Niloufer's movements, but couldn't see any clear evidence.

'Wow.' Anjoli's thoughts churned. 'So, what do we think? Niloufer did it? She was having an affair and killed him to keep it secret? With arrows? Stole some incriminating evidence from his room?'

Kamil shook his head. 'She wouldn't have had time to kill him and return to his room in that brief span.'

'So she had an accomplice. Someone who did the killing while she retrieved stuff – emails, maybe?'

Kamil nodded. 'She has questions to answer.'

Anjoli pulled out her phone and recorded the footage. 'You need to question her soon. And maybe I can come?'

Love and other revelations could wait.

Kamil

Friday, 2 December.
Two days to go.

'You know where we're going?' I ask Imran the next morning.

'Yes, saar. Sunil already told me,' he replies, waving his phone with a confident grin.

'Sorry for the rushed breakfast, Anj. I wanted us to get a head start.'

I brush crumbs from my lap. The mutton patty I grabbed for our journey to Dharavi leaves a flaky trail.

'Don't mess up the car. Imran will have to clean it. And stop calling me Anj,' she retorts, stuffing a corner of toast into her mouth. A blob of jam lands on her chin, precariously close to her *Penguins Are On Thin Ice* T-shirt. Before it falls, I reach over, swipe it off with my finger, and lick it clean.

She smiles. 'Disgusting!'

'Yes, you are. Anyway, everyone calls you Anj.'

'Not you. It sounds weird.' She turns her gaze out the window, chewing thoughtfully. 'Have you heard from Niloufer?'

'Not yet. I left two messages saying I needed to speak to her.'

'She probably knows we're on to her. Supersleuths and all. Where were Daru and Zara last night? I wanted to tell them what we'd found.'

'At some function. I'll catch up with him later this morning. He's not going to like it.'

Anjoli shakes her head. 'Bet he didn't see it coming. Niloufer and Ronnie, both hiding things. I can't believe he's partying with this curse hanging over him. B-Day's only forty-eight hours away.'

'Got to keep up appearances, I suppose. I barely slept last night, thinking of all the what-ifs.'

'Me too. What if something happens and we can't stop it? Hopefully, Zara will send the watchman and Victor away.'

'At least they cancelled the party. We'll stay close to him on Sunday, bucket of water at the ready.'

'Not funny, Kamil!'

'I'm serious. Did you talk to Chanson last night?'

'Tore into him. He didn't like it. Said he's reached the end of his feather. Lol.' She chews her lip, suppressing a smile.

'How are the waiters handling it?'

'They say he's a tyrant and are threatening to quit. Not a good sitch, honestly. I'm really not sure about us taking a holiday.'

Bloody Chanson. Always a fly in the ointment. Or liniment, as he'd say. The evening before had ended so positively. Because the others were out, we had an intimate dinner celebrating our breakthroughs in Bell's case, with Anjoli being surprisingly affectionate.

'We're going, *Anj*. I found a lovely hotel on Ashwem Beach in Goa, with a spa and everything.'

'Did you book it?'

'Not yet. But I will. Today.'

'All right. But just two nights. I need to get back and . . . why are you smiling?'

'No smile!' I pass my hand over my mouth. Don a serious expression.

She stifles a grin. 'While you were hunting for hotels, I was researching spontaneous combustion. There's a lot written about it, but no proof it's an actual thing.'

'Imagine living with that fear. Every birthday a countdown to death.'

'Isn't everyone's birthday a countdown to death?'

'Good T-shirt slog . . .' My phone rings. 'Speak of the devil. Hi, Daru, what's up? Shit! Okay, text me the address. We're coming.'

I take a moment to collect myself, then turn to Anjoli. 'There's been another murder.'

Her eyes go round. 'What? Who?'

I shake my head and tap Imran on the shoulder. 'Do you know Tarkeshwar Shiva Mandir in Mazagaon?'

'Yes, saar.'

'Take us there, immediately.'

Anjoli's voice drops to a whisper. 'It can't be . . . Ronnie, can it? The swami making good on his threat? I *told you* to tell Karve!'

The light-heartedness evaporates. We sit in a leaden silence, as I hope against hope that I haven't screwed up again. Fifteen minutes later, we stop at the head of a narrow lane, too tight for the BMW. The street is lined with cycles and motorbikes, sandwiched between a tall wall and a shabby building. Clothes hang to dry from balconies, some barred with iron railings that give them a prison-like feel. The air thrums with an electric quiet.

We rush to the temple at the end. A constable at the entrance stops us, demanding in Marathi what we want. I raise my hand in a placating gesture and text Darius. He emerges a few minutes later with Karve. The inspector's eyes run up and down Anjoli. 'Madam, you wait here.'

'No thank you. Daru, who's dead? It's not . . . Ronnie is it?'

Darius frowns. 'Ronnie? Why would he be dead? It's a stranger. They've not been able to identify him yet.'

Anjoli exhales in relief. 'Thank god!'

'But why would . . . never mind. Come with me.'

We follow them into the temple – a ground-floor space in a bland building, its walls lined with alcoves holding statues adorned with flowers. The ceiling is draped with garlands and fairy lights. The cheeriness contrasts with the temple's rear, where a black stone statue of Shiva looms. His eyes seem to glow with primal rage. His four arms clutch a trident, a drum, a skull and a flame. The figure casts a chilling shadow, its presence unsettling. An undefinable fear rises inside me, inch by inch. Beside me, Anjoli stands, arms crossed, staring at the floor with her jaw clenched. I follow her gaze and gasp.

Supine before the statue lies the corpse of a man. A massive trident pierces his body, its prongs embedded in his throat, chest and solar plexus. Blood has pooled around wounds in the crown of his head, between his eyes, his belly and crotch.

I swallow hard, my mouth dry, a bitter taste rising from my stomach. The room seems to close in, till nothing's left except for me and this gruesome sight. This is no ordinary crime. The violence, the sheer brutality, speaks of a malevolent force, a darkness that's reached out and consumed this poor soul. I glance at Anjoli, expecting the same intense horror I'm experiencing. Instead, she's studying the scene almost clinically, brow furrowed.

'Stabbed in seven chakras,' Karve says with a note of satisfaction. 'This is the same killer as Eapen, the Bandra lottery seller, and your Bell.'

'This victim isn't connected to Mehta & Sons, thank heaven,' Darius adds. 'I mean . . . well, you know what I mean.'

Karve seems pleased with himself. 'I said to you, this murderer is making sacrifices. Now the papers will be interested.'

I find my voice. 'Who found him?'

'Priest from temple.'

'Is the temple locked at night?'

'Any devotee can come and pray any time, isn't it?'

Or prey. 'I saw a trident like that at the swami's mandir.'

'We will investigate. You go. FFPS squad will be here soon to secure the site.'

I touch Anjoli's shoulder as we walk out. 'Are you okay?'

Her voice is preternaturally calm. 'That was . . . inhuman.'

Before I can ask what she means, my phone buzzes with a text. 'Damn. It's Sunil. He's waiting for us at Dharavi. I forgot to call him.'

'Dharavi's the last place you want to see after that,' Darius says. 'Go home. Have a drink. This killing proves Bell's murder had nothing to do with us. It's definitely a serial killer. Probably the swami, if that's his trident. Leave it to Karve now. Wait, why did you think the victim was Ronnie?'

I compose myself. 'I'll explain when we get back from Dharavi. There are still questions that need answering.'

'Suit yourselves,' Darius says, looking slightly exasperated. 'I have to return to the office. How was your meeting with Arjun yesterday?'

'Interesting.'

I text Sunil that we're on our way. As we drive off, I see Darius watching us, a troubled look on his face.

Kamil

'You're very quiet,' I say, glancing at Anjoli as we head towards Dharavi. I worry she might be processing some latent trauma after witnessing that gruesome scene.

'That was . . . odd,' she finally says, her voice trailing off as if she's trying to make sense of her own emotions. 'He looked more like a specimen in a lab than a person. I kept expecting to feel something – revulsion, horror – but . . . nothing.' She gestures vaguely, searching for the right words.

I nod, understanding her confusion. 'It was grotesque. Not quite real.'

'Maybe if I allowed myself to think of him as a man, it would be different. Is this how you cope with dead bodies?' Her tone is more curious than accusing.

I consider my answer. 'You need distance. Desensitisation is part of it. But it's a double-edged sword. You lose something human in the process.'

After a pause, she adds, 'It has to be the swami, right?'

'He left the body in public again. Almost as if he wants it to be found.'

'Proud of his handiwork? A sacrifice left at Shiva's feet?'

'Maybe. Or another statement to leave his temple alone.'

'Why this guy, then? Whoever he is. And the Bandra fellow had nothing to do with the temple?'

I shake my head as Imran drives on. The silence between us grows more contemplative. 'Why are we going to Dharavi?' she asks finally. 'What's the point?'

'Call it a hunch. We've got three murders, all tied together by these bizarre weapons. We just happen to find a stash of them at the swami's place? He met one victim right before he died? It feels too neat, too . . . staged.'

'Or maybe you're overthinking it?'

'Maybe. But why was Niloufer in Bell's hotel room that night? What's the deal with Ronnie's bribery? Why did Bell make two trips to Dharavi? Visit Arpin? Who's Felix? There are too many loose threads.'

Imran, our driver, speaks up. 'What happened in mandir, saar?'

'Another murder.'

'Y'Allah! Who?'

'We don't know yet.'

'Y'Allah!' he repeats. 'Shaitan is working in Mumbai. We all be careful. I tell my daughters. I know . . .'

The car jerks to a stop on 60 Feet Road, in front of the meeting point Sunil's given us: *A-One Jeans Tailor: Specialist in Jeans, Cotton Trouser & Jackets.*

'Gullies very narrow for car, saar. You hire rickshaw or walk. I take you?' Imran offers.

'No, it's fine. Wait here for us.'

I spot Sunil talking to a teenage girl in a crisp red and white school uniform, her long plaits swinging as she listens. She carries a backpack almost as big as she is.

'Sorry we're late,' I say as we approach. 'This is my colleague, Anjoli.'

'This is my sister, Sunita,' Sunil says. The girl gives us a shy smile.

'What year are you in, Sunita?' Anjoli asks.

'Tenth standard. I finish school in two years,' she mumbles, glancing down.

'And what do you plan to do after that?'

'Lawyer.'

'Wow!' Anjoli turns to Sunil. 'You must be very proud.'

He beams, gently tugging one of her plaits. Sunita pulls away, playfully slapping his arm. 'She's the smartest in our family. Topper in her school. Go to class now, Suni. I'll see you later.' He waves her off, and she scurries away with a quick wave.

'This is where you took Peter Bell?' I say, getting down to business.

'Yes.'

'Why?'

'He was interested.'

'Interested in what? Did it have anything to do with the Coastal Road project?'

Sunil shifts uncomfortably. 'N-No. He wanted to see it.'

'So why come back a second time? You never mentioned that before?'

He waits a couple of seconds too long before answering with a non-answer. 'Just.'

'Why?'

A shrug.

'Did he meet anyone here?' Anjoli asks.

A pause. 'He asked to see Patil of the Jamaat Trust.'

'Who's that?'

'Jamaat Trust govern the area.'

'Why did Bell want to meet him?' I say.

Another shrug.

'Did he meet him on the first or second visit?'

'Second.'

'Can *we* see Patil?'

Sunil's face is unreadable. He gives a slight head-waggle and starts walking. We follow him across a narrow bridge over train tracks. Below us, a chaotic scene unfolds – ramshackle buildings made from cement blocks and corrugated steel. Dirt roads teem with people dodging goats, chickens and cats.

'This area is so peculiar,' Anjoli says. 'You've got massive residential skyscrapers right next to tin shacks. It's mad. Like a refugee camp in the middle of Docklands.'

'Dharavi is one of the largest slums in the world,' Sunil says. 'Over a million of us live in less than a square mile. It is a city within a city.'

'I suppose it is kind of poetic, seeing the top and bottom one per cent living so close together,' she says. 'How come they haven't developed this area? It must be worth a fortune. Surely these dwellings aren't all legal?'

Sunil remains silent, staring ahead.

'Sunil?' she presses.

'Many developers would like to,' he finally says. 'We pay ten thousand rupees – a hundred pounds – a month to rent a room. The people in those towers pay fifty times that amount for a small flat. There's a lot of money to be made.'

'How's it surviving, then? How do you fend off the developers?'

'Dharavi falls under the Coastal Regulation Zone.'

'What's that?'

'No development is allowed if an area is within a certain distance of the sea's high tide line. For environmental reasons. Dharavi is just inside that zone and that has protected us for decades. The Supreme Court has stopped people from touching us as long as we are inside the zone. It has kept us safe. Let us keep our homes and businesses.'

'Lucky.'

'Yes. Very lucky.'

We continue walking, the heat and fumes solidifying the air.

Anjoli suppresses a cough, while Sunil seems unfazed, casting us blank looks whenever he checks if we're still following. We pass through narrow, dimly lit alleys lined with open-fronted workshops and multi-storey mini-factories. Tangled wires dangle precariously overhead. Anjoli navigates carefully, avoiding the gifts left by stray cats. We cross over a river, and my stomach churns. It's a putrid grey sludge, choked with garbage and sewage, inching its way to the sea. To my horror, I see people washing clothes in this cesspool. I turn away, struggling to comprehend.

'Was Peter Bell's visit connected to this? Did this river affect the project environmentally?' Anjoli asks, her voice tinged with disgust.

Sunil shakes his head. 'No. This is far from the coastal road construction site.'

We move into a residential area. Steep metal ladders connect rooms stacked precariously on top of each other. The alleys grow darker, narrower and more uneven. We walk single file, squeezing past doorways where slippers sit outside tiny homes. I peek into one, seeing three kids sprawled on the floor, watching TV. A woman breast-feeds her baby. A man glares at me and spits a jet of bright red betel juice, narrowly missing me. I jump back, startled.

Sunil grows visibly uncomfortable. I feel a pang of guilt for dragging him here, for turning his home into a spectacle. We're intruding, like tourists in a zoo. I focus on the people around us. A mother brushes her daughter's hair, a toddler gets a bath from a cooking pot, a child stares at Anjoli and she smiles warmly back. 'We should have brought something for the kids,' she murmurs.

Men shave each other. Children laugh, clutching colourful kites. A man precariously balances on a stool, patching his roof. Another brushes his teeth. A girl waves at us. Green Muslim flags flutter in the breeze. Everywhere, people smile, chat, work.

I stop, tapping Anjoli's shoulder. 'Look at the people, not the surroundings. They're not living in wretchedness. They have energy, purpose, community. More than we have in London, I'd bet.'

Sunil's face brightens. 'Yes! *This* is our life. Working, studying, eating, sleeping, just like anyone else. This is our community. We look after each other. In those high rises, no one sees anyone. No one knows their neighbour. Here, everyone knows everyone. It's not heaven, of course, but it's not the hell everyone thinks it is. Inside, our houses are clean. Only the gullies are dirty. That will change with time. Younger people want better lives. They have motivation. Look beyond the obvious and you'll see the reality we inhabit. Most people don't. This is what Mr Peter understood. And why . . .' His voice trails off.

'Why what?' I press gently.

'Why . . . he cared.'

We reach some railway tracks and enter a more modern part of the slum. The buildings here look sturdier, the people better dressed. The stench of rubbish is replaced by the overwhelming smell of fish. We find ourselves in an open area filled with rows of seafood drying on bamboo stands. Nets hang like curtains, and seagulls circle overhead. Women sit around, cleaning and gutting fish, tossing heads into pink piles that glisten in the sun.

'This is where I am from. Dharavi Koliwada.'

'Koliwada?' Anjoli echoes.

'Where we Kolis live. Our fishing community. Even Mazagaon, where Mr Darius lives, was Koli once.'

'Does your family still fish?' she asks.

'Yes.'

'Why didn't you go into fishing?'

'It's not a good life anymore. I wanted something different. And so does Sunita.'

'Why do you still live here now that you've got an excellent job?'

A small shrug. 'My people are here. My mother, father, Sunita. Where else would I go?'

'Sorry, I didn't mean to be rude. I was just wondering, why not take them out of here to live with you?'

'Madam, this is our home. My roots are here. We would be outsiders everywhere else.'

A sharp pang hits me. In a way, Sunil's lucky. I've never felt that kind of connection to any place I've lived. Always an outsider, always will be. Anjoli might say I'm romanticising their poverty, but there's something undeniably compelling about Dharavi, despite its contradictions.

'We'll go now?' Sunil says. 'I have to return to the office.'

'Just one more thing. Can you tell me about this Jamaat Trust that Bell met with?' I say.

'They own and manage this Koliwada. Our fish markets, marriage halls, temples. We even have a gym.' There's pride in his voice. 'We rent our homes from them. We do everything collectively. Patil runs the trust.'

'How do I meet him?'

'You will need an appointment.'

'Let's try to see him now, since we're here.'

'He will not be there.'

'Let's try, anyway.'

Sunil reluctantly leads us to a squat, boxy building. Inside, he speaks with a receptionist in a language I don't understand, then turns to us. 'He is not in.'

'When will he be back?'

Before Sunil can answer, an older man in trousers and an untucked pink shirt emerges from an office. He gives Sunil a look, and Sunil subtly shakes his head. As the man re-enters his room, I call out, 'Excuse me, Mr Patil?'

He stops. 'Yes . . . ?'

I step forward, extending my hand. 'Kamil Rahman. I'm a detective from Scotland Yard. I'm investigating the death of Peter Bell. I believe you met him?'

Patil says something sharply to Sunil. Sunil gives a quiet response. Patil turns to me and says abruptly, 'I'm sorry, I have a meeting now. Please make an appointment.' Before I can reply, he shuts the door in my face.

'What did you say to him?' I ask Sunil.

'Nothing. Just introduced you. I told you, he's very busy.' Sunil pulls out his phone. 'I'll call the driver to pick you up.' He walks off, leaving us to follow.

'What the fuck is going on?' I mutter to Anjoli.

'Relax, Kamil. He obviously doesn't want to talk. Make an appointment. Maybe he'll see you tomorrow.'

'Yeah. Sorry. This place. It's overwhelming. Are you okay?'

'I keep thinking about the Willingdon Club.'

'Wishing you were there right now? Today's been too much?'

'No, you idiot. I mean yes, of course, it's overwhelming. Especially after that horrific body. But I meant the contrast between this and the club. It's a lot to process. Darius was right. It is awful. But you were right, too. The people seem happy. There's some kind of positivity here. God, what point am I making? I don't even know.' She rubs her eyes. 'Anyway, I suppose I'm glad I came.'

'I get it. I wouldn't want to live here, but . . .'

'But what?' she says.

'There's something about Sunil – his pride, his sense of belonging. He knows who he is, who his people are. Do you know what I mean?'

'He's secure in his identity.'

'Yes. And in his purpose. I'm not sure I am . . .'

The car pulls up. Sunil says, 'I will go now. I have work in the office.'

'We're heading there too. We can take you.' I motion him to get into the BMW. 'By the way, I haven't received Bell's diary yet. You said you'd email it to me?'

'I will do it today.' He walks away, saying over his shoulder, 'I have some other work. I'll see you later.'

I run after him and grab his arm. 'Sunil, what's going on? You clearly know something. What did you tell Patil? Why did Bell meet him? You can tell me. I'll keep it confidential. I'm not working for the cops. Or for Darius. I just want to get to the truth. Another man was just found dead, killed similarly to Bell and the man in Bandra. The police are sure it's a serial killer. It's possible Bell's death has nothing to do with Mehta & Sons.'

He looks stunned. Then relieved. 'Is this true?'

'Yes, I swear. Now tell me what you know.'

He hesitates, blinking nervously. I wait, giving him time. Finally, he whispers, 'I thought I knew who killed Mr Peter. But if it is a serial killer, then I was wrong.'

'Who did you think did it?'

'That doesn't matter now. I was wrong.'

'Tell me!'

He stares at me. The relief drains from his eyes to be replaced by something I recognise only too well. Before I can react, he says urgently, 'There is . . . a document. I believed Mr Peter died because I showed it to him. But after what you said, maybe I made a mistake. Mr Darius knows about it. Ask him.'

'What document? Do you have it?'

A tiny nod.

'Show it to me!' My voice is too demanding, and I regret it immediately.

He hesitates. 'I need to think, sir. If Mr Peter's killing really is unconnected, then I will show it to you tomorrow. Maybe you will be able to help like Mr Peter wanted to.' He takes my hand

and presses it between his palms. 'Thank you, sir. Thank you.' He scurries away. I watch him disappear into the crowd.

Back in the car, I ask Imran to take us to Darius's office. Tell Anjoli what Sunil's just revealed.

'He *actually* said he thought he knew who Bell's killer is?'

'Yes.'

She processes this for a moment. 'Shit. What do you think's in this document?'

'No idea. Sunil says he has it and Daru knows about it. He said he'll give it to me tomorrow. It could be what those emails between Bell and Daru were about. One mentioned "consequences" if Bell didn't return it. Maybe it's what Niloufer was looking for in Bell's room. Something that could affect her chance at becoming CEO? Proof of bribery? Photos of her and Bell?'

'Lots of maybes. But it seems unlikely that Niloufer or Daru are running around killing people in such elaborate ways for this document.'

'I'm starting to think there are two separate issues here. The three murders might be the work of a deranged serial killer, possibly the swami. And Daru and Niloufer are after this document for a different reason. I need to get them to open up.'

'Well, once you get the document from Sunil, everything will make sense.' She laughs. 'Watch out, though. If this were a TV movie, Sunil would get bumped off before then.'

'God forbid.'

I look out the window. Relive that shift in Sunil's eyes.

Relief turning to fear.

Anjoli

Darius's face was a mask of stone as he stared at Kamil and Anjoli. The atmosphere in the room was as dense as the prelude to a Mumbai monsoon.

'Say again.'

'Niloufer Cama was having an affair with Bell, and Ronnie Engineer took a bribe from the swami,' Kamil repeated.

Anjoli, still feeling the residual grime of Dharavi on her skin and in her eyes and throat, gulped down a glass of water. She watched as Darius blinked rapidly, trying to absorb the news.

'And you think one of them killed Bell?' He shook his head, almost as if attempting to rattle the thought loose. 'Not possible. Karve identified the new body. A Muslim shopkeeper from the area. No connection with Mehta & Sons. These are obviously ritualistic killings by the swami.'

Kamil leaned in. 'I'm not saying they murdered Bell, but they had reasons to want him dead. There's something going on and you know what it is, Daru.'

Anjoli saw the flicker of something – pain? guilt? – cross Darius's face. She said, 'What would you have done if you found out?'

His reply was immediate, but there was a catch in his voice. 'I'd have sacked Ronnie on the spot.'

'And Niloufer?'

Darius hesitated, his gaze dropping to the floor. 'Probably her too. Our guidelines are very strict. But you don't kill three people because you might lose your job.' He turned abruptly, opening his office door and shouting into the hallway, 'Get Niloufer and Ronnie in here. Immediately!'

Kamil raised an eyebrow. 'Really? Together?'

He reconsidered, then adjusted his instruction. 'Ronnie first. What do you mean, I know what's going on?'

Kamil said, 'Sunil told me Bell saw an important document. What was he referring to?'

Darius's response was too quick, too rehearsed. 'I don't know.'

'He said you knew about it,' said Anjoli.

His jaw tightened. 'Did he?'

Kamil's patience snapped. He thrust his face inches from Darius's, and yelled, 'Daru, I'm not stupid! It's been obvious since I arrived that you're hiding something. If you genuinely want me to untangle this mess, then talk to me. I didn't come all the way from London to waste my time. I have my own fucking problems.'

Anjoli's pulse sped up at Kamil's sudden explosion. Darius recoiled, his confidence crumbling under the onslaught, his facade of control shattered. 'Okay. Okay.' His voice was almost a whisper as he bowed his head in submission. 'Peter showed me a document. I needed to see if it was connected to his death. That's why I asked you to investigate.'

'You could have told me that earlier.' Kamil's voice was low and controlled, the anger receding, but the tension still high. 'What's in it?'

'It's sensitive company business. Now that it's unlikely to be linked to Peter's murder, the fewer people who know about it the better. It could lead to serious legal issues.'

'I'm not about to broadcast it,' Kamil growled.

'I'm sorry, Kamil. I can't divulge it. I've been trying to find out where Peter got it from. You say Sunil showed it to him?'

'Yes,' Kamil replied curtly.

Darius muttered under his breath. 'Oh! He must have acquired it from— I was hoping–the little . . . he swore he didn't have it.'

Kamil interjected, 'Sunil also said he thought he knew who killed Bell.'

Darius went silent, his expression shifting from defensive to troubled. 'But . . . how could he? We know it's not linked to us.'

Anjoli glanced at Kamil. 'He knows the swami and did admit he might be wrong. Could Niloufer have been looking for this document? We saw her on the CCTV going to Bell's hotel room the night he died.'

Darius's eyes widened. 'What?'

'Do Niloufer or Ronnie know about Bell's document?' she repeated.

'I asked them about it today. They claim not to. I need to understand who created it. There's someone else I want to speak to. I'll talk to Sunil.'

'Created it?' Anjoli echoed, the phrasing striking her as odd. 'What do you mean?'

'It's complicated.' Darius rubbed his temples. 'What did Arjun Sharma say to you?'

'Is *he* the person you need to speak to?' Kamil asked, not letting him off the hook.

Darius was sweating now, blinking rapidly. Anjoli felt a pang of sympathy. He was clearly under immense stress, with his birthday and the dark family history that came with it looming. They shouldn't be browbeating him in this way.

'He could be involved. I'm meeting him this evening. I'll know more after that.'

Anjoli put a hand on Darius's arm. 'Maybe we should come with you? I know him quite well.'

'Better I see him alone. He's more likely to open up.'

'Is he linked to this Felix?' she pressed.

'There is no Felix,' Darius said quickly, and moved away. She exchanged a glance with Kamil. Something wasn't adding up. What was Darius hiding? 'This is a hugely stressful period for me,' he continued. 'My birthday, Bell's death, these revelations about Ronnie and Niloufer. It's like I'm disconnected from everything happening around me. It's not the first time either.'

Kamil's expression softened, but only slightly. 'Meaning?'

Darius shut down. 'I'm not thinking straight. Let me get through this weekend. I'll be clearer in my head on Monday. We can revisit things then.'

'Why wait till then?' said Anjoli.

'I have to be certain.'

'Of what?'

'Just certain. This has implications far beyond me. Serious consequences for Mehta & Sons. Monday. Please leave it. Okay?'

Kamil stared at him long and hard. 'Of course it's not okay, Daru. But if that's the way you want to play it, there's not much I can do. I have no jurisdiction here. No authority.'

Before Darius could respond, there was a hesitant knock on the door. 'Come,' he called, composing himself with visible effort.

Ronnie's entrance was tentative, his steps faltering as he saw the three of them. He took a deep breath and walked in, head bowed like a chastised child.

Darius motioned him to sit. Ronnie perched on the edge of the sofa, looking anywhere but at his boss. Anjoli settled on the adjoining seat, and after a moment, Kamil joined her. Darius remained standing, towering over Ronnie. 'Talk,' he growled, more an accusation than a request.

Ronnie gave his automatic smile, but his voice wavered. 'What, Darius?'

'What's happening between you and Swami Yogesh?'

'I'm trying to persuade him to let us relocate his temple. You know this.' His eyes were darting nervously. Darius's silence was cold, unyielding. Ronnie couldn't meet his gaze. 'I know I first recommended the tunnel go around the temple, but that was for environmental reasons. I wanted to avoid lawsuits. The swami has powerful friends. We didn't want protests, remember?'

Darius remained a statue.

Ronnie's voice grew desperate. 'But you and Peter were right. I've created the new plan.' He held out a folder with a shaking hand. Darius ignored it, and he let it fall onto the table. Anjoli could hear the heavy transit of breath through Darius's nostrils. Saw sweat beading Ronnie's brow.

'How much did he give you?' Darius's tone was almost curious, as if he couldn't quite believe what he was hearing.

'Sir, he . . . he . . .' Ronnie looked up at Darius's piercing gaze, then crumpled. To Anjoli's consternation, he fell to his knees, clutching Darius's legs. 'Twenty-five lakhs,' he cried. 'I'm so sorry, sir. It was a mistake. My daughter is sick. I needed the money. Please forgive me.'

Darius stepped back, disentangling himself from Ronnie's grasp. Ronnie stood awkwardly, his head hanging in shame, like a dog that had been admonished for peeing in the living room. Anjoli watched, feeling like she was witnessing some bizarre play.

'Ronnie,' she said softly, trying to break through his misery. 'You know the swami. Could he have killed these three people? He had the weapons.'

Confusion clouded Ronnie's face. 'Three people? I thought there were only two. Who else died?'

'A shopkeeper in Mazagaon was murdered by a trident this morning,' she said.

Ronnie looked at her in horror. 'It's possible. Swami Yogesh is violent. My god, maybe it's my fault! I took Peter to see him. Are the police questioning him?'

Darius's countenance was unreadable as he watched Ronnie's torment. 'Mehta & Sons has built its reputation on integrity. You've destroyed that in an instant. You're finished. Get out.'

Ronnie stumbled away, wiping his face with his sleeve. Darius sat heavily in his chair, defeated. 'This will kill Faraz. He's worked so hard to keep us from becoming like all the other corrupt companies in this country.'

'You had no idea this was happening?' said Anjoli.

'It seemed odd, the way Ronnie pushed for the tunnel to avoid the temple. When Peter said we could demolish it, I thought Ronnie had just made a mistake.'

'Bell never mentioned Ronnie taking money?' Kamil's tone was sceptical.

Darius raked his fingers through his hair. 'No, he didn't. Send Niloufer in,' he instructed through the intercom. 'I need this like a hole in the head.'

Kamil's voice softened. 'Sorry for shouting earlier, Daru. I was frustrated. It's like a . . . a mad itch and I had to let it out. The trip's been way more than I bargained for.'

Darius sighed heavily. 'I should have listened to Zara and never involved you.'

'How's she doing?' Anjoli asked.

'On edge. I tell her not to worry, but she keeps remembering my dad burning up on that stage.'

'In two days, this will all be over,' Kamil said, trying to reassure him.

Niloufer entered without knocking. Anjoli assessed her as she sat, crossing her ankles, her posture perfect. She was much taller than she had seemed on CCTV.

'Niloufer, I'm sorry to raise this, but I've heard a disturbing rumour,' Darius began, his voice faltering slightly.

'Which is?' Niloufer's gaze was steady, unflinching.

He shifted uncomfortably. 'It's about you and Peter.'

She looked at him expressionlessly.

He sighed. 'Kamil?'

'Were you sleeping with Peter Bell?' Kamil asked bluntly.

'Who told you that?' Niloufer's voice was calm, almost detached.

'That doesn't matter. Is it true?'

She paused, considering her response. Then pointed at Anjoli. 'Who is she?'

'My partner,' said Kamil. 'Please don't deflect.'

With a dismissive wave, Niloufer said, 'We had a fling.'

Darius muttered, 'Oh, for fuck's sake!' and slammed his fist on the desk. He poured himself a whisky, downing it in one gulp.

'When did it start?' said Kamil.

'A week after he arrived. We were spending a lot of time together, and it just . . . happened.'

'You're married, Niloufer,' Darius's voice was tinged with disbelief. 'You have a child.'

'You don't need to remind me,' she retorted. 'It wasn't planned.'

He sat, nursing his drink.

'How did it happen?' Kamil continued.

'These things do, sometimes. There was chemistry. We got together a few times, that's all.'

'Where?'

'In his hotel. Then I ended it.'

'You said you'd never been to his room?'

She gave him a look that said, *duh*.

'When did you end it?'

'A couple of days before he died.' She paused. 'I couldn't believe it when I heard what happened to him.'

'How did he take the break-up?'

'He was disappointed. He wanted to continue. But I would never leave my family for him. It was just a fling. I knew he'd go back to London.'

'What did he say he'd do?' Kamil asked.

'Do?' She looked puzzled. 'Like what?'

'Tell Daru? Your husband? There's a strict non-fraternisation policy here, isn't there?'

She fiddled with her watch strap, then looked up, her decision made. 'He asked me to come see him on Thursday evening. Said it was urgent.'

'Why?'

'I assumed to discuss us. He was very agitated when he called.'

'When did he call?'

'Around six. I said I'd meet him as soon as I finished my meetings.'

'Where?'

'His hotel.'

'And?'

'I arrived at seven-thirty. He'd given me a key to his room. But he wasn't there. I tried calling him, but there was no answer. I waited half an hour, then went home.'

'And your husband and daughter will vouch for you coming back after that?'

'Yes, of course. My driver too.'

The timeline matched what they'd seen on camera. Anjoli scrutinised Niloufer's face, searching for signs of deceit. Had she searched Bell's room while she waited?

'Did Bell mention anything about a document he was worried about?' Kamil asked.

Niloufer hesitated, glancing at Darius. He nodded. 'No. Peter didn't mention any document. The first I heard of it was from

Daru this morning. Look, I'm sorry about this. It was foolish, but it's over. And as for non-fraternisation . . .' She locked eyes with Darius.

He flushed and didn't respond. Anjoli watched them, realisation dawning. As she processed this, Niloufer spoke again. 'I heard there was another death?'

Darius nodded 'Yes. A Mazagaon shopkeeper.'

'Not connected to us or Bell?'

'No, thank god. It seems to be the work of a madman. Maybe Swami Yogesh.'

Niloufer's surprise was evident. 'Ronnie's man? Why him? I thought he was dangerous, but why kill Peter? And the others?'

'We don't know. All right, you can go now,' Darius said wearily.

As Niloufer left, Kamil swivelled to face to Darius. 'What the fuck, man? You had a thing with her too? When?'

Darius looked ashamed. 'Earlier this year. Zara and I were having problems. I was freaked out about the curse. It was brief.'

'How long?' Anjoli asked.

'Three months.'

'Nice job, idiot,' said Kamil. 'And you plan to make her CEO? Does Niloufer know about the curse?'

'No. Why would I tell her?'

'Does Zara know about your affair?' asked Anjoli.

Darius hesitated. 'Yes. She found out. That's the reason I broke it off.' He let out a groan. 'What a fucking disaster.'

Kamil rose. 'It's been a long day. I'm exhausted. We'll pick this up tomorrow.'

Once they were out of the office, Anjoli said, 'Shouldn't we check the CCTV again? If it wasn't Niloufer searching Bell's room, the killer might be on there.'

He stopped. 'Shit. You're right. I'll call Karve.'

But there was no response from Karve that evening.

Kamil

Saturday, 3 December.
The day before.

The sky above burns with a russet glow. A low rumble of thunder weaves through the quaking trees that surround the blood-soaked battlefield. Dust from the skirmish chokes the air, and my wheezy lungs struggle for breath. Bodies lie scattered, their wounds still seeping around the projectiles that felled them. I watch in horror as they begin to move. Imperceptibly at first, then with growing determination. They rise, clutching the arrows embedded in their flesh, walking like dread zombies towards me, whispering in an unintelligible hiss. Looming over them is a giant figure, his hair writhing with snakes, a necklace of skulls rattling ominously . . .

'Kamil!'

I jerk awake, the vivid nightmare dissolving into the dim reality of my room. I sit up, disoriented, the remnants of the dream clinging to my senses. 4.48 a.m.

'Kamil, wake up!' The voice cuts through the fog of sleep as someone bursts in and flicks on the light.

'What the fuck?' I shield my eyes against the sudden brightness. Through the haze, I see Darius.

'Get dressed. There's been another murder.'

'What? Who?'

'I don't know. Karve just called.'

'Why did he call you?'

'The body's in exactly the same place as Peter's. Apparently, there's something odd about it.'

'What?'

'Dunno. Let's go.'

Anjoli appears in the doorway, rubbing her eyes. 'I'm coming too.'

The scent of burning wood mingles with the damp night air as we step outside Behesht. Imran pulls up, looking as worn out as I feel. He's had to put his uniform on, ready for duty at a moment's notice.

Wipers sweep the thin mist from the windshield as we navigate through the shadowy streets. Sleeping bodies stir in doorways, disturbed by our passing. Street lamps cast a jaundiced glow over the lane. We speed through the silence, each of us locked in our thoughts. I fear it's Ronnie who's dead, but keep this worry to myself.

A small knot of people have gathered near the construction site in Marine Drive. A cop shoos them away from the seawall as Karve spots us approaching. He signals the constable to let us through.

'Who is it, Karve?' Darius demands.

'Not yet identified, because . . .'

'Because what?'

'Look yourself.'

We scramble onto the embankment and peer over the edge. Camera flashes punctuate the darkness. Far in the distance, like fallen stars, the lights of anchored ships shimmer on the water.

'Torch!' Karve shouts.

Three cops switch on their torches, illuminating the photographer's subject. The beams converge on a pair of legs sprawled

on the rocks below. They move up the torso in perfect synchro-
nisation to the shoulders.

Then . . . nothing.

Just bare rock, slick with trickles of darkness.

'Oh my god.' Anjoli turns away.

'Beheaded,' Karve says grimly. 'Like Eapen. Arms chopped off
too. Another tantric murder, it looks like. Since he was again
found at your site, I phoned you.'

'Not our site. Arpin's,' Darius mutters.

'Who discovered the body?' I ask.

'A couple sitting on the seawall. Engaged in . . . amorous
pursuits.'

A shout from below. 'Doka milala!'

The light skitters to something near the waterline. Sunil's
face stares up at me, hair matted, eyes wide open, reflecting the
light like an obscene selfie.

No. No. No.

I lose my balance and stagger back into Darius, who nearly
falls himself.

'What is it?' he asks, alarmed.

'Sunil,' I choke out. 'It's Sunil.'

'What? No!' He peers over the side and collapses onto the concrete embankment. I grab Anjoli's arm, pulling her away before
she sees the full horror. 'We have to move. Forensics will need to
examine the area for signs of where he was thrown from.'

The three of us walk ten metres down Marine Drive and sit
on the wall in a row, silence weighing us down.

Anjoli's voice is shaky. 'I can't believe I made that stupid joke
about him being bumped off.'

'Daru,' I say, my stomach tight with frustration. 'Enough is
enough. Bell. Now Sunil. This is *not* a random serial killer. Sunil
was killed because he could identify the murderer. You were the
only one I told. Who did you tell?'

Darius looks stunned, unable to meet my gaze. He whispers, 'Arjun Sharma. I told Arjun Sharma.'

'*Why?*'

'We were talking about the document. I said Sunil had it and . . . I'm such a fool.' He buries his head in his hands, muttering, 'You don't think—'

I grab his shoulder, shaking him. 'Wake up, man! Why are you protecting him? I thought you hated him.'

'I'm *not* protecting him! There are repercussions I need to understand.' He looks up, devastated. 'What about the lottery seller in Bandra? The shopkeeper yesterday? They're not connected to any of this. It has to be a coincidence. Or that swami has gone mad.'

'Daru.' I stand and face him, my anger boiling over. 'I'm going to tell Karve—'

His face contorts as he mutters to himself. 'It's inconceivable. Impossible to comprehend . . . how is it even possible? How could—'

'Comprehend what, for fuck's sake? How is what possible?'

He shakes his head, eyes wild. 'I . . . I can't. This changes everything. I thought it was just about profit . . . but this? It's much, much worse. This is madness.' He stands and grabs my arm, his grip tight. 'Please. Leave it. This has serious consequences. For me. My company. My family.'

I snatch my hand back. 'No! That's bullshit. Two people have died because of you. Maybe more. You might be next. You asked me to keep you safe.' My voice rises. 'How can I if I don't have the facts? What's in this document that someone would kill for?'

Anjoli, who's been watching the drama unfold, warns softly, 'Kamil.'

Darius's gaze flicks from her to me. Then he steps back, raises his hands in surrender, and sits back down on the wall. I take my place between him and Anjoli as he mumbles, 'All right.

I'll tell you what I can. Years ago, I initiated a scheme. Then I shelved it because it wouldn't work. Someone has resurrected it without my knowledge. It's now in motion. And it's extremely dangerous. I have to stop it before it destroys everything I've built. Before it destroys the lives of millions. Arjun admitted last night he was part of it. I have to find out who in my company is working with him. He wouldn't tell me. There are people I must speak to. I can't say more until I'm sure. Then I'll do what needs to be done.'

Anjoli says, 'What exactly did Arjun say?'

'Peter showed him the document. After showing it to me. Arjun told Peter it was my plan and he should speak to me about it.'

'But it wasn't your plan?'

'It is, and it isn't. It's like an evil twin of my original plan. That's what's so diabolical about it.'

'Who'd want to conceal this scheme?' I ask.

'Lots of people. It affects all of us. Even me. Especially me. The consequences of it going ahead would be devastating. Arjun's own company could be destroyed.'

'And Bell was planning to make the scheme public?'

'He threatened to if we didn't stop it. He was planning to meet Arjun again on Friday with his decision.'

'So these devastating consequences – were they devastating enough to kill to avoid them?'

'No!' His voice is hoarse. 'I refuse to believe someone would murder because of . . . no. I will not believe it. And in such a brutal manner? Why? I'm sure Karve is right. It has to be some mad tantric serial killer. The swami!'

'Who's this Felix that Bell said you had to kill?' says Anjoli.

I'd forgotten about that.

'It's not Felix . . . it's . . .'

'What?'

208

Darius takes a deep breath, stands up, and says decisively, 'Leave it. I can't tell you any more. I'm dealing with it.'

I stare at him in frustration as Anjoli asks gently, 'And you're absolutely sure Niloufer and Ronnie don't know what's in the document?'

Darius looks at her. 'She . . . says she doesn't. But it's possible she . . . Arjun and she work together . . . And Ronnie. He's so ambitious. Prepared to take shortcuts. It could be him. And there are others. I don't know who to trust anymore.'

'Maybe that's why Bell wanted to see her on Thursday night,' Anjoli says. 'To spill the beans.'

'That makes sense,' I say. 'If they were close, he might have wanted to tell her. But got killed before he could. Unless he told her earlier and she had him murdered.'

'Or the swami's in cahoots with Ronnie.'

Darius groans. Presses his fingers against his temples. His face sags, looking like melting candle wax. 'I should never have got you involved. Stupid. Stupid. And now Sunil . . .'

He walks away.

What will Karve do if I go to him now, talking about a document I haven't seen and barely know anything about? He'll pat me on the head and tell me to fuck right off. I feel like I'm burning up inside as I look at Anjoli, who's staring at the dark sea.

I breathe in and out, forcing myself to exhale my ire. I sit and put an arm around her to offer some comfort. She leans into my shoulder. 'That poor, poor boy. He was so proud of himself and his sister. He worked so hard to achieve what he did. We were just with him yesterday. How could his life end like this? How will his family take it? Who's going to look after them all? This is all utterly and horrendously shit.' I squeeze her to me. 'Do you think he might still be alive if we hadn't started digging around?'

The question slices through me like a scalpel. How many times have I pursued the truth, leaving casualties in my wake?

I just hold her, like I did after her parents died. The night thins as dawn creeps in, turning the ocean's surface silver and painting pink feathers on the horizon. Traffic noises grow louder, and Marine Drive becomes busy with cars and people, unaware that a young man's future was just snuffed out.

I release Anjoli gently. No good will come from us getting sucked into a vortex of self-blame. 'We're spiralling down a dark hole here. This is a brutal killer. If he needed to kill Sunil, he would have done so, regardless of anything we've been doing.'

Darius returns, having regained his composure. 'We should go.'

'Maybe you should ask the inspector to open up the Arpin site?' I suggest. 'They most likely beheaded Sunil elsewhere and then threw the body and head over the wall.' The image of Sunil's skull bouncing down the rocks almost makes me retch.

We walk over to the cluster of cops. Darius speaks to Karve, who beckons to another policeman. They stride past us towards the yellow hoardings that cover the construction area.

'You have key?' Karve asks Darius.

'No. We have nothing to do with this part of the building works. It's Arpin's.'

'We cannot wait.' Karve speaks to someone who speaks to someone, and within minutes, a man arrives with bolt-cutters, snipping through the chain.

'Careful of—' None of them are wearing the proper gear, but before I can say 'forensics' Karve pushes open the gate, and they march in. We follow, the idle cranes looming over us like silent watchmen. Beneath them is a tin shack.

Karve's man opens the door and shines his torch inside. The beam sweeps across sacks of cement, scattered pieces of machinery and spare parts. In my sleep-deprived state, shadowy figures lurk in every corner. Karve directs his torch downwards, and the light reflects off dark liquid pooling on the floor. He steps inside carefully.

Flicks a light switch.

The iron smell of blood hits my nostrils. In the centre of the room lies a large, curved sword, its bloody blade and the jewels on its ornate handle gleaming in the light. Next to it, crossing each other in an X, are Sunil's arms.

Anjoli retches. Runs off. Karve's face hardens as he takes in the scene.

Darius's tone is icy. 'Karve, if this is where Peter Bell was killed as well, you should have found it a week ago. There's no excuse for this level of incompetence.'

Karve immediately becomes defensive. 'We looked. I even spoke to Arjun Sharma. There was nothing. Leave it for FFPS. You should not be here.'

'I'll speak to the commissioner about this,' muttered Darius.

'Inspector,' I say when we're back on the main road. 'That sword. There was one exactly like it in Swami Yogesh's temple in Priyadarshini Park. I recognise the handle. In fact, he threatened me with it. I told you I saw the trident from yesterday's killing there, too.'

He looks at me speculatively. 'You cannot be sure. All these types of swords look same.'

'I'm certain. You need to bring the swami in. Figure out why on earth he would kill Sunil. Take fingerprints. Inventory his weapons.'

'Sunil? Who is Sunil? You know whose body it is?' Karve snaps. 'Why you not say?'

'Sorry,' says Darius. 'The shock ... His name is Sunil Tandel. He works for me. He was Peter Bell's assistant. You interviewed him.'

'The killer would have been covered with blood,' I say. 'This is one of the busiest roads in Mumbai. Someone must have seen something. Is there CCTV around here?'

Karve ignores me and addresses his answer to Darius. 'No CCTV. This is for certain another ritual. Like the other three deaths. The Bandra lottery seller has a zero carved on his forehead. Your Bell has eighteen arrows. The Muslim shopkeeper from yesterday has seven wounds. This Tandel's head and arms are cut off with three strokes. Zero, eighteen, seven, three. All sacred Hindu numbers.'

'What is three symbolic of?' Anjoli says. I turn to see she's returned.

'Holy trinity. Brahma, creator. Vishnu, preserver. Shiva, destroyer.' The swami's words echo in my mind. *The anger of Shiva will fall on you like thunder and lightning.*

We watch the forensic squad, in their white overalls and boots, converge on the murder site like a flock of egrets. As we walk towards the car, Anjoli says, 'Do you think Bell was murdered in there, too?'

'Probably. He could have been lured here the same way as Sunil.'

'I have to tell his parents,' Darius says. 'They'll be devastated.'

'Shouldn't we leave that to Karve's men?' I say. 'He'll want to question them.'

Darius looks grim. 'He worked for me. He's my responsibility. Karve won't show any respect to the Koli slum-dwellers.'

Some uncharitable part of me wonders if my friend has some other agenda. 'Do you even know his parents?'

'I'll have my assistant find the details.' He pulls out his phone and fires off a message.

'Will he be up?' asks Anjoli.

'He works for me. He's always up.'

'Okay. We'll accompany you,' I say.

Darius looks despairing. 'There's no way we can keep our name out of the papers now. I have to sort things out before it gets really ugly.' His mobile pings. 'I have the address. Come on.'

We leave as the Marine Drive traffic crescendos in a symphony of horns, the sky as grey and murky as my mood.

Kamil

All I can think about on our way to Dharavi Koliwada is how Sunil's sister's life is about to be shattered. Telling Sunita her brother's been murdered is bad enough – but the dismembered state of his body when it was found? That's too much for a sixteen-year-old to bear.

Anjoli, seated beside me in the back seat, is ashen, her gaze vacant and unfocused. Darius, sitting next to Imran, is staring out of the window, lost in thought. The driver glances at him a couple of times, obviously wondering what's happened, but doesn't dare ask.

The deathly silence feels like an invisible fifth person occupying the gap between Anjoli and me. We pass some kind of structure on a hill surrounded by a forest of green trees, gently aglow in the oblique rays of the early morning sun now breaking through the clouds. To expel the silent interloper and distract Anjoli, I ask, 'What's behind there? That massive wall on the left?'

Darius gives it an indifferent glance. 'Doongerwadi.'

'Oh, your funeral grounds. Wasn't your tunnel going under – what was it called – the Towers of Silence? That's what the priests were protesting about, right?'

'Yeah.'

'What are the Towers of Silence?' asks Anjoli, her voice dull.

Darius sighs heavily. 'It's where we leave our dead.'

'A cemetery?'

'Not quite. We consider dead bodies to be unclean.'

'Unclean how?'

'When we die, Nasu, the corpse demon, rushes into our body and pollutes it. Earth, water and fire are all sacred to Parsis. So we can't bury or burn these unclean bodies.'

Unclean bodies and demons are not the distracting chit-chat I was hoping for. I'm about to interrupt, but Anjoli says, 'So, what do you do instead?'

'We expose them to the elements. Used to put the bodies in the Towers and let the vultures have them.'

Anjoli regains her focus. 'You're kidding? Right here in the middle of the city?'

'In one of the poshest areas, in fact – Malabar Hill. Residents around Doongerwadi used to find body parts on their balconies, dropped by vultures, believe it or not.' I see Sunil's arms on the bloody floor and shudder. The conversation is straying into territory I'd rather avoid.

'Used to?' asks Anjoli, oblivious to my discomfort.

'There are no vultures left. They all died out because of disease.'

'So what happens now?'

'It's complicated. Solar reflectors dry out the corpse. Once it's desiccated, it's thrown into a pit, where it dissolves naturally. Ultimately, the body parts make their way to the sea through a series of shafts.'

Anjoli's jaw clenches. The car falls silent. To distract from the distraction, I say, 'Parsis are originally from Iran, right?'

Darius turns to look at me, wearily, not wanting to start a history lesson. 'This isn't the time—'

I make a tiny movement of my head in Anjoli's direction. He cottons on.

'Yes. We were persecuted there because we worshipped Zoro-aster and weren't Muslims. So we fled to India around thirteen hundred years ago.' A smile comes into his voice. Maybe this is helping him, too. 'The bones of all my ancestors are there some-where, mingled with the bones of all the other Parsis from Mumbai who died. That's something, I suppose.'

'So your grandfather and father were interred there?'

'Yes. So will Faraz. So will I. Next week, for all I know. Birth-day followed by a funeral. Maybe I should have got a two-for-one deal on catering.' He snorts a short, morbid laugh. It's proving impossible to keep this conversation from head-ing down dark alleys.

'Don't worry,' I say with as much positivity as I can feign. 'We're here. We'll keep you safe.' It's banal and insincere, but it's all I can muster as solace. I don't know how to ensure my friend's safety. Who knows what's out there and who'll be the next victim of his family's ghostly vendetta?

'We've done so much for this country.' Darius's voice is wist-ful. 'Built hospitals, schools, endowed charities. We've always been inclusive. We celebrated Diwali with a massive firework display at Behesht a few weeks ago. Had an Eid party earlier in the year. Planning a Christmas celebration soon. Yet, Parsis will always be considered outsiders.'

We arrive at Koliwada. The air is heavy with the scent of salt and seafood mingling with the morning fog. Darius speaks to a passer-by, and after a lot of arm-waving, we're pointed in the right direction. It's still early, but life's in full swing here. We skirt the edge of the slum, passing emaciated dogs scavenging for scraps and a group of children playing cricket. Eventually we come to a ramshackle ground-floor dwelling, between a shop displaying colourful sweetmeats and a doctor's office with an enormous billboard that proclaims, *Dr Chandrashekhar Tambe, Physician & Surgeon. All Vaccines are given here.* Sunil was right.

The people here are free to pursue anything they want. I hear his earnest voice telling us to *look beyond the obvious and see the reality most people don't.* I blink back a tear.

Darius rings the doorbell. After a few minutes, a thin, middle-aged woman opens it, hastily covering her head with the end of her sari while saying something incomprehensible. Darius speaks slowly in Hindi. 'Is there anyone who can speak Hindi or English?'

The woman holds up a hand – wait – and goes back inside. After a few seconds, Sunil's sister comes out in her school uniform, a glass of milk in her hand, looking apprehensive. She stares at us. 'Hello.'

'Hello, Sunita,' says Anjoli, then turns to Darius. 'This is Sunil's sister. She wants to be a lawyer.'

'I . . .' Darius's voice trails off. 'Kamil, maybe you could . . .'

There's no way in hell I'm going to tell this young girl having her breakfast that her brother's dead and dismembered. *And* then get her to translate the news for her mother. We have to find another way.

Anjoli takes control. 'Sunita. Do you know Mr Patil from the Jamaat Trust?'

'Yes. He is my father's friend.'

'Could you find him and ask him to come here, please? Tell him it's very urgent.'

Sunita looks puzzled, then hands her mum her milk and rushes up the lane. We're ushered into the flat. I see shoes lined up outside and make a gesture to remove my own, but Sunil's mother shakes her head and beckons us to sit down. The interior is cramped but clean. Adorned with photographs of Sunil and Sunita. Some capture his achievements – graduation from college, winning a cup at a sports event, standing side by side with his sister on the beach. Others show Sunita accepting a prize at her school and speaking at a debate. A TV in the corner plays a song and dance programme. A washing machine clatters noisily in the background. Sunil has clearly tried to make his family's life as comfortable as possible, and they obviously take immense pride in his accomplishments. Just as my parents do in mine. Suddenly, there's little distance between our lives.

We wait on the sofa as Sunil's mother brings in a tray of stainless-steel tumblers filled with water. Anjoli and I each accept one hesitantly. She says under her breath, 'Don't drink it.'

We sit in silence. The undrunk water weighs heavy in my hand, like the knowledge of the devastation we'll soon mete out to this poor woman and her family. I can see the mother's concern growing as time passes, the ticking of the clock on the wall sounding like a knell. After ten interminable minutes, Sunita returns with Patil. She goes and stands by her mother as he comes over to us and shakes our hands, giving me a chance to put the tumbler down on the small table next to the sofa.

'Good morning. I am Chetan Patil of the Jamaat Trust.' A flicker of recognition as he looks at me. 'Are you looking for Sunil? He is not here. Hasn't been all night. The family is a little worried.'

Darius, Anjoli and I stand simultaneously. 'Mr Patil, I'm Darius Mehta. Sunil worked . . . works . . . worked for me.' The words struggle out of Darius's mouth, each one weighing a ton. Patil's gaze sharpens, a storm brewing. 'This is my colleague, Kamil Rahman, and his friend Anjoli Chatterjee.'

'I know who you are,' Patil says to Darius, his voice flat but layered with some unspoken accusation.

'I'm afraid I have some bad news.' Darius glances at Sunita, then at her mother. 'I'm deeply sorry to inform you that Sunil is no more.'

The room freezes. Sunita's eyes search his countenance, as if hoping to find a lie, her mouth opening, but no sound coming out. Patil goes pale. He whispers, 'Haré Ram. What happened?'

'It was an unnatural death. I am terribly sorry.' Darius's voice drops to a whisper, almost swallowed by the suffocating silence.

Patil looks at him, bewildered. 'What do you mean, unnatural?'

Darius swallows hard. 'Murdered. He was murdered.'

Sunita grips her mother's chair as if it's the only thing keeping her from crumbling. Patil mutters a prayer, the words barely audible, then goes over to Sunil's mother and whispers to her. She looks up at him, confusion and terror etched in her eyes. Then realisation dawns, and a guttural cry escapes her lips. Sunita drops to her knees, clutching her mother's hand, tears streaming down her face.

'Please tell us what happened,' Patil says, his voice tight with barely contained emotion, his hand resting on Sunil's mother's shoulder, grounding her in the midst of her grief.

Darius hesitates, then speaks, his words carefully stripped of the most gruesome details. 'Sunil was found dead this morning on Marine Drive. The police are investigating. They will come to question the family.'

A heartbreaking wail fills the room. Sunil's mother shakes her head back and forth, refusing to believe the truth. Sunita holds on to her as if by sheer force she could keep her world from shattering.

'I'm so sorry for your terrible loss. And I will personally make sure you and your family are looked after. You will have nothing to worry about. This is my vow.' Darius's promise hangs in the air, a brittle lifeline that will do little to mend their fractured future.

Patil's gaze hardens, a flicker of something darker lurking beneath. He leads Sunita and her mother into another room, their sobs trailing behind like ghostly echoes. We stand awkwardly, the weight of grief and guilt bearing down on us. After an eternity, he returns, his expression set in a mask of grim determination. 'Please excuse me. I will find someone to stay with them, then go to the fishing grounds to inform Sunil's father when he comes back with his morning catch. We will need to organise the funeral for tomorrow.'

The impossibility of his words strikes me, but I can't bring myself to prick the fragile hope that they might bury their loved one so soon. Instead, I mutter, 'Can we go with you? I have a few questions I'd like to ask that could help catch his killer.'

'I have my car,' says Darius. 'We can take you to the fishing grounds.'

Patil strides out the door, his steps heavy with purpose. The muted sobbing from the inner room is a haunting counterpoint to the everyday noises filtering in from the street. It's a cruel contrast, the world continuing its mundane business while theirs is irrevocably changed. He returns with a woman who hesitates before knocking on the bedroom door, then enters.

'Let's go.' Patil's voice is clipped and distant.

We follow Darius to the BMW. At the car, I motion for Anjoli to take the front seat, while I slip into the back, wedged between Darius and Patil. I turn to him. 'When I saw you with Sunil yesterday, he seemed anxious to avoid my speaking with you. Why was that?'

Patil's face is rigid, full of barely restrained fury. 'He found out certain things that were dangerous to know. He confided in me. I was trying to learn more.'

'What things?'

'The *real* reason for the Coastal Road project.'

Darius interrupts, an edge to his voice. 'What's that supposed to mean?'

Patil's gaze shifts to him, eyes blazing. 'Stop pretending, Mr Mehta. You wrote the proposal.'

Darius looks down at his fingernails. 'No. It was not me.'

'Really?' Patil's fury is a living thing, filling the car. 'The eradication of the Koli fishing grounds was your plan, no?'

'We sorted that out. Our company agreed a deal with your Trust.' Darius's words are weary, a man tired of the same battle.

'Deal off. I know the truth.'

'You can't just "deal off".' Darius sounds more resigned than angry. 'We have a signed contract.'

'And *you* know what I have!' Patil's shout makes me jump. Anjoli's eyes flick to me in the mirror, wide with alarm.

I try to defuse the situation. 'Why did Peter Bell come to see you, Mr Patil?'

'Ask him.' Patil nods at Darius, disdain dripping from his voice. 'But he will only lie. They all just lie, lie, lie.'

'I didn't even know Peter had met you,' protests Darius.

'So Sunil told you what he was worried about?' I ask, hoping to glimpse the truth.

'Sunil was always worried,' Patil snorts. 'Worried he would lose his job. Worried for his family. Worried for his community. Worried for his very life!'

'Why was he worried for his life?'

'Clearly he had reason to be! Ask *him*!' Patil gestures at Darius again. 'You come here. Lie to his family. Say you will look after them. That they will have nothing to worry about. But you and I both know the truth.'

'What truth?' I cry, my frustration bubbling to the surface.

'Ask him,' Patil repeats.

The layers of secrets and lies are suffocating me. Everyone seems to know more than I do, and it's driving me mad. Patil's tirade continues, a relentless barrage of accusations. 'You will not get away with it. I will not forgive you for what you have done to Sunil. He was blameless in this matter. As was Bell. You may exterminate them to protect your secret, but you and the rest of your corrupt class will soon see the collective power of our people. You won't succeed with your immoral plan. Let me out.'

The car screeches to a halt. Patil jumps out, and I scramble after him, not willing to let this chance slip away. 'Sir, you clearly know what's going on here. I understand you don't want to speak in front of Mr Mehta if you think he is involved. But you can tell me. I won't pass it on.'

'You work for him. Why should I trust you?'

'I work for Scotland Yard in London. I was sent here by Peter Bell's family to find out the truth about his death. I admired Sunil. What he achieved and what Sunita's doing are incredibly impressive. What happened to him was more than a tragedy. It was wickedly unjust.'

He shakes his head, scepticism clouding his features. He's not ready to talk.

'Believe me, I'm only here to get justice for Sunil and Bell. Here's my card. If there's anything you want to say to me privately, please get in touch without delay. Sunil said he knew who the killer was, and that he had this document. If you know anything, please tell me.'

Patil takes my card, his expression unreadable. With a curt nod, he hands me his own card, turns and walks away.

'What was that?' Anjoli asks as I slide back into the car.

'Nothing. Just trying to get him to talk. What's the issue with the Koli fishing grounds, Darius?'

'They created a tremendous fuss when the Coastal Road project was first launched, saying that building in the sea and reclaiming the land would affect their livelihood. That their boats could not reach the sea because of the expressway. They held continuous protests. The government got nervous because of the upcoming elections and threatened to pull our contract. So we changed the design and agreed on fair compensation. It stalled us for months.'

'Who dealt with that?'

'Niloufer.'

'But that's not what this document is about?'

'No.'

' You may as well tell me what's in it, now. Sunil obviously told Patil. Maybe he even has it.'

Darius hesitates, a battle waging behind his eyes. 'Sorry. It is private.'

There's no getting through to him. 'Tchah! What kind of friendship is this? No trust.'

'Were you going to fire Sunil?' Anjoli cuts in, her voice sharp.

'Of course not! He is – was – a valuable asset to our company. Let's go home. I've had enough of this place.'

'What time did you get home from meeting Arjun last night?' I ask.

'One? One-thirty? I showered, went to sleep. Then Karve woke me. Why do you . . .' His phone rings. He answers, 'Mehta . . . Yes, Inspector. I see. Thank you.'

He hangs up, his face ashen. Silence stretches thin and taut.

'What?'

'That was Karve. Sunil was brutally tortured before he died. They cut his limbs off while he was still alive.'

Kamil

Back at Behesht, I collapse, the weight of the day seeping into my bones. Sleep comes hard and fast, sweeping me under without a single dream. It's ten o'clock when I finally surface. The ceiling fan spins lazily, each rotation hypnotic, dragging me into a trance as my mind churns over the damn document that's the key to everything. Was Sunil tortured for it? Darius's whims can't dictate my next move. I grab my phone, shoot off a message to Patil, asking him to call, then drag myself out of bed. It's time to face the morning.

The shower strips away the remnants of my fatigue, the water pounding life back into me. I head downstairs, drawn by the promise of breakfast. Approaching the closed living-room door, I catch the indistinct murmur of voices – Darius and Zara. My hand hovers over the knob, then stops. Could the document be here, in the house, possibly even in Darius's room?

Pulse quickening, I retrace my steps, and tiptoe to Darius's end of the corridor. His bedroom is a museum of elegance, adorned with old Indian furniture. A massive, carved, four-poster bed draped in a vibrant brocade dominates one side, while the opposite wall is claimed by a colossal painting – a grotesque scene of a lion-headed beast in brutal combat with an ancient, bearded man. The violent imagery claws at my nerves. Why would anyone want to wake up to that?

I don't have much time. They could come up any second. I zero in on a briefcase perched on a red velvet-covered ottoman. Blood pounds in my ears as I kneel beside it. I flip it open, rifling through board papers, a glossy brochure for flats in Dadar, a coastal road map and a sales strategy presentation. Useless. I stuff everything back in. If I'm caught here, Darius will see it as a betrayal.

I turn to the wardrobes next. Zara's is a gallery of expensive dresses. Darius's is equally orderly, suits on one side, neatly folded clothes on the other. Nothing useful. I pivot to the dressing table – a chaotic display of Zara's life: cosmetics spilling from a velvet pouch, a silver hairbrush, makeup scattered like a careless confession. A jewellery box sits under an antique brass mirror. I shake my head. Not here.

The bedside table is my last hope. I open the drawer and freeze. There it is – *New Mumbai Relocation and Redevelopment Plan*. The same one from Darius's office. My fingers tremble as I flick through the pages. A submission to the Brihanmumbai Municipal Corporation. Is this the original of the 'evil twin'?

Voices outside the door. Panic surges through me. I drop the folder back in the drawer, my eyes darting around for a hiding spot. The bathroom? Too obvious. Under the bed? I'm not in a sitcom. The wardrobe! I dart into Zara's closet, cursing my choice immediately. How will I explain if they catch me? Inspecting for moths?

'Zara, I have to do it! It's the only explanation.' Darius's voice slices through the door. My breath catches.

'But you can't be certain. It's too dangerous. I won't believe it. It has to be Niloufer. She was sleeping with Peter. And dealing with Arjun. It's possible that they did it together. Or Ronnie. He's friendly with the swami.'

'But it's also possible that . . .'

'I wanted you to fire her after you . . . I shouldn't have let you and Puppa persuade me otherwise. And now you want to make her CEO!'

'I've apologised a million times for my lapse.'

'Lapse!'

'She's the most qualified person to run the company. Why let Mehta & Sons suffer because of my stupidity? And she's only there till one of the kids is ready to take over.'

Silence. The bed creaks under someone's weight. I'm feeling claustrophobic. My leg cramps.

'Whatever. So, what are you going to do?'

'Look, if I discover she's behind it, I *will* fire her. Will that make you happy? But I need to be certain. Arjun was so triumphant. He literally waved it in my face.'

'And you can't find it?'

'I have the old one here. But I've searched everywhere for the other version. Peter showed it to me, then took it away. I shouldn't have let him. But I was so stunned. Kamil says Sunil has it. And now this Patil also knows. I won't be able to keep it quiet for much longer.'

'So Peter and Sunil . . .'

'. . . had to be dealt with. I have to face up to it now. I wish I hadn't asked Kamil to come. He's getting too close to the truth. It could destroy us all.'

'I told you not to. What about the other deaths?'

'Senseless. Just senseless.'

A pause. Then Zara says, 'Look, make it through tomorrow. Once you're safe, tell Kamil to go back to London. We'll sort things out on our own. Nothing needs to come out. And . . . it's good for the family, isn't it?'

'Well, yes. It's worth millions. And good for Mumbai. Of course I want Mehta & Sons to be number one in the country. But not this way! I won't do it this way.'

Moving my hands as silently as possible, I text Anjoli.

Stuck in cupboard in Darius's bedroom. U need 2 get them out WTF?

Do something!!!

I've no idea what she can do. Pretend to have a fit? I'm so nervous I can hardly breathe. My bullet wound is hurting badly now.

'Get some sleep before lunch and gather your strength for this evening. You're so exhausted. Is there any way you can cancel? I have to stay home to look after Puppa. He's taken Sunil's death so badly. Won't eat. Won't talk. He was terribly fond of him. I'm worried. He may just have hours left now. And this document . . . it'll kill him if you tell him. You can't, Daru, you can't!'

'I know. I know. Why do you think I haven't till now? It's fine. You stay. I have to go tonight and pick up the award. But I'll be back before midnight. Let me change into a T-shirt. I'll have a quick nap.'

Footsteps approach the wardrobe. My heart slams against my ribcage.

Now Anjoli!!!!

I can barely breathe. The handle jiggles. The sliver of light under the door widens.

What the fuckety fuck am I going to say?

A massive crash.

The door hesitates, then clicks shut.

My leg buckles. I grab the rail to keep from falling. The hangers clatter.

'What was that?' Darius's voice is sharp.

Shit. Did he hear?

'It came from downstairs.'

The bedroom door opens and footsteps rush away.

I crack the wardrobe open. The coast is clear. Relief floods through me, and I almost laugh at my narrow escape. I consider taking the folder but think better of it. He'll notice it's gone. There'll be another time.

I stumble out of their bedroom and down the stairs. Anjoli, Darius, Zara and Victor are standing around the shattered remains of a floor vase.

'I'm so, so sorry,' Anjoli says, her voice a mix of panic and apology. 'I tripped and crashed into it. Zara, I'm really sorry.'

Victor collects the shards as Zara blinks at the mess. She finally says, 'Don't worry about it, Anjoli. These things happen. Are you okay? Did you hurt yourself?'

'I'm fine.' Anjoli glances at me. 'Look at what I did, Kamil. I'm such a klutz.'

'We'll pay for it, Daru,' I say quickly.

'I doubt you can, old chap,' he says with a dark laugh. 'It was only a priceless antique presented to my grandfather by Faraz.' Seeing Anjoli's stricken face, he adds, 'It's fine. I never much cared for it.'

Everyone disperses. I follow Anjoli to the library, my pulse still racing.

We sit on a plush sofa. The table in front of us is scattered with remnants of her interrupted snack: a chessboard shoved aside to make room for a pot under a tea-cosy, a delicate bone-china cup, and plates of cheese toast with chillies, spinach pakoras and a small fruit cake on a doily.

'What the hell?' she whispers fiercely. 'Here I am, quietly minding my own business, and I get this bizarre text! What did you think you were doing? Now they're going to hate me for destroying their irreplaceable artefact.'

'Sorry. But thank you. That was quick thinking.'

I recount my fruitless search and what I overheard. She listens, her eyes defocusing as she processes the implications. She grabs two pieces of toast, sandwiches them together, and stuffs them into her mouth. 'I comfort eat, you know that,' she says around the mouthful.

I nod, barely able to understand her, but soothed by the familiarity of her quirks. My stomach growls. She pushes the plate towards me. I grab a toast, savouring the bite of chillies against the rich cheddar.

'So Zara's not happy about Niloufer?' she says. 'Not surprising. Have another.'

'I don't know what it all means. Daru said the document would be devastating if it became public. Would Niloufer kill to avoid it harming the company?'

'Kamil ... you don't think ... I mean ... Daru couldn't be behind it all, could he? Because you told him Sunil knew the killer. He could have got rid of him to stop it from getting out.'

'Honestly, I'm not sure what to believe.' I wolf down a pakora and pour myself a cup of tea. The warm liquid soothes my nerves, settling the churn in my gut. 'This tea tastes like a unicorn consommé Chanson might make.'

A slight smile. 'It's Earl Grey.'

My phone buzzes. Rogers, asking for an update. It's Saturday, for god's sake! I decide to ignore him. As I scroll through my emails, I feel a jolt. There, in my inbox, is an email sent by Sunil. It has an attachment.

Could it be the document?

Anjoli

Sunil had sent Kamil Peter Bell's diary before he died. He put his phone on the table in front of them and they scrolled through the dozens of appointments Bell had before his death.

'So, he had daily meetings with Niloufer,' Kamil murmured, his finger tracing the repeated entries. 'A few with Ronnie, and a bunch of names I don't recognise. Let's note down the main ones and see what jumps out.'

Anjoli's pen scratched against the paper as Kamil dictated:

Thursday Oct 27	Eapen decapitated in Bandra
Monday Nov 7	Bell arrives in Mumbai
Thursday Nov 17	Bell at Doongerwadi (met Parsi priests to convince them tunnel didn't infringe on the Towers of Silence)
Friday Nov 18	Bell visits Dharavi
Monday Nov 21	Bell meets Swami Yogesh with Ronnie and Sunil (finds out Ronnie is taking bribes. Swami issues threats)

	Bell goes to Dharavi again and meets Patil (Why? Because Sunil gave him the document?)
	Bell starts to act differently.
Tuesday Nov 22	Bell shows Darius document. They argue. Bell asks Darius if he will kill Felix
Wed Nov 23	Bell secretly sees Arjun about document (Not in diary.)
Thursday Nov 24	Bell sees Niloufer. Ronnie.
	Tells Niloufer he wants to see her. Gets call to hotel room.
	Bell stabbed and killed with (swami's?) arrows. Niloufer goes to room. Room searched
Friday Nov 25	Bell's body found.
	Bell planned to meet Arjun again
Monday Nov 28	Darius asks Kamil to come to Mumbai
Friday Dec 2	Shopkeeper murdered with swami's trident
	Darius speaks to Niloufer and Ronnie about document
	Darius meets Arjun re document.
	Kamil tells him Sunil has it and knows who the killer is
Saturday Dec 3	Sunil decapitated with swami's sword. Does Patil have the document now?

Anjoli stared at the list as she absorbed the sequence of events. 'Two deaths connected with Daru, and two unconnected. Is there any other link between them?'

Kamil leaned back, his fingers tapping a restless rhythm on his chest. 'All killed in bizarre ways with the swami's weapons.'

'Maybe Sunil knew the swami was the killer and that's why he was killed?' she suggested. 'He was at the meeting the swami had with Bell.'

'Which means Ronnie could be next?' Kamil let out a frustrated sigh. 'We should warn him. This fucking document. It's obviously the reason Bell started to act differently. He confronted Daru with it on Tuesday, but Daru only saw Arjun about it yesterday? Why wait so long? And why didn't he speak to Niloufer about it before?'

'Ask him.'

'I will. The swami is the obvious suspect if the murders aren't about the document. But I feel we're missing something. I need to talk to Patil. He knows what's going on. I must get him to trust me. He clearly doesn't trust Daru.'

'And check the CCTV from the hotel,' Anjoli added, her gaze drifting to the walls, feeling like she was trapped in an escape room.

'Karve's ignoring me. My bluff about the commissioner is wearing thin. I'll have to get Daru to apply some pressure.'

The room seemed to grow smaller, the dark wood shelves packed with books and mementos from other eras closing in on them. Anjoli wondered if Kamil felt it too, the weight of unsolved mysteries swirling around. She glanced at him, seeing the fatigue etched in his features, the stress lines deepening with each passing hour. Was it this case? The fear for his friend's life? Or something deeper? He had grown harder over the previous years. Less tolerant. Quicker to anger. How could she help him? Maybe his love for her was what was keeping him from losing it after the sadness and horrors they had experienced. And now it was affecting her, too. She didn't want to get hard and desensitised. 'What's your true self, Kamil?' she asked, breaking the silence that had settled like a thick fog.

He looked at her, startled by the sudden introspection. 'Huh? I dunno. Policeman, I suppose. What's yours?'

'That's what you *do*, not what you *are*. What are you at your core?'

'What's this? A therapy session?' he snapped. Her face fell, and she saw regret fly into his eyes. He softened his tone and attempted an answer. 'I guess I've been searching for meaning my whole life and am no closer than when I started. Sometimes I think the imam can help me. Then I think my job can. Or that you can. What are you at your core?'

Her eyes welled up. She turned away, ashamed of her sudden vulnerability. 'I don't know.'

'Maybe we can help each other figure it out?' He reached for her hand, his touch warm and reassuring.

'Maybe. Kamil, can I be honest? This entire trip has freaked me out. Not just what happened to Bell. Seeing that body in the temple. That horrible bloody room with the sword and Sunil's arms.' She hugged herself, trying to fend off the images crowding her mind. 'That mad swami took me to the edge, and Sunil's death pushed me over. I can't deal with it. Thinking of them torturing him. After we'd sort of got to know him. He was so sweet. I know you'll think it's stupid. I mean, it's not like he was our friend or anything. This curse. What's going to happen tomorrow? If it's real, how do we save Daru? I think maybe I'm not cut out for this.'

She turned away to stare at the bookshelves, her confession hanging in the air. Kamil's voice, when it came, was gentle. 'It's not stupid. I understand. Believe me, I've had my own moments since I started this work. But the fact is, you need empathy to be a good detective. To put yourself in the shoes and mind not just of the victims, but of the perpetrators. They're not always the psychopaths you see on TV. Often it's people driven by extreme circumstances to do something they wouldn't normally do. Although if it is the swami, some insane god is driving him.'

Anjoli turned to him, her eyes searching his face for reassurance. 'And it's not just that. It's the whole country. I feel like I've really experienced both sides of India, here in Behesht and in Dharavi. But it just seems like the surface is dissimilar. I mean, how different is the warmth Sunil had for Sunita from the way Faraz is with Percy and Jasmine? The hospitality Sunil's mother showed us – okay, it was water in two battered steel glasses – but how different at heart is that from Zara welcoming us with brain curry on porcelain dishes. The pride Sunil took, that Imran and Victor take in their jobs. Wanting to do better for their children. And then Sunil goes and . . .' she sniffled. 'I don't know what I'm saying. I'm not good around death and loss. Maybe running a restaurant should be enough.'

Kamil nodded slowly, his gaze never leaving hers. 'I think perhaps you're still processing your own losses. It takes time. But you're the smartest, most beautiful, funniest person I know. You can do anything you put your mind to, you know that. And if you don't, I do. I may not know my true self, but I know you've pushed and prodded me to become a much better version of myself. Kamil 2.0.'

Was he really better, she thought as a wobbly smile tugged at her lips. '1.5. Don't get ahead of yourself. Thank you. You've always been a good person.'

They sat in silence, the ticking of the grandfather clock next to them counting out the beats of their thoughts, echoed by all the other clocks scattered around the house. Time froze, holding them in a moment of shared understanding and unspoken fears.

Finally, she straightened up. 'Okay, enough navel-gazing! Let's get out of here. There doesn't seem to be much more we can do for now. Tomorrow's going to be fraught, because we'll have to keep Daru under observation all day. We need to relax a little. Show me a bit of Mumbai?'

'Let me just try Patil.'

Kamil dialled Patil's number, only to get voicemail. He left a message urging him to call back urgently. 'All right. Anjoli's magical mystery Mumbai tour coming up.'

They spent a sultry afternoon wandering around Colaba, the air thick with the scent of the sea and the chatter of tourists and locals mingling under the shadow of the Gateway of India. Their exploration culminated in the Harbour Bar at the Taj Hotel, where they sipped super-spicy Bloody Marys and nibbled on keema tostadas and stir-fried water chestnuts with garlic and pepper. Anjoli felt the weight lift slightly from her shoulders, laughing for the first time in hours at Kamil's tales of his Kolkata misadventures.

As the evening shadows lengthened, they returned to Behesht, finding Darius out and Zara sitting vigil with Faraz. The house was hushed, an uneasy quiet settling over them as they climbed the stairs. At the top of the landing, just as they were about to part for their rooms, Anjoli paused. She whispered, 'Shall we go look?'

Kamil frowned. 'At what?'

'Daru's room. Make sure there's nothing there that could be dangerous for him tomorrow. I don't know, a bomb or something.'

He hesitated for a second, then nodded. 'I can search for the document as well.'

They tiptoed past Faraz's room and the study to reach the end of the corridor. Anjoli knocked softly on Darius's door. Getting no response, she gently turned the knob and pushed it open. Kamil headed straight for the bedside table, while Anjoli began rifling through the wardrobes and drawers, her heart pounding with every rustle of fabric and scrape of wood. She felt like an intruder in a sacred space, and guilt gnawed at her as she searched.

'The document's here,' Kamil whispered. 'At last, we can see what this is all about.'

Anjoli moved over to him. 'Let's see.'

'*What the hell are you doing?*'

Anjoli jerked around, her heart leaping into her throat. Zara stood in the doorway, her face a mask of fury and betrayal.

Anjoli froze as Kamil stepped forward, trying to recover his composure. He waved the folder at her. 'What's this document?'

'It's none of your business.' Zara's voice was icy, cutting through the tension like a blade. She walked over and snatched it from him. 'How dare you snoop around in my bedroom? I think it's time for you to leave Mumbai.'

'Zara, I'm so sorry,' Anjoli managed to say. 'We weren't snooping. We were worried about tomorrow and checking for—'

'Get. Out. Of. My. Bedroom!' Zara's voice rose to a near scream, each word dripping with controlled rage.

Anjoli bowed her head, her cheeks burning with shame as she scurried past Zara, followed closely by Kamil.

'That's the last vestiges of our friendship destroyed,' he muttered as they hurried down the corridor to their rooms.

Anjoli's heart was still pounding, her hand shaking as she fumbled with her door. 'Shit. That was horrible.'

'We were so bloody close!' Kamil added grimly.

'What a fucking day. I'm going to bed. Good night.'

Later, she lay in her bed in the dark, staring at the shifting patterns on the ceiling created by an uplight shining through the ferns in the garden below. She wasn't superstitious, yet she felt a frond of foreboding unfurling deep inside her and spreading like a fractal in her gut. The vase – was that seven years of bad luck, like breaking a mirror? The Mehtas had already suffered a multitude of misfortunes. Or maybe it was just this house, Behesht, with its ghosts lurking around every corner, the wrathful painting in Darius's bedroom . . . it was all too much.

She got up and drew the curtains, snuffing out the shadows that played across the room. Tomorrow was Sunday. Darius's birthday. In twenty-four hours, she would know if the curse was real.

Anjoli

The harsh cry of a peacock in the garden tore through the morning stillness, jolting Anjoli awake. She sat up, her breath quickening as realisation hit. Today was the day Darius had dreaded all his life.

The disquiet that had been building in her since she'd arrived in Mumbai five days ago overflowed, coursing through her veins like electricity. Her heart pounded in her chest, her hands were damp with clammy sweat, and her stomach churned with a nervous energy that made her feel as if a swarm of bees had taken up residence inside.

She took a deep breath to calm herself, and the rigidity in her muscles eased slightly. The previous night's confrontation with Zara replayed in her mind. They hadn't finished inspecting Darius's room, let alone slept in it as a precaution. She should have insisted on completing the search. What if her carelessness had left them vulnerable?

She strained to listen for any sounds from down the hall, hoping to catch an early sign of the day's outcome – cries, screams or sobs that might signal disaster. But all she heard were the birds outside, their chirps and calls an incongruous soundtrack to her mounting anxiety.

A shower calmed her down, and her mind drifted to Kamil's

inadvertent declaration of love in the police station. A smile tugged at her lips. What an idiot. She'd enjoyed their brief excursion the previous afternoon and was looking forward to their trip to Goa once Darius was safe. New beginnings. She towelled herself off and prepared to face whatever the day might bring.

Darius, Zara and Kamil were already in the dining room when Anjoli walked in. Darius's eyes were bloodshot, either from drink or lack of sleep, and he was in mid-conversation with Kamil.

'. . . caught you searching my bedroom? Come on, Kamil. That's just not on!' His voice was a mix of mild anger and weariness.

'Sorry, Daru,' Anjoli said, sliding into her seat. 'We were just checking for anything dangerous. The curse, you know.'

Darius's sceptical look spoke volumes. 'That's not what Zara said. She told me Kamil had the document in his hand. I can't fathom how you could think it was okay to do that. Now, just give me one day of peace without having to think about this shit. And without being interrogated by you, Kamil. Can you do that?'

Anjoli nodded her agreement as Kamil hesitated, a flash of defiance in his eyes. But then he said, 'Deal. No third degree today. Promise. And sorry again, Zara.'

Zara's cheek was twitching involuntarily. She gave a small, tight nod, her gaze frosty.

'Are you okay, Zara?' Anjoli asked gently. 'Did you not sleep last night?'

'I haven't slept in weeks. Maybe after today . . .' Her eyes flicked to Anjoli's T-shirt, which read *People who have more birthdays live longer*. 'That's not very sensitive.'

'I was just trying to . . . happy birthday, Daru.' Anjoli quickly passed him a wrapped present, hoping to defuse the situation.

'Oh! There was no need for that, but thanks.' Darius tore off the wrapping paper to reveal a framed photograph of three

Indian women chatting on the side of a busy road while a dog slept in the foreground.

'It's lovely! Thank you.' He smiled, holding up the picture for Zara to see.

'It's called *Let Sleeping Dogs Lie* by a Parsi photographer – Sooni Taraporevala. I bought it when we were out and about yesterday.' Anjoli threw a look at Kamil. 'It's from both of us.'

Kamil nodded enthusiastically although it had been her idea. Darius hugged Anjoli, and she felt the tightness in her gut ease momentarily.

'Maybe I should let sleeping dogs lie,' he said with a wry look.

'Meaning?' asked Kamil.

Darius wagged a finger at him. 'Nope. Akoori okay for breakfast?'

'I'm starving,' said Anjoli. 'What is it? Gall bladder? Testicles? Not sure I can handle those so early in the day.'

Zara managed a strained smile. 'Just spicy scrambled eggs.'

She rang the bell. To Anjoli's surprise, Victor appeared a moment later, and placed a steaming plate of eggs in front of each of them. She poured herself some coffee. 'Your dad and kids not joining us?'

'The children are at a sleepover. Puppa had a relapse yesterday. Sunil's death . . .'

'I'm so sorry.'

'He's devastated,' Darius said, his voice cracking. 'Sunil was his protégé.'

Zara's face hardened into a mask of controlled emotion. 'He's in so much pain. I'm doing my best to make things as comfortable as possible for him. It's terrible to say, but I wish Ahura Mazda would take him peacefully.'

'No one wants to see someone they love suffer,' Anjoli offered.

'Strange to think I'll be an orphan once he passes. Daru lost his mother two years ago. Cancer as well.' Zara's voice wavered, and she looked away.

Darius reached out and covered her hand. 'She was Mehta & Sons' general counsel till she retired. Helped me a lot when I took over as CEO. I miss her.'

Anjoli watched the exchange, feeling a lump rise in her throat. 'But you won't be alone, Zara. You have Daru. And your lovely children.'

Zara's gaze lingered on Darius, a mixture of love and fear in her eyes. The thought of losing the two most important men in her life on the same day must be unbearable.

'I just want to get through today, that's all. I wish I'd never heard about this bloody curse. It's the hardest thing I've ever had to bear. I'm sorry . . .' She stood abruptly and left the table, her footsteps echoing through the silent house.

Darius's shoulders slumped. 'I'm worried about her mental state. She's barely holding it together.'

'It'll be over soon,' Anjoli said. 'By the way, didn't Zara tell the watchman and Victor not to come in today?'

'She told Ali it was a special holiday for my birthday. Sent him away on a day trip.'

'And Victor?'

'She's organised a special dinner and nothing will run without him. He's not a threat, surely. He's worked for me forever.'

'I don't know,' Anjoli said, uncertainty gnawing at her. 'Can we at least check Ali's definitely gone?'

Darius rang for the butler. 'Victor, did Ali leave this morning?'

'Yes, sir. With his family. The other servants are wondering why they didn't also get a holiday.'

'We'll sort that out later. Thank you.'

The silence that followed was filled only by the clink of cutlery on plates. Despite her nerves, Anjoli's appetite asserted itself. The bittersweet coffee paired perfectly with the melting scrambled eggs, spiked with onions, chilies and tomatoes. The familiar comfort of food eased some of the tension in her jaw.

Zara returned, looking more composed. 'I'm sorry. I went to check on Puppa.'

'How is he?' asked Darius.

'Same. He'll try to come down in the afternoon. We'll have a quiet day here at home with the children.'

'To ensure your safety today, Daru, can we do a few things?' Anjoli asked, her voice calm but firm.

Darius raised an eyebrow. 'What?'

'First, can we make sure that there's someone with you all day? Sorry, I know it's an imposition, but it's important.'

Darius chuckled, a rare glimmer of humour breaking through. 'Sure. As long as Kamil doesn't go into hostile-interrogator mode.'

Kamil mimed zipping his lips shut.

'Next,' Anjoli continued, 'if we assume the curse is about fire, we need to ensure there are no candles anywhere and everyone needs to be vigilant about open flames.'

Zara nodded. 'I'll instruct the staff.'

'What, not even on my cake?' Darius protested playfully.

'Especially not on your cake,' Anjoli insisted.

'Spoil sport!'

'Anything else?' Zara's tone was resigned but cooperative.

Anjoli thought for a moment. 'Do you mind if I check all the other rooms for anything that could be a danger?'

Zara nodded.

'Thanks. And no strangers allowed in today. No workmen, friends, postmen, nobody. Strict quarantine. In fact, lock the gates and don't allow anyone in or out.'

Darius saluted. 'Yes, ma'am. Now I'm going for a shower. Zara, you better come with me, since I can't be alone in there.'

Zara shook her head, but followed him out of the room.

'Nicely done,' Kamil said to Anjoli. 'Sorry. I should have been helping more.'

'It's fine. You've been busy with other things. Come on, let's get ready as well.'

The day unfolded under a charged tension, everyone forced into a semblance of birthday levity. The children returned after lunch and added a layer of normalcy that the adults desperately clung to. Faraz joined them, his condition visibly worse. He moved slowly and his speech was halting, but he made an effort, a silent presence at the end of the table, his oxygen nebuliser hissing softly in the background.

Anjoli felt a wave of relief when the children demanded a game of Monopoly, and their laughter and squeals as their grandfather secretly passed them bank notes momentarily dispelled her worries.

Faraz ruffled Jasmine's hair. Wheezed, 'Keep building houses like that and Darius will have to rename the company Mehta & Daughter.'

'Hey, what about me?' exclaimed Percy as he moved his dog five spaces to land on Vine Street.

'I thought you wanted to captain the Indian cricket team?' teased Faraz.

'Oh yes, I forgot. Will you buy me a new bat, Motta Pappa?'

Faraz's face glowed with love for the boy. 'Of course. And we'll play together in the garden just like I did all those years ago.'

Percy laughed. 'But how will you play, Motta Pappa? You can't even walk?'

'I'll have to get better then, won't I?'

A lump rose in Anjoli's throat as Zara darted a glance at Darius.

Since they weren't having a party, Zara had organised a fancy evening for the family. At seven, they gathered in the living room under the ornate chandelier, its soft glow casting a warm light over the scene. They snacked on golden fried prawns, masala liver on toast and prunes wrapped in bacon while she kept their champagne glasses filled.

'Five more hours,' Anjoli said to Kamil as he munched on spiced Goan cashews. 'Save some space for dinner.'

He patted his stomach. 'Bottomless pit.'

She slapped his backside. 'Pitiful bottom more like.'

He pushed away the nuts.

Instead of receding as the minutes ticked by, Anjoli's unease grew. The grandfather clock's rhythmic ticking seemed louder, more ominous, with each passing moment. She glanced around the room, noting how even the children's joyful chatter couldn't completely mask the adults' anxiety. 'Why aren't Daru and Zara screaming in agitation?' she whispered to Kamil.

His face mirrored her concern. 'You feel it too?'

'Obviously. But just another four and a bit hours to go.'

'We've done all we can. There was nothing suspicious in the rooms?'

'I didn't get a chance to check Faraz's. He was asleep. And I didn't want to ask when he was at the party.'

'I'm sure it's fine,' Kamil reassured her, though his voice lacked conviction.

'I'd like to check, anyway.'

'Okay. We'll ask.'

As the evening wore on, the pressure continued to build, an invisible cord tightening around them all. Anjoli knew they had done everything they could to safeguard Darius. All that was left now was to wait and hope.

Four hours to go.

Anjoli

The grand dining room at Behesht was a tableau of opulence and tradition, bathed in the soft light of the chandeliers. The table was dressed in a hand-embroidered white muslin tablecloth and placemats adorned with mythical creatures, a nod to ancient Parsi legends. Vases brimmed with fresh roses, and added a fragrant elegance, their scent mingling with the rich aroma of the starters already laid out – asparagus and tuna mousses, a vibrant red and yellow tomato salad, a whole cooked ham, and fish in mayonnaise resting on a bed of shredded lettuce. Victor moved with a quiet efficiency between them, pouring glasses of Puligny-Montrachet, the wine sparkling in the crystal goblets.

The atmosphere was that of both a party for Darius and a wake for Faraz. Hopefully not a double wake, Anjoli thought, then berated herself for her negativity. Kamil leaned over to her. 'You were right. I should have paced myself.'

The meal unfolded like a grand procession, dish after dish arriving in a steady, mouth-watering parade. Chicken escalopes, vegetables au gratin and mutton chops with shoestring fries followed the starters. Just when Anjoli thought she couldn't eat another bite, the Indian food appeared.

'Dhan dar patia,' Zara explained, her voice tinged with pride. 'Rice with creamy dal and sweet and sour prawns. We eat it on special occasions.'

Anjoli saw Kamil surreptitiously loosening his belt and suppressed a giggle. She wished she could do the same, her stomach feeling stretched to its limit.

The meal culminated in a traditional Parsi dessert. 'Sev and dahi,' said Zara, setting down the bowls of warm vermicelli with nuts and raisins alongside icy-cold, sweet yoghurt. 'It's for good luck. God knows we need it.'

Anjoli found room for the dessert, the contrasting textures and flavours slipping down smoothly. She realised she was a little tipsy, thanks to Victor's silent refills of her wine glass throughout the evening.

Finally, the birthday cake made its grand entrance, wheeled in on a trolley. It was a multi-tiered confection mimicking the cityscape of Mumbai, adorned with edible gold leaf and crowned with a sugar replica of the Parsi Fire Temple.

'Where are the candles?' the children chorused, their faces alight with excitement. The adults exchanged glances, a shared moment of anxiety. Anjoli quickly stepped in. 'It's a tradition to close your eyes and imagine candles on your forty-seventh birthday. So everyone do that!'

Darius tipped an imaginary cap to Anjoli. 'A wonderful tradition! This has been a superb meal, my darling. All my favourite dishes!' He sliced into the cake and fed a piece to Zara, catching stray crumbs with his hand under her chin. 'I couldn't have asked for a better last supper.' Zara hurriedly spooned some cake into his mouth to silence him, glancing nervously at the kids, but they seemed blissfully unaware of the dark undertones.

'Come on, let's toast Daddy,' Zara said, moving to the sideboard to pour drinks.

'Let me help,' Anjoli offered as Zara picked up a bottle of Dom Perignon.

'Thanks for saving the moment there. I've got it. Just relax.' Zara poured champagne into everyone's glasses, including a small amount for the children, who looked thrilled to be part of the adult toast.

Anjoli ruffled the children's hair, laughing. She imagined how she and Kamil might treat their own kids someday and giggled. Maybe the wine was getting to her.

'Puppa?' Zara turned to her father, who had eaten very little and remained silent, his breathing laboured. 'Will you have some?'

Faraz looked confused. 'What, maari jaan?'

She waved a glass at him.

He nodded. 'A drop. To keep the children company.'

'Are you okay, Puppa?'

'Yes. This rich food and drink doesn't agree with me anymore. It's a difficult day, but it's almost over.'

Zara nodded, unable to meet his eyes.

'And . . .'

His daughter looked up, bracing herself. 'And?'

'This is the room where Xerxes died because of Salim Sinai's curse.' Faraz pointed shakily. 'He was standing right there when . . .'

A cold draught whipped through the dining room. Zara stared at Faraz, her face tight with anxiety. She quickly poured him half an inch of champagne. Handing Darius his glass, she raised her own with a forced cheeriness. 'To my wonderful husband. The best father to our children. He has brought us so much happiness over the years. We couldn't have hoped for anything . . .' She gasped, her voice cracking, and sat down abruptly.

'Mummy, what's wrong?' Jasmine asked, climbing onto her lap.

Zara hugged her daughter, face pale. Darius embraced them both. 'Nothing's wrong with your mummy. She just had too much champagne, that's all.' He raised his glass. 'To me!'

'Happy birthday!' everyone chorused, the children's voices ringing out in the room.

As they sipped their drinks, Faraz spoke again, his voice a frail whisper. 'I saw a rainbow today. It was a sign.'

'A sign of what?' asked Anjoli, sipping the air-dry champagne.

'Chinvat Bridge.'

'What's that, Uncle?'

Faraz seemed to gain a second wind from the alcohol. 'The bridge of judgement. It separates the living from the dead. All souls cross it on death. It is guarded by two four-eyed dogs. None can avoid it. What must be done must be done, whatever the price, the cost, the pain. One day, we all must walk through fire.'

Percy added, 'The good go to the House of Song and the bad go to the House of Lies. We studied it.'

'And I must go to my bedroom.' Faraz turned to Zara, who was looking down, hands clasped, almost as if she was at prayer. 'Will you take me, maari jaan?'

She must know it's his time, Anjoli thought, as she saw the grief on Zara's face. To help her friend out, she rose and said, 'Time for bed, kids. School tomorrow. Say goodnight to your daddy and grandad. Give them big, big hugs and kisses and let your mummy put you to bed.'

The children did as they were told, then dutifully followed Zara and Faraz out of the room.

Anjoli

Anjoli checked her watch. So far, so good. She felt her shoulders drop; the strain easing slightly. Darius was safe. The curse was just an old superstition, after all.

When Zara returned, she looked more composed, but still wan. 'Is he okay?' Anjoli asked gently.

She nodded, filling her glass with champagne again and draining it in one go. She refilled it immediately.

Darius watched her, concern etched on his face. 'I know it's hard seeing him at the end of the line like this, jaan. Soon he'll be out of pain and in a better place.'

'I know,' Zara's voice broke as she handed Darius another glass of champagne. 'But I can't even concentrate on him properly. These precious last moments are tainted with worry about . . . everything else.'

Darius knocked back the drink, then wrapped her in his arms. 'It's all fine, jaan. Nothing will happen. Kamil's making sure of that.'

Anjoli bristled at Darius's words. Kamil had done nothing to ensure his safety. She'd been the one piecing together the puzzle of the curse. Then guilt washed over her. The important thing was to keep him safe, not worry about who got the credit.

'Anjoli's been doing the heavy lifting,' Kamil said, as if

reading her mind. 'The kids are so cute! Are you grooming them to succeed you, Daru? Family business and all?'

'In time, maybe.' Darius smiled at the thought. 'It's essential it stays in Parsi hands. My granddad. Faraz. Me. Niloufer. Then the children.'

'So you will become chairman once he passes?'

Darius glanced at Zara, then back at Kamil. 'I might keep the CEO role as well. I'm less sure about Niloufer after . . . I won't hold a candle to Faraz, though. He's the one who transformed this company into one of India's great industrial giants. We're up there with the Tatas, Godrejs, Mistrys and Poonawallas. And this Coastal Road project will make us . . .'

He trailed off, lost in thought.

'Make you . . . ?' Anjoli prompted gently.

'Nothing,' he said abruptly. 'It's almost ten. So far, so good. I just have to make it past the next couple of hours, then I'm home free.' He gave a weak punch to the air, trying to muster some enthusiasm.

'Have you told Niloufer she may not get the CEO job?' Kamil asked, watching Darius closely.

Zara stiffened.

'She was at the function last night. I told her I was reconsidering a few things in light of her affair with Peter. I think she got the message.' He yawned loudly, rubbing his belly. 'God, I'm so full. And exhausted. Zara and I will bid you goodnight . . .'

'You can't go to bed now!' Anjoli exclaimed. 'Let's stay up together. It's just a few more hours. Better safe than sorry.'

'Anjoli, I can barely keep my eyes open. Zara will look after me.'

Zara looked stricken. 'Daru . . . I need to pray with Puppa. So he'll depart peacefully and not be tied to us. His breathing has become terrible. That rainbow dream . . . he doesn't have long now. I think eating in this room upset him. Brought back memories. I told him I'd return. Kamil and Anjoli will take care of you.'

Anjoli felt a wave of sympathy for Zara, caught in the emotional tug-of-war between her father and her husband.

'It's okay,' Kamil said gently. 'We'll stay in the bedroom with Daru till you return.'

Darius shook his head. 'I'll never be able to sleep with you two sitting there like guard dogs. What's going to happen to me in my room?'

'We don't mind,' Anjoli insisted. 'At least I don't have four eyes. Please.'

He hesitated, then sighed. 'Tell you what, if you feel so strongly about it, sit in my study outside the room. Lock me in and give Zara the key when she finishes with Puppa.'

Anjoli considered his offer. 'All right. But let us inspect your bedroom first. Ensure there's nothing dangerous there.'

'I thought you already did that last night,' he said with a wry smile.

'Humour us.'

'It's a good idea,' Zara agreed. 'Do what she says, Daru.'

'I have no energy to argue with all of you. Come on then.'

They made their way to Darius's bedroom. 'Why do you have that scary picture?' Anjoli said, walking over to examine the painting opposite the bed.

'Ahriman fighting Ahura Mazda,' Darius explained. 'Bought it at auction some years ago.'

'I hate it,' Zara muttered. 'I wanted to put up a nice landscape painted by my mother. But Daru says we have to remember the duality of good and evil. Why, I don't know.'

Anjoli carefully pulled the painting away from the wall, revealing only dust bunnies. While Kamil ensured the windows were securely locked and drew the curtains, Anjoli checked the wardrobes, mouthing 'sorry' to Darius and

Zara. She rifled through them quickly, finding nothing suspicious.

On Darius's bedside table, a water jug, a glass and two unopened blister packs of tablets sat in neat rows. Anjoli picked up the medicines – Pravastatin, Lisitec. 'Quite a few pills. Are you alright?'

'Just for my cholesterol and BP.'

'Maybe skip them tonight? Kamil, can you get some fresh bottled water from the kitchen, please? Open it yourself.'

She opened the drawer of the bedside table, noting the file that Kamil had mentioned. Taking the bull by the horns, she took it out and said, 'Is this the mysterious document?'

Darius took it from her gently. 'The original, yes.'

Kamil came over. 'Are you going to tell us about it now?'

Darius gave a short laugh and, to Anjoli's astonishment, grabbed Kamil in a bear hug. Releasing him, he patted his cheek and said, 'This is why I love you, man. You never give up. Let's make a deal. If I don't self-immolate in the next couple of hours, I'll tell you everything tomorrow. Deal?'

Kamil grinned and gave his friend a hug. 'Deal.'

Anjoli suppressed a smile at their intimacy as Darius tossed the document on his bedside table. She continued her inspection, examining the red brocade canopy over the bed. Nothing. She peeked under the bed. Spotless. Checked the wardrobes. Zara's dressing table held nothing but the usual assortment of cosmetics and jewellery. Kamil returned with a bottle of Bisleri and placed it on the bedside table, looking amused at Anjoli's thoroughness. They moved into the sump-tuous bathroom, where she locked the window and examined the claw-foot tub and the neatly arranged toiletries. Every-thing seemed in order.

'There's only the one entrance to the bedroom, right?' she asked as they returned.

'Yep,' Darius confirmed, yawning again. 'It really will have to be a ghost walking through walls to get to me in here.'

Anjoli felt as satisfied as she could be. 'All right. I think it's safe. What do you think, Kamil?'

'Looks secure. We'll love you and leave you. Zara, I'll lock the door so no one can enter. You can have the key back when you're ready for bed.'

'What if there's a fire?' Darius joked. 'I'll be cooked alive.' Zara lifted a hand to her mouth.

'Are there any matches around? Lighter?' Anjoli asked quickly.

'Nothing. Not even a candle.'

Kamil grinned. 'Try to avoid spontaneously combusting, then. Don't worry. We'll be right outside. Just shout, and we'll open the door in a jiffy.'

'My life is in your capable hands.' Darius gave a tired smile. 'I'll have a quick shower, then crash. See you in the morning. When I sleep, I'm dead to the world.'

'Stop saying things like that,' Anjoli chided.

'This nightmare's almost over.' Zara held Darius's face and kissed him firmly. 'You don't know how bad it's been waiting for this day, jaan. Years and years of fear. Just building and building.' Tears glistened in her eyes and she could barely speak. 'I love you, you fool. Thank you for listening to us and not arguing too much. I'll be with you as soon as I've settled Puppa. He's exhausted. I'm sure he'll go to sleep quickly. I love you.'

They left the room. Kamil locked the door and pocketed the key. Anjoli gave the knob a rattle to ensure it was secure.

'We'll be just outside, Zara,' Kamil said. 'Don't worry. We've done everything we can. You're being incredibly brave. Look after your father. We'll do the rest.'

'Actually, Zara,' Anjoli said. 'I realise it's an imposition, but your dad's room is the only one I didn't get a chance to check. Do you mind?'

Zara seemed about to refuse, then nodded. 'Just be sensitive.'

'Thanks. Kamil, will you wait here?'

As they walked down the corridor, Zara confided, 'I went to the agiary and prayed yesterday. For both Daru and Puppa.'

'Did it help?'

'Not really.'

Faraz's room was a stark contrast to the opulence of the rest of the house. The white walls and minimal furniture gave it a serene, almost monastic feel. The only light came from a bedside lamp, casting a soft glow over him as he lay in bed, wheezing.

Zara tiptoed in. 'Puppa?'

No response.

She moved closer, her tone more urgent. 'Puppa?'

Faraz woke, blinking in confusion. 'Maari jaan. Are you still all right? Darius?'

'Yes, Puppa. Anjoli is here and wants to take a quick look around. I'm going to sit with you for a bit. Are you in pain? Do you want to say some prayers? Or shall I read to you?'

Faraz gestured weakly at the nebuliser and a battered book on the bedside table. Anjoli noticed his dentures in a glass, his hearing aid next to them. Zara gently placed the oxygen mask over his mouth and picked up the book – *Complete Works of Oscar Wilde*. She read softly. 'High above the city, on a tall column, stood the statue of the Happy Prince. He was gilded all over with thin leaves of fine gold, for eyes he had two bright sapphires, and a large red ruby glowed on his . . .'

Anjoli moved quietly around the room, checking the wardrobes and the furniture. Everything was in its place, nothing seemed out of order. Nothing flammable that she could see. The bathroom was similarly innocuous. She nodded her thanks to Zara and left, joining Kamil outside Darius's room.

'All good?' she asked softly.

Kamil knocked on Darius's door. 'All okay, Daru?'

'About to shower,' came Darius's voice through the door. 'Would you care to watch to make sure I don't slip on the soap?'

Kamil laughed. 'I'll pass. Sleep well.'

He hesitated, then unlocked and opened the door a crack. Darius was taking off his shirt, and looked at Kamil with amusement. Kamil raised a hand in apology and closed the door again, locking it securely. They moved to Darius's study, leaving the door open for a clear view of the corridor leading to his room. Anjoli uncorked a bottle of Pinot Noir from the drinks trolley, poured two glasses, and they settled on the sofa.

Kamil swirled the wine in his glass. 'Thank god it's all turned out to be a weird myth.'

'It's not over yet. But experiencing this with him reminds you the end can come at any time. Know what I mean?'

'I do.'

Her voice softened. 'We should enjoy life when we can, Kam.'

His gaze was intense. 'Agreed. I was thinking that once Daru's safe, and he tells me the whole story tomorrow, we can leave things to Karve. It's been a really tough week, so let's just go to Goa tomorrow after I send Bell's body back. Be with each other.'

Anjoli nibbled at the corner of her mouth. 'But what about Sunil? Surely we should find out why he died?'

'I'd like to, but Rogers isn't going to let me hang around here for weeks. I'm being realistic.'

A pang of desolation went through her. She wasn't responsible for Sunil's death, so why did she feel such a powerful pull to uncover the truth? She forced her doubts down. Kamil was right. They had to be practical. 'All right. Chanson continues to cause havoc, so at least I can get onto that.'

'What's he done now?'

'He wants to replace all our napkins with ones from Anya Hindmarch. At thirty-five pounds a pop.'

'Who's Anya Hindmarch?'

'A famous designer. Anyway, it's beside the point. Our napkins are good enough.'

'What did you say to him?'

'Not to be stupid. I'm not about to allow the tiny margin of profit we make to be mopped up by extravagant linen. But he insists he won't get a Michelin star unless he has the right napery.'

Kamil's befuddled expression made it clear he had no idea what napery was, but he nodded sagely. Anjoli swallowed a giggle. 'And you're right. We need to save money for our business. So you can book a double room in Goa.'

She watched him flush, trying to act casual as he leaned back with a smile. She sipped her drink, feeling a warm glow spread through her that wasn't just from the wine. It was time to make a commitment. She could do this. She twirled her glass between her fingers. 'So you love me, do you?'

Kamil started, spilling some wine on his jeans. 'What?'

'You said you loved me in the police station,' she said, trying unsuccessfully to hide her delighted smile.

'What? Did I?'

'Uh-huh.'

He took a deep breath. 'Well, I do. It's not a surprise, is it?'

'It's not.'

He held his breath. 'And you? What do you feel?'

Instead of answering, she inched closer, her eyes shining with a mix of uncertainty and resolve. He put an arm around her, drawing her to him. Her eyes closed as she tilted her face up, ready for the kiss.

Then abruptly pushed him away. 'Do you smell smoke?'

Anjoli

A njoli took a tentative sniff when a piercing scream from Darius's room shattered the stillness of the study. She shoved Kamil aside, their footsteps echoing like thunder as they sprinted down the hall, skidding to a halt in front of Darius's door. Another, fainter cry seeped through the thick wood. She froze, terror and confusion whirling inside her, as Kamil's fingers fumbled with the key.

A thudding sound behind made her whirl around. Zara was running towards them from Faraz's room, her face a mask of horror, as if she already knew the dreadful truth. 'OPEN THE BLOODY DOOR! NOW!' Her scream was a raw, desperate command slicing through Anjoli's paralysis.

The key stuck. Anjoli's heart stuck too. Each beat a painful explosion in her chest. Kamil rattled the key. It finally turned. He threw the door open, and a wave of scorching heat blasted into Anjoli, forcing her back a step.

Darius's bed was engulfed in flames, a roaring conflagration consuming the four-poster. He was sitting up in the centre, a dark silhouette amid the blazing inferno. His mouth opened in a silent scream of agony, his left hand pointing towards the painting of Ahriman on the wall. His face blistered, the skin peeling away to reveal raw, discoloured flesh. His howls grew weaker until he collapsed, the flames curling around him in a monstrous embrace. The noise of the fire came to the fore – creaks and groans as it devoured the wood and fabric.

Anjoli stood rooted to the spot, her mind unable to process the nightmare unfolding before her. Images from three years ago flashed – her friend and employee burning in his bed in her flat over Tandoori Knights. Not again. She couldn't let it happen again. She dug her fingernails into the palms of her hands, the pain snapping her out of her trance and forcing her to confront the satanic scene.

Kamil rushed forward, attempting to reach Darius, but the heat drove him away. 'Stand back!' he yelled. 'Get a fire extinguisher!'

Zara didn't move, her eyes wide and unblinking, transfixed by the blaze. Anjoli grabbed her shoulders, shaking her violently. 'Fire extinguisher! Go!' Zara snapped from her daze, and sprinted off. The flames danced hungrily, licking at the edges of the carpet. Anjoli darted into the room, frantically searching for water. She stumbled into the bathroom, turned the tap on full blast, and grabbed the nearest container – a mug. Totally inadequate, but it would have to do.

Kamil burst in with a wastepaper basket. She snatched it from him. Thrust it under the gushing tap. It seemed to take an eternity to fill. She raced back, water sloshing over the sides, and hurled it at the flames devouring the bed, the steam hissing and rising like an angry spirit.

'Stem the flow!' Kamil's shout barely pierced the roaring inferno.

'What?' Anjoli screamed, her voice straining to cut through the noise.

'Stop the rest of the room from burning!' He dashed out.

Anjoli ran back to the bathroom, refilling the wastepaper basket. The process was excruciatingly slow. She splashed the water onto the smouldering carpet, stamping on the wet patches to extinguish the embers.

Kamil returned, clutching an ice bucket from the study, and threw the cubes into the fire – no effect. Zara appeared, dragging a heavy red fire extinguisher, two servants trailing with buckets of water. Kamil seized it from her as the servants doused the bed. They ran back to the bathroom for refills while Kamil struggled with the extinguisher's mechanism. After a few infuriating seconds, he pressed the lever. A jet of white foam erupted, smothering the flames. The servants continued their back-and-forth with Anjoli, each splash and stomp a desperate dance against the fire. Minutes stretched into eternity until, suddenly, the flames relented. Kamil kept spraying until the extinguisher was empty, then discarded it with a metallic clang.

The room was a charred wreck, the acrid smell of burnt fabric, flesh and foam hanging heavily in the air. Anjoli, panting and drenched, glanced around, her heart still racing. She gagged, her eyes watering. Had they saved him?

Darius's blackened body lay on the burned remnants of the bed, covered in foam, looking like a grotesque sculpture. The wooden poles of the canopy had burned through, the remains of the brocade hanging in tatters. The reds and blues of the fabric glistened amid the black debris.

Anjoli struggled to breathe in the intense heat. 'Daru, can you hear me?' she called, her voice choked with smoke. She moved closer, trying not to retch at the smell of burning flesh. Did his eyelids flutter? Was there still life in him? She leaned in, her heart pounding.

Yes! There was a faint movement. 'He's alive! Call an ambulance. Bring more water!' she yelled over her shoulder.

Zara's keening wail reverberated across the room, followed by a whispered, 'I'm going to be sick,' as she bolted for the bathroom.

'Water! Now!' Anjoli shouted to Kamil. He ran to the bathroom and returned with a bucket. Anjoli carefully poured the water over Darius's burnt body, using her cupped hand to control the flow. The foam slid off, revealing horrific wounds—carbonised skin, exposed muscle, the bone of his arm. Her stomach turned. Was she making things worse? She felt helpless, unsure if she was doing the right thing. But she couldn't stand by and do nothing. She had to save him. She would not let him die.

A quavering voice came from the doorway. 'What . . . ?'

She turned to see Faraz in his wheelchair, his face sculpted with confusion and fear. 'What's happening? Why this noise? Where is Zara? I rang and rang, and nobody came. He had to help me.' He gestured weakly at Victor standing behind him.

'Darius has been badly burned. Zara's in the bathroom. Call for an ambulance,' Anjoli replied, her voice breaking.

Faraz's wheelchair hummed as he came closer to Darius's bed, rolling over the soaked carpet. He stared down at his son-in-law, his expression twisted in agony. His lips moved over toothless gums, whispering a prayer.

'Ambulance! Dial 112. Now!' Kamil barked at Victor.

The butler nodded and pulled out his mobile phone.

A tear slid down Faraz's cheek. He whispered, his voice barely audible over the dying crackle of the blaze, 'The curse of fire. Xerxes. Cyrus. Darius. You all were my family. I couldn't stop it. I fought so hard. But the power of the curse was too strong. Salim called for lives and he has got lives. I am so sorry, dikra. Forgive me.' He sobbed, his words dissolving into muttered prayers.

Zara stumbled out of the bathroom, her face pale and streaked with tears. 'Is he gone?'

'We have to wait for the ambulance. Moving him might worsen his condition.' Kamil's voice was steady but strained.

'He's still alive. Talk to him, Zara,' Anjoli urged.

Zara moved to Darius's side, eyes vacant. Faraz looked at her, his expression a mixture of sorrow and resignation. 'There was nothing we could do, maari jaan. The curse . . .'

'No, no, no,' Zara's voice broke. 'Why? Why did it have to end this way?'

Faraz reached out, taking her flailing hands in his and holding them to his heart. 'Shhh, maari jaan. Shhh. It was written. Shhh.'

Zara's sobs turned into unintelligible utterances. 'This curse has destroyed our family. What do I do now?'

Faraz looked up at his daughter, lost for words, his eyes filled with a depth of sorrow Anjoli couldn't fathom. She rested a hand on Zara's shoulder. 'Try to talk to him. Keep him with us.' But Zara only moaned, her mind trapped in a spiral of despair. Victor and the two servants hovered in the doorway, their gazes moulded to the tragic scene unfolding before them.

Anger surged through Anjoli, hot and fierce. How had she let this happen? Darius had entrusted her with his safety, and she had failed. She had been outside, lost in dreams of a kiss while he was burning alive. What kind of protection was that? What kind of person was she?

Kamil's voice cut through her turmoil, sharp with urgency. 'We have to treat this as a crime scene. Everyone, please wait outside.'

The servants left as Anjoli squeezed Zara's arm. 'I'm so, so sorry, Zara. Kamil's right. We should go out.'

Zara was resolute. 'I will not leave him!'

'There's nothing we can do till the paramedics arrive.'

'No!' Zara knelt on the burnt carpet by the bed. Whispered prayers. Her father remained beside her, praying too.

Anjoli followed Kamil as he opened the locked windows to

ventilate the room. She breathed in the night air. 'How could this happen?'

'I don't know.' Kamil's voice was filled with frustration. 'I saw nothing that could have caused a fire. We checked everywhere.'

'Why didn't he jump out of bed when the fire started?'

'I don't *know*.'

'Unless he . . . spontaneously combusted?' The absurdity of the suggestion only heightened Anjoli's sense of helplessness.

'That's not a thing!'

They turned back to the tragic tableau at the bedside. Zara's murmurs were louder now. 'Don't go. Don't go. Please, stay with me. Fight for me. Fight for the children. It's over now.'

Anjoli wiped her eyes angrily. 'He was pointing at the painting.' She gazed at the untouched image on the wall – a battle between a monster and a god. Did it mean something?

'Probably a spasm. I doubt he would have seen anything between the flames and the smoke. Are you all right?'

'Not really. The smell. It's like we're back there in the restaurant when it burned . . . I feel sick.' She collected herself. 'Take Zara out. This is not good for her. I'll stay with Daru in case anything happens.'

'You go. I'll stay.'

'Please. I want to. I feel like I let him down.'

Kamil hesitated, then knelt beside Zara, whispering softly. She shook her head fiercely, but he kept murmuring. Finally, they rose, Zara's steps dragging as she followed Kamil and Faraz out of the room. Anjoli closed the door behind them and returned to the bed. Darius groaned, his body twitching slightly.

What the hell should I do? she thought. I have to assume this is a crime scene, like Kamil said. I need to control my pain. A good detective has to compartmentalise. 'The ambulance is on its way. Hang in there, Daru,' she whispered, hoping he could hear her.

She looked around the once elegant room, now blackened and charred. Darius's glass held water, a sooty film on its surface. Next to it were ashes, mixed with bits of burnt cardboard. The folder that had been consuming them for days. It didn't matter now. 'I'll be right back, Daru. Hold on.'

She walked into the bathroom, the sour stink of Zara's vomit mingling with the scent of floral soap. The contrast made her stomach churn. Water droplets spotted the shower cubicle. Darius had showered before bed. The razor, soap, toothpaste, toothbrush and nail clippers were undisturbed. She touched the toothbrush's head. Dry. A damp bath towel and clothes lay discarded on the floor.

She checked the bathroom window. Locked from the inside, just as she had left it. She returned to the bedroom and forced herself to look at Darius, feeling bile rise in her throat. She swallowed it down. Her friend's skin was a horrifying blend of red and black, swollen and blistered. His scorched sudra and pyjamas were fused to his body. 'Can you hear my voice? What happened, Daru? You need to live. Prove this curse wrong.'

She looked around the bed. The pillow and mattress had burned through. Darius was lying on bare, twisted, blackened springs. The thought of him waking to find himself in flames was too much to bear. She forced herself to stay focused, to not let the past consume her.

What had caused the bed to ignite so violently? A match couldn't have done this. Something electrical? She flicked on the bedside lamp, half-expecting it not to work. The light came on, casting a harsh glow over the devastation.

Where was the red silk bedcover she had seen earlier? Surely he would have taken it off before he went to sleep. The bed had fragments of a white sheet and the mattress, but the bedcover was missing. Could silk burn to nothing so quickly?

Commotion outside. The door burst open. Two paramedics

ran in, followed by Zara and Kamil. One leaned close to Darius's mouth and nose, listening. He nodded to his colleague and gently fitted an oxygen mask over Darius's face. They prepared to lift him onto the stretcher.

Anjoli turned away, unable to watch. She prayed that Darius's unconsciousness shielded him from the pain as they lifted him from the bed.

'Where are you taking him?' Zara asked.

'D S Hospital.'

'I'm coming.'

'No, you stay with the kids and your father, Zara,' Kamil said. 'I'll go.'

'No. I have to be there if . . .'

'What about your dad?' Anjoli said gently.

Zara was torn. 'He will survive. Daru may not.'

Anjoli nodded. 'Kamil, you stay here with Faraz. I'll go with Zara.'

Kamil looked like he wanted to argue, then acquiesced.

They followed the paramedics out, and Kamil locked the door. 'Are there any other keys, Zara?' She shook her head. 'All right. I'll keep this one.'

The paramedics carried Darius down the stairs and into the waiting ambulance. Zara and Anjoli climbed into the back, the siren wailing as they sped away. Darius's eyes were closed, his form a motionless shadow on the stretcher.

'I'm sorry, Daru,' Anjoli whispered, as Zara sat beside her, staring blankly at the walls of their vehicle.

In a few minutes, the hospital loomed ahead, a beacon of hope and dread. The paramedics rushed Darius into the emergency room, leaving Anjoli and Zara in the sterile, brightly lit waiting area. Zara collapsed into a chair, her body wracked with silent sobs.

Anjoli approached the reception desk, trying to marshal her

thoughts. The attendant handed her a stack of paperwork, eyeing her curiously. She glanced down at herself. Her body, hands, legs were all blackened with thick soot. She looked over at Zara, who was similarly soiled. She sat next to her, filling out the forms, anything to keep her mind occupied. All she wanted was for Darius to live.

After handing in the paperwork, she washed her face in the bathroom, wiping off as much grime as she could. She offered Zara a chance to freshen up or get something to eat, but Zara ignored her, lost in her own world of grief.

Three hours passed in a haze. Anjoli dozed off, exhausted. When she awoke, two more hours had slipped by. Zara hadn't moved, her expression unchanged. Anjoli stretched, her muscles stiff and aching. As she was texting Kamil to update him, a doctor in a white coat approached them. 'Who's here for Darius Mehta?'

Zara leapt to her feet. 'I'm his wife. Please tell me. How is he?'

The doctor's mien was a mask of professional sympathy. 'I'm sorry. He is no more.'

Zara's face crumpled. 'You were supposed to keep him safe,' she whispered to Anjoli, her voice laced with accusation.

Anjoli's heart shattered. Guilt and sorrow coursed through her, replacing the faint hope that had sustained her for hours. She sat beside Zara, putting a trembling arm around her as they both wept.

The doctor's voice entered the fog of their grief. 'What happened? I've never seen burns this severe. We tried our best with IVs and topical creams, but he was too far gone.'

Anjoli cleared her throat. 'We're not sure. Somehow, his bed caught fire. I can't believe he's dead.'

'Maybe it's a blessing. If he had survived, he would have been severely disabled for the remainder of his life. What should we do with the body?'

Anjoli stared at the doctor, stunned by her bluntness. She said to Zara, 'Wait here,' and led the doctor aside. 'Can you keep him here for now? He was the CEO of Mehta & Sons. An important man.'

'Princes and paupers all end up in the same place. I'll store him in the mortuary.' The doctor nodded towards Zara. 'Is she okay?'

'What do you think?' Anjoli said bitterly.

The doctor looked away, ashamed. 'Sorry. Difficult day. Do you wish to see the body?'

Anjoli returned to Zara, who gave her a dead stare. 'It's not him anymore.'

They took an Uber back to Behesht, the ride a silent journey through the darkened streets. Zara sat rigid, hands clenched tightly in her lap. Anjoli whispered comforting words, but they felt hollow, even to her. She didn't know if Zara heard them.

Back at Behesht, Zara rushed indoors, leaving her alone at the entrance. The house, filled with life and light just hours ago, was now a shadow of itself, shrouded in the darkness of loss.

Anjoli

Monday, 5 December.
The day after.

Kamil sprang to his feet as Anjoli entered the living room, his face scored with anxiety. Faraz sat beside him in his wheelchair, a cigarette hanging limply from his fingers. He had dressed since Anjoli had last seen him, his teeth back in, hearing aid in place. But the strength in his posture seemed like a façade.

Anjoli shook her head. Kamil's eyes shut tight, a whisper escaping his lips. 'Oh god.'

Faraz groaned and stubbed out his cigarette with a shaking hand. 'Where is Zara?' His voice was frail, cracked.

'I don't know. She disappeared into the house. She's in a bad way.'

'My poor baby,' he whispered. The old man seemed to have tapped into a reservoir of resilience somewhere deep within, though the pain drawn on his face was overwhelming. It was as if every movement, every breath, was a battle against the weight of his grief. 'I must go to her.'

Anjoli experienced a surge of admiration and sorrow for Faraz. He had faced so much loss, yet here he was, summoning the strength to be there for his daughter. 'I'm so sorry. It's a dreadful tragedy. You must be in agony.'

He looked at her, eyes heavy with heartache and fatigue. 'One does what one has to. My family . . .'

Kamil cleared his throat. 'We need to find the truth behind Daru's death.'

Anjoli turned to him, annoyance flashing across her face. How could he think about that now, at a time like this?

But his expression was resolute as he spoke to Faraz. 'Daru asked me to investigate. To keep Percy and Jasmine safe. I mean to keep my promise. Sir, do you truly believe Salim Sinai cursed Xerxes for not helping his family?'

Faraz's eyes closed, his skin appearing almost translucent, as if he was disappearing in front of Anjoli. 'Yes.'

'Will this curse pass down through the generations?' Kamil asked. 'To Daru and Zara's children?'

Faraz shook his head helplessly.

'Is there anyone else who can help us understand?' Anjoli asked.

Faraz took a breath from his nebuliser, the sound loud in the quiet room. 'All gone. I'm the only one left.' His voice was distant, lost in the past. 'And Annie.'

'Annie?'

'What?' Faraz was confused, his focus wavering.

'Who is Annie, Uncle?' Anjoli asked softly, leaning closer.

'Annie? She is Ava's maid. Why do you want Annie? She's not here.' Faraz's words were disjointed, his mind struggling to connect with the present.

Anjoli felt a pang of guilt at questioning him, but Kamil was right. They needed answers if Darius's death was to mean anything. They had to save his children. 'Was she there when Xerxes was cursed?'

'Who?' Faraz's eyes were blank.

'Annie. Ava's maid. Was she in the house when Salim cursed Xerxes?' Anjoli repeated, trying to cut through the fog of his memories.

A vague shrug was his only response.

'But she's alive?' Anjoli pressed. 'This Annie?'

'I think so.'

'Do you know where Annie lives?'

Faraz looked bewildered. 'Why would I know?' His eyes disappeared somewhere into the past. 'Salim Sinai's family was slaughtered. Xerxes lied about that night. Perhaps he felt guilty. Maybe he forgot.' His voice trailed off. Anjoli fell silent, imagining the horror. The silence became unbearable.

Then Kamil spoke up. 'I'm sorry. But I need your help. We should conduct a post-mortem on Daru to determine the exact cause of death. Could you use your connections to expedite the process?'

'What? What do you want me to do?' There was a frightened look on Faraz's face.

'Do you have someone you can call to perform a post-mortem on Darius?' Kamil repeated slowly.

Faraz looked up at him. 'But why? The police said nothing about it. We must start the funeral rites. It is very difficult with a burned body and . . .'

'It's necessary.'

He nodded wearily. 'If you say so. You are the policeman, no?'

'Yes. From Scotland Yard.'

'All right. I will call the commissioner.' He dialled. His voice grew stronger. 'Naik? Faraz Davar here. I am sorry to phone so early. We have had a . . . tragedy here. My son-in-law passed away suddenly last night. Yes. Thank you. Your people have been, and I believe a post-mortem may be necessary. Can you facilitate? We want to prepare the body for a funeral today, so if it's possible . . . thank you so much. He is . . . where is he?'

'D S Hospital,' Anjoli whispered.

'D S Hospital. And Naik . . . if they can be as non-invasive as possible . . .' He hung up with a heavy sigh. 'He will get it done this morning. I will make the funeral arrangements for this afternoon. Now I must go to Zara.'

As he left, Kamil turned to Anjoli. 'The police came and looked around. Can't say they filled me with confidence. Are you okay?'

'Numb. I can't fathom how we let it happen.' Her voice was hollow, the enormity of their failure heavy on her. 'He was in a locked room. Nobody went in or out.'

'Maybe it is a curse.'

She swallowed hard. 'Zara accused me of not keeping him safe. I should have done more.'

Kamil wrapped his arms around her, holding her close as she leaned into his chest. 'Don't blame yourself. There are strange forces at play here. We'll talk to this Annie. I'm going to get to the bottom of these murders.'

'I thought you wanted to leave it to Karve?'

'That was before.'

Anjoli nodded against his body, finding a measure of comfort in his embrace. She wanted to stay there forever, but his phone chose that moment to ring. He put the phone on speaker.

'Mr Rahman? Patil here. From Dharavi Koliwada. You left me some messages.'

Kamil steadied his voice. 'Yes. Thank you for calling back. I was wondering if we could meet.'

'I need to see you and Mr Darius Mehta. There is something I have to discuss urgently.'

'I'm sorry to inform you Mr Mehta passed this morning.'

The words felt unreal, hanging in the atmosphere like a dark cloud.

Silence followed on the other end of the line. 'How?'

'A tragic accident.'

'Accident? Like Sunil and Mr Bell?'

'Accident,' Kamil said firmly. 'I would still like to meet and—'

Patil interrupted. 'Sunil's parents' house was broken into. Nothing was taken.'

'When?'

'Yesterday. Everyone was out.'

'Didn't anyone see who did it? It's a pretty crowded area.'

'No.' Patil's voice was flat, resigned.

Anjoli and Kamil exchanged a look. She spoke up. 'Peter Bell's hotel room was also searched. The killer was obviously looking for the document.'

The line went silent.

'Mr Patil?' Kamil prompted.

'Yes, I am here.'

'What is it you wanted to discuss?'

'Who is taking over from Mr Mehta?'

'We don't know yet. He only passed away a few hours ago. Can we meet? Do you know something about the deaths of Sunil and Peter Bell?'

'No.' The denial was too quick. Too firm.

'Why did you want to see Darius?'

'Just about . . . about the fishing grounds.'

'Can we meet this morning?' Kamil said urgently. 'I'm piecing together some facts which I believe may lead to Sunil's killer.'

'You know Arjun Sharma? From Arpin?'

'I do. Why?'

A long pause followed. 'I have to go.'

Kamil stared at his phone after Patil hung up, his face a mask of confusion. 'What the hell was that about?'

'I don't know. Call him back.'

Kamil dialled Patil's number again. Voicemail. 'Mr Patil, Kamil Rahman here. We got cut off. I really think we should meet. I have some information about Arjun Sharma that might interest you.' He disconnected. 'Let's see if that does the trick.'

They sat.

Stared at nothing.

The phone didn't ring.

Anjoli

Anjoli had to do something. Had to understand. 'Shall we check Daru's room again?' she said to Kamil, who was slumped in a chair staring at the ceiling, his face a mask of weariness.

'Sure.' He rose slowly. 'The cops gave it a cursory look, but it was clear they thought it an accident.'

The dread of what they were about to revisit churned in Anjoli's stomach as Kamil inserted the key into the warped lock. The door was swollen and splintered from the fire's intense heat and the water that followed.

The musty reek of charred wood and damp soot hit them as they stepped inside. The sunlight streaming through the window made the destruction more surreal, illuminating the scene with an almost ethereal glow. Dust motes floated in the air, glinting in the light, adding a strange beauty to the devastation. Anjoli's voice wavered as she took in the sight. 'It's surprising the fire remained so contained. It's lucky the entire house didn't go up in flames.'

'Yes. I don't understand how a fire can remain so concentrated in one part of the room. I can't think of anything that would cause something like that.'

'And the folder got burned.' She stepped closer, lowering her voice. 'You don't suppose it was some bizarre type of suicide, do you? Maybe Daru killed Bell and Sunil, felt guilty and . . .'

'It's possible. I didn't check the contents of his pockets.'

'Exactly. We didn't. Who's to say he didn't have matches and lighter fluid with him?'

'But why this way?'

'The curse was weighing on him? Perhaps he felt death by fire was appropriate? There's the whole Parsi fire worship thing. Maybe that's why he was pointing at the painting. He saw himself as the evil monster the god was fighting.'

They searched the room again but found nothing. Anjoli surveyed the mess in the bathroom, her frustration mounting. Kamil seemed listless, the horrific events of the previous night still holding him in its grip. She wished he would snap into his detective mode, but he appeared adrift, unsure of where to start. Fine. If it was up to her, it was up to her. 'Okay. So we left him. You locked the bedroom. He said he was going to have a shower. He did. Left the towel and clothes on the floor. Changed into his nightwear.'

'The room was so tidy. Daru didn't seem the type to just chuck his stuff around.' Kamil's voice was a mix of puzzlement and sadness.

'True. Also, his toothbrush was dry. He didn't brush his teeth.'

'What does that mean? Someone faked the shower?'

'Why? And who? There was definitely nobody in here with him. Maybe he was tired and couldn't be bothered. He said a few times he was knackered.'

'And a little drunk. How long were we next door before we heard him scream?'

'Twenty, twenty-five minutes?' Anjoli replied, her mind struggling to reconstruct the sequence of events.

Kamil seemed to regain some of his energy. 'Okay. Say he takes ten minutes to shower. Then goes to bed.'

They returned to the bedroom. 'So he gets into bed and goes to sleep. Another odd thing. The bedcover isn't anywhere.'

'He probably didn't take it off. Must have got burnt as well.'

'You wouldn't normally sleep on a thick bedcover like that.'

'If he couldn't be arsed to brush his teeth because he was so tired and drunk, it's not surprising he wouldn't have removed it. Fifteen minutes later, he's on fire.'

Anjoli pressed her thumbs to her temples, trying to suppress the throbbing in her head. 'Okay, but would someone who's tired, drunk and contemplating suicide bother with showering?'

'Probably not. And anyway, Daru wouldn't commit suicide and leave the family thinking the curse had continued. He wouldn't put the children through that.'

She inspected the charred remains of the bed. The canopy posts had collapsed, the fabric was completely gone, the mattress a tangled mess of springs and ashes. Switching on her phone's torch, she pointed it into the jumble.

'Can you pass me something I can poke around with?'

Kamil handed her a long nail file from Zara's dressing table. She prodded the mattress coils, squinting in the dim light. 'What's that there?'

'Where?'

She directed her torch into the depths of the mattress. 'It looks like some black sludge stuck in the middle of the springs.'

'Oh god. Is that . . . is that melted skin?'

Bile rose in her throat. She poked at the substance with the nail file. 'It's stuck fast. Feels solid, like melted plastic.'

Kamil leaned closer, his face contorted with disgust. 'It has some metal bits embedded in it. Must be part of the mattress.'

'Maybe.'

'We need to get forensics in. You've just contaminated the scene. Although you're probably doing a better job than Karve's boys.' His attempt at levity fell flat.

Anjoli stepped back, leaned over, and photographed the black material without touching anything.

'There's some more of that stuff over here.' Kamil pointed to the head of the bed. Similar black gloop with shards of metal in it lay on top of the springs.

She scraped some off with the file, scrutinising it. 'This has some other colours in it. Brown? Red? Still no idea what the hell it is. It's hard, too. Can you get me a bit of loo roll?' She folded the scrapings into the toilet paper and tucked it into her pocket. Kamil looked at her with a wry smile. 'You've got this investigator thing down pat.'

'Watched lots of *CSI*.'

'So Ms CSI, a bomb of some sort? Remote controlled?'

'Bit fanciful to think there's a villain on the grounds with a remote, setting off explosions.'

'True. There'd be a lot more debris as well. And we didn't hear an explosion before the scream, did we?'

'No.' Anjoli coughed, the acid stench of burnt material searing her throat. 'Ugh. Let's get out of here. The stink is getting into my lungs. I need a shower.'

Kamil sniffed his fingers and rubbed his leg absentmindedly. He took another whiff.

'What is it?'

'Don't know. Felt a twinge in my leg from my old bullet wound. There's a familiar smell under the odour of burning, but I can't place it. Something very specific.'

She took a deep breath of the sulphurous, metallic smell. *Was* it familiar?

Kamil rubbed his calf again, muttering to himself, 'Where have I smelled that before?'

'I don't know.' They stepped out, and Kamil locked the door behind them. Anjoli felt close to collapse. 'I need to wash up.'

'I'll be next door if you need me.'

She went to her bathroom, stood in the shower, and tried to make sense of the day. Suddenly, she was sobbing uncontrollably, the water from the shower mixing with her hot, grief-stricken tears. She covered her mouth with her hands, hoping Kamil wouldn't hear. She wept for Darius. For Zara. For Faraz. For their children. For Sunil and his family. She wept for herself and Kamil. She wept for her parents and for the years she wouldn't have with them. Her tears went down the plughole, but the grief remained. Drained, she swaddled herself in a huge, soft towel and collapsed onto the bed.

Kamil

What happened in Darius's bedroom? My leg still hurts. It hasn't troubled me for ages. Why now? My friend. I'm so sorry. Is there anything I could have done? I should have insisted we stay with you. The ache in my heart is physical. Who knew grief actually causes your body to hurt? Thank god for Anjoli. She was so with it. Took control. While I . . .

I jolt awake to urgent knocking. 'Kamil, we have to go down. The funeral's starting.'

I blink, disoriented. It takes a moment to shake off the fog of sleep and the weight of the dreamless void. Four-fifteen. I've been out cold for over five hours. A missed call from Patil. 'I'll be right there,' I croak out, voice thick with sleep, and dial Patil's number. He answers immediately, his tone sharp.

'What information do you have about Arjun Sharma?'

'A lot. Let's meet and I'll tell you.'

'I tried to speak to him, but he refused to take my call. Will he talk to you?'

'Yes. In fact, I'm seeing him for dinner tomorrow.'

'All right, let us meet. I have something to show you. Seven o'clock tonight. Nageshwar Machiwala Mandir in Cleveland Bunder.'

My heart races. 'You have Sunil's document?' Another pause. 'You can trust me, Mr Patil.'

'Yes.'

Adrenaline courses through me. 'I'll see you at seven o'clock. WhatsApp the location to me.'

After a quick shower, I head downstairs and grab a slice of cake from the fridge, the memory of Darius feeding a piece to Zara nearly overwhelming me. To my surprise, I find a dozen people gathered in the living room. Ronnie Engineer, Niloufer Cama and Arjun Sharma are among them, all dressed in white. They sit with Zara, her children, Faraz and Anjoli, who's also found light clothes. I hurriedly stuff the cake into my mouth, acutely aware of my jeans and T-shirt. 'Sorry, I'll go change.'

'No time. The priests are here.' All of us follow Faraz's wheel-chair out of the room in a silent procession.

'What are you like!' whispers Anjoli, giving me the side-eye.

'Why didn't you tell me?'

'*I did.* I said the funeral was beginning. Everyone's here to pay their respects.'

We stand at the front door as a large van rolls up the driveway. Two pairs of burly men emerge from the back, all in pristine white, from their cotton-capped heads to their gloved fingertips and shoed feet. Only their faces are visible. They carry Darius's corpse on an iron mesh bier, covered with a white sheet, each pair sharing a white handkerchief.

They bring the body into a side room, now empty except for a table in the centre. The bier is placed on it, and Zara leads us into the room, her eyes raw and red from crying. Percy and Jasmine cling to her sides, their faces torn with grief. The sight of their father, now an inanimate form covered by a sheet, must be incomprehensible to them. Faraz follows, his composure crumbling, wheelchair humming. We walk in behind them, a sombre cortége.

I steel myself. I can't believe Zara is going to let her children see this horrendous, charred effigy of their dad. The priests lift off the white sheet, revealing Darius dressed in a white vest and pyjamas, a white cloth over his face and a rope tied around his waist. Not an inch of his skin is visible, hiding all signs of his immolation and the post-mortem. Anjoli leans towards Niloufer. 'What are those hankies they are holding together?'

'It's called a paywand. It signifies their unity in this task.'

The priests light a solitary oil lamp next to Darius's head, then exit the room. To my astonishment, they return with a dog. The animal sits silently in front of the body, its eyes fixed on it. I glance questioningly at Niloufer.

'The look of the sagdid restores purity.'

Must be linked to the rainbow bridge Faraz mentioned. Two priests enter, carrying a jar within which a fire burns, and take their seats about a yard away on each side of Darius. We stand, heads bowed as they recite prayers in perfect synchronicity, their mellifluous chants a balm and a torment. The smoke weaves its way around the room, wrapping us in sandalwood and incense.

I sneak a look at my watch. Half-past five. My impatience grows with each passing minute. I need to meet Patil, and time is slipping away.

After another half-hour of prayers, we file past Darius's body to pay our last respects. The flickering lamp casts eerie shadows on the walls, and the heady fragrance overwhelms my senses. I tear up as memories of my friend flood back – the laughter, the late nights in Mumbai's bars, his booming voice echoing through the years.

Muffled cries break the silence. Zara looks like she's about to throw herself on the body, but her father stops her. 'No, maari jaan. You cannot touch him. It is impure.' His voice is hoarse with grief. 'It will be all right. It will be all right. The curse is over now.'

'It will never be all right. Never!' Zara's voice is raw with anguish.

Her children stand on either side, their hands gripping hers tightly. Faraz shakes his head, unable to speak, his hand fumbling in his pocket for a pack of cigarettes. He takes one out and holds it, unlit.

'What happens now?' Anjoli asks Niloufer.

'Darius will be taken to Doongerwadi.'

The priests return and carry the body back to the van. We stand in a row to bid our last farewells. The staff of Behesht – watchmen, drivers, gardeners, cleaners, and housekeepers in their white uniforms – all line up behind us, their faces solemn. I notice Ali, the watchman, whispering to Victor. The butler did it. I wish it were that simple.

Anjoli hisses at me, 'Stop looking at your watch. It's rude!'

'Patil wants to see me at seven,' I whisper back. 'At some place called Machiwala Mandir in Cleveland Bunder. I don't know where it is, but I have to get there. He has the document.'

Arjun approaches Faraz, who is avoiding eye contact with the mourners, his cigarette sending up a thin ribbon of smoke. 'What a terrible tragedy. On top of all these other killings. The papers are full of it. Bad for business.'

Faraz's response is a cold, hard stare. He flicks ash off his cigarette, narrowly missing Arjun's polished shoe. Arjun continues. 'I'm afraid I must go. Will you be taking over the project?'

'Me? You'll be at *my* funeral soon. Speak to Niloufer. She is in charge now.'

Niloufer, catching the conversation, looks up from her phone and nods at Arjun. 'Have your assistant call mine.' Ronnie, standing beside me, shoots her a furious look but remains silent.

Zara, in a sudden fit of rage, snatches the cigarette from Faraz's fingers and throws it to the ground. A gardener quietly scoops it up, as Faraz lets out a short, bitter laugh. 'What harm can it do me now? Let me enjoy the few pleasures I have left in life. There is nothing more for me to do. My time has come. Get the cars. We must go to Doongerwadi.'

Imran drives off with Faraz, Zara and the children, as I get into Niloufer's car with Anjoli. The other mourners follow in a convoy of their own vehicles.

Niloufer says, 'Have you made any progress on the murders? Is it the swami?'

'Sunil dying changes everything.'

'Why?'

'The deaths are now definitely connected to Mehta & Sons. Do you have any idea about what's in the document that Darius spoke to you about?'

'No. We were supposed to discuss it again today. He didn't say what it was.'

'Do you think Bell wanted to tell you about it the night he died?' Anjoli asks Niloufer.

'He was very upset about something. I thought it was us. Maybe it was that.'

'Well, you're CEO now. If anyone can get to the bottom of it, you can,' I say.

'It's not official yet. It has to be ratified by the board. And, whatever you may think, just know I didn't want it this way,' she says quietly.

We sit in silence as the car winds its way up the narrow road from Kemps Corner to the funeral grounds. Doongerwadi is a green oasis amidst Mumbai's skyscrapers. Darius's body is laid on a bier outside the prayer halls. We join the mourners as pall-bearers lift the body. 'This is as far as you go,' Faraz says to Anjoli and me. 'Only Parsis are allowed on the final journey. The nassesalars will carry the body to the towers.'

We watch as the corpse is carried up the hill. Faraz's electric wheelchair whirrs loudly, struggling with the incline. Zara, the children, and the others follow, their hands linked with white handkerchiefs. We stand at the edge of the forest, watching until they disappear among the trees. The cars have vanished. I glance at my phone. 'Six forty-five. I'm going to be late. I'll have to call an Uber.'

I send a quick message to Patil, telling him I'm running late and to wait for me. As we await the taxi, I can't help but stare up the wooded slope, wondering what's happening to my friend's body in that dark, ancient forest.

Kamil

The Uber takes ages to arrive. The traffic is a nightmare. By the time we crawl to Cleveland Bunder, my patience is frayed to breaking point. I call Patil. He agrees to wait and tells me to text when we're near. Anjoli and I sit in silence, the events of the day dragging us down like a physical force. After an eternity, she finally says, 'How's Zara going to cope?'

'I don't know. Faraz looked really unwell. He barely spoke two words. If he dies—'

'You mean when.'

'When. She'll have to do that stuff all over again.'

'I wonder if they use the same dog for all funerals . . .' Her gaze is distant, fixed on the headrest of the driver's seat. She looks exhausted, shadows under her eyes, her face pale.

'So Niloufer's CEO now,' I say, trying to shift the topic. 'Daru never told Faraz he'd decided not to give her the job. Zara won't be happy about that.'

'Maybe she can veto it?'

'I doubt she's in the frame of mind to deal with anything at the moment. Who else is there? Ronnie? His days are numbered. Anyway, it's not our problem. Let them play their stupid office politics. It hardly matters now.'

Silence descends as the sun sinks below the horizon, casting the city in a twilight glow. The oppressive heat of the day gives way to a sticky, suffocating evening. There's no air conditioning in the cab, so the windows are open. The air is scummy. Oily.

Finally, the Uber driver pulls over. 'Cannot go further. Street too narrow. Mandir there.'

I text Patil we've arrived. We step into a cramped alley, flanked by weathered brick walls of old godowns, scooters lined up like guards. The atmosphere is malodorous with the stench of fish and salt. We walk on, the alleyway narrowing, the ground beneath our feet uneven and treacherous. Lonely palm trees sway in the breeze, their fronds rustling like whispers in the night. The path eventually opens up, revealing a small inlet dotted with colourful fishing boats bobbing gently on the murky waters. 'Those must be the Koli boats,' Anjoli whispers.

The evening has dissolved into a gritty darkness, swallowing the light. There are no streetlights here. We rely on the dim glow of our phones to navigate, casting long shadows that stretch and warp around us. The emptiness is unnerving, the persistent squawk of seagulls echoing through the air like a dirge. I squint into the gloom. 'Where is this damn place?'

Then I see them – fairy lights twinkling in the near distance.

The temple is a modest structure, more shrine than building. A raised yellow room, barely eight feet tall and as wide, topped with a corrugated metal roof. To the left stands a colourful statue of Shiva, three-headed and six-armed, a mace in one hand, his bull at his feet, puppies playing around him. In the centre, beneath the glittering lights, is a black shivalingam garlanded with wilted flowers. A cobra's head rears above it, and a trident stands guard by its side. The cloying scent of rotting petals mingles with the fishy stench, making my nostrils twitch.

'Shiva again.' Anjoli's voice is strained. 'Human and phallic.'

I call out. 'Mr Patil? It's Kamil Rahman. Sorry I'm late.'

Silence.

Anjoli glances around, unease etched on her face. 'Why did he ask to see us here? It's so deserted.'

'Maybe he has a boat moored at the docks. Mr Patil! Where are you?'

Only the seagulls answer.

Anjoli scans the area, brow furrowing. 'I have a bad feeling. He must have left. Should we go to the Koliwada?'

I don't like it either, but I don't want to freak her out. 'Let me call.'

I dial. The phone rings and rings. I'm about to hang up when she holds up her hand. 'Shh.'

We go silent. Straining to listen. And there it is – the faint, familiar four-bar melody of a Nokia ringtone.

The call disconnects.

I exhale, relieved. 'We took so long; he probably needed a pee.'

I dial again, and we follow the ringtone around the temple, past some overflowing bins. It's even darker here, the shadows thicker and more menacing.

The ringing grows louder. I expect to see Patil's grumpy face any second now, zipping up his flies.

'What's that?' Anjoli cries.

A massive shadow looms on the wall next to me. It grows. A hulking figure hurtles towards us. White face. Ashen hair. Saffron robes. A huge rod slams into my arm. Pain explodes through my bones. My phone flies from my grip, its light spinning into the night.

Anjoli screams as the man punches the back of my head, then knocks her to the ground. I crash into the mud, face first, his blows raining down on my back. The soil smothers me. I'm in agony. All I can pray is that Anjoli escaped.

The man bends over me, his breath hot and foetid in my ear. 'Bharat chhohdo aur un cheezon main apni naak mat ghusao jinka tumhara koi lena-dena nahin hain. Baat sun, bhosad. Nahin to tum dono pachtaoge! Yeh tumhara aakhri chetavni hain.'

One final blow and he's gone. Anjoli crawls over to me as I try to rise.

'Are you okay?' I mumble. 'Did you see him?'

'It was the swami. My god. He kept hitting you. Are you all right? We need to get you to the hospital.'

My back spasms. I grit my teeth, the pain ebbing slightly. 'I'll live. Are you hurt?'

'No. I just fell. Let me help you up.' She shines her torch on me. I blink in the glare, taking her arm to haul myself upright. My legs are wobbly. My head throbs.

'It must have been a trap.' I lean on her shoulder for support.

'What did he say?'

'He spoke in Hindi. Told us to leave India. Not to stick our noses in what doesn't concern us, or we'll suffer the consequences. This is our last warning.'

'Shit. He warned Ronnie, too. Why would Patil set a trap for us?'

'Dunno.' I find my phone. Its screen is cracked. 'Come on, let's go.'

As we turn to leave, Anjoli freezes. 'What's that?'

I stop. Listen.

A groan.

She whispers, 'Another trap?'

I lift my finger to my lips.

Another faint moan, weaker this time.

'Someone's hurt,' she says. 'I think it's coming from there.'

Fear grips my gut like a vice as we track the sound.

I stop dead in my tracks. Anjoli bumps into me, sending a jolt of pain through my back. 'Fuck.'

On the ground, dimly lit by my torch, is the body of a man.

'Is that . . .' she whispers, peering over my shoulder.

'Shit!' I limp towards the body.

'Oh my god! What's that sticking out of him?' she says.

An axe is lodged in the man's chest, the blade embedded between his ribs, the handle angled grotesquely like some monstrous lever.

I shine my torch on his face.

Patil.

Blood dribbles from his mouth. He blinks weakly in the light, a guttural moan escaping his lips.

'He's alive!'

His eyes flicker, his gaze wild and unfocused. What do I do? Should I pull the axe out? My pain fades in the face of this grotesque reality.

Anjoli kneels beside him, taking his hand. 'He's saying something!'

I get on my knees, my ear close to his mouth.

'Phoenix. You have . . . to . . . stop . . . Phoenix. Tell every . . . one. The world . . . has to know.'

'Know what? What is Phoenix?'

'Find the pape . . . papers in . . . now.'

'What do you mean? Where is Sunil's document?'

His grip tightens on my forearm, a death grip. 'Now. Now. Now. Tyanna thambava. Tyanna thambava.'

'I don't *understand!*'

His hand falls away. His eyes glaze over. He's gone.

Anjoli holds his other hand, biting back tears. Trying not to look at the axe, I search his pockets, my fingers shaking.

'What are you doing?'

'I have to find the document.'

Empty.

I direct my torch to his face. His dead eyes stare up at me. 'Do you see something on his forehead?' I ask, my voice barely a whisper. 'Is it . . . the number five? Someone's written it there. In pen.' I snap a photo with my phone. The screen flashes briefly, illuminating the grim scene for a heartbeat. I dial the emergency services, then Karve. 'He says to wait here for him.' My voice sounds distant, even to my own ears. Anjoli's breath is coming in short, uneven gasps.

'What's Phoenix? What did he mean, get the papers now?' she whispers, her gaze locked on the horizon, as if searching for answers in the encroaching darkness.

'Something he wants everyone to know?'

'Yes, but what? Does the five mean he's the fifth to be killed? Why is the swami doing this?'

I shake my head as we stand, the pieces of the puzzle scattering further away.

'Kamil, how could the swami know Patil was meeting us here?'

I rewind the events in my mind, each step replaying like a scene in a movie. 'Patil said he tried to call Arjun, but Arjun wouldn't see him. Arjun was standing next to us at the funeral when I told you I was meeting him at this address. I even said he had the document. Damn it!'

Anjoli's eyes widen with dawning realisation. 'You think Arjun and the swami are in cahoots? Who else was near you?'

'Niloufer? Ronnie? Zara? Ali the watchman? Victor? Everyone!' My voice edges on panic. All I know is that we know nothing.

'Do you think Daru's death could be connected to these other murders? I mean, the Phoenix rose from the ashes of a fire and he . . . is it a coincidence?'

'There's no way Arjun or the swami or Niloufer could have set Daru on fire. They're not ghosts. We were watching him all evening.' But deep down, some part of me trembles at the thought of something more sinister, something beyond our comprehension. I push the fear aside. 'Look, we're supposed to see Arjun for dinner tomorrow night. I was going to ask if we should cancel, but we should go. We can grill him then.'

'Are we in danger? Arjun tried to finish you off that time in London, remember?'

'He failed.' I glance around the darkened landscape, every shadow a potential threat. Is the swami hiding somewhere, watching us, waiting for his next move? I pull Anjoli closer, our arms linked, seeking comfort in our shared fear. Her eyes dart to the axe, then look away. 'The swami's acting like he wants to get caught. Why would he let us see him?'

'Maybe he knows Karve will protect him. I need to check Patil's office to see if he's hidden the document there.'

'Yes.' Her voice is small, almost lost in the stillness. The oppressive weight of the night presses down, and I hear the distant wail of an ambulance.

'We're here!' I shout, my voice echoing against the brick walls. A few minutes later, two paramedics arrive, rushing over to Patil. One of them feels for a pulse, then shakes his head.

'We've called the police.' Anjoli's voice is steady despite the surrounding chaos.

'What happened?' the paramedic asks, his eyes widening at the sight of the axe. He pulls out his phone and snaps a photo. I feel a surge of anger. What's he going to do with that? Share it with his buddies for a laugh?

Anjoli speaks up before I can. 'We just found him.'

'We will wait,' the paramedic says. The four of us stand in silence, a respectful distance from the corpse.

Twenty minutes crawl by before Karve arrives with his men. He takes in the scene with a practised eye, then counts off on his fingers, a grim recital. 'Saw, arrows, trident, sword, axe. Behind another Shiva temple. This is tantra at work.'

'We saw the swami fleeing the scene. He assaulted us. Did you interview him about Sunil's death? Anything from the sword that decapitated him? Also, I want to see the CCTV from Bell's hotel again. I think the killer may be on it.'

Karve takes his time, weighing his response. Finally, he speaks, each word carefully chosen. 'Sword from his temple. Swami's fingerprints on it. Same with trident that killed shopkeeper.'

'Did you arrest him?' I demand, my frustration boiling over.

'These are delicate matters. We must proceed with care.' His voice is calm, infuriatingly so.

'Yeah, right.' I can't keep the sarcasm from my voice. 'Well, it'll be fascinating to see if the axe came from his hardware collection as well. Looks like you have blood on your hands, Karve.'

'Meaning?'

'Isn't it obvious?' I feel my temper slipping. Anjoli tugs at my sleeve, a silent plea for me to stop. 'I told you about the swami. If you had him in custody, he wouldn't have been able to kill anyone else! Or attack me. What about the CCTV?'

'Do not concern yourself.' He raises a hand to silence me. 'And before you say you will speak to Commissioner Naik, know that he has taken over the case personally now.'

My heart sinks. Naik hates me. Karve continues, his voice impersonal, 'He say you are useless. We should not give you more support. To remind you, you are not supposed to be in Mumbai. So go back to London.'

'*Please* check the CCTV,' Anjoli pleads. 'I'm sure you'll see the killer going to search the room. It could be the swami. Then you'll have the proof you need.'

'*Please*, madam, do not tell me how to do my job. We have now checked it. We saw Niloufer madam on it. She has told us why she was there.'

'But who went in after her?'

'Nobody.'

Bullshit. The cops didn't bother checking any more after they saw Niloufer. Just as we hadn't. We give our statements, my voice hollow as I recount Patil's words on the phone. 'He said he had information about Sunil and wanted to meet us.'

'What information?' Karve's gaze sharpens.

'I don't know. He was dead when we arrived.'

Anjoli shoots me a look, but I ignore her. This is the Mumbai police, not the Met. If I tell Karve about Phoenix and Patil's dying words, he and his men will only cover it all up, and I'll never get to the truth.

'Why did he not come to the police?'

'Maybe he didn't trust you.' The words slip out before I can stop them.

Karve's eyes turn icy. 'You are here to shadow me and now I am shadowing you as you find dead bodies.'

'If you don't need us anymore, we'll get back to Darius's home.'

'I hear even he is no more.'

'Yes.' I try a different approach, hoping to salvage something from this mess. 'I'm sorry, Inspector Karve, for any disrespect. We are in shock. Tell me, does the number five on Patil's forehead mean anything?'

'There are five significant elements in Hinduism. Ether, air, fire, water and earth. I am telling you, you are not listening. This is definitely the same maniac.'

'Can we go now?'

'Yes. Back to England. I have released Peter Bell's body.'

I check my watch as we walk to the main road. 8.35. My stomach growls, a reminder of the mundane amidst the madness. 'Let's find something to eat.'

'How can you think of eating? After seeing that. And you must get your injuries seen to.'

'I'm fine. I'll just have some bruises tomorrow. We have to keep our strength up.'

My phone buzzes. *Kamil. Not sure if ur home. Puppa taken a turn for worse & we rushed him to DS Hospital. I'll stay nite w him. c u tomorrow Zara*

Anjoli

The news from Zara's text sat heavily on Anjoli as she followed Kamil through the corridors of the hospital. The scent of antiseptic and the hum of medical equipment pressed in on her, but she pushed forward. There was no way she could return to the house with Faraz's life hanging by a thread. The ICU door loomed ahead, and she braced herself.

Faraz's frail form was almost swallowed up by the hospital bed, his face ghostly pale, eyes closed under the burden of his suffering. An oxygen mask covered his nose and mouth, and the steady beep of monitors filled the room. Zara and Niloufer sat beside him in a tableau of grief.

Zara rose as they entered, her movements slow, as if underwater. She looked in surprise at their dishevelled state, taking in the dirt on their clothes and the exhaustion on their faces. 'Are you all right? You didn't have to come.'

'Fine,' Kamil replied tersely. 'Just a fall.'

Anjoli stepped forward and pulled Zara into an embrace. 'Of course we had to come. What happened?'

Zara's face crumpled. 'He collapsed at Doongerwadi after the ceremony. He's so weak now. They wouldn't let me ride with him in the ambulance, so Niloufer brought me here and Ronnie took the children home. Where were you?'

Anjoli gave a slight shake of her head, but Kamil pressed on, ignoring her silent plea. 'Actually, I'm sorry to say this, but there's been another murder.'

Zara blinked, her sunken face reflecting the harsh hospital light. Anjoli's heart tightened at Kamil's bluntness. Did he really need to bring this up now?

'Who?' The voice from the bed was weak but clear. Faraz's eyes were fluttering open behind the oxygen mask. Zara rushed to his side, her hands hovering over him, unsure whether to touch or hold back. 'Puppa! You're awake. How are you feeling?'

'Who died?'

'I don't know if we should . . .' Anjoli began.

'Tell me,' Faraz insisted, his voice gaining strength with his demand.

Kamil stepped forward. 'It was a friend of Sunil's. Mr Patil from Dharavi Koliwada. Do you know him?'

Faraz shook his head weakly, his breath laboured. 'How?'

'With an axe.'

A pained hiss escaped Faraz's lips. 'O Khodai! What is this madness?'

Zara gasped, 'An axe? My god!'

Anjoli noticed Niloufer sitting in silence, her eyes never leaving their faces, absorbing every word. 'We saw Swami Yogesh fleeing the scene,' she said. 'He attacked Kamil and—'

'—Mr Patil died soon after,' Kamil cut in, trying to control the flow of information.

'Swami Yogesh attacked you? You saw him?' Niloufer's voice was calm, almost too calm, as if testing the waters.

'Yes,' Kamil confirmed. 'It looks like he's responsible for the killings. Do you know him?'

Niloufer was lost in thought for a moment before she responded. 'No. Ronnie dealt with him.'

'Do you know Patil?'

She nodded slowly. 'From the Jamaat Trust. Yes. I negotiated the Koli fishing grounds issue with him. He seemed decent. Straightforward.'

Faraz's breathing grew harsher, his face twisting in pain. Zara's worry turned to panic. 'Are you okay, Puppa?'

He coughed violently. Zara bolted from the room, calling for a doctor. Moments later, she returned with a medic in tow. He quickly assessed Faraz, and reattached the oxygen mask with practised efficiency.

'He's in agony,' Zara pleaded. 'Can't you do something?'

'All we can do is increase the morphine,' the doctor said, his tone clinical. 'His respiratory rate is highly depressed. He's been on the edge for months. Frankly, I'm amazed he's held on this long.' The doctor turned to Kamil, recognition flickering in his eyes. 'You're the Scotland Yard fellow, aren't you?'

Kamil managed a grim smile. 'Back to your day job? No post-mortems today?'

The doctor gave a short laugh. 'Actually I did the PM on Darius Mehta this morning. Commissioner Naik asked me to fast-track it.'

'And?'

'Terrible. Very unpleasant. Burnt bodies are the worst to . . .' He caught himself, glancing at Zara. 'The victim died of fourth-degree burns.'

Anjoli looked at Zara, who was now holding Faraz's hand, her attention elsewhere. But Niloufer was watching closely, her gaze sharp and unwavering.

'Nothing else?' said Kamil.

'He had ingested a significant amount of sleeping tablets.'

'What does a significant amount mean?'

'Several hundred milligrams. Enough to knock him out, but not enough to kill him. He was unconscious when the fire hit. Maybe that was a mercy.'

Anjoli thought back to Darius's struggles with sleep. It made sense he'd taken pills that night. Had there been sleeping tablets on his bedside table? She couldn't remember.

'Anyway,' the doctor continued, 'there shouldn't be so many of you in here. Only immediate family now.'

Niloufer nodded, her composure unbroken. 'Zara, if there's anything you need, please let me know.' She glanced at Faraz, her voice softening. 'He was like a grandfather to me. And Darius . . . well, I'll call you later.'

Zara looked away, offering only a stiff nod.

'We'll see you at home, Zara,' Kamil said gently as Anjoli squeezed her hand before following them out of the room.

'Do you have a minute, Niloufer?' Kamil said, as they walked down the hall. 'Maybe we could grab a quick bite in the cafeteria?'

Niloufer hesitated. 'It's been a long day. I should get home . . .'

'Just a chai,' Anjoli urged, infusing her voice with all the sweetness she could muster. 'We won't take much of your time. Promise.'

Reluctantly, Niloufer agreed, towering over Anjoli as they made their way to the nearly empty cafeteria. Kamil went to fetch their teas, leaving Anjoli alone with Niloufer. 'How was the rest of the funeral?' she asked.

'It went as planned until Faraz collapsed.' Niloufer's voice was flat, detached. 'I called the ambulance and brought Zara here. Where did you find Patil?'

'Cleveland Bunder,' Kamil replied as he returned with their teas. 'He mentioned something called the Phoenix papers. Have you heard that name before?'

Anjoli's voice rose. '*Phoenix*! That must be the Felix Ronnie heard Bell say to Darius. *Kill Phoenix*. Stop this project, whatever it is.'

Kamil snapped his fingers. 'Of course.'

Niloufer's brows knitted together. 'How did Patil know about these papers?'

'Sunil gave them to him.'

'Did you locate them?'

'No. But Sunil's house was searched.'

'And what did you find there?'

'Not by us,' Kamil clarified. 'His house was ransacked, just like Bell's hotel room. Was everything in its place when you went there? Or had it been looted already?'

Niloufer's eyes glazed over momentarily. 'Everything was fine,' she said absently. Then, almost to herself, 'Ronnie had the most contact with the swami.' She stood, her tea untouched. 'I have things to check.'

'Patil said something before he died,' Kamil said, consulting his notebook. 'Tya-nna-tham-ba-va. Do you know what that means?'

'It's Marathi. It means stop them.' She walked out.

Anjoli shivered, wrapping her arms around herself as if warding off a spell.

'Why is she here?' Kamil muttered.

'What?'

'Something about Niloufer being here with Zara bothers me.'

'Because of her affair with Daru?'

'No, not that. I can't place it. It'll come to me.' He rubbed his stomach. 'Can we eat now? I'm famished.'

He returned with a plate of vada pav and ragda pattice. Anjoli wrinkled her nose. 'I said something light.' She took a delicate spoonful of the potato. 'Oh. Not bad.'

She pulled the plate closer and dug in. Kamil devoured his vada pav, dipping it into the green chutney until it was gone.

'Oh. I forgot to say,' said Anjoli. 'Arjun texted me, saying he had to cancel.'

'Why?'

She took out her phone and read the message. ' "Got to cancel dinner. Sorry, it's just not convenient." That vague message isn't suspicious at all, is it?'

Kamil's eyes darkened. 'If he's involved, he won't want us sniffing around. Call him back? Say you really want to see him and Pinky. See how he responds.'

Anjoli dialled Arjun's number and put the phone on speaker. It went to voicemail.

'Try again.'

This time, Arjun answered. 'Anjoli?'

'Hi, Arjun. I got your text. Is there no way you can do dinner tomorrow? I was really looking forward to seeing Pinky Aunty and catching up with you.'

'I'm sorry, it's not a good time and—'

She cut him off. 'We've got some intel about Peter Bell's death. And the Phoenix papers. Thought you might find it useful.'

There was a long pause. 'I suppose I could rearrange some things. All right. Eight p.m. tomorrow. I'll text you the address.'

As he hung up, Anjoli looked at Kamil, a triumphant smile on her face. 'I knew that would do the trick.'

'Well done.' Kamil's face was lined with worry.

Anjoli leaned back with a groan. He looked at her with concern. 'Are you okay? Do *you* need a doctor?'

'No, it's just . . . everything's hitting me now. Patil with that axe in him. Faraz so close to death. The swami might have killed you. If Arjun is involved . . .' Her voice trailed off, a shudder running through her. 'I've known him my whole life. I know he did those awful things years ago, but his dad had just died. He wasn't himself.'

'It's a lot to take in.'

'And Zara. Having to deal with all this on her own. Curses. Spontaneous combustion. I mean . . . what the fuck?'

'I know. I know. I'm sorry. I shouldn't have asked you to come to Mumbai.'

She shook her head, frustration giving way to determination. 'I wish you'd stop apologising. I'm not complaining. I just need to say how I feel, sometimes. I'm glad I came. I need to see this through. What about the maid Faraz mentioned? Annie. The one who worked for Darius's grandmother. We should track her down. She might be the only other link to that time.'

'How would we find her?'

'Shh. Look.'

Zara entered the cafe, looking pale and drained. Anjoli hurried over. 'How is he?'

Zara's eyes were blank, as if she didn't recognise Anjoli. 'He wants to come home. They're prepping him. I just came to get some tea.'

'I'll get it,' said Kamil.

Zara sat next to Anjoli, who said after a while, 'What did Daru do with his red bedcover before he slept?'

Zara looked confused. 'What?'

'Sorry, I know it's an odd question. But what did you both do with your bedcover every night?'

'We folded it up and put it on the ottoman next to the dressing table. Why?'

'It wasn't there after he died.'

'It must have burned.'

'Don't you think that's odd?'

'I really don't know what you're saying.'

Kamil had returned with the teas and was looking at her curiously.

Anjoli ploughed on. 'Daru was quite neat, wasn't he?'

'Anjoli, what . . .'

'His clothes were on the bathroom floor the night he died. Would he do that?'

'I suppose not. He didn't like mess.'

'No, he didn't.' Anjoli held up a hand, stopping herself. 'Sorry, it doesn't matter.' They sat in the desolate cafe, sipping their drinks in silence. The faint sounds of the hospital's life and death echoed around them; the clatter of dishes as the staff cleaned up, punctuating the stillness.

Anjoli said, 'One more thing, Zara. Faraz mentioned a maid. Annie? Do you know where she is?'

'A maid?' Zara looked at Anjoli as if she were crazy, bringing up these random things.

'Yes. Daru's grandmother's maid? Do you have her details?'

'Why?'

'Maybe she knows something about all this. You didn't mention her when we lunched at the club?'

'I forgot all about her. I've never met her. Ask Niloufer. Xerxes insisted we pay a pension to all our servants after they retired. Because ... because of what happened to Salim Sinai. Now Daru's gone. And Puppa ... I can't answer any more of your weird questions. I just wanted a quiet cup of tea before I take Puppa home. I didn't know you were here. You two should return to London. Not that I don't appreciate having you here. It's just . . .'

'Of course,' Kamil stood. 'I'll sort out the paperwork for Bell's repatriation tomorrow and we'll be gone.'

Anjoli remained seated, barely hearing their exchange. She couldn't shake off the image of Patil's burning eyes. His last words echoed in her mind. '*Tyanna thambava. Stop them. Stop them.*'

Kamil

Tuesday, 6 December.
Two days after.

I force myself to relegate the murders to the back of my brain as I get stuck into what I've actually been sent to Mumbai for: a merry-go-round of official paperwork – embalming certificates, no-objection certificates, transportation of human remains certificates, customs forms and a myriad of other permits and clearances whose functions I can't discern, each document a stepping stone through this bureaucratic purgatory. My back aches, my arm throbs, and my hand cramps with every signature. By four in the afternoon, I'm teetering on the brink of madness, ready to dive headfirst into the coffin I've arranged for Bell's final journey home.

The undertaker beams with pride as he unveils the casket. Despite my protests, he insists I view the body, perfectly embalmed, lying in the oak-veneered, zinc-lined, suitable-for-international-transportation casket he had recommended. His satisfaction in his morbid craft is commendable, but I'd prefer not to be part of his showcase. To be fair, he's done an excellent job; you can hardly tell Bell became a human porcupine before his death.

Rogers calls as I'm about to leave the funeral home. His silence on the line stretches as I recount the latest grim events, culminating in a sharp intake of breath when I mention the weapons used. I omit Darius's immolation and the curse; explaining that over the phone would be a bridge too far.

'Are you serious?' he rasps. 'What's coming next? Snake charmers and rope tricks?'

I ignore his casual stereotyping. 'Things have escalated quickly. I feel I should stay and continue shadowing the police to uncover what happened to Bell.'

There's a pause as he considers. 'No. Let them handle it. Your job is to accompany Bell's body back to London.'

Not good enough. I have to keep my promise to my friend and solve these killings. 'It's been incredibly stressful, sir. I'd like to take a few days of unpaid leave. The coffin can be sent unaccompanied.'

'You just had paid leave after being shot,' he says waspishly. 'Fine. But I want you back at your desk Monday morning.'

I hang up and breathe. If five days is all I'm getting, I'd better make the most of it. I contact the airline to organise the shipping. The rep assures me she'll treat the transportation of Bell's body with 'utmost dignity', then immediately undermines her own statement by cheerily asking when the cargo will be delivered. Peter Bell has gone from being a Fellow of the Institute of Civil Engineers to airline cargo in less than two weeks – ask not for whom the bell tolls, it tolls for thee. I forward the flight details to Rogers for Bell's family and call Karve as I head back to Behesht.

'You have not gone yet? What do you want?'

'I've organised Bell's repatriation. Thank you for all your help.'

He thaws slightly. 'Okay.'

'Any progress?' I ask casually.

Silence. Then, 'Swami Yogesh's fingerprints are on the axe that killed Patil.'

'Have you arrested him? What did he say?'

302

'He has absconded. But we will get him. Don't worry.' He hangs up.

I've accepted the swami's the killer, but I'm convinced he's following orders, connected to these elusive Phoenix papers. I need to check Patil's office. But tonight, let's see what Arjun knows.

Later that evening, Anjoli and I are standing in the opulent lobby of Arjun's flat in Bishop's Gate, a new skyscraper overlooking the sea in Breach Candy. A security guard whisks us up to the fifteenth floor, and a servant opens the door to a lavish, marble-floored apartment. We're directed to the sitting room with two major features – a massive portrait of Arjun's late unlamented father, Rakesh Sharma, on one side, and a stunning floor-to-ceiling window offering a breathtaking view of the ocean on the other. The glow of ships in the distance and the moon's reflection dancing on the waves offer a stark contrast to the gaudy interior decor.

'Anjoli!' Pinky's voice booms as she barrels into the room. She's a large woman in a crystal-studded kaftan, her bouffant hairdo defying gravity. She envelops Anjoli in a massive hug.

'Hello, Aunty.' Anjoli's voice is muffled in Pinky's heroic bosom.

'You look so nice, darling. Come, sit, sit.' Her tone cools as she turns to me. 'Hello, Kamil.' Clearly, my role in investigating her husband's death still rankles.

Arjun emerges, dressed in a smart blazer and jeans. He embraces Anjoli and shakes my hand briskly. 'Scotch?' he offers, and not waiting for an answer, pours two generous pegs of Chivas Regal, handing one to me. He sloshes white wine in glasses for Anjoli and his mother, and we settle on a velvet sofa as a servant brings a tray of snacks. There's a definite charge beneath the superficial warmth of the welcome.

'Have a samosa, Anjoli,' Pinky says. 'I had them made specially. Remember how you loved them when you visited us in Watford?'

'Ooh, yes, I did.' Anjoli bites into a fat, flaky samosa. 'Still the best I've ever had. Thank you, Aunty. What a lovely flat. Have you lived here long?'

'Since we moved back. But I miss London. All my friends are there. After what happened . . .' Pinky's eyes flick to me, a hint of accusation lingering. This evening's going to be hell, and I haven't even started on Arjun yet.

Anjoli nudges him. 'So, are you still single? No nice Punjabi girl on the horizon?'

Pinky sighs dramatically. 'Where does he have time for anything except work? I'll be dead before I see a grandchild.'

Arjun's face remains impassive. 'Give Anjoli a tour of the flat, Ma. I have business with Kamil.'

Pinky gives Anjoli a *see what I mean* look. 'Come, beti. Let the men talk.'

'I'd like to stay, Aunty,' says Anjoli.

'No, no. You come with me.' Pinky's tone brooks no argument.

Anjoli shoots me a look of frustration, but I give her a slight nod. Best if I have it out with Arjun alone. Reluctantly, she follows Pinky into the bedroom.

Arjun and I are left alone, the silence between us crackling with unspoken animosity. He sips his Scotch, watching me over the rim of his glass. I match his gaze. 'I know about the Phoenix papers.'

His expression remains unreadable. 'You mentioned that on the phone. What are they?'

'Don't play dumb, Arjun. Darius told me he discussed them with you on Friday night.'

'Did he?'

'And I know you've been looking for Bell's copy.'

I'm bluffing, but Darius had implied as much. Arjun's reaction will tell me if I'm right.

'Why would I do that?'

'Because you don't want them going public. I've found them, and I'm going to publish them, just as Darius wanted. It'll ruin Arpin.'

He laughs. A cold, mirthless sound. 'Oh, Darius wanted that, did he?'

My patience frays. 'Arjun, three, maybe five, people have been killed because of these papers, and—'

'I thought Darius's death was an accident. Are you saying he was murdered?'

'Not Darius. The lottery seller. Bell. The shopkeeper. Sunil. Patil.'

He frowns, genuine confusion clouding his features. 'Who's Patil? I read about the others in the paper.'

'He ran the Jamaat Trust in Dharavi Koliwada.'

'Oh, that's right. He's trying to get hold of me. He's dead?'

'Don't pretend you didn't know.'

Arjun stands abruptly, crossing to the window. His reflection blends with the night, creating a shadowy double. 'I didn't. What happened?'

I join him by the window, the lights of Breach Candy Hospital twinkling below us. 'I found him with an axe in his chest. He had the papers. They're with me now.'

He turns sharply, his face inches from mine. 'An axe?'

'An axe. Swung by Swami Yogesh on your instructions. He almost killed me, as well.'

He doesn't rise to the bait. 'And you're sure Darius's death had nothing to do with this?'

'Why would it?'

He stares at the floor, lost in thought. 'No reason.'

This conversation is getting us nowhere. I take a deep breath and push harder. 'Stop pretending, Arjun. I know what you're capable of. Bell's and Sunil's bodies were found at your construction site. You left Darius's funeral early the night Patil was killed. You had your minion – the swami – do your dirty work to get the Phoenix papers. Can you account for your movements last evening?'

His playful facade drops, and the beast underneath emerges. He shoves his face closer to mine. I inhale the sharp stink of whisky. 'Who the fuck do you think you are, you, you . . . two-bit waiter!?' Drops of spittle spray my cheek. 'Coming into *my* house and accusing *me*? Of murder? Fuck's sake, not enough for you to go after my father's reputation. Now you want to take me down? What on earth does Anjoli see in you? Can't she see you're using her?'

Pinky and Anjoli rush back in, drawn by the commotion. Arjun grabs my throat. 'I've killed nobody. I don't know your swami. Do whatever you want with the papers and get out of my country before I have you thrown out.'

He shoves me away. The edge of the coffee table catches my bad leg. My vision blurs with pain. I stumble, but manage to stay upright. 'Yes, that would be very convenient for you, wouldn't it? Just as I'm getting close to your dirty little secret. You know, Arjun, you haven't changed. You're exactly like your father.'

He swivels, bares his teeth in a vicious grimace, and before I know what's happening, punches me on the side of my face. My head whips back. Agony lances through my jaw. I dimly hear Anjoli scream as I fall to the ground. Arjun looms over me, breathing hard. Lifts me by my collar. Pulls his arm back for another blow.

Anjoli yells, 'Arjun! What the hell . . .'

The fury drains from his face. He releases his grip. I collapse back on the rug. He stands above me, clenching and unclenching his fists. Walks away.

Pinky remains frozen in horror as Anjoli bends over me and extends her hand. I brush her off and stand. Beaten up twice in two days. That's a record, even for me. I rub my smarting face. 'Did you get into the same rage when Bell found out your secret? Is that why you killed him?'

'Do you want an ice pack?'

'Answer me.'

His voice calms. 'I'm sorry. I shouldn't have done that. It's just . . . when you mentioned Daddy . . .' He trails off, turning to Pinky. 'I'm sorry, Mummy.' He looks genuinely distraught, shoulders slumped. 'Darius and I were working on a deal together, but now, with him gone . . . we'll have to see what happens.'

Either he's a great actor or is telling the truth.

'What deal?'

He gives a weary smile. 'I thought you had the Phoenix papers? Look, it's best you and Anjoli return to England. This is bigger than you know.'

'Arjun, just tell us what's going on,' Anjoli pleads. Pinky stands silent. A stunned statue.

'*Nothing's* going on. This dinner was a mistake. I was trying to be nice, but you two clearly have an agenda. You should leave. Do you have a driver, or should I call you a taxi?'

'But beta, khana is ready and we haven't eaten yet. We can't just . . .'

'Sorry, Mummy. I'm not in the mood. You all eat.' He disappears into the depths of the flat.

'I think we better go,' I say, rubbing my bruised jaw.

Pinky's eyes widen with embarrassment. 'Then I insist you take the food with you.' She gestures to a maid who's been standing in the corner, watching agog. 'Khana pack karo.'

The maid hurries off, and I almost laugh at the absurdity of it all. We stand in awkward silence until Pinky speaks again. 'I'm sorry. He's been under so much pressure. The business isn't going well. He has a major project and is very anxious.'

'The Coastal Road?' says Anjoli.

'Something bigger. He says it will put him back on top, but it's causing so much stress . . .'

'What is it?' I ask.

'Something for the good of Mumbai, he says.'

The maid returns with a plastic bag filled with containers.

'Aunty, we really don't need . . .' Anjoli begins, but Pinky presses the bag into her hands. 'You eat my home-cooked food later.'

We exchange strained goodbyes and make our way back to the car.

'He's hiding something,' I say as we drive through the night streets of Mumbai. 'But the killings? I'm not sure. He seemed genuinely offended. Maybe the swami is acting on his own, for some twisted reason unconnected with this Phoenix deal Arjun and Daru are doing *for the good of Mumbai*. Daru used similar words speaking to Zara.'

'The papers Bell had must still be out there. Patil knew Sunil's house was searched, so he could have hidden them.'

'We'll check his office tomorrow. I'll need to find somewhere for us to stay if we make progress, since Zara wants us out.'

We sit in silence, the city lights flickering outside, as we speed through the dark streets.

Anjoli

Wednesday, 7 December.
Three days after.

Anjoli had just stepped out of the steamy shower, droplets clinging to her skin, when she heard Kamil knock. 'You packed?'

She wrapped a towel around herself and opened the connecting door. 'Yah.'

His eyes widened slightly. 'You look . . . fresh.'

'Don't be fresh. What's the plan?'

'Niloufer's sent me Annie's address. We see her. Check out Patil's office. Then decide what to do next.'

'Okay. Gimme a sec.'

Ten minutes later, they dragged their bags into the dining room, the wheels squeaking loudly in the silent house. Zara, rising from the table, glanced at them and managed a tight smile. 'Oh. The servants could have done that. Have some breakfast.'

Anjoli felt the weight of Zara's courtesy, sensing it was more a formality than a genuine offer. 'I think we'll just get out of your hair. Is it okay if Imran drives us?'

'Of course. As long as you like. I'm not going anywhere, just looking after Puppa today.'

'How is he?' Kamil asked.

Zara's face was a mask of controlled grief. 'Not good. He has maybe a day or two left.'

'I'm so sorry.'

An awkward silence fell. Anjoli moved forward, wrapping Zara in a tight embrace. 'Are you going to be okay?'

Zara returned the hug briefly, then stepped back. 'I'll be fine. Thank you for everything.'

'I wish . . .' Kamil started, then faltered.

'Yes. So do I,' said Zara.

Another uncomfortable silence stretched. Anjoli shifted, breaking the stillness. 'Well, then . . .'

Zara nodded, her gaze distant. 'See you.'

In the car, the air was thick with unspoken thoughts. Anjoli finally let out a sigh. 'Oh god. That was horrible. I really felt for her, but didn't know what to say.' She glanced at Kamil, who was staring out the window. 'Everything okay?'

'I'm still wondering why Niloufer was at the hospital with Zara and Faraz,' Kamil muttered, more to himself than to her.

'What are you getting at? Zara said Niloufer drove her there because they wouldn't let her ride in the ambulance with Faraz.'

'Right. But why Niloufer? Why not someone else?'

'You think Niloufer wants Faraz dead? With him and Daru gone, she'd have free rein as CEO. Are you saying she manoeuvred her way to the hospital for some sinister reason?'

He drummed his fingers against his knee. 'I don't know. It's just a feeling. Something about her being there doesn't sit right. It's probably nothing. But yes, that wasn't nice. I feel awful. They were good friends of mine.'

The car slipped through the streets, shadows of buildings looming over them like silent watchers. An hour later, they stood outside a nondescript building in Andheri, its façade faded by years of Mumbai's relentless sun and rain. A voice squawked over the intercom. 'Yes?'

'Is that Annie Menezes?'

'Yes.'

'My name is Anjoli Chatterjee. I was wondering if we could speak with you about Darius Mehta.'

There was a pause, then the door buzzed open. 'Fourth floor.'

The creaky elevator groaned under their weight as they ascended. They stepped out to find a tiny, toothless woman in her nineties standing in the doorway. She wore a faded blue dress, her eyes sharp and assessing despite her frail appearance.

'Why do you want to discuss Mr Darius?' Her voice was surprisingly strong. 'How is he? I haven't seen him for many years.'

'We're friends of his,' said Anjoli. 'I have some bad news. I'm afraid he passed away last weekend.'

Annie crossed herself and whispered, 'Salim's curse.'

A tremor of unease coursed through Anjoli. 'That's what we want to talk to you about. May we come in?'

Annie led them into her tiny, immaculate flat. The space was filled with the scent of old wood and lavender. Family photos adorned the sideboard, but the room was dominated by a massive 3D picture of Jesus on the wall, an LED candle flickering beneath it. They sat on a sofa under his watchful gaze, the weight of past years pressing down on them.

Anjoli said, 'Thank you for seeing us. I understand you worked for Xerxes Mehta when you were young?'

'I worked for Mrs Ava. I was fourteen. She was only a few years older than me. Like a big sister, though of course, I was her maid.'

'Do you remember what happened the day Xerxes Mehta was cursed?'

Annie's face was a mask of old pain. 'It was the happiest night and the saddest night. Happiest because that was when Master Cyrus was born. Saddest because so many people died.'

'Please tell us about it?'

Annie crossed herself again. 'No one ever asks me about

those days. I don't like to think about them. Very bad. Very, very bad.'

Kamil's voice was soothing. 'Take your time.'

'Then you must wait. I will make us some tea.'

When she returned with a tray, Anjoli took it from her and set it on the table. Annie's hands shook as she poured the tea, the hot liquid trembling in the cups. She told them the story, her voice a soft murmur against the backdrop of the ticking cuckoo clock.

Although Anjoli had heard it all before, Annie's firsthand account made it far more visceral. She imagined herself there on that fateful night, hearing the screams of the dying, the harsh smell of smoke in her lungs, the burden of fear and helplessness dragging her down. But one thing didn't hold true. 'Darius told us Xerxes let many people into the mansion and saved them. He just couldn't fit everybody in.'

Annie shook her head vehemently. 'Not true. He let *nobody* in. I was there. He was very frightened, just a young man himself. Joseph and Mustafa begged and begged, but he was adamant. Mrs Ava had just given birth. Mr Xerxes was a good man. It wasn't his fault.'

'Faraz said he lied. Do you believe in the curse?' Kamil asked.

Annie nodded with surprising vigour. 'Of course. The ghost took Mr Xerxes and Master Cyrus, and now he's taken Mr Darius. I warned Master Cyrus, but he didn't listen. I will tell you something strange . . .' She leaned closer, her eyes narrowing to slits.

'What?' said Anjoli.

'Many years later, I saw Salim Sinai, alive and well. *He had not aged at all*. Even though almost three decades had passed. He was living as a ghost to kill Xerxes.'

Anjoli's skin prickled. The room seemed to grow colder, the shadows deeper. 'Where did you see him?' she finally asked.

'I left Mrs Ava's service when I got married, seven years after Mr Cyrus was born. Twenty years after that, I saw Salim at Churchgate station. The very year Mr Xerxes died. He had come back from the afterlife to kill him. I never forget a face. I recognised him at once. Walked up to him and said, "Salim?" But he looked right through me and got on a train. Maybe he didn't recognise me because I was older. But he looked exactly the same as when he died almost thirty years before. I swear on my grandchildren it was him. Mustafa once told me he saw Salim walking in the grounds of Behesht after he had died, as well. That's how I know the curse is real. Only the devil doesn't age.'

Anjoli forced herself to remain rational. This was impossible. There was no way Salim Sinai was alive in 1974. What? He emerged every forty-seventh birthday to kill off the progeny of his boss? And in Behesht's attic was a portrait of an ancient, wrinkled half-dead Dorian Gray face. Ridiculous! She stole a glance at Kamil, who was listening, impassive. 'What did you do after you saw him?'

'I wrote to Master Cyrus after Mr Xerxes passed. Warned him I had seen Salim's spirit, and it had killed his father. We met. But I don't think he believed me. He was still in shock from his father's death. And even if he had believed me, what can you do against the devil?' She murmured a prayer.

Silence descended. Not knowing what to think or do, Anjoli looked at the framed pictures dotted around the room. 'Who are these?'

'That is my son Anthony and his wife and children. That is me as a young girl, outside Behesht. That is my daughter, Rakel.'

'These are wonderful pictures, Annie.'

'I have more! Come, come.' Annie's face lit up with excitement at the attention. Kamil gave Anjoli a look that said, *can we go now?* She ignored him, following Annie to a shelf where the old woman pulled down an album.

They sat on either side of the old lady as she leafed through it. She paused at a sepia-toned photograph of a man in a three-piece suit with a woman in an evening gown and a young boy in a sailor's outfit between them. 'This is Mr Xerxes, Mrs Ava and Master Cyrus. See how happy they look. I left their service after Master Cyrus's navjote later that year. They were very good to me. Looked after me even though I did not work for them for many, many years. I always sent Master Cyrus a card every Christmas until he died. And I sent one to Mrs Ava until she passed.' Annie turned the pages until she came to a group photo, brown and faded, showing a line of people standing in front of the garden at Behesht. 'They took a picture of all the servants with Mr Xerxes and Mrs Ava. I'm the only one left now. There's Joseph, Mr Xerxes's butler. Mustafa, the watchman. There I am, standing on the side, in my white uniform. And there's Salim. He looked just like this when I saw him on the street after Mr Xerxes died. Just the same. Believe me, the curse exists. And now it has worked its black magic on Mr Darius. Maybe I should have warned him, too. Maybe he would have listened to me.'

A chill traced its way along Anjoli's backbone as she stared at the photograph of Salim Sinai.

It couldn't be! She whispered, 'When was this taken?'

'Decades ago. Some months before Salim died. He was only thirty-five, with a young family of his own. But of course, they all perished with him.'

Anjoli could barely believe her eyes. 'I've . . . seen this man.'

'Who?' Kamil asked, his voice sharp with disbelief.

'Salim Sinai.'

'That's impossible!'

'I don't understand.' Anjoli turned to Kamil, her face filled with wonder. 'I swear I've seen him. Recently. Annie's right. He looks exactly the same as in this photograph.'

Kamil

' Do ghosts really exist?' Anjoli's voice wavers with a mix of wonder and disbelief as she stares at the photo of Salim Sinai that she's taken on her phone.

I grip the car seat as it speeds towards Dharavi Koliwada, the rational part of my mind wrestling with Annie's certainty. 'I don't believe in ghosts, but . . . I don't know anymore. Where did you see him?'

She furrows her brow, eyes locked on the photo. 'In an office? Maybe in Behesht? Could Salim have survived and be the one taking revenge all this time?'

'Not unless he's over a hundred.'

Anjoli's face lights up with an idea. 'Imran,' she calls to our driver, 'do you know the watchman at Behesht, Ali? Does he have any children?'

Imran glances in the rearview mirror. 'Boy and girl. Parveen is teacher and Omar works in reception in Darius saar office.'

'The receptionist!' I exclaim, catching Anjoli's triumphant look. 'That must be where you saw him. He must resemble Salim. Let's check him out after Patil's office.'

Imran parks near the Jamaat Trust building and, on my request, follows us inside to translate. We approach a young woman at the reception and ask to see Patil's assistant. A gaunt man with a narrow face emerges after a few minutes. 'Mi Rathod ahe,' he says cautiously.

'English?'

He shakes his head. I turn to Imran. 'Please tell him I'm a policeman. I knew Patil and need to look in his office.'

Imran relays the message, and Rathod responds, his expression wary. 'He is asking why, saar.'

'Tell him I believe Patil had an important document. That may be why he died. It could be here.'

After a moment's hesitation, Rathod nods, motioning for us to follow him into a small office near the reception. The room is sparse, with a metal desk, two chairs and steel filing cabinets lining the walls. A map of the Koliwada is pinned to the wall, houses marked with names in Marathi.

'You take the desk. I'll look through the files,' I say to Anjoli, as I roll up my sleeves. We dive into the search, pulling open drawers and sifting through stacks of papers. The documents are mostly in Marathi, and I can only hope the ones I'm setting aside aren't crucial. My frustration mounts as the minutes tick by with no sign of the Phoenix papers.

Rathod leaves us to our task, as Imran stands patiently by the door. 'He probably thinks we're mad,' Anjoli whispers, glancing up from a pile of folders.

'I'm sure he's seen crazier.'

An hour later, we're no closer to finding anything. I close the last cabinet and turn to Anjoli, deflated. 'That was a complete waste of time.'

'We had to try. What about Patil's home?'

'Not sure we can just show up there.'

'A detective's gotta do what a detective's gotta do, right? Let's ask Rathod.'

He reluctantly agrees, leading us to a small house with a bright red door. A woman in a white sari with mournful eyes opens it. At the sight of us, she covers her head and looks away.

'Patil's wife, saar,' whispers Imran.

'Ask if we can look around for any papers he might have kept.'

Imran makes the request, and she nods slowly, leading us into the flat. It's larger and busier than Sunil's, with a forty-inch flat-screen TV and a stereo system beneath it. A packed bookshelf lines one wall, and various photographs hang around the room. A shrine to Lakshmi sits on a side table. Incense fills the air with the scent of sandalwood.

Patil's wife points to a box under a table. As Rathod and Imran watch, Anjoli and I kneel to sift through its contents. I feel a pang of guilt, invading the privacy of a grieving widow, but push it aside. This is necessary.

We go through the papers meticulously, but it's another dead end. I stand, rubbing the back of my neck. 'Is there anywhere else he could have hidden something?'

Imran translates. She shakes her head.

I look around the room, my eyes lingering on the bookshelf. If Patil knew Sunil's flat had been ransacked, he would have attempted to hide the document. Flicking through all these books feels daunting, especially under the watchful gaze of his wife, but it might be our only option.

I walk over to the shelf, the fragrance of cloves wafting from another incense stick beneath a photo of Patil, this one showing him smiling in front of a boat. His wife notices my interest in the picture and says, 'Tyala ti naav khub avdaychi.'

I raise an eyebrow at Imran. 'She say he loved boat, saar.'

Patil appears so joyful in the photograph. I have to damp down the memories of seeing him with the axe in his chest, his death grip on my hand, his whispered words. *Now. Now. Now. Tyanna thambava.*

Fuck!

Could it be . . .

I spin round to face Imran.

'Tell me what she said again.'

Confused, Imran repeats, 'He loved boat, saar.'

'No. In Marathi!'

'Tyala ti naav khub avdaychi.'

'And naav means boat?'

Imran nods, clearly thinking I've lost it completely. Anjoli's also staring at me, perplexed. I turn to her in excitement. 'Not *now, now*! Patil was saying *naav, naav*! He was telling me the papers were in his boat. He was speaking Marathi when he died. Take us to his boat!'

I can barely contain my impatience during the drive to Cleveland Bunder. As soon as we arrive, I leap from the car, following Rathod through the narrow lanes to the shore. We pass the shrine where we found Patil, the police tape still fluttering in the breeze. Rathod leads us to a bright yellow and blue wooden motorboat, about twenty feet long, resting on the muddy shore. 'Hi Patilchi naav ahe.'

'He must have asked us to meet him at the temple because he hid the document here,' Anjoli surmises, as she climbs aboard.

My heart pounds as I spot a locked wooden box beneath the seat. With shaking hands, I pull it out. The police should have found this. I curse Karve's incompetence, but thank fate for the oversight. If the Phoenix papers are in here, they might hold the key to this whole mess. I hook a fishing gaff into the small padlock and snap it open. Lift the lid. My breath catches.

There, right on top, is a bound folder with the words 'Project Phoenix' emblazoned in bold black type.

I let out a sigh of relief and scan the first page.

Suddenly, everything clicks into place. I know now why Peter Bell, Sunil and Patil were murdered.

Kamil

I have the motive.

Now I have to work out who's pulling the swami's strings.

I clutch the Phoenix papers, the revelations within them exploding like a storm in my mind. We drop Rathod back at the Jamaat Trust, and though he presses for details about the document, I hold firm, asking Imran to convey that we've found what we needed and will update him later.

'Come on. Let's go to Daru's office and finish this. First Salim Sinai's double, then Niloufer.' I'm finally unravelling this tangled web.

Anjoli snatches the Phoenix papers from my hands and begins reading. Her eyes widen as she flips through the pages. 'Oh, my god . . .'

'You can see why they killed to keep it from becoming public.'

She scans the last page. 'But it's signed by . . .'

'I know.' My jaw tightens. 'We need to find out why.'

We take the lift to Mehta & Sons, tension thickening with each floor. I march up to the reception, ready to confront Salim's doppelgänger. Except he isn't. The receptionist looks nothing like Salim's photograph.

He says with a sombre expression, 'Can I help you?'

'Omar?' Anjoli steps forward, searching his countenance.

'Yes, madam. Who are you here to see?'

'Your father is Ali? Darius Mehta's watchman?'

A flicker of concern crosses his face. 'Yes. Has something happened to him?'

'No, no. He's fine. You've heard about Mr Mehta's passing?'

His shoulders slump. 'It's the most terrible thing. We're all very distressed. He was very good to us.'

'Are you aware of the curse on his family?'

He looks confused. 'I'm sorry. Did you say curse?'

'Yes.'

'Erm, no. Who do you wish to see?'

I gently grip Anjoli's arm. 'Niloufer Cama. Tell her Kamil Rahman is here.'

'Please take a seat. I'll let her know.'

Anjoli's frustration grows as we sit. 'I've definitely seen the young guy in Annie's photo. If not the receptionist, then who?'

'Must be one of the servants at Behesht. You've been nowhere else. Let's focus on this for now.'

'I've been to the club. Zara's boutique. Arjun's. All the places you took me to?'

'Was he in one of those locations?'

She runs her fingers through her hair in vexation. 'I don't know.'

A secretary leads us to Niloufer's office. She rises, the stress lines on her face deepening. 'I'm sorry, things are crazy here. I only have a few minutes. Have you found out anything?'

I drop the Phoenix papers on her desk. 'This is what it's all about.'

She sits back down, her fingers grazing the document before flipping through it. She looks up, a single eyebrow arched in inquiry.

'Let me summarise it for you.' My voice is tight with fury. 'It's a detailed plan drawn up by Mehta & Sons and Arpin Construction to raze Dharavi to the ground and build skyscrapers in its place. A three-billion-pound project. The pictures are quite beautiful, aren't they? Lots of green spaces, parks, children's playgrounds. You're even going to clean up the river. In fact, it won't be called Dharavi anymore, it's going to be renamed Phoenix City. And you're generously going to give the right of first refusal on the properties to the current inhabitants. The problem is the minimum price of a flat is one crore rupees . . .'

'That's a hundred thousand pounds,' interjects Anjoli. 'How are they supposed to afford that?'

Niloufer stands, walking to the window, folder in hand. Her silence is unsettling.

'And the maximum for a penthouse apartment with a beautiful view of the ocean is twenty crores,' I continue. 'Two million quid. So what happens to the people who can't afford to live in this paradise you're creating? Let me save you the trouble of looking in the appendix at the back. You're even more compassionately going to relocate them. Relocate them where? To a lovely suburb where they can keep living their lives? No. You're sending them all – that's a *million* people – by cargo ships *to a currently uninhabited island in the Arabian Sea.*' A searing rage ignites within me. Niloufer's back is to us, her gaze fixed on the city below. I snatch the document from her and jab my finger at the page. 'You're going to build facilities for them on the island and give them, what do you call it? Oh yes, *basic amenities.* Very magnanimous of you and Arjun.'

Anjoli chimes in. 'How can you destroy the livelihoods of a million people and forcibly move them hundreds of kilometres away from where they currently live, just so the rich of Mumbai can have even more marble bathrooms and sea views? What kind of cruelty and greed does it take to do that?'

'And look at what it says here,' I say. 'All the political permissions are in place as long as it happens *after* the elections. How many millions did you have to put in the politicians' Swiss bank accounts? What did Daru tell me? Mehta & Sons has built its reputation on decades of integrity. What a laugh!'

'These are communities,' says Anjoli, quietly. 'Families. Girls like Sunita will lose their dreams of becoming lawyers, doctors, accountants. Sunil got out. Prospered. Thousands more could as well. But not interned on an island in the middle of the bloody sea.'

Niloufer finally turns, her face unreadable. 'It's not possible. Dharavi is in a protected area, the CRZ law.'

'That's what makes this plan so diabolical.' I flip to the right page. 'Look at this map. Building the coastal road *changes the sea's high tide line and moves Dharavi outside the coastal regulation zone*. The people living there lose all the legal protection that has prevented grasping people like you from doing this for decades. This coastal road allows your bulldozers to move in. Brilliant! You get the billion-pound contract for the road and, like magic, the multi-billion-pound redevelopment of Dharavi is also up for grabs. For the good of Mumbai, my arse. This is purely to line the pockets of Arpin and Mehta & Sons. I can't take in the pure cynicism of it. *That's* what Bell meant by the *real* reason for the project. Traffic management, my foot!'

Niloufer's calm demeanour is freaking me out. Have I missed something? I push harder. 'Sunil must have stumbled on these papers, realised the homes and lives of his people were at risk and given it to Peter Bell. Bell was planning to go public with it, so he was killed. Then they had to get rid of Sunil and Patil as well. Because if the media got hold of this, Dharavi would start large-scale protests and sit-ins before the elections. The government would run scared and the project would be dead in the water. Mehta & Sons might survive, but Arpin was counting on this to prosper.' I give a bitter laugh. '*Phoenix*! Rising from the ashes. Even the name is a joke. The only question is, whose instructions was the swami taking? Yours? Arjun's? Ronnie's? Darius's?'

Anjoli says softly, 'The document is signed by Arjun and Darius. He must have told you about it. You are the Chief Operating Officer responsible for the Coastal Road project, after all.'

Niloufer's lips tighten. 'I knew nothing. Darius never mentioned it to me. He had a similar plan years ago and must have resurrected it. I'll investigate.'

Resurrected it. The very words Darius had used. The fury I've felt since I read the document ebbs and I start to think rationally. Darius *had* told me he'd created a scheme, but said someone else had made an 'evil twin' of it. And he needed to stop it. In fact, I saw the old scheme documents on his desk and in his room – *New Mumbai Relocation and Redevelopment Plan.*

'What's New Mumbai?' I ask.

'A suburb of Mumbai,' says Niloufer, flipping through the document. 'Under Darius's original scheme, accommodation would have been built there.'

I need to think. I grab the folder from Niloufer and we leave.

In the car, I ask Imran to take us to Behesht. Anjoli says, 'What do you think?'

'Moving the Dharavi slum dwellers to New Mumbai under Daru's original plan might have been acceptable, but the CRZ stopped it. So he shelved the scheme. Someone resurrected it, as he said, and forged his signature.'

'And Daru didn't find out till Bell got the document from Sunil and accused him?'

'Right.'

'Where did Sunil get it from?'

'I don't know. But the reason Daru was cagey about it was that he was trying to find out who had done the forgery. That's why he went to see Arjun.'

'So, *Arjun* fabricated the whole thing?'

323

I shake my head. 'No. It had to be someone inside Mehta & Sons. Most probably Niloufer.'

'But why? Even if Bell hadn't told him, it would all come out after the elections, and then Daru would kill the project.'

'Unless with Daru and Faraz gone, Niloufer as CEO could push it through.'

'Everyone knows Faraz is dying. But how would she know Daru was also going to die? Do you think she murdered him using the pretext of the curse? And where does the swami fit into this? And the other deaths?'

My mind is spinning in circles. I rub my eyes. 'I don't see how she could have killed Daru. The swami could have been working for her and she got Peter Bell, Sunil and Patil out of the way so as not to reveal her and Arjun's secret. Maybe the other deaths were window dressing to obscure the true motive.'

'Why are we going to Behesht?'

'I need to show this to Faraz. If anyone knows what was going on in Mehta & Sons, it would be him.'

Back at Behesht, Zara is by Faraz's bed. The room is heavy with the scent of antiseptic. His wasted body is lying in bed, his breaths shallow.

'How is he?' I whisper to Zara.

She looks at me in surprise. 'Not good. Did you forget something?'

'Can we speak with him? We have some information.'

Faraz's eyes flutter open, and he gives a weak nod. There are copies of the Gita, Koran, Torah, Bible and the Parsi holy book, the Avesta, on his bedside table.

'You're interested in religions, sir?' I say, easing him into it.

He can barely talk. 'At core, all religions say the same thing. Once we were part of god. Then we got separated from that life force. We live our lives in longing and grief, trying to reconnect with it once more and never succeed. I will soon join with him again.'

I hand him the Phoenix document. 'We found this.'

Faraz looks through the pages, then passes it to Zara. 'Where did you get this?'

'That doesn't matter. Is it true? Your company is going to develop the slums?'

He shakes his head, confusion and disbelief clouding his eyes. 'I can't believe it. But Darius signed it.'

'He said his signature was forged. Darius couldn't have planned this without discussing it with you and the board.'

Faraz takes a deep breath of oxygen, the effort visible. 'I've been chairman in name only. Darius and Niloufer ran everything.'

I turn to Zara. 'Did you know about this?'

She hesitates, then nods. 'Daru told me Peter showed him the document, and he was shocked. He believed Niloufer or Ronnie, plotting with Arjun, forged his signature. He was horrified by the plan to relocate the slum dwellers to a desolate island. It would ruin our reputation. He was going to stop the scheme and fire whoever was behind it.'

Just as I thought. 'But why did they bother? Surely they knew Daru would have stopped it once he found out.'

'That's what he couldn't understand,' Zara says quietly.

'All right. I need to speak to Arjun and sort this out. Sorry to disturb you.'

As I turn to leave, Anjoli stops me. 'We met Annie.' She shows Faraz the picture of the servants and points to Salim Sinai. 'Have you seen this man before?'

He glances at it. 'No. Who is he? I recognise Xerxes and Ava, of course.'

'That's Salim. I'm sure I've seen a person who looks just like him recently. Could it be someone in your office or at Behesht?'

He stares at the photograph for a long time, then hands it to his daughter. Her eyes flicker before she returns it to Anjoli. 'I've never seen him. There's no one here like that.'

In the car, Anjoli's frustration bubbles over. 'Zara knows the man in that picture. I could see it in her face.'

'I noticed that too. Let's deal with Arjun first, then figure out the rest.'

Anjoli

The basement car park of Arpin felt like a tomb as Kamil and Anjoli stepped out of Imran's car. The dim overhead lights cast long, eerie shadows, amplifying the surrounding emptiness.

Anjoli turned to their driver. 'Imran, get some dinner. We might be a while. After this, you can drop us to a hotel and go home. Thank you for looking after us so well.' Her voice echoed off the concrete walls.

'Okay, madam. Message when you need.'

Arjun was standing outside the lift and took them into his office. 'I'm sorry again for hitting you, Kamil. It was inexcusable. What do you want now?' Weirdly, he appeared sincere, thought Anjoli. Or did she just want him to be?

Kamil tossed the Phoenix papers onto the table between them. Arjun didn't even glance at it. His gaze remained fixed on Kamil, unwavering.

'We found Phoenix. We know everything,' Kamil declared, barely concealing his anger.

'Ah.' Arjun's response was eerily detached, his stare cold and calculating.

'You don't seem surprised, Arjun,' Anjoli observed, crossing her arms.

He shifted his gaze to her. 'Kamil's a good detective. I expected he'd find it.'

'Enough with the flattery,' Kamil snapped. 'What do you have to say about it?'

Arjun let out a sigh that felt almost rehearsed, his shoulders sagging as if under an invisible burden. 'It was Darius's plan. He approached us with it. After nearly a year of negotiations and securing government permissions, we signed the deal. Everything was set to go after the elections. Then Bell found it.'

Kamil leaned forward. 'So you had him killed?'

'Don't be absurd!' A flash of irritation crossed Arjun's face. 'Yes, I would rather it hadn't come out. The redevelopment is important to us. We don't want it delayed by endless court battles from activists. But believe me, we will win in the end. The politicos have their money. Once they secure their elections, we'll have a free hand.'

Anjoli exchanged a glance with Kamil. Arjun's arrogance was infuriating, yet his confidence was almost convincing. She struggled to reconcile his description with the Darius she had known. There was a lie here, but where did it lead?

'Why did Daru come to see you on Friday night?' she pressed, trying to peel back another layer of the truth.

'To strategise on how to handle it if the plan became public,' Arjun replied smoothly.

'Who do you think killed those people?' Kamil asked, his voice tight with controlled anger.

Arjun shrugged, his indifference like a slap in the face. 'I assume it was that Swami Yogesh. He's disappeared. I heard all the murder weapons were his.'

'What's his motive?' Anjoli shot back.

'Who knows?'

'How did you persuade Daru to partner with you in the first

place?' Kamil's eyes bore into Arjun, searching for any crack in his facade.

A sly smile crept across Arjun's lips. 'You're right. We didn't get along. But when we lost the original coastal road bid and sued, we could have stalled the project indefinitely. I realised moving the CRZ border gave us a new opportunity in Dharavi. I proposed to Mehta & Sons that we drop the lawsuit in exchange for us being subcontractors for the Coastal Road and a joint venture on the Dharavi redevelopment. Darius had considered redeveloping it years ago but couldn't bypass the CRZ restrictions. This was his chance, and he took it.'

Anjoli's patience snapped. She balled her hands into fists. 'Arjun, don't you care about the million people you're displacing from their homes?'

'They'll have lovely new homes,' Arjun replied, as if it were the simplest solution in the world.

'Are you fucking kidding me?' Her fury spilled over. 'It's going to be an internment camp on a mosquito-infested island. No jobs, no community, no hope. You'll be happy if they just die off and stop being a problem.'

Kamil's voice joined hers, dripping with sarcasm. 'Which, given the island will be underwater in ten years because of global warming, is a safe bet.'

Arjun grinned, holding up his hands. 'That's why we'll put them in high rises.' His smile faded as he saw the rage on Anjoli's face. 'Joke. It was a joke.'

Anjoli's disgust felt like gall rising in her throat. 'We'll go public.'

Arjun shrugged. 'Please do. As I told Peter Bell, you'll never win. There's too much money at stake, and nobody cares about slum dwellers. My advice? Go back to London. Do what Peter should have done. Now, if you'll excuse me, I have dinner plans.'

Kamil's voice was a low growl. 'Darius's signature was forged, Arjun. Who did it?'

Arjun stared back, his expression blank. 'No one. He signed it in front of me.'

'Why are you lying? Who are you protecting?' Kamil pressed.

Without another word, Arjun stood and escorted them out of his office, leaving the questions hanging in the air.

Kamil exhaled sharply. 'That guy. He . . . he . . .'

Anjoli put a calming hand on his arm. 'I know. Text Imran to pick us up from the garage, and we'll discuss it back in a hotel over a drink.'

Kamil pulled out his phone, quickly texting their driver. 'He'll be here in five minutes.'

As they rode the lift down, Anjoli turned to Kamil. 'Have we got it wrong? Was Daru behind it?'

Kamil rubbed his face violently. 'I don't know what to believe anymore. I think Arjun's lying, but to what end?'

'Fuck them all. We will go public,' Anjoli said with steely resolve.

Kamil let out an enormous sigh. 'Arjun's right. They'll just wait it out. The politicians have been bought. Once they have their elections, they'll deliver. He's won. We can't fight it. The rich in this damn country always win. Let's just go to the airport and get out of here.'

Anjoli stared at him, fury all over her face. 'How can you even *think* that, Kamil? It's the *homes of a million people*! Their livelihoods are there. Their memories are there. The Koli fishing is there. Who's going to buy their fish in the middle of nowhere? What about social mobility? Do you really believe Sunil's little sister will become a lawyer on a remote island? You may not like the place, but it's not *your* decision to make. How would you like it if the government built luxury skyscrapers all over Brick Lane and forced us to move to, I don't know, the Outer Hebrides?'

He raised his hands defensively. 'You're right. As always. We'll figure something out.'

The garage was silent and empty, the day's workers long gone. The harsh fluorescent lights cast stark shadows across the concrete floor. Anjoli scanned the area for Imran but saw no sign of him. Kamil dialled, his patience wearing thin. Before the call connected, a rush of air and a glimmer of saffron caught Anjoli's eye.

She screamed, 'Kamil!'

He whirled.

The swami smashed a mace into the side of his head.

He crumpled to the floor, blood pooling beneath him.

The swami turned towards Anjoli. She got a glimpse of a red face surrounded by tiny skulls, bulbous eyes, flaming eyebrows and bared teeth. She ran, but he grabbed her from behind, and a wet cloth smothered her nose. A sickly sweet scent filled her lungs as the world spun violently around her.

The ground rushed up. Her forehead slammed into the cold concrete. She caught a last glimpse of black shoes and white trouser cuffs beneath saffron robes before everything faded to nothingness.

Kamil

Thursday, 8 December.
Four days after.

M y eyes snap open, but the darkness remains absolute. Where the hell am I?

I feel like I've been asleep for a thousand hours.

I'm lying on my right arm in a foetal position. My head throbs, a steady pulse of pain at the back of my skull.

Cold, unforgiving concrete under me.

The air is thick, stifling, and reeks of something rotten.

I try to move, but a painful tug tells me my hands are bound behind my back.

Panic surges. Am I buried alive? I thrash, straining against the coarse, putrid material covering my face. Realisation hits. There's a bag over my head.

Glimpses of what happened return. The swami. The brutal blow.

Anjoli.

Is she all right?

I force my untied legs to cooperate and sit up, feeling the ropes digging into my wrists. I attempt to steady my breathing, fighting the rising tide of terror.

A muffled whisper cuts through the darkness. 'Kam? Are you awake?'

'Anjoli?' Relief floods through me, but it's tempered with fear. 'Are you okay? What happened?'

'The swami knocked you out in the garage. He chloroformed me. I remember nothing after that.' Her voice is shaky, but she's holding it together.

'Are you hurt?'

'Just a pounding headache. You?'

'My head's killing me, too. Are you *sure* it was him?'

'I think so. It was all so fast. He wore a terrifying mask.'

'What kind of mask?'

'The Shiva one he had hanging in the temple.'

'Hmm.'

'What?'

'Nothing. For a second I thought . . . nothing. Arjun must have had him on standby. All that bullshit about not caring if it comes out. Of course he does. Where are we?'

'I can't see a thing. This bag on my head is making me want to vomit. I woke up and thought I was alone until I heard you. I've been calling your name, but you didn't respond.'

'Shit. How long have we been here?'

'I don't know.'

'Keep talking. Let me come to you.'

She recites a nursery rhyme, her voice a lifeline in the dark. 'Mary had a little lamb . . .' I inch forward on my knees, feeling the rough floor beneath me, cautiously navigating the void. '. . . everywhere that Mary went—Ow! My foot!'

'Sorry.' I drop next to her. There's a wall behind us. I lean against it, shoulder to shoulder with her. 'Are your hands tied as well?'

'Yes. It hurts.'

'Okay. Turn around. Get this bag off my head first.'

We shuffle around until we're back-to-back. I wriggle my way down her spine until my head is near her hands.

'Can you pull it off?'

Her fingers fumble at the coarse fabric.

'There's a rope tying it around your neck.'

'Untie it.'

She struggles, her fingers clawing at the tight knots. I gag. Her hands pull away abruptly. 'Sorry. Am I choking you?'

'No. Go on. We have to get it off.'

She works at the rope again, her fingers scraping against the rough hemp. Finally, she whispers, 'I think it's loosening.'

The pressure around my neck eases, and the bag slips off. I take a deep, shuddering breath, grateful for the musty air of the room. 'Brilliant. Thanks.'

I blink my eyes and adjust to the darkness. I make out vague shapes and shadows. The only sounds are our laboured breathing, the distant howling of the wind, and the faint crashing of waves. A pungent, manure-like odour fills the air.

'My turn,' Anjoli says. I manoeuvre behind her, my fingers working quickly to untie the knot around her neck. I yank the bag off her head, and she gasps, sucking in deep breaths.

'Breathe slowly. We'll get out of here.'

Once she calms down, I turn my attention to her hands. The ropes are tight, biting into her skin. 'Can you undo mine?' I present my wrists to her.

She struggles with the knots. 'It's really tight. I can't do it with my hands bound like this.' After a few moments, she gives up. 'It's no good. You try.'

I fumble with her ropes, but they're expertly tied. Whoever did this knew what they were doing.

I survey the room. There's a pile of something in the corner. Burlap bags, some boxes and a spade lying flat on the ground. I crawl over and inspect the spade. It's not sharp, but it's all we have.

'I found a spade. Hold it steady. Let me try to cut the rope against its edge.'

She takes the spade and sets it upright. Working by feel, I slide my bound wrists around the blade and start sawing. After several agonising minutes, the rope frays and finally snaps. I pull my hands apart. Free at last.

I quickly untie Anjoli, and she collapses into my arms, shaking. 'I thought you were dead. He hit you so hard.'

'I'm all right. Takes more than that to bring me down.'

She lets go. I can just make out the whites of her eyes looking into me. 'I think we're in real shit here, Kam.'

She's right. We're in shit so deep the stench of it is penetrating our sinuses and constricting our throats. And it's all my fault. But I don't tell her this. I can't bear the thought of her filled with hopeless terror. 'We have to stay calm. I'll get us out of here. I'm sure people will be wondering why we've disappeared.'

'Who's going to tell them? Imran? You're counting on Imran? He's probably lying in a gutter somewhere with ... with ... I don't know – with his eyes and ears scooped out and stuffed into his own mouth! I don't want to die a horrible, painful death by some psychotic nut job. I'm not done yet. I want to do something with my life. I want a family.'

She's gasping for breath. I gently pull her down to the floor. Hold her close. 'Breathe.'

'I can't! It stinks!'

'Breathe through your mouth.'

I pull back. We lie on our sides, facing each other. Breathing in and out slowly in unison. Her breath is warm on my face.

'I've been sitting here remembering all the ways those people died and wondering what he's going to do to us. Break our thighs with that mace and let us bleed to death? Burn us alive?

Impale us with a spear? Cover us with scorpions? Are there scorpions in India?'

'Shhh.' I put my finger to her lips. 'Don't think like that. We will get out of this. We've got dinners to serve, crimes to solve.'

'No, Kam. I think this might be it.'

'It's not, I promise.'

'You can't promise.'

She shuffles closer and leans her head against my chest. I think she's crying and doesn't want me to see. 'Don't you have any regrets?' she whispers.

I've inhaled a measure of her panic inside my own breast. I can feel it, amplifying my heartbeat like a boom box. 'Regrets? Mostly you and me, I guess. We wasted so much time when we could have been together.'

'Yeah,' she says into my neck.

'But also ... shadows. From the past. Constantly surrounding me. Whispering.'

'What do you mean?'

'Lives I could have saved if I hadn't missed silly details. The homeless people in London. The folks at Aishtar. If I'd basically been better at my job. I know it sounds mad. What do you regret?'

She leans back and looks at me. 'Always running.'

'Towards something or away?'

'Away.'

I'm overwhelmed by a deep sadness that has nothing to do with our situation. 'I've been running towards but never reached. What else?'

'Not taking more chances. On life. On us. I'm sorry ...'

She closes her eyes. I do the same.

Darkness envelops us like a shroud.

We lie entwined. Desperate.

Her lips are soft. Her body warm. Her hair silk. Her perfume jasmine.

All my senses are alive. My being electric.

Time stops.

Why have we waited so long? A feeling of profound sorrow and overwhelming love washes over me.

My mind hits pause. Just as it had that time I'd sat on Marine Drive all those years ago. I don't want this kiss to end. But somewhere in my consciousness lurks the fear I can't even think of articulating.

This may be the last kiss we ever share in our lives.

I open my eyes and look at her. She's blurry. Out of focus. Eyelids shut. They open. She looks into mine. Complete surrender. With a candour I've not seen before. She strokes my face, untangles herself, and sits up. 'You're right. We can't just wait to die. What are we gonna do?'

I give my brain a few seconds to unfuzz. Another few for my heartbeat to get to something approximating normal.

Right.

Do something.

I pat my pockets. Empty. No phone. Nothing useful. I stand. Legs wobbling. Head floating. Dopamine and adrenaline overflowing. 'Stay here. I'll look around.'

She gives a small laugh. 'I'll give you two minutes, then I'm off.'

I walk to the door and test the handle. It's solid, thick wood, securely locked. I look around the room again. No windows. Rough concrete walls. Inside a gunny bag, I find only damp, malodorous fertiliser. Wiping my hands on my jeans, I open the boxes – seed packets, plant pots and some long, thin boxes.

I look closer, squinting to focus. Open them. Fireworks. That's weird. 'I've found two rockets, three fountains, two Catherine wheels.'

Anjoli finds her way to me. 'What are they doing here?'

'Probably left over from Diwali last month. Maybe we can use them.'

'What's this?' She holds up a small plastic box with buttons. I take it from her. Hold it close to my face.

'Looks like some type of remote detonator. I guess you press this red button and it sets off the fireworks with a wireless signal. Needs a similarly controlled fuse at the other end. That's how they were doing it at the last firework display I was at.'

'Where you got . . .'

'Yeah.'

I feel a twinge in my leg where the bullet hit me all those months ago at the High Commissioner's Diwali party.

I prise open another box and feel around carefully.

'No fuse. No matches. No batteries in the detonator. They must have used them all. There's no way to set them off.'

'Could we fashion an explosive? Maybe use it with the fertiliser?'

'I've no idea how.'

I break open a rocket. Pour out gritty, black powder into the palm of my hand. 'There aren't very many fireworks here, just half a dozen, and they're damp. They wouldn't do much, even if I knew how.'

My leg's hurting more now.

'This is more useful.' I pick up the spade, testing its weight. 'It's the best we have. We'll wait by the door and take him by surprise when he comes back.'

We take our positions. I set the spade by my side. Rub my leg. Grimace. Then sniff my hand. A fugitive memory tugs at my brain. What's bothering me? Something in Darius's bedroom? Zara's wardrobe?

'You okay?'

'Yes, my bullet wound flares up sometimes when . . .'

'Listen. I can hear the ocean in the distance. Seagulls. Are we near Arpin's construction site?'

I know she's thinking about where our mutilated bodies will be dumped. I shake my head. 'No sounds of Marine Drive traffic. This seems to be a gardener's shed or something. We must be in some remote part of the city.'

'Then they'll never find us. Some detectives we are.'

I go silent.

Smell my hand again.

Whisper, 'Holy shit!'

'What?'

'Daru *was* murdered.'

'What?'

'I know how it was done.'

'How?'

'Give me a second. Let me work it out.' I think back to the day and night of Darius's death. Then it falls into place. 'So that's how . . . But *who*? And *why*? And how is it connected to the other deaths?'

'*Tell me*,' says Anjoli urgently.

'He *had* to be killed because he'd stop Phoenix. The curse was the excuse. Are they in cahoots? But how would they know . . .'

'Kamil. You're driving me crazy. If you don't tell . . .'

I put a finger on her lips. 'Shit. Shit. Shit. *That's it!* Driving you crazy! Listening. *That's* why Sunil was killed. It was all my fault! *That's* what I saw in the garage!'

'What?'

'Always listening. Always silent. Fuck. How could I have been so damn careless? My bloody preconceptions!'

'*What are you saying?*'

I see everything as if through a pane of glass.

'The killer of Sunil, Patil . . . they've been one step ahead of us all along. As if they knew exactly what we were doing and thinking at all times. There's only one way that could be true. *That's why Zara asked Niloufer to the hospital!* I've been so stupid. So fucking stupid. Anjoli, this is *my* fault. Sunil. Patil. The shopkeeper. I should have kept my damn mouth shut! The killer has to be . . .'

The handle squeaks, returning me to the present. I press a finger to my lips, signalling Anjoli to stay quiet.

Tiptoe to the side of the door.

Grip my spade tightly in both hands

Raise it above my head and wait for the killer to enter.

Kamil

A beam of light slices through the darkness.

It jerks around.

Blinds me.

I swing the spade with all my strength.

And hit air.

A violent blow to my arm sends my makeshift weapon clattering to the ground.

Blinking against the glare, I make out the outline of a gun pointed at my face. IOF 9mm. Standard issue for Indian police. Civilians can get them too, but it's rare.

I back into the room, hands raised in surrender, squinting at the figure in the doorway. Saffron robes. Wrathful Shiva mask. Gloves. He steps inside, languidly swinging a mace in one hand, the gun and pen torch in the other.

I look closely at him. I was right!

An ebb of failure. What does being right matter if we're going to be dead in minutes? 'What do you want?' I demand, my voice steady despite the fear coursing through me.

He moves silently, eyes cold behind the mask. Looks around. Notices we've untied ourselves. His calm, almost casual demeanour is chilling. Anjoli presses closer to me, her breath hitching with every step he takes.

'What do you want with us?' she asks.

He gestures with the gun for us to move towards the door.

'We're not going anywhere,' I say, rubbing my throbbing arm.

The man raises the mace, its steel head glinting ominously in the dim light, and twirls it in a menacing circle. I stand my ground, just as I had when the swami put the sword to my chest. He steps closer, and I consider jumping him. The mace looks heavy – it might unbalance him. But the gun. If he fires, the ricochets in this concrete room could hit Anjoli.

The decision is made for me when he slams the mace into Anjoli's belly. She doubles over, a gasp of pain escaping her lips, and crumples to the floor. He backs off, the gun pointing steadily at us.

'Oh my god!' I bend over her, my heart pounding.

'Ugh.' She struggles to her feet, clutching her stomach.

He steps forward. I lift my hands. 'All right. We're coming.'

I support Anjoli as we exit the shed, her grip on my arm tight with pain and fear. The cool morning air is a relief after the stifling confines of our jail. The sky is painted in hues of purple and pink as dawn breaks. The breeze carries the scent of the sea, and the sound of crashing waves is faintly comforting. For a moment, I'm grateful to be outside, even under these dire circumstances.

We're in a small clearing beside a cluster of tin shacks with thatched roofs. Colourful laundry hangs between trees, fluttering in the wind. A tall palm tree stands guard, its branches swaying gently. In the distance, a wooded hill rises steeply, a narrow path winding upwards into its depths.

Our captor gestures for us to follow the path. As we start up the hill, my fear hardens into dread. I've grown used to Mumbai's constant noise – the hum of traffic, the chatter of people. Now, the silence is unsettling. Only the sound of our footsteps, the waves and distant birds break it. There's no one here to help us.

I hold Anjoli's hand, pulling her along as we ascend. She's breathing heavily, each step a struggle. Sweat trickles down my forehead. The temperature rises quickly with the sun, turning the air uncomfortably warm. Our captor follows us, his saffron robes swaying, unaffected by the climb.

We push through the undergrowth, zigzagging higher and higher. My throat is dry, and my head throbs with the effort. Glimpses of the ocean below remind me of our isolation. After what feels like an eternity, we reach a flat clearing dominated by a massive bronze cannon on a raised platform.

I collapse onto a bench, trying to catch my breath. Anjoli sits beside me, holding her stomach, her breaths coming in slow, painful gasps. The view from here is stunning – mangrove forests line the water, small boats bob by a jetty. A moo from somewhere hints at a nearby cow. The incongruity of our surroundings is jarring.

Suddenly, a sharp blow strikes my shoulder. I whirl around, expecting another attack, but the man is standing still, looking down the path. Another thwack. This time on my head. I look up to see two monkeys in the trees, one clutching a fruit, ready to hurl again. I stand, pick up the hard, unripe mango that hit me and stuff it into my back pocket. The monkeys lose interest and swing away.

The man finishes his inspection and signals us to continue. We follow him. The sun is fully up now, its heat relentless. The path leads downhill, winding through rocks, sand and litter. My eyes survey the area for a chance to escape, but the terrain offers no options.

After another ten minutes, we arrive at a massive cave entrance flanked by colossal pillars. I realise where we are – Elephanta Island. The same place I'd explored a week ago, thinking it might be a delightful spot for our mini-break.

I squeeze Anjoli's hand to calm her. Our captor signals us to enter the cave. Inside, a gigantic stone carving of Shiva's three faces looms in the shadows. Creator. Preserver. Destroyer. How fitting.

The man surveys the cavern, his eyes darting through the mask. I imagine us laid out beneath Shiva's impassive gaze, our legs shattered by the mace, bleeding to death. Another ritual sacrifice in his mad scheme.

No. Not today.

He changes his mind. Maybe it's too close to the entrance. He guides us deeper into the cave, his torch illuminating the path. We pass carvings that watch us with silent eyes. We finally stop in front of a sculpture of Shiva performing his dance of death, one arm and leg missing but still exuding a raw, visceral power.

The man looks around. Nods. This is it. He motions for us to sit. I see Anjoli flinch as a bat flutters overhead.

'How much is Arjun paying you?' I ask to buy time.

He taps the mace on the ground, the sound echoing ominously. Points down. Sit.

'No.' I stand firm.

Anjoli glances at me, fear streaked across her face. I try to convey some semblance of reassurance, but I know we're in deep trouble. She takes a breath and speaks up. 'Is this what a truly religious man would do, Swami Yogesh? We know about Project Phoenix. We'll expose everything and save your temple. It's over. Darius is dead. You've killed Peter Bell, Sunil and Patil. Your sacrifices to Shiva,' she gestures to the statue behind us, 'are done. No more death.'

Her words seem to reach him. The mace trembles in his grip. I see a flicker of doubt in his eyes. I edge away, creating distance between us. We're now in a rough triangle, a few feet apart. The cave is silent except for our breathing. The man's resolve hardens. He aims the gun at Anjoli.

This is it.

344

I look at his polished black shoes again.

Listening. Always listening.

Driving.

A plan forms.

Risky. But I'm out of options.

I reach into my pocket.

Shout, '*Imran! Wait!*'

He turns, startled. 'I know it's you. Take off that mask.'

He stares, unblinking. Then pulls off the mask and throws it down. His face and hair are smeared with white ash. His eyes gleam. 'Hello, saar.'

I knew it! He's been driving us around ever since we arrived here. I shoot a quick glance at Anjoli, whose mouth has fallen open.

'Why?' I ask. 'Who are you working for?'

'No matter . . .' He raises the gun, finger tensing on the trigger.

Anjoli cries out, 'But, Imran, what about your daughters? Your wife? Would they want this?'

He falters, the gun wavering. 'I do this for them. Sunil know it was me. He was going to tell Darius saar. I had to stop him. To save Faraz saar. And now . . .'

The gun points at Anjoli again.

It's my last chance.

I say a silent prayer.

Then hurl the mango straight at him.

It hits him square in the face. He stumbles, dropping the torch. The light goes out.

The cave plunges into near darkness, the only illumination a faint glow from a hole in the ceiling that casts a dim halo at Shiva's feet. My eyes adjust, and I launch myself at Imran. Time slows as I leap through the air, reaching for the gun. My fingers brush cold steel. I seize the weapon, twisting it in his hand, and drag him to the ground. In that fleeting moment, my mind races, calculating angles, anticipating his next move.

Chaos erupts as we fall onto the cave's unyielding floor, a tangle of limbs and raw desperation. He tries to pull his hand away. I rotate the gun as hard as I can. His index finger is trapped in the trigger guard. He grits his teeth in agony. One more turn and I'll crack his finger. He opens his hand. The gun falls. He lifts the mace with his other hand, but it catches in his robes. I grab his arm. Sink my teeth into his wrist. Taste blood. A thud as he drops the mace.

Okay. Now we're even.

I pull my arm back to punch his face, but he gets there first. My head reels. He hits me again and again. I raise my arms to parry his strikes, but I'm losing ground. He flips me over. Straddles me. He's immensely strong. Even with my adrenaline in full flow, I don't have a chance. My face is mashed in the floor's dirt. His hands are around my neck. Squeezing. I choke. My legs beat helplessly against the ground. My vision goes black.

A sharp crack.

He falls off me, and I gasp for air, scrambling to my knees. Anjoli stands over us, the mace in her hands. Imran lies prone, blood oozing from his head. He attempts to rise, but she brings the mace down again. He collapses, unconscious.

As the cave settles into an eerie calm, my breath slows. My body's in agony, but I'm alive.

'Shit,' Anjoli whispers, switching on the torch. 'Are you okay? I didn't know you could fight like that.'

'Neither did I. Thanks for . . .' I gesture weakly. 'I thought he had me.'

She looks at the driver, satisfaction all over her face. 'I got the bastard good. I hope I haven't killed him. He's still breathing. I can't believe it was Imran.'

'I figured it out in the shed. I saw his shoes and trousers in the garage. He's been listening to us the whole time, always knowing our plans. Now we need to find out who he's working for. I have a theory, but I need to confirm a couple of things first.'

'I saw his shoes too! Tell me your theory!'

'There's no time. He could wake up any minute. We have to go.'

'What do we do with him?' She glances at the unconscious body.

'Leave him. Take the mace. Let's go. Actually, wait.' I approach Imran cautiously. He's still out cold. I grab the gun, then search his pockets. My fingers close around the keys to the BMW and his mobile phone. I take the keys but put the phone back. It may help me test a theory.

We sprint out of the cave into the blinding sunlight, leaving Imran unconscious under Shiva's empty stare.

Kamil

I stop to get our bearings outside the cave. There are long, steep steps descending to the sea, lined with stalls covered in blue tarpaulin. 'That way,' I point.

Before I can react, a flash of fur streaks towards me. A small, nimble hand snatches the gun from my grip. I gasp as the culprit – a mischievous monkey – leaps into the nearest tree. It swings effortlessly, the weapon dangling from its tiny fingers, its black eyes gleaming with playful defiance.

'Shit,' says Anjoli. 'Get it back!'

I look at the simian, grinning impudently at me. 'How? Let's go.'

'We can't leave a monkey with a loaded gun. It might kill itself. Or worse, someone else.'

'I can't chase it in the trees. And Imran could wake up at any minute. We have to go.'

'Throw the mace at it.'

I toss the weapon, but it doesn't come anywhere close to hitting the target. The monkey twirls the IOF like a small brown gunslinger, flashing a toothy grin.

'Forget it.' I grab her hand, and we bound down the steps.

At the jetty, a fishing boat's crew lifts nets onto their vessel. We run towards them, waving and shouting for help. Startled, they look at us, and through frantic gestures and the sight of our wounds, they understand we're in trouble and need to get to Mumbai.

The fishermen are unexpectedly gentle as they help us climb into their malodorous boat. We perch on the side, panting, trying to avoid the foul water and fish guts sloshing around our feet as we set off.

Anjoli catches her breath. 'How are you feeling? You've been beaten up thrice in as many days now. You should change your name to Kamil Reacher.'

I touch my bruised head and wince. 'Kamil Underachiever, more like. If you hadn't brained him, I'd be toast.'

'That's why we're a good team. What the hell was Imran doing?'

I shout over the boat's engine, 'It was all about keeping the secret of Phoenix. He was right under our noses the whole time. His English is better than he let on. Always listening – to us, to Bell. The driver becomes part of the car. You ignore him.'

'*I* didn't. I tried to ask him about his life. And even then . . .' She wraps her arms around herself.

'He must have phoned Bell at the hotel that night. Lured him to the construction site. Said he had something to tell him. Then killed him to stop him from revealing what he knew about the document. Probably got the idea of making it look like a sacrifice from that lottery seller's death. When I started sniffing around, he diverted attention away from Mehta & Sons and Arpin by killing the shopkeeper. But it didn't work. I still went to Dharavi with Sunil, who told me he had the document and knew the killer. I was a fool. I told you that in the car with Imran listening. So he had to get rid of Sunil. But he didn't find the document on him either. Patil was next. Shit, he was even there when we found the Phoenix papers on Patil's boat. That's what was bothering me about Niloufer being at the hospital. Why didn't Zara get Imran to drive her there? Why did she need a ride with Niloufer at all? Because Imran was off killing Patil after the funeral!'

'But how did he know where Patil would be that night?'

'He was standing right behind me at Behesht when I said where I was meeting him. He framed the swami, staged the deaths to look like sacrifices. Saffron robes and an ash disguise make it hard to identify features. And once he knew we'd worked it out, he had to get rid of us.'

'Fuck.' She goes silent. 'So, he was working for Arjun?'

'I'm not sure about that.'

I shift to the side, trying to keep my balance on the speeding boat. The adrenaline subsides, and my body aches from the blows. Anjoli's probably in a similar state. She looks at Elephanta Island receding behind us. 'How did he get us there?'

'He's big. Knocked us out. Put us in the BMW, transferred us to the boat, then hauled us up to the shack where we woke. He wanted to kill us under the Shiva statue to frame the swami. I'm sure the swami's fingerprints will be on the mace. Imran was wearing gloves. The same ones Daru's domestics wear. When I saw that, I knew I was right.'

'Do you think he'll come after us?'

'He'll be scared we'll go to the police. He needs medical help. You split his skull. If we're lucky, he might bleed to death.'

'Oh my god, do you think I actually killed him?'

She looks horrified, so even though I think she probably has, I soften it. 'Not necessarily. He may just try to disappear, like the swami.'

'Why did the swami run if he didn't do any of it?'

'When Karve questioned him, he realised his weapons were missing and knew he was being set up. Imran probably stole the weapons after Sunil, Bell and Ronnie went to see the swami about the temple's destruction. Gave him a ready-made means and motive.'

We fall into silence. The sea breeze is calming after the humidity of Elephanta. One of the fishermen offers Anjoli a black, dried morsel that looks like beef jerky. He grins. 'Eat. Good. Bombay Duck.'

He hands me a sliver. Anjoli looks at me, questioning if it's safe to eat. I shrug. After what we've just been through, how much harm can this do?

I chew on the salty tidbit, trying to figure out who paid Imran. I have a theory. Just need to test it.

'This is good.' Anjoli takes more from the fisherman. 'Chanson would love it. He'll pickle it and serve it with his special dal.'

'He'd probably name it "call of the sea" or something,' I say absently. 'I wish he'd just call a spade a spade.'

'Well, they call this fish duck. And . . .'

The fisherman interrupts. 'Ami pohochalo ahot!'

We've arrived at the Gateway of India. I have nothing to give the fishermen, but they wave us goodbye and speed off.

Finally, some luck. Darius's BMW is parked opposite the Taj hotel. Imran's peaked cap sits on the dashboard.

I set the satnav to Darius's house.

Anjoli looks in the glove compartment. 'Our phones!'

I take in the joy on her face. It takes so little to make us forget we almost just died.

'So have you figured out who was pulling his strings then?' she says. 'Arjun? Niloufer? Ronnie?'

'I need to ask Faraz something. If he's still alive. Then I'll know for sure.'

I can't remember the last time I drove in Mumbai. The thought of Imran sitting where I'm sitting, listening to everything I said, appals me. How could I have been so stupid?

We stop at a traffic light outside the Zakaria Patel Orphanage. Anjoli throws it a look and says, 'Poor Zara. I know what it's like to lose a second parent. It feels weird to say you're an orphan at our age, but you really do feel it and . . . holy shit!'

'What?'

The light turns green and I beep my horn to get the scooter in front to move.

'I *know* where I saw the person in Annie's picture. But how can . . .'

'Where?'

'At Behesht. But I have to be sure.'

'Tell me!'

'I'm figuring it out. Your turn to wait now. You do this to me all the time.'

I can't argue as she becomes lost in her thoughts.

Ali opens the gates at Behesht, his brow wrinkling at seeing me driving, but says nothing. I park in front of the main door, and Victor lets us in, unfazed by our bruised, bloody and bedraggled appearance.

'Is everything all right, Mr Kamil?'

'Please take out our luggage and park the car. Imran won't be returning.' I toss him the keys as Anjoli rushes off into the house. 'Where are Zara and Faraz?'

'In Mr Faraz's bedroom.' He lowers his voice. 'It is his time.'

Anjoli returns carrying a newspaper, and we head to Faraz's room.

We enter quietly. Faraz and Zara are both asleep – the old man in his bed connected to an IV drip, breaths shallow and laboured. His daughter snores gently in an armchair beside him.

She jerks awake. Blinks. 'You're back. Again.'

Faraz stirs. Says faintly, 'Water.'

Zara wets a swab and moistens his lips.

A mobile on his table rings. He glances at it, but doesn't pick it up.

'Who's calling so early?' mutters Zara. 'Don't they know you need your rest?'

'It'll be Imran telling you we escaped,' I say to Faraz.

Zara stares at me, astonished. Anjoli looks stunned.

Faraz waves me off with a weak hand.

'*You* were behind it all, weren't you? You, Niloufer and Arjun planned the entire project before you got sick. Arjun admitted it, though he pretended it was Daru he designed it with. He let slip he met you when you were in the hospital. I missed it at the time. You knew Daru wouldn't go along with your island plan, so you had Niloufer forge his signature. Imran was always your man, totally loyal. Hell, you gave him his job. Always looking out for the underprivileged. Unless you're sending them off to a godforsaken island. Sunil was your assistant. He found the Phoenix document amongst your papers and gave it to Bell. It's the only scenario that makes sense. Then, when Daru questioned you about it, you killed him because he was going to stop your crazy plan.'

Faraz lets out a deep breath, as if releasing something inside him. 'Let me be,' he whispers. 'I will face the ultimate justice now. What can you do to me that he cannot?'

Zara says fiercely, 'Leave! He's dying. Stop tormenting him like this.'

'Just tell me why, Faraz? Why was it so important to protect the secret of Phoenix? Why these brutal killings?'

Another weak wave. Go away.

'Tell me, Faraz. Confess.'

He shuts his eyes. Reopens them. His spectral cataracts glow, revealing his inner demon. Or maybe it's just the blow to my head making its after-effects known. 'Arjun and Niloufer told me we could make Mehta & Sons the number one company in India. Legacy. No harm.'

'No harm! You killed five people! Including your daughter's husband. Seven if Imran had murdered Anjoli and me.'

Faraz seems to gain some strength. He sits up with difficulty. Zara stares, eyes opaque. What is she thinking? Realising her father is a monster? 'I did not tell Imran to kill those people. He was trying to help me. But he went too far. I wanted nothing to happen to Sunil.' A tear trickles down his cheek. 'He was a dear boy.'

'What about Bell?'

He closes his eyes, either in pain or to avoid my glare. 'Niloufer kept whispering Bell had to go. That I must have my legacy before I die. I was on so many drugs. Wasn't thinking. I told Imran to take care of it. I was so tired. I just wanted it to be over. No fuss. There's always so much fuss.'

'Why did Imran do it? What makes a driver a serial killer? Were you trying to warn me off? Was that it? You and Niloufer were worried I was getting too close to the Phoenix papers?'

Zara and Anjoli stare at me. Frozen. Faraz's voice seems to come from another dimension. 'Imran is loyal. Loyalty means so little these days. We always look after the families of our servants. His children having good lives was his legacy. He loves me. Loves his family. My regret is I didn't stop Niloufer from making him go as far as he did. I'm tired.' He raises his head. 'Once you are on the road of revenge, it is difficult to see what might be on either side. Your gaze is just fixed ahead of you on your goal. Allah already knows everything that will happen, and nothing happens unless it is according to Allah's will.'

'Don't quote the Qu'ran to justify your evil. This had nothing to do with revenge. Just money. Who the hell were you taking revenge on?'

Zara says weakly, 'Please . . .' Her words fall away. Faraz remains silent. How can this frail old man with only hours to live be so evil?

'Daru suspected you, didn't he? He couldn't talk to you when Bell showed him the document because you were in the hospital. That's why he wouldn't tell me what it was about. He was waiting to speak with you. Presumably, you denied it. So he thought it was Arjun acting on his own. But why kill him? Arjun said you would have got Dharavi in the end, now that the CRZ was no longer an issue. After the elections. Why did you have to kill Daru? Who you said was like your son? And in such a baroque way. Was it because he would have stopped the project and stymied your dream of Mehta & Sons becoming number one? Is that why you needed Niloufer to be CEO? Was it because he had scruples and cared about the Dharavi people? Even though you would be dead before the scheme came to fruition? It makes no sense. Are you mad?'

Faraz remains so still I think he's died.

Anjoli's expression hardens. She twists her hand around the newspaper she's held since we entered the room, knuckles whitening. She leans forward, staring into Faraz's eyes. 'Daru's death wasn't connected to Phoenix, Kamil. Faraz achieving his legacy was a by-product of his murder. He said it. Revenge. That's why Faraz killed Darius. And Xerxes. And Cyrus.'

Anjoli

Kamil looked at Anjoli, stunned. 'What did you say?'

Faraz squeezed his eyes shut. He spoke through his discomfort. 'Medicine, maari jaan.'

Zara took two tablets from the table. Handed them to him, along with the water. He swallowed them with some difficulty. 'Thank you.'

Anjoli's voice was flat. Sorrowful. 'Faraz is Salim Sinai's son. He didn't die in 1947. Somehow, he survived the Hindu pogrom. Maybe he played dead. He heard his father curse Xerxes. Decided to make the curse come true. I finally remembered where I'd seen Salim's picture before. It was the photograph of Faraz when he was a young man. Dedicating that orphanage. In the *Parsi Times* profile of Daru.' She unclenched her hand and opened the newspaper she had been carrying. The young Faraz was the spitting image of Salim Sinai.

'It was Faraz who Annie saw at Churchgate station. She thought he was his dad.'

'Why didn't Xerxes recognise him then?' said Kamil.

'It was years later. Maybe he'd forgotten what Salim looked like. When someone's with you day in and day out, you don't think they look like someone else. I think Faraz got himself adopted by a Parsi, then wormed his way into Xerxes's life. Bided his time. Mustafa, the watchman, knew about the curse. They all kept the secret. And there were lots of other little things. Look, he keeps the Qu'ran here on his bedside table.'

'He quoted from the Qur'an as well – the day of judgement passage,' said Kamil. 'Every soul shall taste death and you will be paid in full only on the Day of Resurrection. I was also surprised to hear him recite the shahada when Daru was dying in his bed. He never gave up his original religion.'

Faraz murmured, 'I was seven when my abba and mumma died. Hiding in terror under the sheet in that blood-filled room. He told me not to move. Not to make a sound. When I heard him curse Xerxes, I knew I had to bring his last wish to fruition. Uncle Mustafa brought me up. Then Mr Davar took me in. Adopted me when he saw me waiting tables in Mazagaon.'

'Annie said Salim's son's name was Zafar,' said Anjoli. 'An anagram of . . .'

'Faraz.' His eyes stared into some distant past. 'Zafar is not a name I have heard in a long time. It is good I am Zafar again before I die.'

Zara spoke for the first time. 'And Zara is part of Faraz and Zafar.'

Kamil stared at Zara in astonishment. 'You knew?'

'Yes, she did.' Anjoli's voice was heavy with sadness. 'How did you set fire to Xerxes at the party?'

'Ava asked me to buy him a new suit from London,' said Faraz faintly. 'I made thermite out of aluminium filings and iron rust. Added a magnesium fuse. Sewed it into the collar of the suit. All I had to do was touch it with the lit cigarette in my hand when I hugged him and . . .' He shut his eyes in pain. 'Hate is a funny thing. You start with a reason. What he did to my abba, my sister, my mumma. Xerxes could have saved them. Chose not to. That could not stand. Three Sinais died. Three Mehtas had to die. A life for a life. My grandchildren were always safe.' He let out a hacking cough. 'After years, the hate just becomes part of you. Like breathing. It constantly regenerates. It is there every day when you wake. Every night when you sleep. I liked Xerxes. He was good to me. Sometimes I even forgot I hated him. Can you love someone you hate? I came to hate the hate itself. But when his birthday was coming, I remembered my abba dying. The hate took over again and . . .'

Zara's voice broke, 'Puppa, don't.' Faraz's voice trailed off. They all stayed silent, his words curling around them like a ghost.

Anjoli's shoulders were tense and rigid, like a coiled spring ready to snap. 'At first, I thought maybe you got your uncle, the watchman, to kill Cyrus. But then I realised you must have inculcated that hatred in Zara. Groomed her from when she was born. Made her booby trap Cyrus's magic box. You told me you went backstage with Daru before the show, Zara. Almost like you wanted to confess something to me. Was it some kind of remote-control device you hid in the box?'

Kamil turned to Zara in horror. 'But you were a child!'

Zara stayed mute. Faraz placed his hand on hers. 'No. No. It was Mustafa. I was supposed to do it. Then had to go to London. I gave him the remote bomb. I knew all about demolitions, you see. It was part of my job at Mehta's. All he had to do was press a button.' A tear trickled down Zara's cheek.

'Maybe Mustafa pressed the button, but Zara put the bomb in the box.' Anjoli was relentless, her eyes dark with a mix of anger and sorrow. 'I just don't know how you killed Daru, Zara. It was you. It had to be. You drugged his champagne so he couldn't get out of bed. He kept saying he was tired. That post-mortem doctor said he had many sleeping pills in his system, even though there weren't any by his bed. Stupid of me to miss that. That's why he didn't brush his teeth or put away his clothes or the bedcover. He just collapsed on the bed after his shower. He was so out of it he didn't realise till it was too late that he was on fire. Was it a bomb again? I think you were having second thoughts that evening. That's why Faraz mentioned Xerxes's death and that Chinvat Bridge thing. To steel your resolve. How did your father make you hate your husband so much? Was it easier because Daru had slept with Niloufer?'

Kamil took over. 'She did it with cordite. That's what I smelled in his bedroom. My bullet wound hurts whenever I'm around fireworks because of when I got shot at that Diwali party. It ached in the room after Daru died. I worked out how it must have been done when I saw the fireworks and detonator in Elephanta. Hide a single firework with a remote fuse inside the mattress. The detonator inside the pillow. When Daru's head hits the pillow, it sends an electronic signal to set off the firework, which sets fire to the bed. The fused plastic and metal bits you saw in the springs, Anjoli, were what was left of the mechanism and the battery after the fire. My leg hurt when I was hiding in Zara's wardrobe. She probably stored the fireworks there. And coated the sheets and canopy with an accelerant as well. That's why you were so angry when you caught us snooping around in your bedroom the night before he died.'

Zara was weeping openly now.

'*No!*' Faraz said emphatically. '*I* did it. I did it all. Leave her alone.'

'You were in the hospital,' said Anjoli. 'And too weak. Zara sews her own clothes. She sewed the mechanism into the mattress. Okay, perhaps you pressed the actual button just minutes after I searched your room, but she was there when you did. Was it in your bedside-table drawer? I didn't want to look because it had all your intimate possessions on it. The sheer callousness of it all.'

'Puppa, did you really tell Imran to kill all those people?' Zara said. 'Daru suspected, but I told him it couldn't be true. And did you and Niloufer want Daru dead for this stupid project? For your legacy? You? You who told me we cannot let evil flourish. You who said we have to defeat Ahriman? You did this?'

Faraz patted her hand but stayed silent. Tears squeezed themselves from under his closed eyelids. 'Some do the deed with many tears / And some without a sigh / For each man kills the thing he loves / Yet each man does not die. Now, maari jaan. It is now.'

'You did it?'

'Now, Zara!'

'No!'

His voice became strong. 'Now!'

'What about me? All my life, I've done what you wanted me to do. Even turned against the husband I loved. Left my children fatherless. All for the honour of our family. For some curse that you had to fulfil. And now you can't stay alive for me?'

'You are strong. My time has come. Give me the tablets. You can do it, my only one.' Anjoli watched as Zara wordlessly crushed a dozen tablets with a spoon, mixed them in a glass of water, put it in her father's hand, and turned away.

'Morphine?' Anjoli whispered. 'Should we stop her?' She looked at Kamil, who shook his head. He was right. There was no reason to bring this old, dying man to justice. Maybe he would be judged on Chinvat Bridge and be transported to the House of Lies. Fitting for the lie of a life that he had lived.

Faraz put a hand on his daughter's head and drank it down. 'I'm sorry, maari jaan. Maybe I could have gone down another path, but . . .' His face twisted, a shadow crossed it, and he whispered, '*Ash-hadu an la ilaha illa Allah, Wa ash-hadu anna Muhammadan Rasulu-Allah.*'

Kamil finished the shahada. '*Inna lillahi wa inna ilayhi raji'un.*'

360

Anjoli waited by Faraz's side as he died. Zara didn't look at him once. She said nothing, cried no more.

They sat in silence, the room thick with unholy deeds, unspoken words and unshed tears. The only sound was the steady, shallow breathing of Faraz, gradually slowing, fading, until it stopped entirely.

Kamil

Goa. Thursday, 8 December.

I take a sip of the drink and wince. 'What did you say was in this Angelica cocktail?'

'Cashew feni, port, whisky and sweet vermouth,' says the bartender, tossing his shaker in the air and catching it expertly. 'Not to your taste?'

'A little sugary.'

'Shall I make you something else?'

'No. It's fine.' I have another tentative sip, grimacing at the overly sweet concoction.

He pours Anjoli's drink into a coupe. 'Here's your Arabian Fantasy, madam.'

We wander down the beach, carrying our bags. I throw myself onto the sand. Anjoli settles next to me, her face reflecting the vivid hues of the setting sun. The tide is receding. The horizon over Ashwem is painted with shades of orange, red and pink, blending seamlessly into the deep blue of the sea. I drink in the scene. Children play in the water, their laughter mingling with the cry of gulls wheeling overhead. Couples walk hand in hand, casting long shadows against the diminishing light. It feels like another world, far removed from the chaos, sadness and death we've left behind.

A young woman approaches us, arms laden with colourful scarves and trinkets. She waves a shell necklace at Anjoli, who shakes her head with a polite smile. The woman moves on, trying her luck with an American tourist who's loudly explaining the spiritual essence of yoga to his disinterested girlfriend.

It's been seven hours since we left Zara by Faraz's deathbed. I booked the first flight to Goa, desperate to escape the suffocating grip of Mumbai. As our Uber wound its way up the driveway, I glanced back at Behesht, once a warm and inviting haven. Now it stood ancient and dilapidated, a relic of a bygone era, its grandeur faded and weary, like the ghosts that haunted its halls.

I called Karve. Told him about Imran. He listened silently, promising to investigate. When I asked about the CCTV footage, he confirmed no one else had entered Bell's room after Niloufer. She had been the one to search his belongings while Imran was killing him.

Anjoli and I didn't say much to each other on the journey here, each lost in our thoughts. The events of the week were a cold, heavy stone in my chest. Had my choices led to these deaths?

Anjoli brushes sand off her *Hindus don't believe YOLO* T-shirt. 'What will happen to Zara?'

'Nothing, I suppose. There's no actual proof she did anything. She'll just have to live with her guilt. I can't imagine it'll be very pleasant. She's lost everything.'

'Hardly everything. She still has the big house, kids, servants . . . I can't understand how she could commit her own husband to such an agonising end. Imagine the terror of dying like that. I'm never going to wear that dress!' She drains her Arabian Fantasy and shudders.

'Faraz cast a powerful spell. But you could tell how conflicted she was throughout.'

'Daru's affair with Niloufer may have strengthened her resolve. She must have felt so betrayed.'

'You were impressive, figuring out he was the curse all along. It was in front of my face, but I didn't see it. You're brilliant, you know, Anj.'

'That's why we're a great team. You get the how . . .'

'. . . and you figure out the why and the who.'

'What was that thing he said about man killing the thing he loves? Is it from the Qu'ran as well?'

'*The Ballad of Reading Gaol* by Oscar Wilde.'

'Oh.' She goes silent for a few minutes. 'I don't know what to make of Faraz. What he experienced . . . seeing his family slaughtered because his father's boss wouldn't give them sanctuary. He must have gone mad. I suppose anyone would.'

'He was obsessed by two things – avenging his father and making Mehta & Sons number one. Arjun and Niloufer manipulated him into agreeing with their plan by telling him they could make the latter happen. He knew Daru was going to die, so Niloufer and Arjun could execute their terrible scheme.'

'Did *they* know he was planning to kill Daru?'

'I don't think so. I think they thought Bell's death would be it. But then Niloufer took over and got Imran to do the other killings to cover up what had happened. I don't believe Faraz knew about that. When he found out, it was too late.'

'And they'll get away with it? Make billions?'

'Unless Imran confesses. He probably believed that Faraz had given his blessing for the murders. Faraz was the man he was close to. We have no proof anyone will listen to. Powerful forces stand to make a lot of money from it. But I will give the Phoenix papers to Rathod. Maybe he can do something.'

'So sick. I don't want to think about them anymore.'

She puts her empty glass to one side, stretches like a leopard, runs her fingers through her hair like a shampoo ad, then lies down on the sand. I wriggle down beside her, feeling the warmth of her body next to mine. We stare up at the sky, fingers barely brushing. My neck throbs where Imran tried to strangle me. I touch it and wince.

'You okay?'

'Why do I keep getting beaten up? Tahir solves crimes with no broken bones, and I can't recall Miss Marple ever getting punched in the kidneys.'

She laughs, a light, soothing sound in the dusk. 'I guess you're not the kind of detective who solves crimes by smoking a pipe while knitting, and using your little grey cells. You're more of an action man. Whereas I use my brain.'

Her teasing stings, but I let it slide. She rolls to her side and faces me. 'What do you think about our detective agency now? You just agreed we're a great team.'

I sit up. 'I've always known that. But I think maybe I should stay with the police a little while longer.' The sand shifts beneath me. My words surprise me. I hadn't realised I'd decided.

She goes quiet, processing. 'How come?'

'I don't know. The past few years have been so chaotic. I need some stability. Also, you were right. The Met is a mess. And maybe my promotion is tokenism. But I left the Kolkata police because they were corrupt. Maybe this time I shouldn't run. I should try and reform it from within?'

'Very noble,' she says drily.

I ignore her tone. 'You asked me the other day what my true self was. I've been thinking about that.'

'And?'

'Maybe finding yourself is a journey, not a destination. Perhaps I'll never know.'

She gives a tight smile. 'Wow. Goa's already turned you into a hippy.'

'How would you feel if I stayed with the Met?'

She blows out her cheeks. 'I want you to be a happy hippy. Maybe I'll make a go of it on my own. Anjoli's Investigations.

You can be my man on the inside. At least you'll have a steady job if things go tits up.' She gets up on one elbow, pointing towards the horizon. 'Look, the sun's almost gone.'

I look at her, trying to decipher the emotions playing across her face. 'Do you want to go inside?'

She turns to me, her expression unreadable. 'Are you hungry?'

'No I meant . . .'

'I know what you meant. But . . . maybe we should wait.'

Something inside me closes.

'For what?'

'It's not you, Kamil. It's me.'

I give a short laugh, tinged with bitterness. 'Your T-shirt slogans are a lot less cliched than that.'

'I mean it.'

Her hand finds mine. Our fingers intertwine. The bustling beach seems to quieten as I watch the sea swallow the last rays of the old sun. My heartbeat slows. 'Our kiss the other night was lovely,' she says. 'Although a less smelly location would have been better. But, let's face it. My relationship history is . . . chequered. There was the maniac.'

'Massimo. Yeah, but that was a one-off.'

'I guess. I don't like to think about it. Then there was Ray.'

'Ray? Who's Ray? You've never mentioned him before.'

'No.' She falls silent. 'I don't talk about him.'

I squeeze her hand. 'You can talk to me.'

She squeezes back. Draws a shaky breath. 'We were together in my last year of uni and some time after that.'

'Was he doing psych too?'

'Yes. We clicked. I think it was the first time I was really in love.'

My heart clenches. But I maintain my composure. 'What happened?'

'We moved in together.'

'And then?'

She pauses, searching for the right words. 'It's like you're crazy about each other. Your love is like, like a river? And then slowly things happen. At first, you ignore them. These minor niggles fall into the river like stones. And the water keeps rushing over them so you don't really know they're there. Then there's another. And another. Then a bunch more. And before you realise it, the river slows to a trickle. Then finally, nothing can get past the stones. It's dammed up.'

I try to make sense of what she's saying. 'So what happened?'

'My feelings got bunged up. I dumped him. Neha thought I was being over-dramatic. That I was looking for perfection I'd never find. That I'm scared I'll be left alone, so I stay alone. Maybe it's better that way. You and I have both changed over the last few years.' She throws me a sad smile. 'When you came to London, you were this naïve, angry, gauche, funny, moral guy. And now . . .'

She takes her hand away, staring out at the sea. The first stars are emerging.

'And now?'

'You've hardened. The Kashmir stuff. It did something to you. Your smart-arse comments are a shield. I understand. I really do. I've hardened too.' She shivers. 'It's getting chilly.'

A spurt of anger winds through me. Hardened? Smart-arse? I want to argue, but bite my tongue. 'You know me better than anyone else. But, however much I may have changed, I will not leave you.'

'I know. But what we have is so precious. Do we really need any more?'

I gaze at her beautiful profile in the darkening twilight, my heart aching with unspoken words. 'I think so.'

She pauses. Takes a deep breath. 'Come on. Let's eat something and then go to our room.'

What the hell does this woman want? I'm hopeful but deflated as I brush the sand off my jeans and follow her, attempting to ignore my sore head and heart.

As the shadows melt on the beach, one thought returns, a nagging worry at the back of my mind.

What did the monkey do with that gun?

Acknowledgements

The genesis of this book came from my old Parsi friend Kaikobad Mistry, who suggested 'Why don't you write a ghost story.' Since I know nothing about that genre, I dismissed the idea. What I was interested in, however, was writing about his community. Growing up in Bombay (always Bombay to me, never Mumbai), some of my closest friends were Parsis and I've always been fascinated by their history and culture. As I started researching this ethnoreligious group, Kaiko's throwaway comment resurfaced and the idea of a cursed Parsi family was born.

So I have Kaikobad and Shireen Mistry to thank for the idea, their wonderful meals (brain *really is* good!) and for the painstaking reading of several drafts and sending me so much great material, personal photos and videos to help me bring their culture to life. This was augmented with fantastic material from several outstanding books and periodicals – *Oh! Those Parsis* and *The Bawaji* by Berjis Desai; *The Good Parsi* by T M Luhrmann; *Parsiana* and *The Parsi Times*.

The other place that looms over this book is, of course, Dharavi. I'd seen it in *Slumdog Millionaire* and read about it in *Q & A* by Vikas Swarup and *Shantaram* by Gregory David Roberts, all three of which influenced *The Shadow*. But it was visiting it that really brought it to life – I genuinely felt the sense of community that Kamil and Anjoli experienced. Strangely, after I started writing the book, an announcement was made that India's second richest man (and close confidante of the Prime Minister) was to spend billions redeveloping Dharavi. In the words of Reuters: *Indian billionaire Gautam Adani aims to convert Mumbai's Dharavi slum into a modern city hub, while acknowledging that resettling its 1 million residents will be a challenging task.*

I find the word 'resettling' deeply unsettling, but will wait to see what happens. If you want to experience Dharavi and Elephanta, I strongly recommend Reality Tours, a social enterprise that funds schools in the area, and whose guides Chetan, Hitesh and Sameer were a fount of local knowledge.

A further influence on the book was from a brilliant article, 'The Autopsy Report', by Rudraneil Sengupta in *Mint*. I found this fascinating and leaned heavily on his piece for the chapter on Bell's post-mortem.

Thanks to great friends Sarang Panchal and Sachin Date for helping with the Marathi translations; Sohrab Ardeshir for his incisive comments, taking us to the Willingdon Club (with Nita Deb) and for introducing us to Ayra Cama, who let us into her wonderful Parsi home, Adenwala Baug, which informed some of Behesht; Salil Tripathi and my sister Nandini for providing cogent feedback on early drafts. Thanks, Alex Wildish from Engineering Forensics, for technical advice on how to make people combust!

Thanks, as always, to my wonderful agent Laetitia Rutherford at Watson Little and brilliant editors Katie Ellis Brown, Hayley Shepherd and Sania Razia at Harvill Secker. The entire team at Harvill and Vintage (enumerated in the credits after this section) have been unflinching in their support and enthusiasm for Kamil's and Anjoli's journey and, for this, I can't thank them enough.

But, as always, the most credit goes to my wife, Angelina. Not only did she traipse around Dharavi, Marine Drive, Priyadarshini Park, Machiwala Mandir and Elephanta with me in Bombay's dusty heat, she also spent months reading, rewriting, crossing out, commenting, researching and making this book far, far better.

> *Who knows what evil lurks in the hearts of men?*
> *The Shadow knows!*
> *The Shadow* (Radio Programme)